"Come ... ze falling to her ... kiss. It canna hurt you."

"One wee kiss?" she echoed, flabbergasted that he would think there could be anything "wee" about him.

"Done!" he said, taking her stunned echo as permission.

"Oh no, I—"

He swooped down and caught up her mouth with his, her protestations muffled into silence. His mouth was hot and demanding, just like the rest of him. He commanded the kiss, crushing anything she might do to resist or gainsay him. He pressed the heat of it onto her until she melted and relaxed into it. *It's one kiss,* she thought. *What harm can one kiss do?* He felt the change come over her and pressed his advantage instantly. He thrust his tongue forward against her, licking the trembling seam of her lips. It was a blatant knock at her door and she was torn between instinctively knowing this was a bad idea and instinctively knowing it was going to be the hottest kiss of her life.

By Jacquelyn Frank

The World of Nightwalkers
Forbidden
Forever
Forsaken
Forged

Three Worlds
Seduce Me in Dreams
Seduce Me in Flames

Nightwalkers
Jacob
Gideon
Elijah
Damien
Noah
Adam

Shadowdwellers
Ecstasy
Rapture
Pleasure

The Gatherers
Hunting Julian
Stealing Kathryn

Other Novels
Drink of Me

Anthologies
Nocturnal
Supernatural

FORGED

The World of Nightwalkers

JACQUELYN FRANK

BALLANTINE BOOKS • NEW YORK

Forged is a work of fiction. Names, characters, places, and incidents are the products of the author's imagination or are used fictitiously. Any resemblance to actual events, locales, or persons, living or dead, is entirely coincidental.

A Ballantine Books Mass Market Original

Copyright © 2014 by Jacquelyn Frank

Excerpt from *Cursed by Fire* by Jacquelyn Frank copyright © 2014 by Jacquelyn Frank

Published in the United States by Ballantine Books, an imprint of Random House, a division of Random House LLC, a Penguin Random House Company, New York.

BALLANTINE and the HOUSE colophon are registered trademarks of Random House LLC.

This book contains an excerpt from the forthcoming book *Cursed by Fire* by Jacquelyn Frank. This excerpt has been set for this edition only and may not reflect the final content of the forthcoming edition.

ISBN 978-0-345-53492-7
eBook ISBN 978-0-345-54674-6

Cover illustration: Craig White

Printed in the United States of America

www.ballantinebooks.com

9 8 7 6 5 4 3 2 1

Ballantine Books mass market edition: May 2014

For Alisha and Mitchell
May your future together be filled with
many blessings

GLOSSARY
AND PRONUNCIATION TABLE

Kamenwati: (Kah-men-WAH-ti)
Menes: (MEN-es)
Apep: (Ā-pep)
Asikri: (Ah-SĒ-crē)
Docia: (DŌ-shuh)
Ka: (kah) Egyptian soul
Hatshepsut: (hat-SHEP-soot)
Tameri: (Tah-MARE-ē)
Chatha: (Chath-UH)
Pharaoh: (FEY-roh) Egyptian king or queen. This is used in reference to both male and female rulers. In this case, the rulers of the Bodywalkers.
Ouroboros: (You-row-BORE-us) A snake or dragon devouring its own tail, a sign of infinity or perpetual life.
Panahasi: (pan-uh-HAS-ē)
Legna: (LĀY-nuh)

Note: All the *h*'s in the Gargoyle's names are silent unless the name begins with *h* or the *h* logically occurs in the name.

FORGED

THE LOST SCROLL OF KINDRED

. . . And so it will come to pass in the forward times that the nations of the Nightwalkers will be shattered, driven apart, and become strangers to one another. Hidden, by misfortune and by purpose, these twelve nations will come to cross-purposes and fade from each other's existences. In the forward times these nations will face toil and struggle unlike any time before, and only by coming together once more can they hope to face the evil that will set upon them. But they are lost to one another . . . and so will remain lost, until a great enemy is defeated . . . and a new one resurrects itself . . .

CHAPTER ONE

Approximately three hundred years ago

His name had been taken from him.

All those years ago, when he had first been forged, they had robbed him of everything that he had been and had left him with nothing . . . stripped and raw, without even a name. From the moment he had been reborn into the thing that he now was he had been called many things. Slave. Idiot. Fool. Those words were his name now. *What do you think, fool? Fetch me that water, slave. Don't you know what you are doing you idiot!!?*

But no longer. Tonight he would be free, one way or another, and he would not flinch from what it would take to grasp that freedom. Whether it be actual escape or whether it be death.

All he had to do was get the stone. That was all. Just one small piece of rock that had been bound to him at the very same moment his existence had been forged into this horrid life. One small stone would mean the difference between life and death to him. Freedom or oblivion. There were no other choices. He could no longer tolerate any other state of being.

But the task was harder than it seemed. His master guarded the stone zealously, as he did all of the stones of his slaves. He felt a twinge of regret that he would be leaving the others behind to wallow in their enslaved states, but he could not worry about them and he could not enlist their help. He would not risk any lives but his own. More important, he did not know if he could trust any one of them not to betray him.

Yes, it was selfish in its way, he acknowledged to himself, but he had no choice but to be selfish. This folly would be his and his alone.

All he needed was one small stone.

He waited until the room had emptied of everyone save himself and his master. He lingered nonchalantly, trying not to look like he was up to anything that could be perceived as remotely rebellious.

His lord was a dark and powerful man. He was very high up in the chain of command, his life busy and focused on the war he was heading against his enemies. However, he was not all-powerful. True, he had been talented enough to forge many slaves like himself, but his master answered to a mistress of his own.

He fawned over her constantly, bidding his slaves to do any number of tasks, both benign and horrific, on her behalf. And though his master was the one who had enslaved him, it was this mistress he directed his impotent captive fury toward. Oh, they were equally responsible for the individual slaves they created, but his master's mistress was the twisted mind that birthed the terrible tasks his master would bid him to take care of.

And no matter how reprehensible the task, as long as his master held that stone, he'd had no choice but to comply. And so he had done terrible things. Things that sometimes he had taken great pleasure in doing, despite knowing how dark the ultimate goals of his master might be. He had stolen things. He had headed raiding parties against his master's enemies.

He had committed cold-blooded murder.

And the night he had realized that he was beginning to take delight in these murderous tasks was the night that he began to see how reprehensible he himself was becoming. He could only blame his master to a point, but he had gone above and beyond the duties outlined to him and he had taken pleasure in it all. He had gone from being a man enslaved and despising his captor to a true and loyal servant who took pride in the way he accomplished these dark, vile deeds.

He had truly become a disgusting reflection of his master. He had so much penance to pay for his deeds that he probably didn't even deserve freedom. But to keep away from freedom meant that he would only continue to perform more harm on others. He would continue to descend into damnation, and that he could not abide.

But it was this loyalty toward his master that made his master drop his guard, leaving the stones unprotected against his very best and most loyal of slaves. Just the same, if he failed, he would never be trusted again, and would suffer everything from cruel torture to absolute death. He had seen his master's wrath in action up close and personal. Hell, he had often been the instrument through which his master had exacted his vengeance on those who crossed him. He knew just how creatively the man could sketch death on another.

The room was empty, but that meant nothing. He walked slowly and purposefully toward the box holding the stones. A simple wooden jewelry box with blue velvet lining and a high polish that made the wood gleam. It was in the shape of a hexagon with another hexagon of etched glass in the center of the lid. The central design on the glass was of a lily. Had it had color, it would have been a black lily. Black lilies were his master's mark. He was sometimes instructed to cast a black lily on the ground near a scene of action; whether it be something as brutal as a vengeance murder or something as benign as an altar of worship, he'd dispatched his master's mark. It was not some corny token, however, like in movies or television—some way of saying "I was here!" or "Fear my wrath!" The black lily was a profound symbol for death, a death his master chased with a single-minded fury. Not the deaths of those around him, but his own.

For his master was a powerful immortal, doomed to live life over and over again, always remembering the suffering that had come the lifetime before. Not many recognized this, but as his master's right-hand man, it was hard to miss how the man craved permanent death.

He hesitated a moment before touching the box. He knew it was ensorcelled, that it would raise an immediate alarm and explode with defensive, painful magic against him. Through the glass he saw the small collection of colorful stones, each ranging from being as gray as granite to being beautiful shades of red and everything in between. His, he knew, was the cinnamon-colored stone just big enough to fit his hand around. It was clear as glass, as brilliantly faceted as a ruby without the deep blood-like coloring. It matched his eyes perfectly. It was what it was. A stone. A protected stone. His touchstone. A stone he would be bound to for the rest of his days. It had been taken from his hide the day he had been forged and now . . . now he was a slave to it. Every day he must sleep in contact with it. If he did not . . . the consequences were horrific. To be parted from the stone for long periods was to risk permanent being.

He fisted his hand, turning his flesh and bloodskin to stone . . . a dark gray stone. With a carefully controlled show of force, he rammed his fist through the glass. He was powerful enough to grind everything within the box into dust if he was not careful, and that would mean not only his end, but the end of all the others connected to all those other stones.

The reactive magic was horrifically painful. It lashed at him, driving him back, pushing him away from the object he so desperately needed. He lunged forward against it, but still the force drove him back.

No! No! I cannot fail this!

He needed to succeed and he needed to do so quickly. The alarm screaming out of the room would bring others in mere moments. Using every last ounce of strength and will he possessed, he lunged forward once more, grabbed for his touchstone, and closed his fist around it.

The box toppled to the ground, the other touchstones within it scattering wildly. But he paid them no attention. He was turning into the push of the magic, letting it shove him violently out of the room. He plowed over two acolytes that had come running at the sound of the alarm. A third lifted a weapon, a gun, and fired at point-blank range into his chest, right over his beating heart, right below the brand that forever marked him. The stone of his skin deflected most of the bullet's impact, but he felt and saw a chunk of it go flying. The pain was brilliant and fierce, but he paid it no mind. He'd felt worse. For now he focused on grabbing the acolyte, yanking him closer and smashing his hand, touchstone within, into the man's skull. The man crumbled and he let him fall, discarding him like trash. As always he allowed no remorse to fill his mind. That would come later. In that moment he needed to fight, for his freedom and for the right to pay penance—for the new sins he was about to rack up as well as for the old.

Shaking that thought off, he made his way outdoors, the night cold and brisk and stunningly perfect as he spread his wings and launched himself into the air with three steady pumps of his wings.

He knew they would be on his heels, but he also knew he was free.

Free.

And no one would ever take that away from him again.

CHAPTER TWO

Captive.

Chained. Like a beast. Like . . . like an animal awaiting butchering. Awaiting those that would devour him.

Ahnvil wanted to scream, but he would give his captors no such pleasure. He moved and the sound of chains
scraping over the cement floor of his prison instantly
came to him. He was shackled at the ankles as well as
the wrists and thrown behind a wall of steel bars for
good measure. His prison was a basement of some sort
that he could sense was fully underground.

The sound of conversation floated to him, and his ears
pricked up. He moved forward as far as his manacles allowed and began to pace, as if agitated. It was what they
had come to expect of him. The feeling of superiority this
supposed knowledge gave them made them sloppy and,
he hoped, would give him an advantage.

"I've got to show you this," the Templar priest was
saying in semi-hushed tones to his companion. He
doubted there was even anyone to overhear them, but
their desire to be secretive was telling and he was going
to make sure to be very attentive . . . while not seeming
to be so. Perhaps he would finally find out why they had

bothered chaining him up and keeping him captive instead of simply killing him and striking a serious blow to their enemies who depended on his strength and abilities. Of course there was always the possibility they were going to let time do it for them . . .

"What is it?" the second Templar, a short, balding male, wanted to know. *Seriously?* Ahnvil thought dryly, *Of all the humans he could choose to be reborn in, this is what he chose? It goes to show that some Bodywalkers are just smarter and stronger and* better *than others.*

A Bodywalker was a body with two shared souls. One was the human that had been naturally born to it. The other soul was that of an ancient Egyptian, a powerful man or woman that could be reborn in the host body of the human, in effect sharing that body with the original soul. Only, these Bodywalkers, the Templars, did not share. They subjugated the innocent human soul . . . just as they had once subjugated him.

The Bodywalker he knew, the ones he was devoted to, the Politic, they were different. They cared for their human hosts, they Blended with them and respected them and shared their lives with them in harmony. The way it should be.

And since Bodywalkers could choose exactly whom they could be reborn into . . . it seemed ridiculous that this one had chosen such an inferior physical specimen.

As they came fully into range of his prison cell, he could see his captor: tall and handsome, if older, with salt-and-pepper hair and a deep dimple in his left cheek. This one had obviously chosen based on aesthetics.

"Oh my! Where did you get that?" Baldie asked with surprise when he caught sight of the captive in the cage.

"Not that," Dimples said impatiently. "I'll tell you why I've caught *that* in just a moment."

"Oh. Well, what then?"

Dimples went to a drawer in a nearby worktable, a table that held any number of things, including all kinds of components for the spells the Templars worked. They were dark, vicious powers that ought not to be messed with. The same dark powers that had created *him*.

Dimples pulled a steel box from the drawer and opened it, the tremulous touch of his fingers revealing exactly how excited he was about what was inside the box. He reached in and withdrew a necklace, the pendant of which glinted sharply when the light from above struck it.

"What is it?" Baldie asked, snatching it out of his companion's hands. Dimples immediately snatched it back, holding it again with reverence.

"It's called Adoma's Amulet," he said breathily.

"Really?" Now Baldie had adopted Dimple's reverent tone. "What does it do, Panahasi?"

"I have no idea," Panahasi said.

Baldie frowned with consternation and impatience. "If you don't know what it does, what's so special about it?"

"What's special is that I found it in Kamenwati's belongings before his things were cleaned away!"

Their captive's ears burned at the recognizable name. Kamenwati was the most powerful Templar priest ever known. He had been the right hand to the most powerful priestess, Odjit.

That is, until Kamen had defected to the other side. *Ahnvil's* side.

Ironic, considering he was Ahnvil's creator. His former master.

Baldie reacted accordingly. "Ohhh! And what makes you think it's special, other than that?"

"Well, apparently Kamen had been researching it virulently. It was with tome upon tome, sitting on his desk. But the only thing he had found thus far was this passage." Panahasi withdrew a small book from the box and flipped it open to a marked page. Ahnvil winced as he watched this, wondering how the book didn't simply fall apart in Panahasi's hands, given how obviously old it was. But neither of the Templars seemed to respect or even notice that. They were too busy trying hard to stand on the shoulders of another's works, someone who was far and away more worthy of reaping the benefits of those works, if by way of his power alone . . . and even Ahnvil had to admit that, despite his own hostile reasons for despising Kamen.

"It reads: 'The slave, born of the infinite Nightwalkers, will set free the power within. The one that harnesses Adoma's Amulet will have such power as to make a god weep.' "

"Oh my," Baldie breathed, clearly finally understanding the scope of what his friend held. "Oh!" he said with sudden animation. "That's what the Gargoyle is for!" He glanced over at their prisoner.

"Yes! And he's not just any enslaved Gargoyle, he's Kamen's Gargoyle. Kamen's creation. I thought if any slave would be powerful enough to unlock the power within this Amulet, it would be one of either Kamen's or Odjit's slaves. And since Odjit has no living Gargoyles that I know of at present, this one will have to do."

"So what do we do next?" Baldie wanted to know, rubbing his hands together eagerly.

"We don't do anything. I am going to try to get this Gargoyle to unlock the power in the Amulet."

"And just how are you going to do that?" Baldie sneered, clearly not liking being cut out of the potential rewards, even if he had done nothing to deserve them. Just as his friend had done nothing to deserve them outside of being a thief. "If you get too close to it, it'll rip your head off. It's not as though it's going to want to do you any favors."

"I know," Panahasi said with a frown as they both looked over at him. He gave them a dutifully vicious smile for their efforts.

"Well, you better think of something soon. You only have a few days before he's no longer any good."

"I *know*," Panahasi growled sharply. "Don't worry, I will think of something. Kamenwati isn't the only priest with power, you know. I did manage to ambush the Gargoyle and catch him, didn't I?" Panahasi said, puffing himself up. But it rang very hollow to both Panahasi's friend and his captive. Probably even to Panahasi himself.

"Never mind." Panahasi said when his companion still looked dubious. He dropped the Amulet into the box along with the book he'd read from and shoved both onto the table. The action made the lid of the box shut sharply. "I'll deal with it later. I merely wanted to know if you were interested in being a part of it. But if all you are going to do is judge . . ."

"No! I won't judge," Baldie said eagerly. He held up a hand, palm flattened out solemnly. "I swear."

"Good," Panahasi said, seeming to be mollified by his friend's newfound respect for him. Or what passed for respect. It was more likely he would try to find a way to snatch the Amulet for himself at the first opportunity. That was just how grasping and disloyal these Templars were.

There was a noise at the door and Ahnvil's keeper came bumbling through in a cacophony of objects and clumsiness. She was not his captor. Merely his warden. She moved forward, approaching him cautiously as she always did, her fear obvious on her face. She was wise to feel trepidation. He had not made things easy on her. She had never actually harmed him, but neither had she aided him in any way except to feed him and tidy his cage. He stood up, his fists clenching, his entire attitude making his body seem bigger than his already massive stature.

"Is it daylight?" he asked, the passing of time so awkward and slow for him in here, shut away from the whims of the sun.

"No. It is turned night," she answered amicably. She was a mousy little thing, in face and form and most certainly in attitude. She was shy and unsure, especially when she approached his cage.

She was incredibly petite. So small and so thin he could break her with a single swipe of his hand. She moved to the lever on the wall across from him and his entire body went tense, instinctively straining against the action to come. She pulled the lever and immediately, with a grinding groan of machinery, the ends of his chains began to disappear into the wall. They shortened and began to drag his powerful, straining body back toward the solid stone of the rear wall of his prison. He glared at her scathingly, and she turned and hid her face under the length of her hair.

He growled as he stepped back voluntarily, knowing that it was inevitable anyway but it was at least an act of freedom, of choice, however small or disillusioned it might be.

"What is my slop for the day, jailor?" he asked. She seemed to flinch under the reference of her being his jailor. Even though they both knew there was little truth to the matter. She was not the one who had put him here and she was not the one who held him captive still.

She moved back to the doorway to fetch the tray she had been carrying when she'd entered the room, then, with a sense of unease he could feel all the way across the room, she came toward him, her steps small and tight. She was so afraid of him things on the tray rattled softly because her hands, possibly her whole body, was trembling. As she approached the steel-barred door of his room, she hesitated. She had good cause to fear him. Even lashed down as he was he was, still a force to be reckoned with. And no doubt she could feel his hatred toward her as it rolled off him. She'd have to be dense not to be intimidated.

"*Mendato dirivitus day-o septoma,*" she said at last, unlocking the heavy door and its lock with the spoken spell. She was not afraid of him hearing it, because his kind could not cast magic. Magic had forged his kind into life. And magic, it was said, could not beget magic.

She turned and butted the door open using the hook of her ankle to control it. She entered more quickly now. He could only assume it was because she wanted to get the whole thing over with and the less time she spent in the cage with him the better off she'd be.

She had no idea, he thought with menace. If he could get his hands on her, he'd snap her rotten Templar neck in an instant. She and her kind had taken the one thing, the *one thing* that he treasured above all other things, and they would pay for it.

They had taken his freedom.

It was driving him insane, being locked away like this. Though it was a very different type of captivity than the one he'd been forged into, this was far worse. Probably because this time it had been his foolishness, once again, that had gotten him in this kind of trouble.

He'd been tracking down another piece of Templar scum, had followed him into a bar, only to make the mistake of being distracted by a pretty girl, a decoy, who had talked to him cheerfully as the Templar bastard had come up behind him and . . . Well, he didn't exactly remember what had happened next, but his head sure hurt and he'd obviously lost consciousness.

She put the tray down on the floor within his reach . . . or rather, within his reach when the chains were slackened. She stood up and pushed back her hair, the shining length of it smooth and clean and rich. Despite his hatred for this Templar, he had to give credit where it was due. God had done right by her when it came to her hair.

Ahnvil growled low and fierce and she jumped in her own skin, quickly backpedaling toward the door. He had been captive here for two days and time was growing short. He needed to act now or risk insanity or, worse, permanent being. Of all the things his kind feared, permanent being was by far the greatest and most universal. Insanity could be healed with time and guidance, but permanent being . . . it meant being a prisoner in stone for all time.

"Before you go," he said hastily, pausing to clear the rough anger in his voice. "Tell me why it is that I'm being held here. I know nothing of value, and wi'out my touchstone you have no ability to enslave me. All this does is risk permanent being. 'Tis senseless! I am just a guard for a low-level Politic Bodywalker," he lied, "I swear I doona know anything!" His desperation was coming through in his voice, his thick Scot's accent growing thicker, and he cursed himself for the weakness.

She put one hand in the other, twisting them together in agitation.

"I don't know," she said, and he knew she was speaking honestly because of the stark worry in her eyes.

Worry for me? he wondered. Hardly, he thought an instant later. She was a Templar. The worst kind of Bodywalker. The kind that robbed its host of all previous life and individuality. The kind that would enslave another being. The kind that would use evil magic to have their way. She was a snake. Perhaps a less dangerous snake in the grand scheme of things, but a snake just the same and her venom would be just as deadly . . .

however small it might come in its doses. He shifted, testing his bonds for the thousandth time, the sting of his raw skin reflecting that. Early on he'd shifted from stone to skin, trying all manner of methods to free himself. Every attempt, no matter how small, reminded him that time was ticking away, and along with it his sanity. For, as strong as he was, the longer he was away from his touchstone, the weaker he became. The longer he was away from his touchstone, the looser his grasp on reality and . . . eventually, his mind. And the longer he was left without the stone, the more sure his impetus toward permanent being would become. Permanent being. Turning to stone and never being able to turn back again. Trapped in one's own stone prison. No way of healing from it, no way of coming back. And these Templars were counting on his fear of that. They didn't need to torture him. They need only wait and let time do it for them.

"Imagine how frustrating this is for me," he said, letting his true desperation come through, trying to appeal to those flickers of humanity he saw within her from time to time. Maybe her host wasn't completely subjugated, he thought with even more desperation. Maybe there was a true human being fighting within her.

Maybe he could use that to his advantage.

"Like you I am merely a servant tae a master. I know nothing. I'm li'le more than a dog playing fetch." He growled. "I fought for freedom only tae find myself li'le more than a slave again," he lied. Quite convincingly, he thought. He deflated with a sigh. "But they will no' believe that. No' even when I turn to permanent being." He shuddered at the words, and he did not have to act the emotion.

"I'm sorry," she said, and he almost believed her. "There's nothing I can do."

She turned to hurry out of the enclosure.

"Wait. What's your name? Just so I know what tae call the only friend I seem tae have in here." That's it, he coaxed in his mind as she leaned back toward him, taking his measure as she tucked a silky strand of that hair behind her ear.

"Jan Li," she said, and he knew instantly it was her host's name, the Asian features of her face telling of it if nothing else. That was unusual. Usually Templars did not adopt their host's names. The less they were reminded of the host within them, the happier they seemed to be.

"Jan Li. Thank you, Jan Li, for talking tae me. My name is Ahnvil." She probably already knew that, but he gave her his name in order to coax her into humanizing him. It would work on whatever part of her was decent . . . if any part of her was. It did occur to him that she might be just as deceptive as he was being, acting the innocent to wheedle the information they wanted out of him using femininity and helplessness to pave the way. But it was worth the risk to play the odds. What other choice did he have?

Jan Li locked his cage back up, testing it with a rattle of metal, as if he could move that far forward in his little pacing acre. Then she went to the chain release and let him have the slack in his chains again. Perhaps . . . was it his imagination or was it a little more than he'd had before? He shook his head, trying not to let the situation toy with his grasp on reality. He would lose hold of that soon enough. What he did notice was that she kept looking over at him. Even as she left the room, she cast a slow look at him over her shoulder.

Then she left him alone.

Alone to wait.

She reappeared five hours later, the only one to breach his solitude, and it was harder and harder for him to ignore the ticking clock they had purposely left within his line of sight.

She was carrying yet another tray, coming toward the cage to trade it for the empty one at his feet. It wasn't until she went for the lock that he realized that she hadn't taken the slack from his chains. Did this mean she was beginning to trust him? Beginning to relax her guard?

She lowered the tray to the table and lifted her dark eyes up to his.

"You have five minutes at most before they notice you are missing. I have constructed a ruse that has brought the guard from his station. There is a camera watching you."

"I figured as much," he said, his breathlessness a result of his disbelieving elation.

"All I ask is that you take me with you. I cannot break free of these people on my own. I beg of you to lend me your protection. I am afraid I am of little strength and use to you and all you have is surprise and my knowledge of the complex on your side."

"Deal. And 'tis enough," he told her.

She wasted no time then entering the cage, making him realize immediately that she had a key grasped within her shaking fingers. She unlocked his manacles with lightning speed, something he found impressive, for all her talk of being weak. It occurred to him that this could all be a ruse, an act to get his hopes up only to crush them later. A way to further stress his mind in order to bend it to their will, but what other option did he have? And whatever else, his hands were unbound and that meant his wings could be called forth.

After freeing him, she wasted no time hurrying out of the room and he had to make haste to follow her. Only . . . he stopped and looked back toward the worktable . . . toward the metal box. On impulse he grabbed for the box, opened it, and snatched the Amulet from within it. Then he hurried out of the room.

They were underground, as he had long suspected for all they had behooded his head on his way to his cage initially. But it was barely a basement, free air hitting them after only two flights of stairs. He heard a lot of shouting and saw people running away from them across what looked to be the yard of an old prison. It was full of fencing and barbed wire at its rims, but the openness allowed him to see there was a fire and a hole ripped into the fencing and the ground. A distraction, he realized as he turned to look back at her. But he was in free air and that was all he needed. He shifted form instantly, his stone skin rippling over him and his wings bursting forth from his back. He grabbed her up against himself and with a thrust of powerful legs he launched into the sky, making sure to protect her from anything that might be thrown at them from the ground. But what he worried about most was that he was burdened and that other Gargoyles they would send after him would not be.

CHAPTER THREE

"It is *not* an ugly monument of metal with no purpose. It's an ugly monument of metal that's allowing us to carry on this interference-free phone call."

That small bit of logic released a tirade of venom about the evils of modern technology from the other end of that lovely connection and Katrina Haynes rolled her eyes heavenward, as if that were going to help deal with her mother for whom logic was a fluid thing. The ugly cell tower they'd just placed on her mother's neighbor's property on the mountain above was a blight and an eyesore and entirely not necessary said she-who-was-infamous-for-bitching-about-dropped-phone-calls and she-who-was-attached-at-the-hip-to-her-barely-understood-smartphone. Her mother had to have the best, whether she could use it to its potential or not.

Katrina's own smartphone had been a gift from her mother for Christmas; otherwise she'd still be making do with her much beloved flip phone, and being quite content with it. Although, she had to admit to an Angry Birds addiction. She had several different variations of the game.

"Well, Mother, then you'll have to be content with looking *down* the mountain and not *up* the mountain where the cell tower is. After all, isn't that what a vista is all about? Looking *down* around you?"

She whistled sharply, looking down her own drive to where Karma had disappeared. She exhaled, her breath clouding on the deep sigh. The air was cold and crisp, just the way she liked it, and as she looked down at her own vista, a breathtaking view of the valley and the small town of Stone Gorge, Washington, where she lived, she guessed she'd probably be a little pissed off, too, if something marred her view in any direction.

"Momma, Karma's disappeared again. I'm going to have to call you back."

"That dog." Her mother tsked. She didn't like the thundering Newfoundland dog. Her mother said it was because the dog reminded her too much of a black bear rather than a dog, and being so close to the wilderness where bears often came down and ravaged her mother's birdfeeders, Katrina could understand the trepidation. Although Karma was a bounding bundle of soft, sweet, slobbering devotion and wouldn't hurt a fly, never mind a birdfeeder.

Kat said her goodbyes and hung up the phone before moving down the steeply sloping drive and whistling again for her dog. But as she came around one of the drive's many curves, she found the dog snuffling into the thick leaf fall left over from that autumn's annual shedding. Karma's big body was blocking her view of whatever it was she had found. Fearing she'd come up with a skunk, Kat hurried forward.

"Karma, come out of there!" she ordered sharply.

And that was when she saw it. Him. It. She couldn't decide and she was frozen in place, rooted with fear and shock, her heart pounding with sudden madness in her chest. He was probably the largest man she had ever seen in her life, and living in nearly wild mountain country that was saying something. He was almost twice as big as the gigantic dog sniffing at him. But the most shocking thing about him was not that he was half naked in the slush of the last snowfall that was half melted yet, but that half his skin was gray, like the coarseness of a stone, and half was dusky, perhaps deeply tanned or maybe racially swarthy with an acre of sculpted muscle. He was lying on his stomach, seemingly dead.

Then he groaned, proving himself alive, and rolled onto his back, and all her fear melted away when she saw a copious amount of bright-red blood. She lurched forward, shoving her dog aside, as she dropped to her knees and reached out to touch him. Her hands fell onto his shoulders, one of which was chilled human skin, the other of which was as rough as stone. *But that couldn't be,* she thought in some corner of her mind. Skin simply did not turn to stone. Perhaps it was a full thickness burn or some other kind of injury . . . But the sectioning of skin to stone fluctuated under her touch and suddenly the shoulder opposite turned to stone and the other to flesh beneath her trembling hands, robbing her completely of any further excuses.

But with that change came a sudden gush of blood down the ridges of his defined abdomen before it dripped heavily into the snow, much of which was already stained a melting red.

"Don't . . . move," she said, fumbling for her phone. "I'll call for help."

"No!" He reached out to grab her by her front, her thick coat suddenly feeling like nothing in the grip of his fist as he jerked her forward. She felt like something fragile all of a sudden, like he could snap her in two at his whim. "You see what I am. I canna control it. The pain . . . They would see what I am." He looked up then, searching the dark predawn skies. She and her mother always spoke in the freakishly early hours before dawn, and they always called each other through a

cup of tea and coffee, respectively, touching base and
bookending their days to the sound of each other's
voice. "I need shelter. Please. I canna be caught out in
the daylight."

Katrina sat there on her knees, the wet snow melted by
her body warmth seeping into her jeans, frozen with fear
and indecision. In the end it was the bright red of another
gush of blood that galvanized her.

"This is crazy, this is crazy," she said under her breath
in a fast, heated whisper. "Okay," she said so he could
hear her. "I'll bring you inside. But . . . that doesn't mean
I won't call for someone. If you try to hurt me . . . my dog
will attack you."

"Oh," he said, his chiseled lips turning into a wry
smile, "the dog that was just merrily licking my face?"

Crap. *Damn it, Karma*, she thought with heat.

"W-well . . . I-I'll scream or call for help."

"Thanks for the warning. Once we're inside I'll snap
your neck to shut you up." She gasped as he gave her
another wry smile. "Doona tell the villain what you're
planning tae do when you doona know what he's capable of. I willna hurt you. I need your help. And fast. I'm
getting weaker by the second and you willna be able tae
move me if I become dead weight. You're far too small."

He mentioned her smallness almost as if it were a terrible failing on her part and that got her back up. People
had treated her like this tiny little missish thing all of
her life and frankly it just served to piss her off. She was
small, no doubt about that, but she could pack a punch
if necessary. And after his warning about keeping her
plans secret, she bit her lip to keep herself from saying
as much.

Instead she reached out to help him up. It was clearly
all he could do to gain his feet, and she realized just
how critically wounded he was. But she couldn't see the
damage just yet with all that blood obscuring her abil-

ity to determine the worst of it. Despite his concerns over her diminutive shortcomings, he leaned heavily into her all the same, making the disparateness of their heights seem suddenly more obvious. As they trudged up the sloping drive she began to fear her ability to get him to safety. Her muscles began to burn under the strain of climbing with his significant weight against her just as the house came into view through the thickness of the pines.

"How much . . ."

Farther, he wanted to know. The blood coming from him was soaking the left side of her clothing and she knew why he couldn't speak. He was using all of his focus to stay on his feet.

"It's here. Right here. Not much farther. You can do it," she encouraged him. It seemed to give him strength and he lifted his weight further onto his own feet and propelled them forward quickly. At the walk of the house, however, he stumbled and went down, staining her stone walkway with his blood. "Come on," she said, fearing he couldn't go farther and, like he had said, she wouldn't be strong enough to get him into the house. She glanced up at the sky, the dawn doing nothing to lighten it because of the bitter cloud cover heavy with snow. Worse still, the wind was picking up, promising a blustering and brutal blizzard.

But the weather was a ways off and it was the least of her worries. Except, a storm could cut her off from any help, and she would be helpless to him . . .

But right then it was he who was helpless to her, and that galvanized her into action.

"Up!" she commanded, yanking at the arm he'd lain across her shoulders. "Get up. Only a little farther. The dawn is coming," she warned him, not knowing why that should trouble him so much. Maybe it was the coming storm that worried him. Rightly so. Washington was known for some mighty mean snowstorms. Especially at this altitude.

She pulled him up and he got his feet under himself in what she suspected was his final act of strength. They stumbled to the door and she hastily juggled him and the doorknob, his weight on her making her fumble at it. Finally it gave way and they staggered into the house.

"Somewhere dark. No light. Protected." His words jolted out of him on groans of obvious pain. Far be it from her to argue.

"I know the feeling," she muttered.

She went for the nearest bedroom, which turned out to be the master suite. All the other rooms were on the second floor and she knew navigating stairs was out of the question for them both. Even without his weight, the burning muscles of her legs couldn't possibly have gotten her up them.

"That's it," she said with a grunt, "I'm getting my fat ass in gear and getting on the treadmill. In the spring it'll be better . . . A few treks up and down the mountain, right?"

After much grunting and bumping into walls, they made it into her bedroom and fell into the bed together, his weight flattening her until she could barely breathe. She shoved at him, but he was barely conscious and she realized that the weird stone thing was once again shifting in and out of being on his body . . . if that were even possible. Hell, it had to be possible. She was watching it with her own eyes. Feeling it against her own skin. Before he turned to stone completely and she found herself trapped under a ten-ton statue, she strained to push him off her with what remained of her strength. But as much as she shoved at him, she knew it was his help alone that allowed him roll to off her.

She wriggled out from under him and gained her feet by the bed, panting hard for breath. *Damn it,* she thought inanely as she saw him lying big and bleeding in her bed, she really loved that quilt set and she was never going to be able to get that blood out.

Thinking he was unconscious, she reached out and poked a finger against the stone-looking skin on his arm. She couldn't believe it, but it really was stone! A rough stone like that of an unpolished statue. How in the hell was that possible? It couldn't be . . . but it was. She was feeling it right under her fingertips.

"No outside light. Please," he said, startling her. Begging her. "The daylight will make it impossible for you to help me, and I will die. I promise you, I *will* die."

She nodded hastily, reaching out to give him an awkward pat of reassurance on the large, curving muscle of his shoulder. "Don't worry. I've already closed the storm shutters." And started a fire in the fireplace that warmed both the master bedroom and the living room with shared sides, its warm light dancing over them both. That and the bedside light was enough.

He exhaled then, a long shuddering breath of his final strength bleeding out of him, and suddenly she remembered what all of that blood meant and forgot about her damaged clothes and quilts. She ran for her bathroom, yanking out the supplies she had squirreled away in dribs and drabs over the years just in case . . . well, just in case. And now, it was in case. She found a basin and loaded it up with gauze, iodine, and 2-0 vicryl sutures. She belatedly washed her hands and snapped on a pair of purple nitrile gloves, even though she was already drenched in his blood. She would work better with clean hands and the traction of the gloves.

She hastened to the bed, moving up to him and hitting both of the bedside lights. She turned him and realized there was no more stone skin on him. He was entirely a flesh-and-blood man. For some reason that comforted her a little. But the idea that that could change at any moment sat heavy on her thoughts. Suddenly she felt the burning presence of her phone in her back pocket. She should call for help, never mind his protestations. He was out like a light and there was nothing he could do about it, he was just that weak. But he had surprised her thus far with his ability to power through his weakness, and even if she called for help, it could take anywhere from thirty minutes to an hour before anyone would make it up the mountain to her. This was what she had feared, and the only thing she had feared, about living alone so remotely. She had imagined things like this, evil men stumbling upon her house and she alone and helpless.

But nothing about him made her sense that he was evil, per se. After all, he had pointed out to her what he *could* do to her . . . inferring the opposite, that he *wouldn't* do anything to hurt her.

In the end she decided to leave the phone silent in her pocket, even as she berated herself for probably being stupid and very likely to regret it. But the healer in her jumped to the forefront, and she grabbed gauze and began to wipe at the source of his blood. She gasped when she finally cleared the field and could see the extent of the damage. A cut deep into his side, as if someone had swung a sword into him, trying to cleave him in half, and down his side and leg he was violently burned, third degree in most places.

Again, she felt the burn of her phone in her pocket.

"Doona," he rasped, as if he could read her mind.

"I won't," she soothed him. "But you are terribly injured. You need a hospital."

His mouth turned grim and his eyes fluttered open. For the first time the golden topaz of his eyes jumped out at her. They were beautiful, she thought with no little awe, as was the rest of him. He had the darkest, deepest black hair she'd ever seen. Not blue-black . . .

not dark brown . . . but purest black. It had the lightest curl to it as it fell in waves to just above his collar. He had an aquiline nose and deeply sculpted cheeks, the cheekbones wide. His mouth was full, like for a woman, only unmistakably male. She imagined a mouth that large had a smile just as wide. A killer smile, she was sure. He was not pretty or boyish by any stretch of the imagination, but was still strongly handsome.

But there was no time to further enjoy the view. She had to clear her field once again and she grabbed her suture kit. As deep as the wound was, she worried about the contamination of the leaf litter and whatever had caused the injury in the first place. She first used saline to wash it clean until she was satisfied there was no debris in the wound, and then she squeezed the bottle of iodine over him and prayed for the best.

"This is going to hurt. I don't have anything to numb the area." The area? Hell, she was practically going to have to do surgery to put him back together.

"Do it," he rasped. And then, fortunately for him, he passed out completely. She felt it ripple throughout his body, almost like the deflation of sudden death. She worriedly checked his breathing and found it, shallow and weak as it was. She turned her attention to his wound, threaded her needle, and went to work.

CHAPTER FOUR

Kat had finished her ministrations a while ago, but then she'd had to shower the blood from her own body and change her clothes. Once she had done that she went about the process of cleaning up the rest of her patient. The wound was clean and neatly sown where it could be sown, but his jeans had been burned onto his body and removing them was no easy trick.

She had a pair of surgical scissors, heavy gauge and meant for cutting through some pretty tough stuff. She'd already cut his jeans down the left side and away from his wound, so now she worked them under his jeans on the right and slowly cut the thick, resistant denim away. It was no easy trick and her hands were burning with an ache by the time she cut through the ankle hem. She didn't know if it was because the material was particularly tough or if it was her adrenaline crashing and her hands were shaking like crazy from it, but she had to stop a couple of times for fear she might accidentally cut him. The last thing he needed was to lose more blood. As it was, he was very pale and drawn around the lips, his skin having a grayish sort of pallor to it, but this time it was not from stone. It was what anyone might look like after leaving so much blood on the ground. He hadn't woken up since the last time, and although that was sparing him a great deal of pain at the moment, that also made him dead weight.

She grabbed his jeans by the ankle and, digging her feet into the wood floors and putting her weight into it, she dragged the cut denim from under his body.

And now she had a naked god in her bed. She hadn't really paid any mind to him while he'd been in dire need, but now she drank him all in, head to toe, and tried to come to grips with the idea that anything human could be built so big and so beautifully.

Wait a minute. *How do you know there's anything human about him?* she wondered. But looking at him now, after having her hands on him and her fingers within his tattered flesh, she wondered if what she had seen before had been merely a trick of the predawn light. But no, she gave her head a shake. Sight was one thing, but this had been touch as well and she had felt the roughness of stone. She had felt the weight of it against her body. Logic screamed at her that it couldn't possibly be true, that she hadn't seen and felt what she knew she had seen and felt.

Impossible. The whole situation was impossible. She took out her phone and for the hundredth time she debated calling her mother.

She shoved the phone back in her pocket at that thought and gingerly picked out the remnants of his jeans from the burn wounds, debriding his flesh meticulously until it was bleeding freshly and clean of all debris and dead flesh.

After cleaning up the bloody mess she'd made, making certain every inch of him was cleaned and tended to, she marched to the kitchen and made herself a cup of hot, liquid java nirvana. She normally didn't drink coffee at this hour, but she figured she would need it if she was going to tend to her patient for the next few hours.

She'd fantasized about mainlining it, hooking up an

IV to get it straight into her bloodstream like any good junkie would desire, but alas, via stomach was the only delivery method to be had, her medical expertise not-withstanding.

Speaking of medical expertise, it was nice to know she still had it. It had been five years since her tenure as a physician's assistant in one of Manhattan's busiest ERs. Like any skill, it was easy to lose one's knack for it. And while she couldn't say she was up on the latest methods of doing things, she was content to know that she knew enough to get by.

She pushed away any other ruminations about her skills and where she had last practiced them, ghosts too easily stirred up whispering mockingly in the back of her brain.

"Five years. You're a whole new you now," she said softly to herself, soothing herself with the mantra. Some-times it worked. This was one of those times, but prob-ably only because she had much bigger fish to fry.

And no sooner had she thought that thought than the naked behemoth himself came stumbling down the hall-way, lurching from side to side like a drunkard, the light of a fever burning in his eyes.

"Is it night?" he croaked. When she didn't answer fast enough he reached for her and slammed her up against the wall with a bone-jarring thud. After working in a city ER for years she had seen this a hundred times, a patient waking up disoriented and aggressive. Just the same, there were no orderlies or security guards there to bring him down. It was just her. Little ol' her. "Answer!"

"No! It's daylight and you need to be back in bed before you rip those stitches!" Everything about him screamed of a superhuman man. His temperament was still up in the air, but everything about him reeked of dangerous power.

Not to mention nudity. A state he didn't seem to notice at all. And being a former trauma nurse, she shouldn't be noticing, either, but it was kind of the elephant in the room. Elephant meant in more ways than one. There was nothing at all small about the man. His wife, if he had one, had to be an equally big girl. Kat couldn't begin to imagine being on the other end of someone so big in so many ways. It was one time where she was happy to admit she was way too small to even consider tackling that particular mountain.

She turned her voice soft and coaxing. "Come," she said gently, her hand running soothingly down one of the forearms trapping her against the wall. "You're going to hurt yourself."

He scoffed. "There's very li'le that can hurt me."

But she could tell he was struggling to remain upright, his brawny body shaking in fine tremors at first then expanding into harder ones. "Please come lay down in bed for me and rest. It's not like you can go anywhere with a storm closing in."

He growled and gave her a shake. "Offer me bed one more time, wench, and I'll be taking you with me." He leaned in close, his nose touching her temple as he snuffled against her rather like her bear of a dog might do. "You smell very tempting, but as li'le as you are I wouldna risk it if I were you. I'll no' be an easy lover." His voice dropped an octave. "I like to grab at my lass, dragging her tight again' me, and devouring her smells and tastes before I even think about fucking her to within an inch of her life . . . but maybe, even as small as you are, you're wanting to be devoured like that?"

Oh yes, please! part of her cried suddenly. *Wait. No!* her saner thoughts prevailed. She shook off the momentary melting craving his sensual threats caused, the bold words having jump-started her brain into illicit musings. *There will be none of that*, she told herself sternly.

Right before he ran a hand up her ribs and completely embraced her breast with palm and fingers.

She yelped, grabbed his hand, and smacked it away.

He growled impatiently. "First you offer me bed, then you push me away. Quit your teasing, woman."

"I am not teasing! I only meant—" She huffed out a breath, realizing she was trembling just as powerfully as he was, and she told herself it was from fear and not because he'd just weakened every bone in her primitive body.

"There will be n-no wenching tonight," she stammered as firmly as she could, pushing at the massive wall of man with an ineffectual palm against his chest. There was some sort of raised burn on his chest, something long healed but purposeful in shape . . . as though he'd been branded. Two snakes, wrapped around a dagger in an infinite figure eight, each snake seemingly devouring the tail of the snake before it in what seemed to be a never-ending cycle. The heavily defined and branded pectoral muscle jumped, ostensibly at her touch. Like a kid seeing something fascinating and new, she wanted to repeat her action just so she could see the reaction once more. Truth be told, there was a wave of virility pounding off him, catching her in the surf of it, dragging her around like a helpless child at the beach. But there was nothing at all childlike about the heat his words sent snaking through her.

Kat worked her mouth into a harsh line and looked him dead in the eye. *Who the hell used the term wench anymore anyway?* she thought, trying to bolster her sternness. "You are going back to bed, *alone,* to rest! Doctor's orders! You've lost a lot of blood and—"

And right on cue he listed dangerously forward, nearly squashing her up against the wall like a bug as all his weight pushed into her. But he recovered quickly and drew away from her, taking a moment to dust her off and check her for signs of life. It was little things like that, little thoughtful kindnesses, that kept her thinking he was not a bad man, whatever his treatment of her thus far.

"Perhaps you are correct," he said, still sounding as though he'd lurched out of the Middle Ages. But for all she knew he had. "I'll be taking a rest, in spite of the insufficiency of your bed."

In spite of what now?

Instantly she became pissed off. "Hey, my bed is just fine. It's not its fault that you're abnormally gigantic! Just be glad I didn't leave you in the brush to die!"

He frowned then and suddenly there was clarity in his eyes. "Yes." His hand went to his wounded side, his fingers running over her stitching. "I'll be thanking you for that," he said. "I think I'll be requiring your help further," he said politely, indicating his unsteadiness. Mollified, she stepped under his arm and, again, despite their disparate heights she managed to help him back into bed. But man, was she going to feel it tomorrow when her muscles began to complain about the serious heavy lifting she'd done in such a short amount of time. And without a sufficient warm-up!

After she got him in bed, she finally pulled out her phone and called her mother.

And got her voicemail. Lovely.

Beep! "Hey Mom. It's me. It's really—" Crackle. Crackle. Click. "Important that you call me," she finished with a sigh even though it was very clear the line had gone dead. "Oh crap!" she exclaimed suddenly, running to the window and, sure enough, there was the reason her cell service sucked. A heavy fall of snow was whooshing around outside. She noticed the creaking of the house for the first time and the wailing of the sudden winds. It had blown up fast and hard, but no one could blame her for not noticing under the circumstances. "Oh crap!" she said again suddenly.

It was obvious her guest had a fever. His gaping wound had been exposed to God knows what and he could easily go septic if he didn't get some strong antibiotics.

Kat ran to the master suite bathroom and started tearing through her medicine cabinet and the under cabinets, even though she knew she was a good girl who always took all her medication right down to the very last pill. But who knew? Maybe she'd been a rebel just once. Of course her rebel days had ended quite abruptly years ago, and any medication from back then would be expired, but it was better than nothing.

Nothing. She found absolutely nothing. A deep groan wafted into the bathroom from the bedroom, a punctuation to her failure. She hurried into the next room and up to the bed. Sure enough, her bed was creaking as he thrashed about, sweating up a storm. God, it had set in quickly. Or maybe not. Who knew how long he'd been lying out there. She hadn't brought Karma that far down the drive in days. The only reason she'd even gotten that far today was because her mother's dismay over a cell tower—one that wasn't working, by the way—had distracted her.

Apparently standing there at his bedside thinking was a bad game plan. A tremendous paw of a hand suddenly swiped out for her and yanked her off her feet, her body flying over his and her back hitting the bed. Her breath left her in a hard whoosh of sound.

"You again?" he growled as he rolled atop her, his hand wrenching her legs apart to make way for himself. He was so strong and she was so taken by surprise she hadn't had a hope of fighting him. Once again she found his face buried deep at her neck as he took a deep breath in through his nose. "God Almighty in the blue sky above you smell good enough tae eat."

"No! No," she cried. "No eating! There will be *no* eating!"

She wriggled under him, trying to push him off her, even though she knew it'd be like a flea bouncing against a dog to try to change his direction.

"Oh, there will be eating," he countered, his voice lowering to an even deeper timber than his already rich tones. "And licking and sucking and quite a bit more than that, my bonny lass."

This whole time she'd been trying to place his accent. She'd never been very good at that, but in that moment, when he called her a bonny lass, she realized he was a Scot. *Ooo*, she thought, *Scots are sexy. Gerard Butler is a Scot and God he is sexy.*

But Gerard Butler was half this thing's size and she couldn't afford to think he was sexy. Even if she kind of did. Maybe he was only part Scottish. His accent wasn't always so thick, and sometimes, when he was truly lucid, it faded to a much lighter version of itself. Just like his civility seemed to appear in those more lucid moments.

"No," she said more firmly this time, "you will not eat me." Then she realized what she'd said and she colored hotly. "I don't even know you. And I don't want you to . . . to do anything to me. I want you to let me up."

"If you dinna want me, lass, then why do you no' stay away? Why do you keep coming tae my bedroom smelling like sweetness and sex?"

"I-I don't . . . sweetness and sex?" she asked, getting distracted from her goal.

"Aye," he rumbled, that low voice trebling into her in a stimulating vibration. "As if you'd poured sugar over your nether bits and are wanting me tae lick it up."

Okay, now the heat coming off her face could warm the polar ice cap. It was quickly matched by the heat suddenly radiating from those aforementioned nether bits. Not to mention she'd gone decidedly wet.

"Come now," he purred coaxingly, his golden gaze falling to her mouth. "One wee kiss. It canna hurt you."

"One wee kiss?" she echoed, flabbergasted that he would think there could be anything "wee" about him.

"Done!" he said, taking her stunned echo as permission.

"Oh no, I—"

He swooped down and caught up her mouth with his, her protestations muffled into silence. His mouth was hot and demanding, just like the rest of him. He commanded the kiss, crushing anything she might do to resist or gainsay him. He pressed the heat of it onto her until she melted and relaxed into it. *It's one kiss,* she thought. *What harm can one kiss do?* He felt the change come over her and pressed his advantage instantly. He thrust his tongue forward against her, licking the trembling seam of her lips. It was a blatant knock at her door and she was torn between instinctively knowing this was a bad idea and instinctively knowing it was going to be the hottest kiss of her life. *There was once a time,* she thought, *when you would have grabbed something like this with both hands and cried* Woo-hoo!

She opened her lips and he dove right in, commanding and fierce. The wet stroke of his tongue in her mouth released an equally wet flood of heat bleeding into her from every which way. His hands came up to bracket her head, only his elbows holding the full press of his weight off her. But that didn't matter to her right then. Because, right then, she was having her socks blown off by the deepest, hottest, richest kiss of her life.

When he finally pulled back a minute distance to give her time to catch her breath, she realized she was panting for it. For breath . . . and for another life-searing kiss. He was so hot along the length of her body, like a furnace turned up high, and he was so . . . hard.

Holy crap! He was naked and the sudden hardness

pressing against her between her legs was most decidedly the most enormous erection ever known to man. And that's when reality slammed into her. She was too small and weak to fight him off if he got it in his head that he wanted more than a kiss and was going to just take that as well.

And you will not think about how much you might enjoy that, she warned herself harshly. *You will realize just how scary the concept ought to be and act accordingly terrified.* And the other thing, the heat of his body was deepening and she wasn't arrogant enough to think that had anything to do with her.

"Okay, let me up now," she said. "You've had your kiss, now let me up."

"Oh, but you're no' really wanting me tae go," he wheedled. "Look at your wee nipples." He rose up enough to put a hand between them, letting him cup her breast through her cotton shirt, his fingers brushing eagerly over the point of her hardened nipple. "They're begging for a suckle, now aren't they?"

"No!" she said, flustered. "They are begging for nothing of the kind!"

"Then what are they begging for?" he countered, a sly smile crossing his lips and feverish gold eyes.

"There's no begging. No begging at all!"

"Liar," he countered, brushing his fingers over her nipple again. "If this isna the prettiest of beggars, I doona know what is. Let me see the wee thing and then we'll decide."

He reached for the bottom hem of her shirt and she squeaked in panic. She grabbed his wrist and tried to stop him, but all she managed was to slow him down to a slow drag as he caught the hem of her shirt and pulled it upward.

"No. Please don't."

There must have been something in the tremble of her

voice that struck him. Or maybe it was another moment of that suddenly rare lucidity. Whatever it was, he looked up into her eyes and read the fear and conflict there and it made him do her bidding. He stopped, releasing his hold on her shirt and moving his hand to the neutral territory of the sheet beside her shoulder.

"Are ye teasing me, lass?"

"Not intentionally," she said meekly. "The kiss wasn't my idea."

He seemed to think about that a moment, then with a scoff of breath he rolled off her. "Go!" he commanded her. "And doona come back until you're ready tae do something about this!" He grabbed his erection in his hand, running his fist down the length of it. "You're far too bonny tae resist. Remember that before you come tae tease me again!"

Katrina scrambled for her freedom, falling to the floor from the bed then struggling up to her feet. She hastened from the bedroom with all speed.

CHAPTER FIVE

She needed to do something. She couldn't just leave him in there to fester with fever and then die. Any medical professional past or present and worth their degree would know this.

Decision made, she grabbed up her car keys and ventured out into the storm. The storm was already brutal and this was an absolute act of suicide. She knew that it was. But desperate times called for desperate measures. Luckily, the nearest doctor was only a mile and a half down the mountain. Equally lucky was that the storm was obliterating daylight.

Kat was bundled up tight to protect herself, but still it was bitter cold when she stumbled out of her car and banged on the doctor's door. Michael Sloan opened the door with a harsh yank and looked at her as though she'd lost her ever-lovin' mind. Which, she figured, she obviously had.

"Urinary tract infection!" she said by way of greeting. "I'm sorry, but I'm dying and I had no choice. They said the storm was going to last days . . ."

"No, I understand," the man said, ushering her in. Dr. Sloan was in his late forties, but looked incredibly good for his age. So handsome, in fact, that he was thought of as quite a catch by the busybodies in their small town who were forever endeavoring to marry him off. They had focused on Kat more than once as a prospective bride for the single doctor, but she had managed to dodge their efforts thus far. She had squelched them every time as best she could. God knew the last thing she needed was the complication of a man in her life.

She might have found the present irony in that funny if she weren't so bent on her task of the moment.

"I know all the signs, and the pain is tremendous," she said, fisting her hand against her innocent bladder and doing the wee-wee dance for effect. "I need some Cipro."

"Cipro? Don't you think that's a bit strong for—?"

"Trust me, it's a bad infection," she cut him off hastily.

He stood there and seemed to brood about it for a moment. "Of course I trust you," he said then. "Of all my self-diagnosing patients, at least I can rest assured you know what you're talking about."

"None of your self-diagnosing patients were a physician's assistant."

"True," he said with a chuckle. "Let's do a urinalysis and I can get you the Cipro."

"Dr. Sloan." She cast a meaningful look outside. "I barely made it down here. With my shy bladder a urinary test could take forever. Please, I have to get back."

"Right! Of course." He hurried back to the rear of his house. There was no pharmacy in town, so he kept his own supply of medications on hand. He filled a bottle with the required pills and she paid for them hastily. "I'll just note your chart and we won't tell anyone we skipped a few steps. After all, it's an antibiotic, not an opiate."

"That's right," she said with a smile. "I better go!"

"You better be careful. You should never have—"

"I know! See you, Doc!"

As she skidded on the steep slope from the doctor's porch to her car she muttered a constant litany of "This is crazy. This is crazy. This is *so* crazy!" And even a little of "You could have told him. You just had to open your mouth and say, 'Hey. There's this guy at my house who can turn to stone, right? Oh, and he's wounded and probably going to die of infection. But before that happens he's probably going to . . .'"

She couldn't leap to the word "rape." He had done nothing to make her think for a minute he was the raping sort. He was just . . . lusty. Yes, that was a good word for it. He was full of lust. Fevered lust. As if all his barriers and filters had evaporated and this was who he would be if all the clutter and nonsense of life were cleaned away. He was something of a throwback. As though he'd dropped in on her from a different time.

Oh great. Not enough for you that he's made of stone half the time, you have to make him a time traveler, too? You've been reading far too many trashy romance novels, Kat! After all, a real woman wouldn't just accept half the shit that goes on in those novels.

She stopped and thought about that for a moment, applying it to her present circumstances. *Well, shoot.* Could she help it if she'd seen crazier shit in an ER than a man who could turn to stone? After all, it was rather a benign thing overall . . .

Katrina shivered her way into her car and, throwing the truck into four-wheel drive, began the treacherous trip back up the mountain. She was inching along, grateful that the snow had shifted from driving pellets of snow and ice to a thick blanketing fall of soft, fat, white flakes. It made it easier for her to see, although she couldn't see more than a few feet in front of her because it was, after all, still a heavy snowfall.

The thickened snow also provided a little more traction, which she desperately needed. At the midpoint to her house she was so tight with tension from creeping up the deadly mountain road that her neck, her arms, and her entire back were hurting. She shrugged her shoulders, trying to work it out, trying to alleviate the pain of it, even though she barely noticed it on a conscious level because all her attention was focused forward.

And at some point she stopped worrying about getting home and started worrying that a man's life might hang in the balance and she was the only means of swaying the odds in his favor. It was a weighty responsibility, one she realized she was glad to take on. If not, why would she ever have taken part in this madness? She could only suppose that instinctively she knew there was something good about him, something worth saving, worth risking her own life for. Then again, she probably would have done the same for even the lowest of men . . . only she would have made sure to call in the cavalry.

Kat didn't even release a sigh of relief when she turned into her drive. The drive to her house was long and even more treacherous than the roads. The drive was dirt and gravel, which could make for good traction . . . unless it was drenched wet and then frozen. Then it was nothing but ice at an incline. Right then it was a mixture of both. The tires slipped and spun in places, the drive dropping off into a gully on the right side and threatening to skid her right off into it. But eventually she reached the final curve to the house, pulled right into the garage, and then came the well-earned sigh of relief. She didn't spend more than a moment at it before she was out of the car and bursting into the house.

Karma was on her like white on rice the next instant. The dog whined and threw her big body into Katrina as if she'd been gone a year. She'd been trained not to jump up only because that kind of love from that big of a dog would most likely kill Katrina. But that didn't keep Karma from body bumping her like a maniacal kid in the bumper cars.

"Yes, yes. Hello, hello," she said, giving the dog a hasty pet or two before plowing past her and heading for her bedroom. She didn't even bother taking off her coat. She fished the Cipro out of her pocket and headed for the master bath to fetch a glass of water.

When she entered the bedroom she once again found the bed emptied of her patient and he was nowhere in sight.

"Damn it to hell and back!" she growled. God only knew what shape he was in and where he was in her house. And so help her, if he went about bleeding on something else she'd kill him herself!

Thumping the antibiotics onto the bedside she then shimmied out of her coat as she marched through the house in search of him.

"He can't have gone far," she said aloud as she stalked through the rooms of the ground floor.

And sure enough, she found him out cold on the kitchen floor, right in front of her refrigerator. Apparently fever had not ruined his appetite and he had come in search of something to eat. There were jars of things like pickles and olives on the floor near him, all of which seemed to be empty. She found herself praying he didn't throw up later. That wasn't going to be a pretty experience for either of them.

Anyway, in the here and now she had an unconscious behemoth lying on the floor and she had the pleasure of trying to figure out how to get him up and back in the bed . . . preferably without his usual groping and fondling and kissing.

Katrina tried to keep from acknowledging the warm,

gooey heat that swirled around inside her as she remembered the kissing and fondling with no small amount of craving for more. A craving that she quickly stomped down inside herself. She had enough to worry about without tripping off into fantasyland. He was a stranger. *A stranger.* There was nothing about any of this that should engender trust in him, never mind the comfort level she required before considering becoming intimate with him. And she didn't *want* to become intimate with him. Not him or anybody, but especially not him. The guy was a Neanderthal for Pete's sake. He kept pawing at her and trying to . . . to screw her ever chance he got. And it was very clear he was an old hand at tumbling "wench"-like persons.

With a sigh, Katrina went back to the bedroom. She took the opportunity to change out the soiled bedding, shoving it all immediately into the washer and dumping a hefty amount of bleach in the dispenser. It might damage the quilt, but so would blood. She had to take her chances.

As for herself, she had showered and changed her clothing before heading to Dr. Sloan's, but she had been covered in blood herself at one point. So much for universal precautions. If he had blood-borne anything, she would definitely be exposed. She suddenly felt a twinge of fear. What if that strange stonelike condition were catching?

She shook that off. Partly because she simply couldn't deal with the idea. She began another debate in her head, weary already from so much thinking, realizing she was tired because by then she would have already been tucked into bed. It was this nearly panicked rapid thinking that she had happily left behind when she'd left her life as a PA in Manhattan General Hospital. It was this kind of stress that had caused her to lose her hair, develop an ulcer, and gestate a major case of anxiety, her whole existence about being on edge for the next thing that walked through the door . . . even when she wasn't working.

Who would have thought she'd be dragging this kind of stress through her own front door years later, ulcer healed, anxiety at bay, and hair, thankfully, regrown. But she wasn't interested in reverting to her previous state so she needed to relieve herself of this potentially high stress environment as quickly as possible. But . . . what if it *were* catching? Oh God! She'd potentially exposed Dr. Sloan to it!

"Okay, don't panic. Don't panic," she muttered to herself rapidly. *He's snowed in along with everyone else. No one is going to come into contact with him.* The odds of anyone else being as stupid and reckless as she had been by driving down the mountain were extremely nonexistent.

She hoped.

She tried not to think about it as she stripped out of her wet, snow-saturated jeans and wriggled into her favorite pair of heather-blue sweatpants. The house had warmed considerably in her absence, what with the fire and all, so she traded her sweater for a T-shirt that said NEW YORK FUCKIN' CITY! on it. It always made her smile for some reason. True, she'd never had the guts to wear it in public, her conscience paining her that some small child somewhere might be able to read it and repeat it. But she loved the idea of it. The idea of being brave enough and bold enough to don it in the first place.

But it was not even a blip on her self-conscious radar as she hurried into the kitchen and kneeled beside her own personal feverish giant. She touched his skin and, as expected, he was burning up. Actually, she needn't have touched his skin at all. He was radiating heat like a furnace and she could feel it all against the front of her body.

Before doing anything else, she carefully capped and moved the empty jars around him to the kitchen counter. "Oh man!" she whined. "You ate all my pepperoncini!" How the hell does someone eat a whole jar of the fiery pickled peppers? They were a favorite of hers, but in small doses. She knew the jar had been nearly full because she'd just opened it two nights earlier, eating a small pile of peppers with her pizza. "Hey, does this mean you picked a peck of pickled peppers?" she joked to her unconscious patient, snickering through her nose as she lightened her mood a little.

The juice in the jar sloshed around as it joined the others on the counter. Six in all. But none of the new additions to her shopping list were anything of great nutritional value. She realized he would have been forced to resort to it because she didn't have very much in the way of fresh food in her fridge. She was content with frozen meals and bowls of cereal. Although cereal appeared to be off the menu since he'd drunk down just about all of her milk.

"No worries. I have powdered. Not the same," she chattered to her rude and thoughtless guest, "but good enough. And I have duplicates of everything in the garage pantries. Be prepared, that's my motto. And a good one, too, when you tend to get snowed in a lot in these parts."

Of course it had more to do with her OCD than it did with genuine preparedness, but she wasn't going to needle herself with that detail.

After about five minutes of trying to wedge him out from between the counter and the refrigerator, enough to close the refrigerator door, she gave up and realized she was never going to move him unless he woke up to help her. And if all her jostling, shoving, and grunting hadn't stirred him, then she wasn't sure she knew what would. She had smelling salts, but she was afraid if she put ammonia under his nose he would wake up and swat her away, sending her crashing into a wall or something equally as painful. She eyed the fridge and her houseguest alternately for a moment when a brilliant idea came to mind.

CHAPTER SIX

Ahnvil felt as though he were on fire. He was trapped, locked down in this horrifying fire that couldn't kill him, but burned him straight to the bone over and over again. But something was creeping into his agony, something faint at first, then stronger and stronger, enough to distract him even from his eternal torment.

Then he realized what it was.

Food. Cooking food. Suddenly the fire abated and he realized just how hungry he was. Starving even. Had those who had put him in the fire also been starving him? He couldn't seem to remember. Was this yet another torture he was going to suffer?

No! He would not let them win. He would not let them trap him and hold him anymore! Never again! And he would kill anything that got in his way!

The big beast in Kat's kitchen came to with a blood-curdling roar of what could only be taken as rage. It frightened her so much that she dropped her cooking fork in the heavy cast-iron skillet she was using and ran out of immediate reach. For good measure she leapt up on a countertop, as if he were a mouse or something she could avoid by removing herself from contact with the floor.

He roared again and rolled to his hands and knees, lashing out at the nearest object, her refrigerator door, and nearly ripping it from its hinges. *Hey*, she thought *that's stainless steel. Don't hurt it.* She certainly didn't have the nerve to say it out loud. She didn't even have the nerve to *think* it with volume.

After a few seconds he seemed to orient himself and he was able to stagger to his feet.

Ta-da! Her idea had worked! Score one for Team Kat! Again, she was proud of herself, but not enough to say so with, like, spoken words or visible emotions. She was trying too hard not to be noticeable. She was small. Small enough to go unnoticed if she played her cards right. When his back was fully to her she pulled her legs up and balled herself on top of the counter.

Ahnvil was barely aware of where he was. He had no interest in the details. Not really. He wanted the thing they had been tormenting him with. Now that he was free, he would have it even if he had to kill an army to get it.

But there was no army, he realize a moment later. All there was was a skillet on an open flame, a steak of massive proportions sizzling away inside it. Heedless of anything but his goal, he ripped the pan from the fire, with one hand and grabbed the steak with the other. He was eating it a moment later, ripping into it with huge gnawing bites, barely giving himself a moment to taste it before he was swallowing it down. It had to be the most delicious thing he had ever eaten in all of his life. He realized it was probably just perception, but just the same, it tasted like ambrosia.

Once the steak was almost halfway gone, he began to look furtively around himself, prepared every minute to fight off whatever army lay in wait. He was aware the steak was probably just bait to trap him again, but he didn't care. He would deal with trouble when it came and not a moment before. He'd never been the worrying sort. He'd make a goal and see it through to its end. He saw no sense in worrying about outcomes or anything else for that matter. Life was straightforward. Good or bad. War or peace. Free or slave. Fight or die. Simple. As simple as he was. Flesh or stone. Simple.

It only took him a moment to notice the wee fey lass curled up in an intimidated ball on a counter across the way from him. He looked over his shoulder to see what she was so afraid of, but he saw only the stove and the refrigerator. Items in a kitchen. He was in a kitchen.

That gave him pause. He swept his eyes over the vast room, with its open area on one side that led out into a sprawling living area with tremendous floor-to-ceiling windows all along the central wall of it. And that led him to fixate on the wild white and gray storm swirling on the other side of it. He pulled in a moment, checking his internal clock. Daylight. It ought to be daylight. But it wasn't. The storm. It was blotting out the sun. It relieved him to know that. It meant he could move about freely without worrying about the touch of the sun turning him.

His attention went back to the little fey thing. It occurred to him then that she must be afraid of *him*. It almost made him laugh. He was a protector of all things good and innocent, not a beast to be feared. Why would she . . . ?

Then he stopped and looked at himself. Really looked at himself. He was towering over her in her kitchen—he had to assume it was hers—naked and fierce and eating her food—he had to assume it was hers—like an animal. There were no enemies. There was no prison.

Not then. There *had* been, but he had broken free of that prison. Again, he checked his internal clock. Three days. He'd been three days and nights without his touchstone. Who knew how much longer he had before the unthinkable would happen?

He slowly put the pan down on the nearest surface and flexed his burned hand a bit, feeling it for the first time, only just then realizing he'd burned himself in his haste to obtain her food. He straightened his stance and, though he tried, he couldn't make himself give up the steak he was gnawing on. It was almost gone in any event. It wasn't likely she'd want it back. He held out a placating hand.

"You've no reason tae be afraid," he said with a swallow of the divine beef. If there was one thing that could be said of his kind, it was that they loved their food. And with good cause. They burned caloric energy three times as fast as humans did and therefore had to replenish just as quickly. Next to their freedom, food was the thing most Gargoyles coveted at any given moment. Freedom and food. In that order.

"Y-you killed my refrigerator. I-I'd say that gives me reason."

Damn, he thought as he looked at the damaged piece of equipment. He swallowed the last of his steak and reached to maneuver the wobbly door. It shut, but not with any certainty that protected the food within it . . . what little there was of it. She barely had a bite in there, he realized as he immediately found himself looking for more food to satisfy his appetite. Then again, as tiny as she was, she probably didn't eat all that much.

He turned back to her. "I'm truly sorry for that, I am. I wasn't in my right mind. Where am I? What is this place?" Then he moved and a blinding, fiery pain came over him, nearly bringing him to his knees. If not for the counter near him he would have fallen straight to the floor with the sudden unexpectedness of it. And quick as that, like the dart of a bee to a flower, she was off the counter and working herself under one of his arms as though to hold him upright. It made him chuckle in spite of the wave of pain. Did she think a wee thing such as herself could help a man of his size by doing that?

"You're injured," she said with haste and, he had to admit, obviousness.

"I can see that," he said dryly. He didn't bother to ask her what had happened. He knew well enough. He had broken free of that devil's prison with the help of another brave lass . . .

Ahnvil shoved away any thoughts of that escape and the woman who had made it possible. He would access his feelings about it later. Right now he had someone else's feelings to consider. "Come, get away," he said, shoving her away from him and looking around at the windows hastily as if his pursuers were right beyond the glass. They might well be, and then he would have brought hell down on this innocent woman and maybe she too would end up . . . dead.

"Stop it," she said, stubbornly dodging his efforts to put her aside. She was up against his uninjured side quick as a flash. "You need to lie down and rest. You're going to be here awhile," she said, nodding toward the storm outside. "So you may as well relax and take the time to rest. If you'll let me get you to bed I'll make you another steak," she tempted him.

And damn it, he really wanted another steak. He was still famished and, he argued with himself, he couldn't afford to be weakened by hunger. She had a point about the storm. Between that and the fact that it was daylight beyond the storm, it was very unlikely he had been followed. But that didn't change the fact that time was running very short for him. Dangerously short. He didn't have the time to spend on eating and convalescing.

But that storm . . . that would hold him back. Especially wounded as he was.

"How long?" he asked, nodding toward the windows as well. "When can you expect a lull?"

"I don't know. Not for at least twenty-four hours, I promise you that much. These storms are fierce and long here. It could last as long as two or three days. And then after that it will take a good deal of time before the plows can come through and allow us the ability to go anywhere. So you need to face the fact that you're stuck here for a while. May as well rest, heal, and," she made sure to add, "eat."

Her logic and her lures were inescapable. With a nod of assent he let her help him down the hall to a bedroom and a freshly made up bed. By the time they got there, he felt as weak as a newborn lamb and his legs were shaking with the effort of remaining upright. As they traveled she told him the story of how she had found him and what kind of state he was in. Fever. Likely infection. Wounded. All of which he could easily take care of . . . if not for the dangerous time constraint looming over his head. It was best to remain as he was, remain human and helpless, than it was to change to his stone self, a state where he would heal far more rapidly. But he had to play it safe. After three days away from his touchstone, he had to play it safe.

She had him tucked in in a flash, her speed and strength pretty impressive. She pressed some pills on him and followed them up with water so fast that he had them swallowed and gone before he could even think about arguing with her. Then she gave him a pat on the hand.

"Now if you think you can manage to stay here this time, I'll go make you another steak. I'll make you some sides as well if you can wait."

He seriously debated that for a moment. Then he said, "Make me two steaks and all the trimmings you can manage." Then he thought to add, "Please."

Her eyes went wide. "That will be three steaks!" she

said with no little shock and even a touch of being impressed.

"Your point?" he countered, a hard look daring her to argue. He wanted that steak and wasn't in the mood to fight about it. But that look meant that he would . . . if necessary.

"All right then," she said, backing up carefully as if she were afraid to startle him. That was when he realized what a gruff ass he was being, and a sheepish sensation washed over him. It must have telegraphed to his expression because she hesitated.

"I'm sorry. I'm just very hungry," he said, all of his regret lacing the words. She had done so much for him, and he was being an ingrate.

"It's okay." Considering his feverish state, she wanted to offer him something lighter to eat, but she didn't have the nerve to do so. "I'll be right back with your food. Please can you try to stay in bed this time?"

"This time?" he echoed, lying back on his pillows and starting to look seriously worse for wear. He had done a lot these past fifteen minutes and it was clear it was more than his body could handle.

"You keep coming out of bed. Last time it was to eat and the two before that it was to . . ." she trailed off, realizing he probably had no memory of the times before and if she was reading this slightly more civilized version of himself right, he was going to be mighty embarrassed by what he'd done. Maybe. She still wasn't sure what he was made of.

"It was tae what?" he demanded to know, sitting back up and narrowing those golden-amber eyes on her.

"You're feverish. It's not important," she dismissed turning back toward the threshold of the door. It was mere steps away and she'd be free of his overwhelming presence. Maybe she'd get lucky and he'd pass out from fever before she got back with his food.

"'Tis important tae *me*," he said, that hard voice demanding she do away with the niceties and get right down to the truth.

"You keep"—she swallowed—"you keep trying to, um, fondle me." She wasn't going to point out that she'd been thoroughly fondled already. Perhaps he had a code of honor or something and learning that would upset him. She didn't want to disturb him any more than he already was.

She thought that right up until the moment a wolfish smile streaked over his mouth and through his eyes. "Aye, I'll bet I did." He chuckled in a deep, rolling laugh. "You're fine for what ye are. And tiny though you be, you're more than a bit juicy at the breast."

She gasped, horrified and insulted. Well, maybe not insulted . . . or maybe she was insulted. She was confused about how she should take all of this. Frankly, she was burning out from being at red alert for so long. Perhaps that's why her temper took over.

"You arrogant, obnoxious ass!" she spat out at him, heedless of the fact that she was poking a bear. "You better keep your hands to yourself from now on, fever or no fever, or I'm going to stab them with whatever sharp instrument is lying handy nearby!"

"Oh well," he said, his humor still high in his eyes, "I'll be sure tae be more careful then."

It was clear he was anything but intimidated by her. In fact, the swine was mocking her.

"Oh!" she huffed, turning hard and stomping out of the room. She wished she had the sharp wit necessary to put an arrogant SOB like him back in his place, but the truth was she simply wasn't that clever. And she had always taken things much too seriously all around. It had made it hard for her to make friends at work. The staff would josh and kid one another, but when they got to her she'd always felt . . . ashamed. Insulted and

ashamed. She'd obsess about the flaws they obviously
saw, big enough flaws that made them want to tease her
about them. It had been just another source of stress in
her daily life when, for others, such things would have
been jovial and relaxing. And eventually they had
stopped trying to get her to laugh at herself and had
instead taken to whispering behind her back about how
she couldn't take a joke to save her life or how stupidly
serious she was.

Careful, here comes the fun police, someone would
mutter as she'd approached the nurses' station, thinking
she couldn't hear them. But she'd been cursed with abnormally sharp hearing, yet another painfully useless
talent in her life, and she had heard every whispered
comment or dry remark.

Now, as she marched off to cook his food, she tried
not to cry, gulping back the urge as it burned in her
eyes, nose, and throat.

Ahnvil could hear her banging violently around the
kitchen and he tried hard not to chuckle, but the urge
was too much to handle. As punishment his side burned
with a fierce stabbing pain, reminding him of much
more sober truths. Eventually he was frowning as he
probed the angry red wound and the neat little stitches
holding it all together.

Stitches? And she hadn't just broken out the sewing
box and made a haphazard job of it. It looked professional. No, better than professional. Professional and
very precise. Very . . . thoughtful. Had he been human,
under her care he could have expected very little in the
way of a scar. As it was, her skill would help his already
rapid healing abilities . . . provided the damn infection
didn't continue to retard the process. He was susceptible to everything a human was susceptible to. The difference being his odds of surviving those vulnerabilities
were much, much higher.

Provided he could turn to his stone self. But this far out from his touchstone he didn't dare. He was afraid that if he did, he'd never be able to turn back again. Even so, as he sat there in bed waiting for her, he felt a ripple of heavy pain race down one of his arms and suddenly his flesh shifted to stone. His heart slammed around in his chest and he held his breath, waiting, praying he would change back. It was the first time he could ever remember changing to stone involuntarily . . . save those times he had been caught unaware in the sunlight. Instances like that, however, were thankfully few and far between. To be caught unaware was to be risking the moment of death. Turning to stone should always be well prepared for and should always be done in safe quarters.

This place was not safe. There was the storm blotting out the sun, yes, but it would not last forever and he didn't trust it to last as long as she had said. Weather was too unpredictable to put all his faith in a forecast. So the first thing out of his mouth when she returned was, "I need you tae close all the curtains. I canna have a bit of sun on me. I . . . I have a condition . . ." he said as vaguely as he could.

"Is that the condition that turns you to stone and back again?" she asked a bit dryly, letting him know that she was neither blind nor stupid and the rippling shift to stone had been happening even while he'd been unconscious.

"I . . . know it must seem strange tae you," he hedged, his eyes falling on the food as a serious war between his appetite and his desire to explain himself brewed. " 'Tis just . . . a medical condition. 'Tis no' catching or anything," he hastened to add, trying hard not to frighten her off. He was going to need her for a while yet. Just until he was strong enough to maneuver on his own. The storm might give him a reprieve, but the truth was he had enemies on his heels. Enemies who would not think twice about tearing through an innocent woman in their effort to reacquire him as a prisoner. And as horrifying as the idea was of being locked up once again, the idea of her coming to a brutal end was even worse.

"Yeah, sure," she said, her tone more than a little dry. "I'd believe that . . . if I weren't in the medical field. And while I've heard of people slowly turning to stone over time as parts of themselves calcified, I've never heard of them turning back to flesh again." She dusted a hand over the foot of the comforter on the bed, straightening the corner almost absently as she spoke. Then she suddenly turned dark, serious eyes on him. They were a pretty sort of red and brown, rather like the color of bourbon, he thought inanely in that brief moment. "Please don't treat me like I'm stupid."

Ahnvil toyed with the fork that had come with his tray, but as hungry as he was and as good as the food smelled, he wanted to make himself clear with her.

"I'm sorry. Just trust me when I say the less truth you know abou' me the better it is for you. I doona want you in any danger. That's part of why 'tis important to make sure no one can see into this house and not even the smallest shaft of sunlight can penetrate."

She stood a moment, absorbing what he had said, and then gave a little nod. "Eat. I'll take care of it. I'm not interested in your secrets, only in seeing you make it through this injury in one piece."

She moved away and went to the sliding glass doors that normally went out onto a deck with breathtaking views of the valley below. She picked up the jacket she had discarded earlier and shrugged into it hastily. Then she toed out of her slippers and stuck her feet back into her boots. The snow that had gotten into them during her previous excursion out in the weather had melted and was cold and wet against her feet, soaking right into her socks. Once she was laced up and buttoned up, she unlocked the deck doors.

"Wait, what are you doing?" he demanded of her. She looked back at him, her features drawn and serious.

"I'm doing what I said I would. And I would appreciate it if you would do the same," she said, nodding toward the tray.

"But . . ."

She didn't give him room to argue. She stepped out into the storm. It was like stepping out from heaven straight into hell. The safe, quiet warmth of the indoors was swept away with a brutal howl of wind and the bitterly cold scouring sensation of ice stinging into every last exposed pore on her face, neck, and hands. Normally she would have bundled up far better than this, but it was only going to take a minute to close the heavy outside storm shutters over the doors. She'd managed to do all of the windows, but had not had the opportunity to get the doors since she'd been summarily distracted. But it wasn't as easy as she had hoped for. The shutters were heavy even under the best of conditions, but in the brutal conditions of the storm and with the already heavily accumulated snow lying up against the doors it was almost impossible. She was going to need a shovel, she realized. She would have to shovel out all the gathered snow around the door and shutters before she would be able to close them, protecting the glass and keeping the light off her sun-shy guest. She let go of the shutter she'd been struggling with and turned to head back inside for warmer clothes and a more thorough game plan. She ran face-first into a branded chest and wall of naked abdominal muscles. He grabbed hold of her with one arm, using himself as a windbreak, protecting her from the worst of the harsh winds, and with the other hand he grabbed the left shutter.

He simultaneously thrust her back inside the house and yanked the shutter closed in one powerful movement. But he clearly paid a price for it. He grunted and leaned to one side. She shrugged off the grip he still had on her arm, figuring by his expression that had he been up to snuff he would never have allowed her to do so. She came back outside and grabbed the other shutter, determine to power it closed on her own, delighted when it obeyed only to look up and spy his hand on the shutter above her head. Resisting the urge to stamp her foot and pout, she turned on him.

"Get back inside! It's too cold out here for you!" She eyed his naked body with purpose. Damn it, the man should at least have the decency to . . . umm . . . shrink from the cold like a normal man would.

"Likewise," he replied, taking her arm once more and ushering her inside whether she liked it or not. But since she was freezing her ass off she didn't argue or resist, however she did use her apparently miniscule strength to tug him in her wake. Once she was indoors, she locked the shutters down and slammed the deck doors shut.

"Get back in bed!" she commanded him, pointing for effect. *Yeah, that's it. No nonsense. All business.* He'd have to take her serious in her well-practiced Nurse Ratchet voice. She'd gotten a lot of mileage from that voice, more than making up for her small stature with it.

The bastard chuckled at her, even as he put a pained hand to his side, making her realize he was seeping blood again. It was crimson against his fingers.

"You certainly are a wee pushy thing," he drawled, his brogue rolling out of him in deep, sexy waves.

Wait! No! Not sexy. Don't even think about sexy! God only knew who he was. God only knew *what* he was. She had no business looking at him like he was somehow attractive to her. He was a powerful stranger, possibly not even a human stranger. Powerful enough to be on his feet even though he was paper white from blood loss.

If not human, then what?

At her glare he held up conciliatory hands and made his way back toward her bed. He was limping, hunched slightly into his wounded side, clearly suffering pain. She wished then that she could have come up with some clever way of getting pain medication for him, but she hadn't been able to think that far. His infection was much more insistently at the top of the list of things that needed to be dealt with. She couldn't even think about the rest of the list right then, either, or she would be overwhelmed by it. The list of things she ought to be doing after finding herself a nursemaid to a dangerous, questionably human being. Like, call for help . . . run for the hills . . . or take a valium . . . something like that. She made herself take even, steady breaths and adopted an all-business attitude.

"Be that as it may, I know best in this situation, and what I say goes. Especially because this is my house."

He gave her a measuring look right before he halted his progress toward the bed, turning around to tower over her. His height and his obvious strength were incredibly intimidating and she heard herself swallow. No doubt he did, too.

"You're a tiny, li'le thing," he pointed out, his voice a low rumble. "But make no mistake. I'm a stranger in your house. Twice your size and a trained warrior. I do nothing I doona want tae do and you know nothing else abou' me. For all you know I'm a serial killer, wee one. Dangerous and a risk I am. One that you, wee as you are, shouldna have taken on."

She scoffed. "I didn't have much choice and neither did you. You would have bled to death and, by now, been covered in snow until the spring thaw! So don't you try and bully me when I'm just trying to help!"

" 'Tis no' bullying," he said, his tone rough and seemingly a little angry. " 'Tis a risk you shouldna have taken."

He listed suddenly, a grunt of pain escaping him as he reach blindly for the nearest object sturdy enough to brace himself against. There was none. None but her, and when he tried to straighten rather than use her to lean on, she thrust herself under his arm and against his good side.

"Stop this," she demanded of him, powering him toward the bed, realizing that he had weakened enough to where he didn't have a choice but to obey. She got him to the bed by force of will alone and by the time they got there he was covered in a sheen of perspiration. He grunted as he hit the bed and she grabbed some 5-x-5s and pressed them hard against his wounds, once again disregarding universal precautions, even though a box of gloves was just across the room. She couldn't afford the time it would take to glove up and neither could he. He had lost too much blood to risk losing much more.

"Eat your food if you still can," she ordered him, nodding toward his neglected tray. "And try to keep it down. You need the nutrition."

"Aye," he said, but it was a weak reply compared to the powerful boom she knew his voice normally worked at. She would bet it bruised his virile male ego to have to depend on a woman, but that was just too bad.

He was stuck with her and she was going to be in charge, whether he liked it or not.

CHAPTER SEVEN

Isabella Russ rolled over in her sleep. Though barely conscious, she recognized the scent that filled her nostrils immediately.

Man. Her man. Her husband. She sniffed a little then took a long slow breath in because he smelled so divine, as usual. It was a nice distraction from the fact that she was still tired even though she had slept the day through.

"Are you sniffing me?" came the deep-throated rumble of amusement near her ear.

"You smell good," she mumbled against his skin, snuggling up against him more tightly. It was chilly outside of the blankets and she had no interest in joining the cold waking world just yet.

And right on cue, the toddler cried.

"Ohhh nooo!" she ground out, ducking her head under the covers as if she could hide from the demands of her son. But unlike her daughter, her son had proved to be everything a demanding child could possibly be. Jason, for instance and much to her dismay, had refused to breast-feed. Bottle-feeding made twice as much work and she hadn't quite got over her pique at not being able to feed him "from her heart." Of course he was beyond breast-feeding by now anyway, but she still wasn't quite over it. And it was only one of the dozens of ways this particular child was determined to use to exhaust her.

For instance, waking up at the crack of dusk. The child had an internal clock that told him dusk was imminent, as did most of the Nightwalker breeds, but rarely was it so highly developed in one so young.

Bella was just lucky that way.

"I'll get him," her husband said with a low chuckle.

"No!" she said when he went to move all of his virile warmth out of the bed and from under the covers. "I want you to stay."

"Well, one of us has to get him or he'll start to scream," Jacob pointed out to her needlessly.

"Let Leah do it," she sighed.

"Leah is nine. She is a little young to be taking care of our rambunctious three-year-old."

"Well, I know that!" She huffed and rolled onto her back. "Fine. Go. I'll be up in a second."

"Bella." Jacob reached out with a long-fingered, strong hand and ringed her around her throat with it. "What is this all about? If you are tired, we will do fine without you while you nap further." He reached to run his hand from her throat down the length of her body in a comforting caress. Comforting. Not sexy or sizzling or any of the things they had once felt every single morning right after setting eyes on each other. There was never any time for that now. Now there was just a toddler to tend to.

"More sleep won't help," she said, ejecting another sigh of frustration. "I'll just have exhausting dreams."

"Exhausting dreams?" he echoed. "What kind of exhausting dreams? Do you mean dreams or premonitions?"

Bella was a Druid, a half-breed of Nightwalker and human. Once upon a time she had been all human, or so it had seemed, until Jacob came along and touched her. His

Demon DNA had interacted with her Druid DNA and turned her "on" to her rapidly growing abilities. One of which had proven to be the ability to sense the coming future. Which could ultra-suck sometimes. Especially when she needed to sleep to compensate for her child's demands on her.

One would think that becoming immortal and all would make it much easier to tend a child, what with their awesome immortal healing and replenishing abilities. But no, just like any other mother she was doomed to perpetual exhaustion. This in spite of the fact that Jacob was the best father in the known universe.

She sighed again. "Don't mind me," she said. "I'm just whiny today."

"You did not answer my question," he pressed.

"Well, I don't know which it is! I just keep dreaming of going on *vacation*. Vacation far away from here, like in the States. Somewhere snowy and cold and crisp with lots of hot chocolate and roaring fires."

"We have fires and cocoa here," he said with amusement. "I can always have Elijah whip up a nice snowstorm for you."

"I don't want a wind Demon snowstorm, I want a natural one."

Jacob blinked. "But . . . it is natur—"

"Don't ask me to be logical! I'm too tired!" she groused. Again, a contrite sigh. "And did I mention that this might be, you know, *alone time*?"

Jacob raised one dark brow and amusement was quirking at his lips again. "Alone time? We can be alone whenever you like . . ."

"But then I just fall asleep because I'm so wiped out. Never mind!" She tossed back the covers and got to her feet huffily, but one touch of bare feet on cold floor and she was jumping into her slippers.

"Bella, come back here and talk to me."

"Screaming child, remember?" she tossed back at him over her shoulder. She marched herself into Jason's bedroom, hitting the lights and making her way to the crib. An instant smile streaked over her lips the minute she saw Jason's face, his eyes lighting up at her approach. His belligerence turned to babbles of delight and, as usual, he melted her cranky little heart.

"Come here, you," she said, scooping him up into her arms. He kicked his feet and wriggled with excitement before wrapping around her like a monkey on a flagpole. Then he laughed. He had what he wanted and that was the end of that. "Spoiled little booger," she said softly, kissing his forehead three or four times.

"Bella," Jacob scolded her as he followed in her wake.

"Let's just feed him," she said, not meeting her husband's questioning eyes as she went to push past him.

"Not until," he said, a hand and arm in the doorframe blocking her path, "you tell me what you want. Just tell me and it is done."

She looked up into his nearly black eyes and saw the determination in them. Immediately she was reminded of why she would love this man until the day she died . . . which, being immortal and all that . . . was a long way off. Hopefully. There were always dark forces out there that could risk their lives the same as anyone else's. Immortal was not the same thing as invulnerable . . . or unkillable.

It was just that being a Nightwalker meant it was just harder to pull it off.

Thank God.

Or thank Destiny, as Jacob would say.

"I love my son," she blurted out.

"I—" he frowned. "I know that, little flower. I have never said I doubted that— Bella! Why are you crying?"

Immediately he was enveloping her face between his elegant hands and tipping her head back so she was looking up at him through the sudden wash of tears in her eyes. "B-because I'm hormonal!" she said, trying to pull away.

"I know you are dealing with exhaustion—"

"No! Not *that* hormonal! I mean . . . *h-o-r-n-y* hormonal," she said bluntly, a little stomp of her slippered foot accompanying it. "And you haven't touched me in four months! Not once! Well . . . I mean you touch me all the time and you're very loving, but you're just all gentle and sweet and nice. Of course I am very grateful that you are gentle and sweet and nice—don't get me wrong. I know how lucky I am. It's just that we used to have s-e-x. I mean, of course we had s-e-x. We have two children," she rambled on, so fast her husband was having difficulty keeping up with her shifting topics, "but I don't think you find me sexy anymore and I can't even find out because I'm so tired all the time or the minute we have two seconds alone the baby cries or Leah jumps into bed with us or we have to save the world or something!"

And somewhere in all of that, Jacob finally got the gist of the problem.

"*Ohhh*," he said, light dawning, "you want to go on *vacation*."

"I could swear I said that. You're a little slow on the uptake tonight." She went to walk past him again but he wasn't ready to let her go just yet. He swiped a thumb through the track of a tear that had fallen when she'd blinked.

"Vacation. Childless. United States. Cold. Cocoa. Fires. Skiing. Consider it done," he said. "We shall leave tonight."

"B-but the b-baby and Leah and—"

"We leave tonight," he pressed onto her. "Noah will watch Leah and the baby. Or we can give the baby to Elijah and Sienna."

That made Bella laugh. "You're evil," she said. Sienna was renowned for being completely stumped by children of any sort. They made her incredibly nervous. Even more so since she'd found out she was expecting her own. She was fairly large and uncomfortable and desperately afraid of what was going to happen next.

Elijah's answer had been immersion therapy. He'd offered to watch any child in a thousand-mile radius, exposing Sienna to all shapes, sizes, ages, and sexes in the hope that it would calm her worries.

So far, not so much. Bella had tried to tell him that the only thing that would make her calm down would be birth. The ultimate immersion therapy. Elijah had not been convinced, much to Sienna's dismay.

"My point is, we know Lycanthropes, Demons, Mistrals, Shadowdwellers, Druids, and Vampires. Out of those six Nightwalker breeds we are going to find someone trustworthy to watch our children, and you and I are going to go away."

Then he leaned in, ignoring the wriggly bundle that was their son and pinning her to the spot with dark, famished eyes. "And I've been waiting for you to get h-o-r-n-y for three months now," he said hotly. "Had I known you were already there, I would have done something about it immediately."

"Ha! Some telepathic connection we have," she snorted. "I thought for sure you knew and that I was too chubby with baby weight and that you didn't want me . . ." And suddenly it sounded ridiculous to her own ears.

"And I thought for sure you knew I wanted you, will *always* want you. I was just . . . toning it way down because I did not want you to feel like you had to. I know how tired you have been."

"Well, okay then," she said with another little sniff. "Vacation."

"Great," he said, smiling wide and a little bit lecherously. "Where? The Catskills? Vale?"

"Stone Gorge, Washington."

Jacob blinked. "Where the hell is that?"

"Stone Gorge, Washington, duh," she said dryly.

Jacob rolled his eyes. "I know that. I meant to say, why there? I know a great place in Vale. It'd cost a small fortune and rightly so. Plush cabins, night skiing . . ."

"Stone Gorge, Washington."

"I'm having a bad feeling about this," Jacob said hesitantly.

"Have all the bad feelings you want. We're going."

End of story. She didn't say it, but Jacob knew she didn't have to, and so did she.

Oh yeah, he was definitely having a bad feeling.

And yet, with copious amounts of scorching sex on the horizon, those bad feelings were easily pushed aside.

CHAPTER EIGHT

He was snoring.

Not your average rumbly little snore, but a fricken freight train that rattled her rafters.

Great. How was she supposed to get any sleep between that and the fact that he was in her bed? Oh yes, there was another bed upstairs, but it wasn't *her* bed, and she didn't want to go too far out of earshot. God only knew what he was going to do this time and it usually ended up with her trying to pick his enormous bulk up off the floor. And honestly, her legs had truly had it. So had her arms. And her back.

God, she was getting old.

Thirty years old and *old*. Retired. Decrepit.

And, apparently, not that dried up. Not if her constant review of his blistering kiss was any indication. She kept finding herself rubbing absent fingertips over her slightly parted lips and in the middle of remembering the feel of his mouth against hers.

No. Forget it! she kept telling herself every time. And every time she was just as unsuccessful as the time before. She was sitting in the chair in the corner of her bedroom, one foot tucked under her and the other pushing rhythmically against the floor so she was rocking and gliding gently. She had a cup of coffee perched on her raised knee, and she blew on it intermittently because it was still too hot.

He'd been asleep for about three hours and in that time she'd checked on him more than half a dozen times, doing things like checking his pulse and his bandages. Never once had he stirred and never once had he stopped snoring.

After hours of the sound it was beginning to have a lulling effect. She found herself drifting off more than once and that was when she had decided on yet another pot of coffee. By this time of day she was usually drinking tea instead of coffee . . .

Hell, by now she was usually asleep.

She had gone out into the living room about ten minutes ago and cautiously peeked outside. It was so dark out for daylight hours that she did something she very rarely did.

She left her house and walked out into it. Karma was utterly delighted, although a half-hour ago she'd been looking at her with consternation wondering why they were still awake and why she wasn't the only big thing lying in her bed. The snow had not lightened in the least, but the driving ice part of the storm was in a lull, it seemed. Karma bounded through the snow, six fresh inches already added to what had already been there. It had been a heavy winter thus far, and there were huge icy piles of previously plowed snow on all sides of her driveway. Fortunately the gully on the one side made an excellent receptacle for snow. And the icy piles made Karma feel like the king of the mountain when she climbed atop them, so she would bark, great white clouds of breath fanning into the air.

The temperature was dropping rapidly, even colder than it had been when the storm had started. She could hear the heavily laden trees creaking as the wind rushed between them.

"Karma! Come on, girl!"

Karma did so happily, another indication that it was getting colder. Normally she would have been hard to get back indoors. But even with her thick coat of fur she had reached her limit, and despite thick down, so had Kat.

After coming indoors, she was a bit at loose ends and quickly became bored. She moved into the bedroom and, since she'd already cleaned up all the soiled gauze and such, she found herself picking up his cut up jeans from the floor. That was when she realized there was something in one of the pockets.

It was a necklace. A very pretty silver and onyx necklace. The silver was an oval disk, polished to a shine so that she could see a mirrored image of herself within. It was rimmed with highly polished black pearl-like stones. She guessed they were onyx, but perhaps their luster meant they were pearls. She wasn't exactly a gemologist so she didn't know. All she did know was that the pendant was very beautiful and very old. She had a weakness for very beautiful and very old things. That was why she felt absolutely no guilt when she hurried to the mirror and dropped the thing over her head, lifting her hair and letting it settle. As if it were made just for her, the pendant rested perfectly flat at the top of her cleavage.

"Ooo. Pretty," she whispered, fondling the thing, feeling the cold metal and stones between her fingers.

She probably should have taken it off right away, but since he was out cold she didn't see the harm in wearing it for a little while longer. He would never know, she told herself. And that was why an hour later she was toying with it, running the loose pendant up and down the chain. The chain had no clasp, no beginning, and no end, just delicate links that shone and glittered.

Suddenly, the freight train screeched to a halt. He awoke with a roar, shoving himself out of the bed in a huge leap until he was crashing into the wall and her innocent little hand-painted bedside lamp was lying like an incandescent murder victim on the floor. He had both hands clenched into fists and at the ready, and his skin rippled into stone and then flesh again like a rolling wave changes the color of the sand.

She leapt to her feet, holding out a steadying hand.

"It's okay! You're okay!" she said quickly and loudly, never knowing what might penetrate into his dubious awareness. He glared at her distrustingly for a full fifteen seconds before his darting eyes had taken in his surroundings and allowed him to relax just a fraction. Then he seemed to reconcile where he was and with a great exhalation he relaxed, slowly releasing the clench of his fists.

It was strange, but of all the thousands of questions she wanted to ask him, at the top of the list seemed to be *Who the hell hurt you?* It shouldn't have been. At the top of the list should have been *What the hell are you?* But in all fairness, it was a close second. And since she doubted she was going to get an answer to the first, she thought she'd shoot for second best.

"C-can you tell me something?" she asked hesitantly. "Can you tell me why your skin does that . . . that stone thing?"

For a second he had an expression on his face like he had been caught with his pants down around his ankles . . . only she doubted such a thing would make him feel self-conscious. He just didn't seem the type to care much about what others thought of him. Then again, she had, like, a total sum of thirty minutes to go by, so how would she know?

For a second she had the feeling he was going to tell her to mind her own beeswax, but after a momentary debate he ran a hand back through his wild black hair and eyed her as if judging just how much truth she could actually handle.

"I'm no' sure you want tae know that," he said cautiously, his body listing to the left. He was bleeding once more. With a tsk of sound she put her cup down and grabbed more 5-x-5s. She came up to him and approaching with a little caution she pressed them over his saturated bandage and leaned her weight into him. It pushed him back against the wall, which was good because it gave her a little counterforce.

"It's kind of the elephant in the room no matter how you look at it," she said, daring a look up at him. His amber eyes glittered in the muted light of the room, reminding her that her lamp lay on the floor. That made her frown. She'd found it in an antique barn for a song. It'd been one of her favorite acquisitions.

"Most humans canna handle the truth of things," he said darkly.

Most humans? Was there something other than humans to be found? She kept in mind what she'd seen so far and swallowed hard.

"Try me out. If I panic you can knock me unconscious or something. In fact, if I panic I'll probably thank you for it."

"Just the same," he said cautiously.

"Try me," she repeated.

"Verra well. I'm a Gargoyle."

She blinked. Like an owl, she blinked again. "I don't understand. You're . . . a mean ugly statue at the top of Notre Dame cathedral? Or more cute like the Disney versions?" She swallowed noisily, hoping for the latter. Knowing otherwise.

"We doona all live on churches," he scoffed, as if she had stereotyped him. She didn't see how that was possible since she knew of only one Gargoyle. One living breathing moving one, that is.

"Okay," she said carefully. "Forgive me for pointing out the obvious," she said after a delicate clearing of her throat, "but despite the occasional flash of stone, you're kind of made of flesh and bone."

He laughed, the gravelly sound of it suddenly taking on a whole new meaning for her. "Aye," he agreed, "that I am. Half of the time. And the other half I'm solid stone with wings and as ugly a face as you ever did see."

"Oh," she said. Then without thinking she asked. "Can you show me? Like, on purpose?"

"Nay, I canna," he said with a slow shake of his head. "No' right now."

"Why not?" she asked, unable to quell her curiosity.

"'Tis a long story. Ye doona want to hear it."

"I wouldn't have asked if I didn't want to know."

"I doona think you know what you want because you doona know what you ask."

"Nice. Way to condescend," she said darkly.

That made his brow furrow. "I only mean tae say if you think you're scared now, an explanation will no' make things better."

"I see," she said, unable to help nibbling on her lip a bit nervously. "But I was just wondering—"

"Jesus, woman!" he burst out, half exasperated, half laughing at her. "Verra well, then. All the wee things that go bumpy in the night are real. Djynns, Phoenixes, and the like, Wraiths . . . and some things you never heard of before."

"Gh-ghosts? You're telling me ghosts are real?"

"Wraiths," he corrected, wincing when she pushed a little too hard into him.

"Phoenixes," she whispered. "What about Vampires? Werewolves?"

"No, no such thing. They're called Nightwalkers. There're six breeds. Wraiths, Mysticals, Djynns, Bodywalkers, Night Angels, and Phoenixes. Six Nightwalkers in all."

"Wait, that makes seven. Gargoyles makes seven."

"No"—he shook his saturnine head—"Gargoyles are no' Nightwalkers. We're . . . more like scions of a Nightwalker breed called Bodywalkers. And if you want a better explanation, I'll need to be off my feet."

"Oh! Oh, of course!" She immediately pulled the gauze back, checking and seeing that the bleeding had stopped again. For now. She helped him the short distance into the bed, tucking pillows behind his back when he was clearly determined to sit up. She pretended not to notice when he made an appreciative sound down around the area of her cleavage.

And suddenly, just like that, he grabbed hold of her by her arms and gave her such a good shake her eyeballs clattered around in her head.

"Where did you get this?" he demanded roughly, grabbing for the pendant.

She had the conscience to color.

"I'm sorry. I found it in your pocket and it was so pretty . . . I couldn't help my—"

"Off! *Now*!" he all but bellowed into her face.

"All *right*!" she snapped. "Jeez, don't have a conniption! I was just trying—"

"*Off!*" He made like he was ready to rip the thing free of her neck and fearful for the life of the pendant she hurriedly went to take it off. Bad enough he'd killed one antique already.

"I know, it's for your wife right? You're right, it was wrong of me to put it on. But I promise I didn't hurt it."

"Why aren't you taking it off then?" he demanded to know.

"I am!"

"No, you aren't, you keep picking it up and putting it back down."

"I am not!" she said, picking the pendant up.

And letting go of it again.

Their eyes met, hers perplexed and his stormy. "I'll do it," he said, grabbing the necklace.

Kat felt a solid punch in her chest and she went flying through the air and into the far wall. The air kicked out of her lungs as she dropped hard to the floor a second later. On the opposite side of the room, her houseguest was scrambling out of bed. She felt dwarfed as he loomed over her and she flinched when he lifted his hands toward her.

"Please don't!" she cried, her body still trying to regain full oxygen to her lungs.

"Christ, I'm sorry," he said, touching her anyway, pulling her upright into a sitting position and gingerly cradling her cheek in one of his large hands. She felt suddenly fragile and far too delicate in the face of him.

"D-did you hit me?" she asked tremulously, more than a little pique in the words. She didn't exactly remember him making contact with her body, but how else would they explain her flight across the room.

"No! I wouldna hit a defenseless woman!" he said, utterly affronted by the suggestion. "Most especially the woman who saved my arse from certain death."

"Oh." She coughed and rubbed at her aching chest. She felt as though she were going to have a solid bruise come evening. "Then what happened?"

"Must be a bloody curse," he muttered under his breath to himself.

"A curse? All right did you say . . . a *curse*?"

"Aye," he said grimly, clearly seriously believing his own supposition. "You doona ken the kind of world I come from, lass. Curses and wishes and the like happen all of the time. I ought to know. My stone self, the beast I became and can become, it's an elaborate sort of curse."

"You mean . . . you used to be h-human? All human?"

"Aye," he said with a tight nod, clearly not happy discussing it. "But I doona want to talk about it. Let's get you on your feet. There's a good lass."

Ahnvil reached out to gently palpate her ribcage and she squealed and batted him away. "Stop that!" she cried. "There's been more than enough fondling for one night."

He smiled as naughty as a wolf plotting to use a shortcut to grandmother's house. "There's no such thing as too much fondling," he said. "But I doona ken your meaning. I've no' fondled you, though I canna say the idea hasna crossed my mind before this. Though I admit I was thinking about you doing all the fondling. Ye've a fair fine pair of hands on you lass, soft and sure. I'd be lying to say otherwise."

"You could have gone with not saying anything at all," she muttered, scrubbing a hand at one of her blushing cheeks. Then she stopped and looked at him oddly. "What the hell is your name?" she thought to ask suddenly.

"Ahnvil."

"Oh." Then a second later, "Seriously? You were born and your mom looked at you and thought 'Ahnvil, that's the way to go!'"

"Nay, lass. 'Tis no' my original birth name. 'Tis the name I chose after my second birth. It's spelled A-h-n-v-i-l. The *h* is silent."

"That's a very odd spelling. Why the *h*? And what do you mean by second birth? Are you, like, a born-again Christian or something?"

"No, lass. What's your name?" he countered, obviously evading her questions.

"Kat. Short for Katrina." She figured first names were as far as she was willing to go.

"Well, Kat lass, I'm a wee bit tired, so I'm going to go back to your fine bed and have a rest."

"But what about this necklace?" she wanted to know, trying twice more to take it off by the time she reached the bed, and both times inexplicably letting go of it the minute she thought of pulling it over her head.

"Well," he said, sitting on the bed and taking a minute to catch his breath. He was so very pale and she realized it was from his blood loss. But she had no basis for comparison because she had no idea if he was normally pale. She might have thought he was tanned, because he seemed so strong and potentially outdoorsy, only he had an obvious aversion to daylight, which was something she completely understood. "We canna do anything about it at the moment. So it's best to let it lie. I doona want tae hurt you trying to take it off again."

"Oh. Okay." She could appreciate that. She fondled it for a second. "It's very pretty, but I don't think I want to be stuck wearing it for the rest of my life," she said worriedly.

"I doona think it will come tae that," Ahnvil lied. "I've a few people I can go tae for help." He listened for a minute to the howl of the wind that had picked up outside again. "But it will have tae wait until after the storm."

She scoffed. "Longer than that," she said. "You're not going anywhere for quite some time." *Although,* she thought, *anyone else would have been unable to even move after those awful wounds.*

" 'Tis cute the way you worry about me," he said with a chuckle.

"Shut up!" she said, flushing under his teasing regard. "I'm just doing what any good person would do. Besides, if I don't take care of you I'll never get this thing off."

She picked up the necklace. It was so shiny and pretty. It felt smooth and cool in the center, but when she touched it, even when she tried, she left no fingerprints on it. She found herself looking into the disc in the center of it, her reflection clear as if in any mirror. Only, somehow she looked different in it. Not distorted per se . . . just . . . hazy. She'd be looking at herself and it'd start off normal but after a moment she would sort of fuzz over.

"Stop," he said suddenly, reaching to cover the Amulet, breaking her eye contact with it. "It keeps entrancing you," he warned. "You doona even seem tae hear what I'm saying tae you."

"It does not!"

"Then what did I just say?"

"That it's cute the way I worry over you."

"That was several minutes ago," he said. "I've been talking to you about how I don't heal like normal people do. Although, I would heal faster if I turned into stone."

"But you've been turning to stone all along," she said, torn between frowning at the reminder that he was less than human and fascinated by every new detail. After all, she'd never met a supernatural creature before. Anxiety aside, it was actually incredibly cool.

"I mean turning into my full stone self. The grotesque. What you're seeing is my body trying tae change tae stone as a reflexive protection, but I am fighting it off."

"Why would you do that? If you can heal . . ."

"It's a long story. Suffice it tae say, it would be bad."

And he had only a couple of days before it would get worse. Possibly permanently worse. He found himself looking anxiously at the shuttered windows. "Any news on the storm?"

"Oh! I didn't even think about the news. I'll turn on the Weather Channel and see what they say." She reached across him for the remote on the opposite bedside table, her entire tiny body pressing into his lap and the curve of her hip coming into pronounced view. Just a few inches more and she'd be fanny up.

He'd already noticed she had a fine little arse. He'd

have to be dead not to, and he wasn't quite there yet. The way her spine dipped before the flare of her backside and the perfect roundness of her cheeks could make a man's hands itch to grab hold. She might be compact, but she was very shapely for her size.

The TV popped on and suddenly she was gone from his lap, flipping through the guide and channels in an expert swipe. "I'd been tracking the storm, along with everyone else, for several days. Give it a few more hours and we will lose electricity. But I have a generator of course. We get so many storms up here on the mountain that it'd be stupid not to."

"Verra good, Kat lass. I'm clearly safe in your hands, am I no'?"

"Yes," she said with a proud lift of her chin. "Frankly you couldn't have found a better place to be sick. I . . . I have experience with serious wounds and such."

"Aye, I can see that you do," he said, lifting his arm and inspecting her work at his side. "Where did you learn tae do this?"

"I used to be a physician's assistant in a Manhattan hospital."

"Used to be?" he asked.

"I . . . left. And moved out here. I don't do that any-more."

She didn't blame him for his puzzled look. Whenever she told someone this story they always looked that way. And then came the inevitable question.

"So you work out here as a physician's assistant now?" But she could tell by the lilt of his voice that he'd caught on to the fact that she wasn't. So she just shook her head. "Why no'?"

"I don't really want to talk about it," she said eva-sively, fiddling with the remote in her hands. He didn't want to talk about himself so he ought to respect her not wanting to talk about herself. "Are you hungry again? I can cook you something else."

"No," he said softly, his big hand settling over hers and the remote, pressing down on them until they all rested together in her lap. "Kat lass, why did you quit? I know your training must have taken a verra long time. Clearly you were good at what you did. And even if it was a matter of relocating, you still could have found a job in a local hospital. So why did you no'?"

"I'm just . . . I just don't want to," she said, knowing he could see it for the lie that it was. She had loved her job. It had been something she could do in the dead of night, in the darkness, and it had been important. She had made a difference. She had helped save lives.

"Doona lie tae me, Kat lass, and I willna do the same tae you." Well, that was a lie, Ahnvil thought with an internal wince. He'd already told her a fib or two. But it had been in her best interest.

She colored, a pretty pink flush that tipped the end of her nose and the upper shell of her ears, dusting over everything in between until her wee freckles were a fair contrast.

"I really don't think this is any of your business," she said, moving as if to get up and get away from his influence over her. But he was not going to let her get away that easily. He took hold of her arm, pulling her back down beside him on the bed. He grunted at the effort, cursing his injured state. He wasn't the sort who was used to limitations. He didn't like them. He never had. Not even when he'd been mortal. Human.

"You canna run away from things, Kat lass. They always find you in the end." He should know. He had run away three centuries ago, freed himself and thinking he would never see his master and maker ever again, and that if he did he would kill the man where he stood. But that was far from what had happened when the time had come. A fact that still grated. But there was a bigger picture than his vengeance against the man who had made him what he was. Vengeance would have to wait.

"Don't lecture me!" she bit out defensively, but she didn't shrug him off and she didn't move away from him. That was when he realized that despite her protestations she actually wanted to talk about whatever it was that had happened. He found himself wondering why he should care. He had far more pressing things he should be worried about. But in all fairness, she had taken care of him, so if it helped her, he should take care of her a little bit in return. The favors were unequal, since she had saved his life, but it was the best he could do under the circumstances.

"I didn't . . ." She stopped, tucking a strand of hair behind her ear in a nervous habit. "People don't like me very much. I don't fit in well."

"Bollocks. You're a fine lass. Fair of face and a good heart from what I've seen so far. What more is there for people to like?"

"A sense of humor," she said dryly. "And not being weird helps. Everyone knew I was . . . weird." She exhaled, her shoulders dropping in defeat, as if she didn't blame them for it.

Ahnvil was shocked by his reaction. He became angry—nay enraged—to hear her speak and, more important, to see her spirit fall away from her. He reached out to take both her shoulders in his hands turning her toward him. "I've been in your company for some minutes now, Kat lass, and I dinna see anything weird abou' you. As far, I've seen someone good-hearted with a care toward others in need. That isna weird, 'tis *rare*."

"You just don't know me well enough. If you did . . ."

"Are you saying that I would find you weirder than a man who can turn to stone at whim? Or perhaps one that turns to smoke in sunlight and calls up magic from things around him? That's a Djynn," he said when her eyes went wide. "Or perhaps a man who shares his body with two souls? That's a Bodywalker. Or how about a woman with skin as black as midnight and eyes as yellow as the sun? That's a Night Angel."

By the last item on his list she was agape with shock and wonder. Wonder at all the things he was telling her and shock because she believed him.

"Y-yellow eyes?" she asked, a bit unsurely. She tucked back a fine lock of that pretty sable hair of hers and Ahnvil found himself drawn to the motion. It moved like silk, that hair.

"That gleam like a cat's," he said, his hand coming to stroke over her jawline, a gesture of comfort, he told himself. But the truth was he found her delicate features fascinating. He couldn't put his finger on it, but maybe that was because he couldn't decide if she looked fragile or like a tough little dynamo packed into a small presentation.

Both, he decided after a few moments. She was both. Tough when she needed to be, and fragile on occasion, like she was right then.

"You better lie back down," she said softly, pulling away from him almost awkwardly. He could see she was flushed again, all pink and unnervingly adorable.

He was getting too close, she thought, drawing away from him. She didn't like it when people got too close. Too close meant too much scrutiny and too many opportunities to find flaws within her. Right now, for some reason, his opinion mattered. She didn't know why, because she had come to live her life unapologetically since the day she'd walked away from her career in Manhattan. But that maneuver had come with a heavy sort of price. The kind of price that had her living alone, in the dark, on a mountain in the smallest town in America.

"Did you want something to eat?"

"What I want," he said, catching up her hand before she could move out of reach, "is for you to come back to me. Keep me company."

It was a bad idea. Company meant talk and talk meant telling her things she probably wasn't ready to hear, things he probably shouldn't be telling her. But he'd come this far already.

She sat back down on the bed and looked at him warily, like he might bite off her hand if she weren't careful.

"What's the deal with the turning to stone?" she asked immediately. Almost as if she knew it might make him shut down . . . send her away. Let her escape.

Ahnvil ought to have done that. He ought to have sent her away and just settled down to wait out the storm in relative peace. Also, the idea of having more to eat was appealing. His metabolism was so damn high that he needed a constant influx of food. Not every second of every day, but at the very least a meal every two hours. Except when he was in stone state.

"A Gargoyle has three states," he found himself telling her, as if he told mortal humans these things all the time. One of the unspoken and harshest rules in the Nightwalker world was that they never revealed themselves to the human world. But she had already seen too much and he hadn't been prepared to explain away what she'd seen. It had simply never come up before. He'd had a flawless record of avoiding being seen in transformation.

"The flesh state"—he indicated his present state with a hand—"the stone state, where I turn completely tae stone from the tips of my hair tae the tips on my toes. Then the third state is the grotesque. I . . ." He hesitated and wondered why.

Because he didn't want to be ugly or frightening to her. And in grotesque form he was exactly that.

"Go on. I'm a big girl. I can take it." She wheedled him

with a small, teasing smile. It made him laugh and he found himself dropping his guard.

"I well and truly look like a Gargoyle. As though you might have ripped me from the top of an old cathedral. It's different for all of us, the way we look, but the one constant is wings. We all have wings."

"Wings! You mean, stone wings? How the hell do you make stone aerodynamic?"

"Wings are wings, and ours are strong enough tae take flight despite the weight of our bodies."

"Oh my God," she said, her jaw dropping open. She was a smart girl. She could easily imagine, he knew, just how strong that meant he was. "So . . . you're ugly?"

"I am," he said with a grim nod. "And when I turn tae stone I'm worse." He winked at her and she laughed in a surprised burst.

"Oh!" She shoved at him slightly. "You're not ugly and you probably know it."

"Aye, but it has been some time since I've heard a lass tell me so."

She seemed to think on that a moment, her teeth coming to worry at her bottom lip thoughtfully.

"Why the *h*? In your name?"

Now this was a touchy topic for him. He deflected instinctively because the answer would only start them down on a wild path that promised to be very painful for him.

"You first. Why did you quit? Doona tell me 'tis because you're weird. Why are you weird? What's so wrong abou' you?"

The worrying turned to full blown biting of her lip. He could tell by the volume of pain in her eyes that she had just as much reason for avoidance as he did.

Stubbornly she stood up and walked away. Ahnvil cursed himself for being cruel to her, but he couldn't have it any other way. He didn't want to talk about how, once upon a time, he'd had no name. No identity. No value as an individual. Perhaps it was because he'd just come so close to being in the same conditions that he was sensitive to it. But he would not have been made a slave this time. This time he would have died. And they wouldn't have batted an eye while allowing it to happen. He still had the taste of fear in the back of his throat because of it. A fear that would not be erased until he got back in contact with his touchstone.

He felt a tremendous urge to trail after her, in spite of his desire to keep his business to himself. The impulse truly surprised him because he was such a close-to-the-vest person. Yet here he was, blabbing about all things supernatural. Although, the horse had already been out of the barn once she'd seen him turned to stone. That and the fact that he was even conscious after so much blood loss.

But a Gargoyle could only die from massive amounts of trauma, like say a spear to the heart or a transected aorta or the ever charming beheading. Complete blood loss was probably deemed a massive trauma. But he knew he'd come very close to death . . . or would have if he'd been left out in the storm bleeding to death. The other way a Gargoyle could die? If someone took a wrecking ball to them in statue form. Or damage equal to that. It was every Gargoyle's worst fear. To be frozen in stone, totally helpless, watching certain death come at them.

Ahnvil shook the morbid trail of his thoughts away, hunkering down into the bed once again, wincing at the blossom of pain the movement caused. He needed to rest and heal and he needed to do it as quickly as possible. When the storm let up he would have to be on his way immediately. But it worried him, this storm. He had to get all the way to New Mexico, and after a storm airports were bound to be shut down for a while. Normally he would fly on his own, but this time he couldn't. Not without risking permanent being. He could put off being away from his touchstone perhaps a few more days as long as he didn't turn into his grotesque state. At this point even his stone state was taking a risk.

And then there was the issue of a compact little beauty with eyes the color of bourbon and hair like nice dark mink. He could not, absolutely not, leave her behind. Not with the knowledge she now had.

She didn't know it yet, but rescuing him was going to change her life as she knew it forever.

CHAPTER NINE

A blizzard. His wife had just sent them dead-on into a blizzard. Jacob wrapped his body around his wife's immediately using his Demon power to transform them both into dust. The trouble with that form, however, was that they were going to be subject to the whims of the blustering winds even more than they had been thus far. But Bella had refused to wait out the storm and had pressed him on almost fervently, making him really start to question what was driving her. His wife's pre-monition abilities were known to be dangerously con-suming, especially if she didn't obey them. She may not realize precisely why she was being driven in a certain direction, just that she had to go at all costs.

This was beginning to feel like one of those situa-tions. Which meant that their so-called vacation was going to be anything but.

They stumbled onto the porch of the cozy little hunt-ing lodge in Stone Gorge, turning solid immediately, getting pushed inside by the driving ice and snow. As they checked in, to the shock and awe of the proprietors who wondered how they had even made it up the moun-tain, Jacob began to fret more and more about why they were there.

They were both exhausted from the trip, him mainly

because so much of it had taken place during daylight hours. The touch of the sun made Demons weary, forcing the weaker ones to sleep. He was of considerable age and talent, on the verge of being a powerful Elder, and so had been able to bear it more than another might, but still it had taken a great deal out of him.

The minute they checked into their room and shed their frozen, wet clothes, Jacob ushered his wife into the hottest shower their icy skin could stand. His curvy little wife immediately snuggled her wet, naked body up to his, her hands running up his back in that inviting caress she almost always used in order to draw him in closer to her. It worked every single time.

"Stop worrying," she said. "I can hear you thinking and worrying."

Of course she could. As imprinted mates they lived constantly in each other's thoughts. They spoke telepathically just about as much as they spoke aloud. Which came in quite handy when they were feeling amorous with a nine-year-old running around. A very bright nine-year-old who could tell what they were saying even if they s-p-e-l-l-e-d words out over her head. It had been quite some time since they'd been able to do that.

It was a wonder he'd missed out on the understanding that she had been feeling neglected. But sometimes, when she put her mind to it, she could hide her feelings and thoughts from him.

"I think you know, as well as I do, what is driving you here."

"I know," she said with a frown. "I don't know why it has to be here and why it has to be now, but you know that if this is premonition driving me then that means it's important that I be here." She pressed forward and drifted her lips across one of his pectoral muscles. "However, that doesn't mean we can't enjoy our child-free existence while we're at it."

Jacob sighed as a very familiar heat began to bleed into him, originating from the touch of her mouth and the stroke of her hands. Even after over ten years of being together, he knew it was never going to cool. They would always be quick to fire to each other's touch. It was the essence of their connection. It was surprising, he agreed, that they had gone so long without touching each other like this. She had been right to feel neglected. And with gentle fingertips skiing down the slope of her breast, he began to rectify the situation.

The meaning and reasons of why they were there could wait.

Panahasi had a dilemma. The Gargoyle had escaped . . . *with* the Amulet. An Amulet that promised to have great power and that, somehow, the Gargoyle could unlock. That is, provided the scripture was accurate . . . and provided he could figure out how. Panahasi knew exactly who the Gargoyle was and exactly what importance he had with the highest ranking members of the Politic Bodywalker faction. If the Gargoyle couldn't figure out how to unlock the Amulet there was most certainly someone among the higher echelon of the Politic who could.

He had even heard rumors that Kamenwati had defected to the other side and was now working with their enemies. *The traitor.* But that meant he would immediately recognize it and would already know what it was capable of.

Initially, he had considered his luck in capturing the Gargoyle twofold. First he would use him for the Amulet to give himself power, then he would turn him over to his mistress, Odjit, in order to obtain the glory of her praises for a job well done in capturing an enemy so close to the Politic throne.

Not that she was actually known for praises. Not

lately. Lately the Templar Bodywalkers had come to have reason, more reason than ever before, to fear the ruthless Odjit; ever since she had changed in appearance, growing somehow larger and more imposing than she had been before. No doubt the result of some kind of spellwork she had discovered and implemented, much in the way Kamenwati had discovered the Amulet. They were always on the hunt for more powerful magics, anything new and possibly able to give them a stronger foothold in the war against the Politic.

Only of late, the Templars had been less about finding new magics and more about pleasing their deadly mistress. Along with her physical changes had come a more powerful need to subjugate her followers. Perhaps some blowback from whatever she had done to herself.

But that made Panahasi's position all the less enviable. Did he risk his neck right off, risk enraging her by telling her what had happened? Or did he simply remain quiet and hope she never found out about it? She might be displeased if he got out ahead of it, possibly enraged, but if he failed to tell her and it got back to her what he had done, then he would no doubt forfeit his life. It wouldn't be the first time she had claimed that sort of price in order to mollify her anger and sense of betrayal.

Panahasi, however, was more along the lines of a coward. He did not readily admit it, but he did so now, telling himself it was only in the face of his mistress's wrath that this side of himself came to bear.

He decided silence was the better solution. Die now or possibly die later, the choice was actually more simple then he had made it out to be.

There was only one problem.

Moribundi. His companion from earlier was privy to the knowledge of his flawed attempt at power. Should Moribundi find himself in the position where he could

obtain clemency for a wrongdoing or position for revealing his friend's failure, he would not hesitate to do so. It
was far more likely Moribundi's betrayal would lead to
his ultimate death than it was likely the Gargoyle and
Politic Bodywalkers would somehow gloat to Odjit about
what had happened. Luckily, the Politic were not the
gloating sort.

But Moribundi was even more of a coward than
Panahasi was and there was no loyalty among the Templars. It was every man for himself.

So Panahasi began to research poisons.

He wasn't about to take any chances.

And then he was going to send some of his underlings
out on a search for the lost Gargoyle. If he could get
Adoma's Amulet back before the Gargoyle got too far,
then all of this would be swept under the rug completely.

None of this would have been necessary if he'd been
powerful enough to create his own damn Gargoyle. But
as it stood he was not. Neither had Moribundi been.
And he was unwilling to trust anyone else with the
quest. No, he had to finish rectifying this. The Gargoyle
had been wounded. Perhaps fatally, if Panahasi was
lucky. Now it was just a matter of time. Time before his
success or his failure was known.

And his first step was taking care of the one loose end
he had left out there.

When Kat returned to the bedroom with a tray of
food, having noted that he seemed to grow stronger the
more he ate, he was asleep. Luckily what she had prepared was cold-cut sandwiches and macaroni salad. It
would keep. She placed the tray gingerly on the bedside
table, not wanting to wake him.

Then the lights went out with an audible grinding
down of all the background sounds in the house, including the television and the weather report. She gasped re-

flexively as total blackness surrounded her. At the sound of her surprise, her patient shot upright in bed, grabbed her right off her feet, pinning her to the mattress underneath him, his large hand grasping at her throat until she couldn't breathe. She choked, her hands pushing hard at the wall of his chest, her whole body trying to buck him off her. But it was like trying to dislodge a mountain. He would not be moved until he wanted to be moved. Obviously in his shocked confusion he had mistaken her for a threat and, even as she panicked for lack of air, a calm part of her mind wondered what kind of world it was that he came from that made him perceive threats around every corner. Considering his wounds, it was probably a greatly dangerous one.

She knew her only hope was to make him realize she wasn't the threat he thought she was. So she went against every natural instinct she had to fight, dropped her hands, and relaxed completely beneath him. At the very least he might think she was already dead, threat neutralized.

It was the hardest thing she'd ever done in her life.

And it worked. Through the darkness she saw his face change as awareness settled onto him.

"Jesus God!" he said explosively, launching himself off her and out of the bed. He stumbled, the bedcovers tangling around his legs, and fell hard onto his backside. Kat meanwhile was dragging for much needed air, her bruised throat rasping as she coughed and tried to breathe in through an equally bruised windpipe.

"Good God, Kat lass, I'm so bloody sorry."

He was scrambling over to her the very next second, back on the bed and running his big hands around her head. Jesus, she felt so small in between his hands. But the way he was touching her now, as if he might break her, made her also feel somehow treasured. It was a ridiculous perception, considering he'd just tried to kill her.

"It's okay," she lied with a cough. Well, in a way it wasn't a lie. She was alive, wasn't she? And she knew he hadn't meant to hurt her.

"No, it bloody is no'! Lord help me, look at your wee throat. 'Tis bruising." Shaking fingertips stroked her along the length of her throat and an inexplicable shiver of warmth trembled through her. Then, out of nowhere, he dropped his head down and pressed a gentling kiss at the corner of her lips, their breaths exchanging as each tried to calm theirs for their own reasons.

"It's okay," she whispered again, her words making the side of her mouth brush against the side of his. She could feel several days' worth of stubble against her lips, could feel the way he was shaking for fear he'd hurt her. It calmed her. Calmed her breathing. Cleared away whatever remaining fear his actions might have caused her to feel.

And through the dark she could see the amber of his eyes. Could see the way they were almost luminescent, in spite of the fact that there wasn't so much as a streak of lighting to be had anywhere around them. She found herself thinking that they were possibly the most beautiful eyes she had ever seen in her life.

His rapid breathing audibly subsided as well. His eyes seemed to study her face as he pulled slightly away from his brush against her lips. And understanding passed between them there in the dark. Forgiveness was given and accepted. Gears shifted. And suddenly fear and regret had melted away and something else was left in its place. Something she wasn't sure she exactly understood. Then, as her eyes drifted over his handsome countenance she realized with an internal groan what it was.

She found him attractive. Appealing. *Arousing*, she thought. *Oh God! I'm one of those women who let a*

66

Jacquelyn Frank

man beat on them and then forgive them for it five seconds later!

But why wasn't that thought keeping her from licking her lips, wetting them with a sort of anxious anticipation.

"Ah, now there's a pretty picture," she heard him mutter softly, his eyes fixated on the brief appearance of her tongue.

Ahnvil wanted to doubly curse himself for the fiend that he was. Oh, he had known for the better part of three hundred years that he was as much beast as he was man, a thing that acted more on instinct than it did the rules of civilization, but never had that bothered him more than it was bothering him right then. He'd just tried to kill her, for fuck's sake! Now what? What was he thinking? He was thinking about how fine her lips might taste. Because the brief touch of his mouth before had done nothing to tell him what it would be like to press his mouth over hers and slip his tongue inside of her mouth. And the minute the curiosity crossed his mind he could no longer think of anything else.

And then, over the idea of a simple kiss, he grew hard. And by the way her eyes widened, she became instantly aware of it.

"I'm a rough beast," he said, by way of excuse and apology. "Make no mistake about it, Kat lass. I'd never be an easy man tae be with and you're such a wee thing."

And instantly he knew it was the wrong thing to say. Or perhaps the very rightest thing he'd ever said because she got her back up in a fiery flash of indignant bourbon eyes.

"I am not small! Nor am I frail! Stop treating me like I'm some kind of porcelain figurine!"

"And you're tough enough to survive a beast that grabs you by the throat in the middle of the darkness?

A beast so used tae fighting for his life he'd crush you wi'out even knowing he was doing so? Wi'out a regret?" he demanded of her angrily.

Her eyes softened in their regard of him. "You sound very much like a man with regret."

Well, it was hard to argue with that when he took a moment to think about it. "But that doesn't change the fact that I'm . . . Ah, God, Kat lass. I know what I am but I canna think of anything but how fine you'd taste right now. What does that make me in your eyes?"

She swallowed visibly and audibly. She didn't answer, but her gaze dropped to his mouth and a sort of answering craving seemed to blossom in her eyes. He could see it and he could feel it. Just as true as he could feel himself grow even harder at the very thought of it.

"Damn me tae hell and back," he muttered as his breath fell hotly over her lips. "You'll hate me and then some one day. Mark my words."

And with those prophetic words, he gave in to his impulses and rushed his mouth against hers. There was nothing gentle about the kiss, nothing introductory. He kissed her as though he'd earned every right to ravage the breath from her body. His words had spoken of caution and concern, but his mouth . . . Oh, his mouth was not holding anything back. It took only a second for utter craving to take the wheel. He pressed into her with a deeply indrawn breath, his weight falling over her, his body propped on one elbow while the other hand gripped her at her hip and drew her tightly against him.

Sweet hell, he thought an instant after he ran his tongue across the plush seam of her lips, the craving she felt for the coming of it reflected in the softest little moan on the back of the softest little sigh. Had he not been so keen of hearing he might have missed it, and that would have been a crying shame. He swept his tongue into her mouth and there it was, instant bliss, the sweet-est of flavors known to man. Oh, and the heat of her. Wet and lush it was searing him to the quick. All of her was searing him to the quick.

He feared he was being too rough with her. After all, he'd not been with a human female in nearly three cen-turies. No. He'd slaked his bodily needs on Gargoyle females. Women as much beast as he was. Women who could readily take him at his worst.

But here was this gentle, delicate thing beneath him and he had no right, no right at all, to be doing this. Yet that lecture, like all the internal lectures thus far, fell on his completely deaf ears. He was too full of longing. Too overwhelmed with the taste and feel of her. And then her hand reached for his hair, her fingers plowing through the thick black locks, her palm pressing against him and . . .

. . . encouraging him? Wanting *more* of him? She was unafraid? Or was she just unaware of the fire she was danc-ing so close to?

That was when her tongue came forward and slipped inside his mouth. Had he thought himself hard before? Oh, what an unsuspecting fool he was. The feel of her aggressing into the kiss was the most erotic thing he could ever remember to that date. But why? Why was she affecting him so hotly?

He didn't care. He grabbed her at her hip, shifting him-self over her, groaning when she parted her thighs and welcomed the weight of him between them. Their kiss took on a new, fiery life, her lips burning against his, the wetness of her toying against his tongue. He felt honored. Couldn't help but to feel it. He knew he was undeserving of her trust after what he'd just done to her, undeserving of *her,* period. But he couldn't make himself pull away, couldn't keep himself from pressing his hips forward against her, his naked flesh rubbing up against the denim of her jeans.

Her hand left his hair, her nails raking down the back of his neck. Every muscle in his body clenched as the sensation rode through him. Then her touch was curving over his shoulder, sliding down his chest and under his arm so she could draw her fingers down his back. The feel of her touching him was more arousing, it seemed, than him touching her was. The idea boggled because right then he couldn't get his hands on her fast enough, hard enough, thorough enough.

He drew back from the kiss, catching his breath, his mouth hovering so close to hers as he groaned with pleasure from her touch. If she kept heading in that direction, she'd soon have her hand on his ass, and the anticipation of it floored him.

He tried to do her one better. His hand drew down to the hem of her sweater and lifting it with quick fingers he slid his hand beneath it, his palm running up over her ribs, his fingertips brushing the underside of her breast. It was far too tempting, far too overwhelming, the craving for more. He hotly embraced her breast, felt the fullness of it filling his hand, her nipple pointed and sweet.

She moaned and lifted into his touch and it was like he'd captured starlight—that was how bright and burning his reaction was.

"There now, there's a willing lass," he groaned against her mouth.

Apparently it was the wrong thing to say. All her pliancy disappeared like the whip of a magician's cloth revealing a trick. She drew back from him, before he could reclaim her in another kiss, as if she suddenly realized what she was doing and who she was doing it with.

Damn, he thought with vehemence. *Bloody hell and damn! I want her too much to stop!*

"Wait! Stop!" she said, her hands leaving his skin to push at him. Pushing him away as if she weren't soft and wet with wanting him. And he could tell, just by the power of scent alone that she was all of that and more.

It was too late for her to suddenly agree he was too much a beast for her liking, he thought fiercely. She couldn't give him just a taste of something that powerful and then expect him to stop wanting it altogether.

"Why wait?" he asked her, his hand leaving her breast to curve around her hip and around to the sweet shape of her arse. He loved the shaped of her, the way she filled his hand so well in spite of how small the rest of her was.

"Because I don't want this!" she blurted out.

A fine and balder lie was never heard, he thought with amusement.

Kat was suddenly awash with conflicting emotions and desires. Oh, he felt so good. So damn good. So male and powerful under the grip and press of her palms. One hand held him in a tight grip around his shoulder, and one hand was pushing against his chest and it was as if she couldn't make herself agree on what to do.

But she wasn't going to be a "willing lass." The kind of willing woman who acted and thought nothing of later consequences. She had made a good life for herself here, and she wasn't going to let him come in and ride roughshod all over it. She wanted things. Things that had nothing to do with big, sexy Gargoyles.

Just then his voice turned deeper, lower . . . guttural, his accent growing thicker with obvious desire.

"I ken you're afraid of me half the time, but the other half," he said, his face turning against her neck until he was breathing her in, "the other half of the time you're wanting me. I know it because I feel it. I *smell* it. 'Tis a thing so ravenous that I canna ignore it." His hand ran up the side of her body in a long, purposeful caress, ending with him cupping her left breast in a hard, insistent hold again that made her gasp. "And I'll be willin' tae bet that if I touched you below and between, you're wet and wanting me as well."

She gasped again, this time with indignation even as her face flamed hot because the rest of her flamed even hotter. "I am not!" she lied sharply. "Don't think so much of yourself! And get your hands off me!" She wriggled as if to throw him off her, but his grip was like iron and it was laughable to think she was any contest to his incredible strength. Even weakened as he was, there was nothing she could do to fight him. And besides, half of her heart wasn't in it because he was right. He was right to say she was overwhelmed with craving. There was a part of her that wanted him to do as he said, touch her there and prove her a liar.

"Li'le liar," he said, as though he could read her mind. His hand ran down from her breast and she began to breathe so hard it was a wonder she didn't pass out. He swept his fierce touch down her belly and over the front of her jeans. He cupped her then with powerful fingers and used his grip on her to jerk her hips up, his erection so bold and hard against her thigh she felt her knees go weak.

"There now," he hissed. "I can feel the heat of you. And how could I be so hard that my bollocks hurt from it if you were as cold tae me as you say you are?"

"I'm not responsible for the state of your . . . your . . ."

"Bollocks," he said with smug amusement.

"Yes. Shut up!" She didn't think she could burn any hotter with embarrassment, not to mention other things. He moved his hand then and ground himself against her and she felt herself responding wetly. A moan escaped her and he chuckled.

"I canna help it. 'Tis my nature, lass. Gargoyles are a lusty lot even under the weakest of circumstances, but

when we sense lust toward us from another . . . you ken
there's no resisting it. In other words, I wouldna be feeling it if you were as cold tae me as you claim." He exhaled against her neck, his breath steamy and rich.
"And there's nothing cold about you," he reminded her,
his grip on her tightening just enough to get her attention. "Now I'm going tae slide my hand under this
denim you're hiding behind and I'm going tae prove tae
us both how wet you are."

"So what!" she blurted out. "Okay, so what if I am.
I-it's been a-a long time and of c-course I'm going to feel
something when you're touching me like this! It's not as
though you're hard to look at and all muscley and tes-
tosteroney! I'd have to be dead not to respond to that.
What girl in her right mind wouldn't want a-a man like
you?" When he exhaled with satisfaction into her hair
she made herself go stiff in his hold. "It doesn't mean I
actually am going to have sex with you! I'm a discerning woman and . . . and you're . . . you're . . ."

"Go on and say it, lass," he urged her, his voice like
churning gravel, a sense of grimness to his tone. "I'm a
Gargoyle. I'm a thing you don't understand. An inhuman
thing. Go on. Say it."

"No," she said, deflating in his hold, half the tension
in her body disappearing. "A Gargoyle, yes. A *person* I
don't understand. But not inhuman. I don't think of you
like you're inhuman."

His hand slid away from intimate areas, coming to
rest low on her belly. "Well," he said, "that's something
I suppose. Something tae start with. And you've admitted you want me. Another thing in my favor."

She huffed. "You don't give up, do you?"

"Nay, no' when it comes tae you. I promise you that."

The promise affected her in unexpected ways. It made
her feel . . . cherished. Did he mean it that way? Everything he'd said up to that point had been just hot hard

lust, but that one statement made it more . . . personal. As if . . . as if it was more about her than it was about his sensual nature. As if her affect on him was somehow special.

"Will you let me go now?" she asked softly, still aware that he held her very tightly and that he was still as hard as steel against her. Good God, she couldn't help but recall how . . . *endowed* he was. It ought to be terrifying, and, she supposed, she *was* a little bit terrified. But that fear meant she was contemplating him actually using it with her and she couldn't let her mind go there.

Only, it was clearly already there.

No. *No*, she lectured herself. *You can do this. You just have to be firm.*

Firm. He was firm. Oh yes . . . very, very f—

Shit. *Shit shit shit! Stop it, Katrina Christina Haynes! This is a slippery slope and you're just going to fall on your ass if you keep this up!*

"I canna let you go when you keep squirming again' me. Feels too bloody good."

"I'm not squirming! And even if I were, it wouldn't be so you could get your jollies with it! It's because I'm trying to escape, you big oaf! Now let me go." *Oaf? Really, Katrina, was that the best you could do?*

"I will, but on one condition," he said, his eyes light with amusement.

"What is it?" she asked warily.

"That you promise me another kiss. No' now, but later on, at a time of my choosing. If I ask, you have to give over. Just a kiss, Kat lass. One wee li'le kiss."

Kat bit her lip, her heart thundering in her chest. Not just because of all that had happened thus far, but because the idea of him calling in a marker like that at any given moment in the future well and truly excited her as if he were already kissing her all over again.

"All right," she breathed. "But just one. And no tongue."

"Oh, there'll be tongue and plenty of it," he countered. "I doona do things halfway and I willna expect otherwise from you. But just a kiss. Whatever comes after, now that's up to you."

"You promise?"

"Aye, I swear it."

"Okay," she assented.

Slowly, with obvious reluctance, he relaxed his hold on her, letting her move away from him in small increments. She was about a foot away from him, sliding toward the opposite side of the bed, still bathed in the infernal heat he was giving off, when he reached a hand to her neck, stroking a long caress against the side of her throat and then up into her hair.

"Good God, you're beautiful," he said on a low breath. " 'Tis no' because I'm tryin' tae make headway with you that I say it, but only because 'tis the truth."

She didn't acknowledge the compliment, or the way it made her feel all melty inside. Still she just moved out of his hold, got to her feet, and walked away. She left the room without so much as a glance over her shoulder toward him, and it was possibly one of the hardest things she'd ever done in her life.

Ahnvil rubbed the heel of his palm down the length of his cock. He had a cockstand that could drive nails and the woman who caused it was walking in the wrong damn direction. Christ above, didn't she understand how this was painful for him? And not just in the physical sense. No matter what her protestations otherwise, he knew she saw him as a thing . . . a thing to be frightened of. And she wouldn't be entirely wrong to think so. It'd been a long time since he'd been human, and now he spent only half his life as one . . . if that much.

He wondered sometimes if he had forgotten how to be human altogether.

He shouldn't be dwelling on this. He shouldn't be doing things to push her away. If he had any hope of getting out of this mess he was going to need her help and his goddamn cock was thinking for him and fucking things up.

Why? Why canna I leave off her and let her be?

His life depended on her. He was entirely in her hands. And he suspected she knew that and that it was a heavy burden for her to carry. God, he wished like hell he could leave her out of this, but he had few choices available to him. He couldn't turn to stone. He couldn't risk it. Being away from his touchstone for this long could mean he would turn to stone permanently if he did. But it was only in his grotesque form that he could have access to his wings, the wings he needed to travel with any speed back to New Mexico. So that meant traveling by conventional means and considering his stripped down state he was going to need funds and resources for that.

And then there was the small issue of leaving her behind or taking her with him. Well, actually, it wasn't an issue at all. He truly had no choice in the matter. The problem was, he didn't think she would come willingly.

Damn him. Damn him to hell for ruining another woman's life. For risking another woman's life. And this one was mortal, human, and far more fragile than the one who had been lost before. At least the other had known what she was getting into. Despite all his revelations to her, Kat had no idea of the danger involved in being this close to him.

CHAPTER TEN

Kat avoided the bedroom like the plague for the next few hours. She was tired, her usual bedtime having come and gone and the stress of the whole situation wearing her out even more. She tried her mother two more times and got the same lacking result. She wished, for the first time in all of the time she'd lived there on the mountain that she had a landline. Normally she wouldn't have needed it, and it wouldn't have mattered to her to be cut off from the rest of the world. After all, it was kind of the whole point of having moved there in the first place. And the cost of a landline on top of a cell bill was prohibitive. She'd had to make a choice and this was what she'd chosen.

Of course, when making the decision she hadn't taken Gargoyles into consideration.

And other things.

She ran through a list of beasties and ghouls in her mind and then shoved it all away. She had enough to worry about with the Gargoyle in her bed. No need to go looking for any more trouble than that.

In spite of all her fretting, she did drift off to sleep for a little while, napping in the recliner in her living room. When she awoke, she found she had a blanket draped over her that she hadn't had when she'd fallen asleep.

She looked around in confusion for a moment, but then remembered there was a Gargoyle in the house. A very considerate Gargoyle, she noted, unable to help the little smile the idea brought to her lips.

Well, she could at least return the favor and make him more food. Hadn't he said that he had a high metabolism? Although at this rate he would eat through all of her stockpiled supplies in a week! Thankfully the storm wasn't supposed to last that long and the roads would be cleared a few days after.

It was only shortly after she started moving around the kitchen when Ahnvil walked out of the bedroom. When she glanced over at him she ended up doing a double take. He had apparently showered, cleaning away all the remaining blood and grime from his injury and from being in the woods. He was wearing one of the white terry towels from the bathroom and somehow looked twice as sexy as when he was completely naked . . . which was saying a lot because a completely naked Gargoyle was nothing to shrug your shoulders at.

"Are you hungry?" she asked, turning her back to him in hopes that it would keep her from running greedy eyes all over his glorious muscles, his wet hair which made him look attractively tousled and that enticing line of hair that began slightly above his navel and darkened the farther down below his navel it went.

Yes, that towel was slung across his hips very low indeed.

Luckily for her he took a seat at the breakfast bar, sliding onto a barstool and putting an entire granite countertop between them as she moved around the kitchen. That was good, she thought. The more things that were between them, the better off she'd be.

"Are you hungry?" she asked again.

"Always," he said, and she was glad she couldn't see the grin that no doubt followed. His smile was an absolute killer all on its own, but add those vibrant amber eyes to the mix and it was utterly devastating. "And yourself?"

"Actually, I think I am a little hungry," she admitted. "I could make some more sandwiches or something hot . . ."

"Hot. With meat. Something that'll stick to a man's ribs."

And better still, Ahnvil thought, *to that already delectable fanny of hers.* Which was, at present, facing him as she did her damnedest to avoid looking in his direction. But he wasn't fazed by her obvious awkwardness. It was actually satisfying for some reason to know that she was so affected by him . . . no matter whether it was a good effect or a bad one.

Honestly, he had no right to be looking at her as a man looks at a woman. He had made her life complicated enough as it was. She certainly didn't need him making advances toward her and, logically, he couldn't afford to do anything that might put her off to him. But as prevailing as his need for her to help him to get back home was, he was finding his unexpected desire for her to be equally prevailing.

All the more reason to let her be. He was a rough, powerful man with equally powerful passions and she was human.

Human and fragile, he reminded himself.

There was a basket of fruit next to him and he picked a tangerine, pulled a napkin over, and began to gently peel it. She was a lot like the fruit he held. He had to be gentle with it or he would damage it and lessen the experience of enjoying it.

On principle, Kat made herself turn around and face him. Principle and the fact that her cutting surface was in that direction. She moved all the vegetables over to the countertop on the opposite side of the breakfast bar and busied herself chopping them. Facing him . . . but not facing him. Staying intent and focused on her task. Not so focused, however, that she didn't see him peeling his tangerine, his hands seeming so graceful despite their size as they completed the task. He slowly began to section the pieces, eating them one by one.

"So do you have a wife?" she heard herself blurt out. "I-I mean . . ." she flushed, knowing it must sound like she was fishing for selfish purposes. "Do Gargoyles take wives like people do?"

"We do everything like people do," he said. Was it her, or did that sound suggestive? "But no, I doona have a wife. Nor a girlfriend. I have . . . partners."

"Oh! You mean . . . like you're gay?" she was incredulous. "Or, I mean, bi. Right? You'd have to be because earlier . . ." Kat knew she was blushing, and his growing amusement at her expense wasn't helping.

"No' gay. Just no' attached. My partners are like me. Heavily sexual beings looking for a way to vent their intense sexual cravings."

"Intense?" she heard herself asking. She shouldn't be even exploring this information. It was a bad idea.

"Gargoyles are as much animal as they are human. When we're forged we are actually blended with an animal."

"So . . . a human and an animal," she encouraged.

"Yes. And then a Templar priest used a vile spell to forge me, using a bear, in my case. I was always a big man, but that made me bigger, as well as faster and stronger. And, make no mistake, more vicious. More territorial and protective of what's mine." The way his eyes moved over her just then made her crave for a moment what it would be like to be his. To be protected by him. He would care for a woman, she decided thoughtfully. The fact that he had checked in on her, been thoughtful enough to realize she would be chilled on such a stormy day with nothing but the fire to warm her and then covered her. Yes, he would be very caring. And then for that libido to come with it, it would be a very intense package.

"What's a Templar?" she asked.

He picked up another tangerine and began to peel.

"Enough about me and my world for now. What of you, Kat? Is there no man to warm your bed?" Now why did the very idea of that bother him, he was forced to ask himself when a visceral clenching of his gut took place.

"No," she said, looking down at her hands even more intently.

"Let me guess," he said quietly. "You're too weird for a man to be liking you."

The way he said it he sounded angry, as if he took offense from it. She was cautious as she nodded.

"What in bloody hell is so wrong wi' you?" he demanded, his hand slapping down on the countertop.

"I don't expect you to understand," she said defensively. "You just don't know—"

"Then make me understand. What's so bloody wrong wi' you?"

He could tell she was very reluctant to speak about it, but he gave her a fierce look, making it very clear that he would not be swayed from this or mollified by half-answers.

"I'm allergic to the sun," she said in a sighing rush. "It's called xeroderma pigmentosum, or XP. I can't go out in even the smallest amount of sunlight. It's why there're shutters on all the glass and I have automatic shades that draw down at dawn every day."

For the first time, Ahnvil looked at his surroundings, and saw that, though the windows were vast and large, there were indeed shades dropped down over every last one of them, even the largest picture windows. Even the sliding door had had shades pulled down, but instead of admitting she had a condition that would make it impossible for sunlight to penetrate inside, she had gone out to close the shutters, pretending rather than exposing herself for the freak she imagined herself to be.

"The slightest touch of the sun can cause terrible blisters on my skin, at the very least a rash. People with XP can get skin cancer easily . . . many often die from it before they get to be my age. I-I'm just lucky I guess."

" 'Tis a medical condition. There's nothing you can do about it so how does that make you weird?" he wanted to know, his tone hard and angry.

"Oh, come on. You know the way the world works. We can be as politically correct as we want, it doesn't change the fact that people who are different are looked on as weird and as something to be avoided. When it comes to blisters and rashes the likes of which I suffer from, it's worse because people are afraid you're contagious or something. They don't even want to"—she swallowed noisily—"touch you. So"—she lifted her chin in a gesture of bravery—"I live nocturnally, avoiding daylight at all costs. I used to work the night shift, but people still noticed that I never wanted to go out in the sun, never wanted to do things in the daytime even on my days off. They thought I was being unsocial, but I was just trying to protect myself."

"I see," he said. "And instead of telling them the truth you let them think you were just weird."

"They would have thought me weird either way."

"Your friends are in the medical field are they no'? Surely they would understand—"

"Maybe. But maybe not. It wasn't anyone's business anyway."

She was hiding behind the fall of her hair. *Just like she hid from the sun,* he thought, *just like she hid from the people around her.* But he could imagine that growing up that way would make it very difficult for her to trust others. The more he thought about it, the more he thought of how hard it must have been for her to work her way through school, avoiding all classes or training that took place during the daylight. It showed a level of strength and fortitude that was very rare in humans.

"I canna go out into the sun, either," he pointed out.

Her chopping slowed, paused. "Well . . ." she said, "you didn't say why exactly."

"I wouldna have would I?" he said with amusement. "But there's little left to hide so . . . The touch of the sun turns me tae stone involuntarily."

Her mouth dropped open in a silent O of surprise.

"In fact," he went on, "there's no' a Nightwalker in the bunch who can stand the touch of the sun wi'out it affecting them negatively. So in a way, that makes you an honorary Nightwalker, now doesn't it?"

She would have never in her life imagined that there could be an entire *species* of people in the world who were just like her! "Like what?" she wanted to know, unable to hide her eagerness. "What happens to them?"

"The Djynn turn tae smoke. The Bodywalkers are paralyzed. Wraiths, I'm told, are turned solid and vulnerable. Easier tae kill them. And trust me, you want tae be able tae kill a Wraith. Night Angels are rendered powerless and turn from having a beautiful skin of black to the palest ghostliest white you've ever seen on a living being. Leaches the color straight out of them, making them look like albinos."

"Oh. Wow." She smiled as he picked up his third tangerine. "That's . . . I just never thought I'd be hearing about so many people who are like me."

"So, Kat lass, no' feeling so weird anymore now are you?" he said a bit smugly. She had to laugh and her smile grew.

"I admit it. I'm not." Just then she elbowed the tomato on the counter beside her accidentally, sending it rolling toward the edge. He shot forward and grabbed it to keep it from falling, grunting softly in pain from the swift movement. He set the tomato back down beside her and gingerly reseated himself.

"You shouldn't be up. You ought to be in bed."

"Men like me doona do well wi' staying in bed." Then he sent her a roguish grin and slid rapacious eyes over her. "Actually, that's no' exactly true."

There was no mistaking his meaning, nor was there any mistaking his thoughts. He looked as though he were contemplating undressing her. *Very* slowly. His hands slowed in their peeling of the tangerine, gentling and turning the lush fruit between his fingers, cradling it in his hand as he might cradle the weight of her breast.

It was hard to imagine that a hand so large and so rough would be capable of such grace and sensuous gentility. Kat felt herself go instantly and thoroughly wet, the moisture rushing from her body feeling so abrupt that she forgot how to breathe, never mind wielding a knife with any dexterity. And then, as if he could tell, his head lifted abruptly and his eyes zeroed in on her in a searingly fierce gaze. He took in a slow breath through his nose, and then on his exhale he released a low, rumbling cross between a growl and a purr.

"Ah, Kat lass," he said, swallowing audibly as his hand began to squeeze the fragile fruit he held. "'Tis no' fair for you tae no' let me look at you as a sexual being when you are clearly verra much one. You canna deny tae me you are thinking of what it would be like tae bed me."

"I—"

"And before you lie tae me, Kat lass, remember I've the senses of a beast, a bear tae be exacting, and I can *smell* you." The way he said smell with that kind of intensity made her heartbeat jump frantically ahead of itself. Her mouth went dry and she tried to swallow, tried to get any part of herself to function properly. Because she *was* thinking about going to bed with him. If she were going to be honest, she had been thinking about it ever since he'd made his first rough pass at her. Even while in a feverish and brutish state there had been, and still was, something viscerally arousing about the man. He just oozed male sexuality. From the rough shadow of his whiskers to the bulging curve of his biceps to the heavy prominence of his cock, whether in clothing or not, he was as virile as they came. And that was if he had just stood there and done nothing. But he never did nothing. Not with those laughing eyes and those cocksure grins of his. Any normal red-blooded woman would have noticed.

For the first time she had to be abnormal. There were so many oddball things about her, why couldn't it be that he *didn't* excite her? *Didn't* make her chest go so tight that she could barely breathe, her whole body suddenly feeling light enough to fly and hot enough to burst into flame. All with a look and a smile.

And why wasn't she immune to him anyway? She'd been largely immune to all other males in the world. Not that she'd never taken lovers, because she had. And she'd even enjoyed herself once or twice. Maybe. But there was a difference between the enjoyment she had felt and . . . and *this*. This feeling, this awareness . . . this response that at times rivaled what she had felt when in full orgasm at the hands of other men. Had she ever truly known the proper point of pleasure? If so, she ought not feel like she'd somehow been missing out all this time.

"S-so what?" she answered shakily. "Just because . . . I mean, I can't always help . . . I already told you you're not exactly hard to look at, you know! And you're always talking about it as if you live, eat, and breathe sex or something."

"Aye." Again, that unrepentant grin. "And I think

about it more and more the longer I'm in your company."
There was a drop in his tone. Not just to make him sound
more lusty, although that was there, but to make him
sound more sober. As though he found the games he
played with her to be very serious.

She shook that thought off. He was clearly the sort of
man who knew his way around women. He probably
knew how to make each one think she meant something,
that she was somehow special in some way.

She glanced back at his hand, realizing that juice from
the tangerine was wending down his fingers and along
the back of his hand. He had unthinkingly squeezed the
fragile fruit just a little too hard. For some reason the
knowledge made her swallow a little bit harder.

For a brief, searing moment she wondered what it
would be like if she could sip the sweet nectar straight off
his fingers.

"I don't want to talk about this anymore," she said in
a rasp between a too-tight pair of vocal cords.

Ahnvil's eyes narrowed on her and she could see him
thinking. God only knew *what* he was thinking. She
never knew what she was going to get next with him. His
golden eyes shifted from her to the fruit and back again.
Then, abruptly, he put it to his mouth and took a huge,
rending bite of it. Juice exploded everywhere, more of it
rushing down his long fingers, runnels of it washing
down from the corners of his mouth, droplets waiting to
drip quivering at the end of his chin.

Then in the next instant he was on his feet and rushing around the counter. She was panting for breath even
before he grabbed hold of her. He jerked her up against
the length of his body and, running fast, fierce fingers
through her hair, he held her for the crushing press of
his mouth. An instant later his tongue was sweeping
boldly into her mouth. The taste of tangerine exploded
onto her taste buds. Tangerine and hot, sexy male. Sud-

denly she really wanted to lick every speck of citrus flavor from wherever it had ended up on him. Lips. Face. Fingers. There had even been some dripping down onto his chest.

Before she could control the impulse, she did exactly that. She started by catching his head between her hands and drawing back a little, holding his head still to keep him from chasing her down. Then she touched her tongue to his lips, this time licking him instead of kissing him. Her tongue ran over his bottom lip slowly and with purpose, until she heard a frustrated growl ejecting from him. It made her smile, made her revel, for that brief moment, in her power as a woman. Her power over him.

Her hand slid away from his face, over his shoulder, down his arm until she was picking up the hand that had held the sweet fruit. Then she drew back from his mouth and lifted his fingers to her lips. He was staring hard at her, breathing like he'd run a marathon, and when she touched her tongue to his index finger and subsequently drew it into her mouth, he ejected one of those savage sounding growls. And the more he made sounds like that, the more his flavor burst across her tongue, the more she wanted him.

"Ah, Kat lass," he ground out heatedly. "Doona look at me like that if you doona want me tae fuck you where you stand."

And what would be so wrong about that? she asked herself inanely as he withdrew his fingers from her mouth and swept her back up into a hot kiss. What would be so bad about taking large handfuls of virile Gargoyle and just having her wicked way with him? Maybe she wanted that. Maybe she wanted to be down and dirty like that.

Oh yes. Yes, she very much wanted to be dirty with him.

A sound of rough frustration burst into her mouth

from his and she suddenly felt his hands on her hips
hauling her feet up off the floor and with a slightly awkward plop she found herself sitting on top of her own
kitchen countertop. He parted her knees roughly and
injected his big body between her thighs, his hands on
her ass dragging her forward over cold granite until the
very center of her core was pressed up against the lower
ridges of his abdomen. An abdomen left bare thanks to
that low-riding towel around his hips. All she would
have to do was grab for that knot and she would get to
see beyond that sensuous path of dark hair leading
down from his navel. Oh, so what if she'd seen him
naked . . . seen him naked and aroused already. This
time it was different. How it was different she couldn't
exactly say, but it was. This time she felt as if he were
truly seeing in the clear . . . no fever or strange circumstance or misconception. He'd come for her, come
across that room in order to take her taste over the taste
of that perfect, ripe tangerine. He'd somehow seen into
the heart of her desires and had acted on them. And
God help her she was acting on them, too. The feel of
him, so big and vital between her legs made her moan
low in her throat. Apparently he liked the sound a great
deal because his hands clenched tighter at her hips.

"Ah hell, Kat, I can feel the heat of you through these
damned jeans." His hand curved forward, running over
the slope of her thigh until his fingers were burrowing
along the center seam of the jeans that were confound-
ing his efforts to touch her intimately. She gasped at the
feel of his touch, the boldness of his fingers pressing
against her as if all they wanted most in the world was
to be running through the wet folds of her eager sex.

"Jesus, you're hot," he breathed into her mouth as he
began to kiss her again in earnest. Had he been heated
before? No. She realized she hadn't known the meaning

of the word. He was voracious against and within her mouth and she felt as though she were drinking pure acid, her mouth was so alive with sensation. It dripped down into her body burning and melting her from the inside out. It was hard for her to comprehend that less than twenty-four hours ago he had been unknown to her and even now, was still a total stranger but yet he knew something about her that she had not known for herself. She had not known she could be so passionate, so hungry for another being. A being she had barely come to know. In the past she had been so cautious, waiting until she was on the verge of true friendship before being brave enough to tell them about herself and her condition. Never mind becoming intimate with them on the level that she was being intimate with this man. But maybe it was because he was just as strange, just as afflicted as she was that allowed all of her defenses to drop.

And now she had his hands pressing intimately against her and it somehow felt more right than any other sexual interaction she'd had to date. Maybe because for the first time she wasn't so hung up so much on the details of what was wrong with her and was more focused on what was feeling so right.

Frustrated by her denim he went for a different level of assault. He grabbed for the bottom of her sweater and whipped it up over her head before she even could think about protesting. She gasped as her heated skin met the colder kitchen air. It was only truly warm in the living room and the bedroom, which shared the cozy heat of the fireplace. Left without heat, the kitchen had grown much colder over the past hours.

He stood away from her for a long moment, his eyes roaming over the freckles on her skin. "Ah, Kat lass, you're a fair sight for some verra sore eyes."

And for some reason she took utter delight in his

words. Took pride in them. She was proud of herself for pleasing him. How insane was that? Pride for pleasing a complete stranger? It was a study in madness.

He reached out then with his right hand, his fingers splayed as he brushed the pads of them down over her breastbone and the beginning swell of her breasts. He narrowed to a single finger, tracing the crease of her cleavage right to the rim of her confining bra. And it was confining. It felt as though it were reining her in, holding her back from feeling all that she could feel. He stood away from her, making her feel all the more exposed for it. It would somehow be easier, she knew, if she could just be swept up in the heated moments of his demanding kisses. Then it was almost as though she were watching it all happen to someone else. This way she was left with nothing but awareness of herself, who she was, and how out of the norm for her all of this was. Then again, wouldn't it be out of the norm for anyone? After all, how many hot, sexy Gargoyles were there in the world?

The thought was sobering and she found herself creeping toward her discarded sweater, which rested in a puddle off to the left of her.

"Ah, I doona think so, Kat lass," he growled, reaching to push the sweater out of her reach while he stepped back up against the countertop. "It will no' come back tae you until I've had a wee taste of this fine fair skin of yours. Look at how pretty and pale you are. No' a touch of sun tae be had. I like that. You're as fair as an Irish lass and a damn sight more pretty, too."

He lowered his face to her neck, nuzzling her there with a purring earthquake of sound rumbling up out of him. His hands had gone to the countertop on either side of her thighs, gripping it hard enough to snap the granite, she was sure. "Just one li'le taste." She loved the way he said "little," his accent dropping both *t*s. It was another reminder of how different they were, but it didn't make her come to her senses in the least.

What she was doing was waiting with all of her breaths held in abeyance for the first touch of his lips against her skin.

"I can see your pulse in your throat. A fine, strong throbbing pulse. I see it racing. Tell me, Kat lass, is that for me? Is it because you want me?"

Oh, why couldn't he just kiss her and be done with it? Why did he have to keep talking to her? It was so much easier when he just kissed her until she was utterly mindless and didn't have to think about the consequences. So all she could do was shake her head.

"No? Does that mean no, Kat? You doona want me?" He backed away from her and her hands shot to his shoulders and she cried out.

"No! I-I mean . . . I mean yes. It's because of you. A-a physiological reaction i-is only normal when in a sexual situation." Oh God! Did she just say that? Did she just babble at him like some kind of freaking dumb-assed textbook?

"I see. So 'tis the situation and no' the man himself," he said, his chiseled lips turning down in a frown.

"No! It's not just the situation," she added hastily. Then, afraid she sounded too eager, she subsided a little. "Why do you have to know this? Why can't you just . . ."

"Just kiss you?"

"Y-yes," she admitted breathily.

He leaned in until their lips were just about to touch, his bright eyes meeting hers intensely.

"Because that would be too easy for you, Kat lass. And I'm no' about tae make this easy for you, no matter how much I'm wanting you."

With that he pushed away from her and moved to the sink. He washed his hands and his face free of the remaining juice from the tangerine, but it wasn't until he returned to his stool that she realized he wasn't coming back to finish what he had started. She realized she was staring at him, completely dumbfounded. Then she felt just how cold the room had grown and she angrily grabbed up her sweater and jerked it on over her head.

"I'm going to check on the generator," she said bitingly, leaving her food preparation to storm out in search of her coat. The problem was she'd have to pass within reach of him to get to the bedroom. *Well, so what?!* He obviously didn't want to take advantage of her.

"Uh-uh," he said just when she thought she was going to make it past him. His hand shot out and ringed her around her biceps on her right arm, yanking her forward between his knees as he turned the barstool to face her. She went to jerk away but he held fast. He grasped her chin in his fingers and turned her face up to his. "Doona pitch a fit, lass," he said, making her want to claw his smug grin off his face. "I'm no' trying tae be mean tae you, Kat. No' rejecting you, either. I'm just telling you, I know I can run roughshod over others tae get my way, and I willna be doing that wi' you. Me wanting you is one thing. You wanting me is all of another. I know it. I'm aware of it. I want tae know what you want and you need tae tell me."

What was she supposed to say to that? He was a stranger. Was she supposed to say that she wanted a total stranger? Didn't he know how ludicrous that was? Did *she*?

"I ken you're no' ready yet. I can wait, lass. 'Tis no rush. Now, let me check the generator and you can finish this fine meal you've been working on. Which way is it, Kat?"

"It's outside . . . you can't—" She ran her eyes down the length of his barely clothed body.

" 'Tis no' a problem, lass."

"It is a problem!" she snapped, shifting instantly into tough medical professional mode. "You will sit right down and you will wait for me to do it myself. Your job is to heal. The sooner you're better the better off we'll both be." The unspoken intent being that she would be happy when she could go back to hiding in her quiet, well-ordered little world.

"I will no'. Come if you like, but I'm going out."

"B-but—" But she was speaking to herself as he ducked around her and headed for the door. "To the left!" she thought to call out inanely just as he was throwing the door open. He slammed the door shut in his wake, leaving her to shiver in the rushing cold left behind.

Ahnvil went out into the blistering cold with nothing but the towel he had on for protection. Ideally he could have donned his stone skin—it would have protected him from the cold—but these were not ideal circumstances. There were few things that frightened him, but permanent being was one of them . . . just as death frightened anyone, he supposed.

The walk out into the crunching depth of fast-fallen snow was just the thing. As it was he was burning up from the heat of the desire he felt for his pretty little Kat.

No. Not his. She couldn't be his. He didn't want her to be his. Being his meant being in danger, and she was already fragile enough in health and in psyche. As he touched the cold metal of the generator, his warm skin sticking fast, he was forced to remind himself of these things. He was no prize. She would win nothing if she thought to pursue him. Asking for her to make the next move was inviting her to set herself up for disappointment. He had to stop this. Stop it now before it went too far.

If it wasn't already too far. There was no explaining it, no way of defining what it was about her that made him want to chase her down like a hound chases a fox. And like those hounds he would be the death of his quarry.

Katrina set her pan over the open gas flame of the stove and began to cook the meal she'd started. She was almost finishing when the door exploded open and Ahnvil stepped inside in a freezing wash of wind and snow. As she hurried over to him she swiped up the afghan she'd been dozing under earlier and swung it quickly around his hunching body.

"Fuck, that's cold!" he cursed fiercely. Kat hurried away and came back with a stack of fresh towels, pressing them onto him.

"You should have let me go!" she said.

"What's done is done," was his only reply. Realizing she wasn't going to get anywhere, she retreated into the kitchen to tend to her neglected pan. When she turned around, she did a sharp about-face right back again. She'd just gotten an eyeful of gorgeous gluteus maximus as he whipped away his wet towel and replaced it with a warm, dry one. From that moment on she studiously focused on the stir-fry she was putting together for them.

"So . . . if the newscasters were no' lying tae us, this storm will blow out in another twelve hours. We can go then."

"First of all, just because the storm ends it doesn't mean we can go anywhere. Not for days, considering how far up the mountain we are and how much snow they are expecting. And second of all, what do you mean 'we'? I'm not going anywhere!"

"First of all, if you want that bloody necklace off you you are going tae have tae come wi' me. Second of all, I doona bloody have days! Two at worst. Three at best. If I doona get back in time . . ." He trailed off, running an agitated hand through his dark hair.

"What? What'll happen if you don't get back in time?"

"I . . . it would be bad. 'Tis all I'm going to say about it," he said, a definitive shutting down of the topic.

"Fine!" she snapped, pushing the meat around in the pan angrily. But after a moment she slowed and reached to fondle the cold metal of the Amulet. "Do you think they can get it off? The people you want to bring me to?"

"I've a fair idea they might. There's a man there, if you can call him a man, named Kamenwati. He is well versed in magics of all kinds. If anyone is going tae know how tae get the bloody thing off, it will be him."

"If you can call him a man?"

"Douche bag is a better word."

She burst out with a sharp laugh. "Tell me how you really feel!"

He grimaced. "We have history."

"What kind of history?"

He moved into the kitchen and retook his stool.

"He was my forger."

"He wrote bad checks for you?" she asked.

"No," he smiled with amusement, but it was a wry sort of smile. "Gargoyles are forged, lass. He was the man who forged me."

"You mean he's your creator."

"No. God is my creator. Kamenwati is the man who made an abomination of that creation."

She whipped around to face him. "You are not an abomination!"

"You are no' weird," he countered. They both frowned, inwardly admitting to themselves that they were hard on themselves as far as their feelings about what the outside world would make of them.

"So how exactly is a Gargoyle forged?"

"You take a man like any other, and you take a beast. Using complex spells you can make a combination of the two, but it cannot be living matter into living matter. You need—"

"A stone statue. A Gargoyle."

"Aye. Usually a Gargoyle. The spell takes the essence of each and combines them into the stone receptacle. The bodies die and only the souls remain. Then the Gargoyle is branded by his maker and becomes slave to his house."

"Slave!"

"Aye," he said. "Kat lass, your food is burning."

"Oh!" She swept the pan from the stove and quickly dished it onto twin plates. She stood on one side of the counter while he sat on the other.

"A slave? You were a slave?" Her eyes fell to the brand on his chest, the burn of snakes wrapping around a dagger like the medical caduceus.

"Aye, I was. For thirty years."

"Thirty years! H-how old are you?"

"Three hundred and fifty-two."

"Three hundred and . . ." She swallowed hard. "How is it possible for him to keep you a slave for thirty years? I mean, you're so big, and if you can turn to stone, you must be practically invulnerable. How . . . ?"

"He created a failsafe. It's called a touchstone. A small stone that they cleave from the Gargoyle at the time of his making. That stone must be imbued with a Bodywalker's energy on a regular basis and every day the stone must be returned to where it was cleaved. The Gargoyle must sleep in contact with that stone again in order to heal and regenerate. If no' . . . if no' they risk permanent being. Turning to stone permanently. Pretty much one of the few ways we can be killed."

"So in order to be free you had to take the stone with you?"

"Aye. And something that small makes it easy tae lock up and tae hide. And since sunlight turns us tae stone, they make certain we're in the sun before bringing it out.

If they want tae punish us they will push us tae risk permanent being, knowing 'tis the thing we fear above all else."

"So . . . how did you escape?"

"My maker had left his stones out of hiding that day. He rarely made such a mistake, believe me. I had been watching and waiting for years before he made this one li'le mistake. But even though it was out in the open it was still protected by spellwork. A lashing out of sorts. Taking the stone meant taking the hit."

"Oh my God. It almost killed you didn't it?"

"Aye," he said softly before turning his attention to the meal she'd made. She let him eat for a short while, although with the speed he was eating at, a short while was more than long enough.

"I was going to say 'so then you escaped' but it wasn't that simple was it? You were badly injured and these people, these Bodywalkers sound very powerful."

He nodded then ventured to look at her. "The details are no' important. Only the result. I've been a free man ever since."

Until recently, he thought grimly. But he didn't feel it necessary to tell her the details of how she had come to find him if she wasn't flat out asking him for them.

"So how many days without a touchstone does it take before permanent being?" she asked with a delicate sort of curiosity, as if she were afraid he might find the query offensive. He did not. But neither would he tell her just how close he was to the condition himself. He wouldn't worry her unless he absolutely had to.

"A few days. Sometimes a week. It can depend on the Gargoyle, who the forger was, how strong the spell work was. How big the touchstone is. Larger touchstones hold more energy, allowing a Gargoyle to store more energy, enough to last for longer periods of time."

"And what about you?" she asked, her eyes nervously looking toward the windows and the storm swishing around beyond them. "Is that why you are in a hurry? Is that why you need to rush out of here?"

"I've got plenty of time," he lied smoothly to her. "My forger was one of the two most powerful Templar Bodywalkers in the world. His Gargoyles are among the most powerful, most invincible of our breed. But it also meant we were held longest in captivity as well because he was not the kind of man to make mistakes or become careless with his touchstones. I need to leave to give my leader some information." To bring him that Amulet. And the girl attached to it.

"But if you need a Bodywalker's energy to rejuvenate the stone, how can you be free from your maker?"

Such a bright, quick thing she was. He marveled at her. The world of Bodywalkers and Nightwalkers in general was a very complex one, a tough one to keep track of at times, and she was keeping up enough to ask well-thought-out questions.

"Let me begin by explaining what a Bodywalker is."

"Oh yes. That might be useful," she said with an eager nod.

"Only if you promise tae eat," he countered looking pointedly at her largely untouched plate of food. "Or risk forfeiting it tae me."

She grinned at him for that, picking up her fork and stabbing at some meat and vegetables. Once she had dutifully popped the forkful into her mouth she gestured for him to continue with no little amount of impatience.

"The Bodywalkers, like me, were once human. Long ago in Egypt in the cradle of civilization. It is believed that their mummification processes and their selfish desire tae bring all their worldly goods along with them into the land of the dead angered the gods. As punishment they

were indeed allowed tae be preserved for all time . . . in
spirit. In the Ether, a place sort of like the way people
picture heaven. Full of clouds and insubstantial spirits.
There they were aware of one another, aware of time
passing in gruelingly slow increments. Aware of the life
that continued on the living plane of existence. A limbo,
if you will. No' heaven. No' hell. No reward . . . but a
great deal of torment simply by nature of being aware of
the passage of time second by second, year by year, century by century, with nothing tae occupy their minds.

"One day one of the souls in limbo discovered that
they could live again. All they need do was find a human
being on the verra instant of death and ask them if they
would mind sharing their bodies with a second soul. If
they say yes they are reborn together as a Bodywalker.
The visiting soul brings with it remarkable healing ability and a very special power, different from soul tae
soul, and immortality. As long as they can stay alive,
they will live indefinitely.

"There are two factions of Bodywalkers," he said,
"the Politic and the Templars. The Templars use spells
and unnatural magics tae get their way in the world.
They also subjugate the host, the original soul, completely taking over the body. The Politic are different in
that they do not like tae use most magics and that they
Blend with the host soul, coming tae a point of equal
sharing and harmonious life together with the host they
are guests tae. Now, tae answer your question, the Templars and Politic are at war and it is we Gargoyles that
were the catalyst of that war. The Templars were already disapproved of for their hijacking of the host
body, and there were other reasons why discontent was
brewing between the two factions, but it was the creation of Gargoyles as slaves that pushed them over the
edge. There was a great war, much like your civil war,
only there is still no winner and those who were the

original tribe of Gargoyles were physically freed in one great fell swoop at the beginning battle of this war. The Gargoyles were led tae freedom by a great man named Herron."

He grew quiet for a moment, toying with a last piece of bell pepper left on his plate. "You see, we are no' allowed tae have names once we are made. They strip us of them. I doona know why exactly. A way of humiliating and subjugating us, I suppose. Herron was the name of the great Politic general that led the charge that freed all of the first generation, or tribe, of Gargoyles. As homage every Gargoyle in the first tribe took a name starting with h. Every Gargoyle in the next generation put the silent 'h' in as the second letter in their names."

"Then third put the 'h' in the third position," she said with understanding. "So that makes you a second generation Gargoyle because the 'h' you use is in second position."

"Aye."

"What defines a generation?"

"A hundred years. If you were forged in the first hundred years you were a member of the first tribe. The second hundred, the second tribe. And so on."

"I see." She frowned at him then handed him her half-emptied plate. He took it and began to finish her leftovers.

"So in answer tae your original question, we each find a Politic Bodywalker tae swear fealty tae. We pledge tae protect them and theirs, stand sentinel outside their walls, and they in turn vow tae recharge our stones, give us a place in their homes and families and protect us in turn as we sit in our statue states recharging in the sun. 'Tis what you might call a mutually beneficial arrangement."

"I see," she said again. "Do you like your Politic Bodywalker?"

"Oh aye," he said with enthusiasm. "Menes is the ruler of the body Politic. A finer Pharaoh there never was. And he has a sweet mate as well. A fiery redheaded lass. Her name is Hatshepsut. Or Marissa. We use Marissa. Wi' two souls comes two names and they choose which one tae be called by. Menes uses his host's name as well. Jackson. You'll meet them before all is said and done."

"I will? A pharaoh?" She swallowed hard. "I don't know if I'm fit for royalty." She swallowed again and her hands began to wrap around each other. "It's just a necklace. A pretty one. I can just stay here and keep it on."

"No! You canna! That's dark magic there," he said, pointing harshly at the Amulet. "You're coming wi' me. The sooner we get that thing off you the happier I'll be. You can be on your way after that, but I'll no' let you run around wi' that on no' knowing what it might do tae you."

"Don't try and boss me around! You can't make me do anything I don't want to do!" Then, before he could argue she seemed to rethink what he had said. "Dark magic?" She lifted the pretty necklace and looked at it, swallowing audibly. "How do you know that?"

"You canna get it off can you?" he retorted.

"Oh. Yes. There is that. But that seems harmless enough."

"For what we see of it. Who knows what's happening behind scenes? 'Tis verra dangerous, Kat lass, and make no mistake about it."

"I'll take your word for it." She retrieved his plate and moved over to the sink. He could see her working things over in her mind. He could only hope she didn't ask something he wasn't able to answer.

"So how many days has it been since you were last in contact with your touchstone?"

And there it was. The one question he really didn't

want to answer. Partly because he didn't want to face up to it, and partly because he didn't want to pile more worries on to her. Especially since the most urgent concern was currently around her pretty little neck.

The slave, born of the infinite Nightwalkers, will set free the power within. The one that harnesses Adoma's Amulet will have such power as to make a god weep.

What the hell did that mean exactly? And if he was supposed to be the one to harness the power of the thing, then why was it trapped on *her* body?

"Oh, doona worry," he lied to her again. "I have more than enough time tae get back tae my touchstone. Doona worry about that."

"Well, of course I'm going to worry about it. I don't want you to turn permanently to stone. And before it looked like you were having trouble controlling it . . ."

He *was* having trouble controlling it. It was actually taking a conscious effort not to turn to stone, whereas before it had been an effortless thing. Usually it was like breathing . . . an automatic ability he paid little attention to. But now, if it got much worse he was going to be afraid to go to sleep, afraid that the unconscious state would allow for him to turn unwittingly. Maybe he was making a mountain out of the symptom, but he had never been away from his touchstone for this long before and he had no idea what it would do and when it would do it. It was a sickening feeling to know that you weren't in control of yourself or your destiny. True, none of them were to any extent, but this was bringing that sharply into focus. For all of his three hundred years, he still wasn't ready yet to die. He was needed. Jackson and Marissa needed him there to protect them even more than ever before. There was a demented god out there, reborn in Panahasi's mistress's body, that was hell bent on destroying them all and he needed to be there to put himself between them and it. That was the way he should die. In battle. With wings spread wide and a weapon in his hands. A sword, to be exact. It was his preferred method of dealing with Templar bastards like Panahasi. It was pretty fucking impossible to recover from having your head lopped off.

No. He would not die by turning slowly to stone. He simply refused to.

"I think I'm going tae have a lie down," he said, realizing that the more effort he expended doing other things the more likely he was burning precious energy away. But what he had noticed was that the more he ate the easier it was to keep flesh form.

"I think that's a good idea. Did you have enough to eat?" She looked skeptical, clearly already having learned that he was a bottomless pit as far as food was concerned. "Do all Gargoyles eat this much?"

"Some more than others," he said with one of those easy grins. "We have high metabolisms. The more we do the more we have to replenish our food stores."

"I can see why that would be." She eyed his massive stature. "Go rest. I'll come check your bandages in a minute."

He nodded and moved back into the bedroom.

For Katrina it was a lot to digest. She felt as though her brain was buzzing with information. It was so hard to believe there was this whole world right beyond her reach that she never knew of. A world that, like her, was subject to the vicious whims of the sun. She didn't exactly know how to feel about that. About any of this. The one thing she was taking away from it though was that time for Ahnvil was clearly running short. It was going to take days for them to get out of there. The end of the storm and then waiting for the roads to clear would probably take the better part of a week. Just how long was too long?

She didn't want to find out.

The big guy was starting to grow on her.

Odjit, also known as the imp god Apep, looked down at the dead body of Moribundi with a frown of consternation.

"Well, now I wonder how this happened. This is so unfair! If anyone is going to kill someone it's going to be me! A perfect opportunity has been completely wasted. I'm sure I could have made an example out of him in some way." She/He sighed deeply. "Oh well, there's nothing to be done about it I suppose. Let's hang his body outside the gate and pretend he did something terribly wrong to offend me." Apep glared at the only two other people in the room. Panahasi and some girl whose name Apep couldn't care less about remembering. "You realize this means death if rumors were to somehow abound otherwise."

"Yes, Mistress," they both said quickly, the young girl literally shaking from fear. It was just the kind of reaction Apep loved to see in his little minions. Apep gave his slightly rounded belly a pat, a strange sort of comfort to the sensation that he had not expected. Ever since he had been reborn into this strange and delightful woman's body he had been enjoying the differences from being male to being female. And now, now that his new female body was impregnated by that poor, unsuspecting Night Angel, it was even more strange and delightful, even more enjoyable.

The Night Angel had been powerful and strong, and his seed was just as strong. But he had not been strong enough to keep Apep from taking that seed by force. He should be very grateful that he had left him alive afterward. After all, it might have been bad luck to kill the father of his child. He was a god so he knew better than to tempt the fates. Even gods were subject to the whims of fate.

"I will do as my mistress asks," Panahasi said with great deference. Today was one of those days where the groveling of his minions delighted him to no end. There were days of course when nothing could mollify him and, strangely enough as his pregnancy progressed there seemed to be more of those than usual, but this was not one of those days.

"Mistress?" Apep asked archly.

"My most glorious and benevolent mistress," Panahasi corrected himself with a low bow and a complete exposure of his neck and back. Most pleasing indeed.

"Yes. Well. And then when you are done you can fetch your glorious and benevolent mistress some crawdads."

"Crawdads, Mistress?" he asked awkwardly.

"Yes," he hissed low, leaning in and narrowing his eyes on the underling. "Your mistress wants crawdads. Cajun crawdads. And plenty of them. The spicier the better. Is there a problem with that?"

"Oh no, Mistress. Your servant only wants to know how spicy you prefer them to be."

What a waste of his talents, Panahasi groused in his thoughts as he went to his computer in order to research where the hell in Washington he was going to find crawdads.

CHAPTER ELEVEN

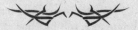

"The storm has stopped," Jacob noted from across the room.

"Huh? What—?" Bella sat up sharply in bed, her curling black hair falling in a rumpled cloud around her head and shoulders and he had to smile at the sight of her. She used both hands to shove back her hair and she grabbed up handfuls of sheets. She scooted off the bed, wrapping herself up in the sheet as her feet hit the floor. "Oh jeez, that's cold!" she cried out, hopping from one foot to the other. They had lost electricity quite some time ago and outside of the fire in the hearth they had no source of warmth save each other. But they had happily been keeping each other warm and then some. Jacob obliged his wife and met her halfway over to him, sweeping her up in his arms and carrying her over to the darkened window. Although he was naked he did not feel the cold quite like his half-human bride did. Just as his half-human bride couldn't grow a seedling to a full-grown oak with just a thought in less than five minutes. But neither could he translate any language, nor could he see the future, both talents his wife did with ease.

He brought her over to the lodge room's window seat, sat down on the cushion, and settled her into his lap. The lack of electricity didn't bother them in the least.

They were used to it because Demon physiology and technology didn't get along very well. They resorted to fires in many fireplaces, just like they had been doing for years in the land of England. She was already missing home. Not home exactly, but her children. She had not been away from them for a protracted period of time before, and even though it had only been a full day, she knew that it was going to be some time before she got to see them again. It was that feeling more than any of the others that told her this trip was being driven by her premonition senses. She didn't want to face up to that. She was enjoying their time alone together and she was afraid of disappointing Jacob.

Just now she had been dreaming about walking in the snow. She had felt herself lifting her legs and pumping them down into the newly fallen snow. She had heard whispers in her head, unintelligible, as though she were getting some sort of message but it was coming out all garbled. Since she wasn't a telepath, that made no sense to her at all.

"I said the snow has stopped," Jacob said softly near her ear, his warm lips nuzzling her in the spot he just knew melted her bones into a big pile of goo.

She sighed with contentment. Then his mouth was on her neck and she went utterly limp in his arms. Heat spiraled through her, a heat that had never waned, not even when she'd been mad at him, in all the years of their marriage.

The Demon King, Noah, had wed them while she had been pregnant with her first child. A fact her bratty sister had pointed out to her, teasing her as being the "knocked-up" sister. What was ironic and a little sad about that was that Corrine now wanted to have children of her own and so far had been disappointed that it wasn't happening. But Gideon, the Ancient Medic and healer had said that everything was just fine and that it was only a matter of time, so they were just in a holding pattern at the moment. As for herself, it was time for them to start thinking about using a contraceptive. It had proven to be equally as difficult to get pregnant between their children, luck of the draw allowing them to hit it out of the park the first time with their first child. It had taken five years of unprotected sex before their son had come along. And she would like to have another child one day, but being immortal they had all the time in the world for doing that and she wanted to enjoy watching these two children grow up some more.

Because at the rate her child's powers were developing, she would soon be leaving their house and going to her foster parent's homes instead. In the Demon culture it was believed that foster parents were better equipped to mold and train fledgling children, since their parents might be inclined to be too gentle and too forgiving. This allowed the parents the opportunity to maintain a purely loving relationship with their child and to leave disciplining and training to a trusted family friend. In Leah's case the foster parents were Elijah, Noah's former Warrior captain and Legna, the Demon King's sister.

The fostering usually took place as soon as a child began to show signs of its powers, usually around the late teens. But Leah was her father's daughter and had been showing signs of power since as young as two years old. It was of course far too young to take the child from her parents so Bella had been working diligently to put off the fostering as long as possible. Both of her foster parents resided in Russia and Bella couldn't bear the idea of her moving so far away. She had already warned her husband that the odds of them moving to Russia after the fostering began were very high indeed.

But she was almost ten now and it was only a matter of time before Jacob made the decision to let their daughter go. She was the first child of the previously undiscovered element of Time. Until Leah there had only been six elemental Demons: Fire, Water, Earth—like her father—Wind, Body, and Mind. Now she had introduced control over Time and another child, Seth, was prophesied to have control over Space. As such Leah needed to be nurtured and controlled very carefully. There was no telling the amount of havoc that could occur if she wasn't raised with proper control. There was also no way of truly knowing what she was capable of. They would all be learning alongside of her.

"Stop fretting," her husband murmured gently against her throat. "I won't let her go until she's ready."

"I know. It has to be when it's best for her," she said softly. "Because if it were up to me she would never go anywhere. I want to go for a walk," she told her husband. The desire was compelled by her morbid thoughts as much as it was compelled by her suspicions that she was having premonitions.

"Are you kidding?" he asked incredulously. "It's freezing out there and the snow has got to be at least two feet deep!"

"It's nice! It's fresh and clean and crisp outside. I love it after a snowfall like this."

He looked entirely skeptical, but he said, "All right, if that's what you want."

And that was why she loved him so much. Because for him, it was always about what she wanted. And she knew exactly how lucky she was.

With the exception of eating a few more meals, Kat almost didn't interact with her guest at all after their first meal together. Apparently his injuries caught up with him and all he wanted to do was sleep. Which she was completely fine with her because she didn't think she could handle much more time in his presence what with him being all gorgeous and overwhelmingly sexy.

It just wasn't fair that he had it all coming and going like that. How was even the sanest woman alive supposed to resist that?

She wondered if he had always looked like that; if he had looked that way before he had been forged. Or had he needed to get used to seeing a stranger's face and body in the mirror along with getting used to being a slave?

"The snow has stopped."

Kat had been at the sink washing dishes when he suddenly spoke in her ear from behind her. She dropped her pot with a clatter and swung around to face him, unwittingly dripping water and suds on his feet. He was so close she could feel the inferno-like heat of his body flowing into her.

"I know. I peeked out earlier." She lifted her hands, wanting to push him back a step and yet somehow afraid to touch him. As though if she started touching all that gorgeous male virility maybe she wouldn't want to stop. And that just wouldn't do. Not after spending the past few hours lecturing herself on all the reasons why it would be a bad, bad, very bad idea to get entangled with him any more than she already had. One: he was a Gargoyle. Two: he was obviously dangerous. Three: they didn't make safety gear for battling back lusty Scottish men. Not since the chastity belt went out of style.

He seemed to notice her dilemma, because one of those heart-stopping smiles spread cockily over his lips. "Is there a problem, Kat lass?" he asked, the throaty rumble of his voice washing down over her as she cocked her head back and looked up at him.

"No. Nothing," she said a bit hoarsely. And there was a gleam in his eye that told her he didn't believe her for a single solitary second.

"Verra well then. Best be getting dressed. We'll be leaving soon."

"Leaving! We can't leave! And if you hadn't noticed

you don't have much in the way of clothes! I had to cut through your jeans in order to get them off you."

"I was thinking maybe you know of a store in town that might have my size."

"That's open at eleven o'clock at night?" she countered. "Right after a *blizzard*? And town isn't just a hop, skip, and a jump away. It's miles between here and there and even with my truck we couldn't make it through this snow."

"I dinna say you were going tae *buy* the clothes for me."

"You mean break in?" She gasped, utterly horrified. "That's breaking the law!"

"Kat lass . . ."

"Don't you 'Kat lass' me! We're not breaking in . . . and the closest store that's open twenty-four hours a day is forty minutes away! Walmart. But—"

"Then we'll go there."

"How?" she demanded to know. "We can't drive! The roads are going to be impassable for days!"

"I noticed you had a coupla fine pairs of snowshoes in the front closet."

"The front . . . when did you get the chance to look in the front closet?" she wanted to know.

"When you fell asleep earlier. Did you know," he said, bracing a hand against the counter and leaning in even closer, "that you have the cutest li'le snore when you're sleeping?"

"I do n—" Well, maybe she did. It had been a while since she'd actually fallen asleep with someone around. And even then they were at least polite enough not to mention it! "Yeah, well you snore like a freight train."

"Aye. I likely do. I'm no' used to sleeping in order to catch my rest. I'm used to being in the sun, baking the stone of my body while my touchstone regenerates me."

He made it sound so beautiful, and she could hear the longing in his voice.

"But then that means you never get to sleep with . . ." She flushed. She had no right to posit about something so personal.

"No, lass. I only need tae regenerate a few hours every day. Four is well enough. So I can stay and sleep with you most of the day and go out into the daylight about four hours before dusk."

"With me? I'm not sleeping with you," she said, trying for indignant and achieving breathless.

"Well, for example then," he said, his grin turning utterly devious.

"Oh. All right. But that doesn't solve our problem. You have no clothes and you can't walk forty miles naked in the freezing cold snow! And that's if the Walmart is even open. The storm was very widespread and we still don't have electricity. And I have a dog here. There's no one to take care of Karma."

At the sound of her name, Karma perked up from where she'd been having a nice long nap in front of the fire. However, she immediately put her head back down, clearly not interested in moving.

"She's a breed meant for snow," he pointed out, looking at Karma who immediately began to wag her tail in loud thumping sweeps against the floor. As if she understood everything they were saying. "We can bring her wherever we need tae go. But what we need tae do is get to a viable airport as soon as possible so we can fly out of here. We can take her with us if you want—"

"I am not flying Karma commercially! Do you know what they do to live animals on flights? They stick them in cargo holds that aren't even climate-controlled!"

"Lass—"

"No! Don't you 'lass' me! I won't do it. And I'm not

coming with you on this snow-covered Bataan death march!"

"She will no' be flying cargo, Kat lass. She'll be on a private jet in the cabin wi' us."

"You . . ." She blinked. "You have a private jet?"

"No. But my employer does. No' that I canna afford my own, but why waste money on two?"

"Y-you can afford your own *plane*?"

"Aye. One or two."

"One or . . ." She closed her eyes and swallowed. Focus. Stay focused. "Again, that doesn't change the fact that you have no clothes now."

"I have a shirt. I found this big T-shirt in your things." He indicated a shirt he'd been holding in his hand. He put it on to demonstrate, shrugging into it and pulling it down.

"That's a nightshirt. And what were you doing in my things?" she demanded.

"Looking for a shirt," he said with a grin. "Doona worry, I only touched your underwear a li'le."

"You—" She was gearing up to yell at him, but then realized he was teasing her. Despite herself, she found herself fighting back a smile. "You have nothing to wear on the bottom."

"This'll do for now." He indicated the towel and the way the shirt came down low on his body.

She eyed him dubiously. "Maybe I have some sweatpants . . ." She trailed off . . . because they both knew that even her baggiest sweatpants wouldn't come close to fitting him. She was too small and he was too big. As it was her nightshirt was busting at the seams.

"Doona worry. I'm no' human, Kat. I willna feel the cold like a regular man would. And if it gets tae be too much I'll change into my stone skin."

The truth was he could be just as sensitive to the cold as any other man might be after a certain level of exposure. And changing into his stone skin was out of the question. He wouldn't risk not being able to change back.

"I gather there's one or two houses between here and there," he went on. "Is there no one you know close to my build?"

"No." No one. Everyone she knew was six feet tops. And she didn't know that many men to begin with. She didn't socialize all that much with the townsfolk. She did her shopping forty miles away in the twenty-four-hour Walmart that didn't care about the fact that she could only shop in the dark.

"Then it is what it is. The sooner we start the better off we'll be. So let's go."

"I don't want to go," she whined as he took her hand and tugged her along in his wake. "It's so cold out there and so warm in here. I tell you what, I'll snuggle with you if we stay by the fire."

That brought him up short, causing her to slam into his broad back. That was how she came to realize just how good he smelled. He seemed to think about her proposal very seriously, but with a sigh he went on into the bedroom.

"I'll take a rain check," he promised her.

And if she hadn't thought she was in hot water before, she now had no doubts about it.

"Snowshoes," she grumbled, stepping wide with every step. Karma was of course loving every minute of the trek, bounding with endless energy ahead of them, her tongue lolling happily. She would tire out eventually, her big body weighing her down, but for now she was happy. They were just passing Huntsmen's Lodge, a very small ski resort farther down the mountain from her. The runs were dark, night skiing out of the question when there were no lights to be had. She could imagine any visitors would be chomping at the bit for daybreak.

It was right about then that she ran full force into something. The impact knocked her over and she went down in the snow, her head spinning. Ahnvil was by her side in a second, helping her out of the snow.

Bella ran full force into something, going down on her ass in the snow. She went so deep that she was covered like a sugar cookie from tip to toe. She spit snow out as Jacob helped her back up to her feet.

"What was that?" he asked with a chuckle.

"Damned if I know," she said. "I ran into something."

Jacob was looking around and seeing absolutely nothing around her save unblemished snow. He grinned and readied to tease her.

"I did not trip!" Kat said indignantly. "I ran into something." She looked around after Ahnvil had helped her to her feet. The snow was swished all around from her flailing, but as she looked she realized there was a set of footprints leading right up to where she was and then as much disturbed snow as there was on her side.

"That's . . . strange . . . ?" she said questioningly, as if looking for verification. "It looks like I ran into someone, but there's no one there."

"Kat lass, there's nothing but unblemished snow all around us. No one has been through here but us."

"No! Look! See the footprints?"

"I doona see any footprints," he argued with her.

"They're right there!" She pointed at them.

"Kat . . ."

"Wait." She cooled her temper and tried to think. For some reason, a reason she would never know, she took off her glove, leaned forward and slowly pressed her hand into a spot of new snow. It left behind a perfect handprint.

To her shock after a moment a second handprint appeared right next to it, pressed there by a seemingly invisible hand.

"Holy shit! Tell me you don't see that!" She pointed. "That handprint."

"Of course, I do. You just made it."

"No, I mean the one right next to it!"

"Kat, there's only one—" He cut himself off, looking at her like she'd lost her mind as she ignored him and slowly drew a heart in the snow. A second heart appeared right next to it and then a name.

Bella.

"Whoa. It's a ghost," she breathed. Any other day, any day before having met a Gargoyle, she would never have believed any such thing. But this wasn't any other day.

"I still doona see anything."

"Well, I can!" Bella said belligerently to her husband. Then she gasped as a name began to appear in the snow.

Kat.

"Look, her name is Kat!"

"Bella—"

"Oh, hush up!" she said irritably. "Let me think! This means something. It has to mean something. It means something, too, that I can see it but you can't! Okay, so her name, and I'm assuming it's a her, is Kat." She then proceeded to have what looked like, from his perspective, a completely one-sided conversation with herself in the snow. She asked questions like *Who are you? Are you dead? Why can't I see you?*

"She doesn't know she's dead or something," Kat said, nibbling one of her chapped lips.

"Kat. 'Tis cold and time is wearing on," he said gently.

"I know. I'm sorry. I just want to try one more thing. Where are we going?"

"For now? Walmart," he said dryly.

"Right. Okay. That's too long. It's going to take us forever. I was thinking if the plows come through by the time we get to town then we could get a car somehow and drive the rest of the way there. The main roads might be better than the side roads . . . plowed sooner anyway. So let's see if she can make it off the property."

She looked around. "Aha!" Then she wrote, "Meet me at the willow tree."

The willow was about fifty yards away on the other side of the road. Then she immediately began to hurry away, her companion tagging along behind her. As she ran she could see a second set of footprints running along beside her, though at a careful distance. After all, they didn't want to run into each other again. The first time had hurt bad enough.

Sure enough the ghost made it off the property just fine. They began to write back and forth again furiously.

"Are you a ghost?"

"Are *you* a ghost?" she responded in reply.

"Hmm. Odd."

"Kat, I'm freezing my bollocks off."

"Right! Sorry. Let's have them meet us at Walmart. It'll take us another couple of hours to get into town and if the roads are better . . . I'd say tomorrow night? Maybe around nine p.m.?"

"Yes, but where? And what if we're late?"

"Do you have any paper? Let's see if she can read from a note."

He looked at himself and his nearly nude state and then back at her as if she'd lost her ever-lovin' mind.

"Oh! Right. Okay, so no paper. But they'll have paper there if we can get there."

Will leave a note at River Ridge Walmart entrance. Right-hand side.

"Those entrances are huge. Inside or outside?" Ahnvil asked.

"Oh right!"

All the way inside immediate right. 9p.m. tomorrow night.

Okay! The ghost replied.

"Wow! Let's go! I want to see if she can make it and if she can find the note. This is so cool!"

Suddenly the woman who had been dragging her feet the whole way was delighted and eager to be going. She whooped out, the sound echoing in the night, as she hurried her way down the mountain. Good thing, too, because Ahnvil couldn't feel a damn thing from the waist down.

It was nearly dawn by the time they got into town. There wasn't a plow in sight. Her disappointment was legendary.

"Doona worry, Kat. We'll make it there come time for her to get the note. Let's find a place to warm up."

"There's a motel." She eyed him up and down. "I'll get the key. You can wait and I'll let you in the room."

By the time he got into the room with her he thought he'd rather be dead. He was so cold he could hardly move and his feet were torn up and bloody, a fact he was going to have a hard time hiding from her once they were in close quarters again. He could only hope that lack of electricity would work in his favor.

"Jesus Christ," he said under his breath once he had excused himself to go into the bathroom. He was hunched over into himself, leaning back against the door. There was nothing for it. There was only one way he could think of to get warm the way he needed to get warm fast. And since sex wasn't likely to be the best idea in her opinion, he would have to settle for less. He took the time to wash his feet in cold water—cold water, which felt a damn sight warmer than his feet right then. He changed his flimsy towel for a clean, dry one then hurried out of the restroom.

"Oh good!" She went to hurry past him. "I snuck Karma in. Took me a few minutes to pull the hunks of snow out of her fur, but she's good now. I'm going to use some towels to dry her. And I have to pee fiercely bad. Needed to for hours but, you know, baring my ass in the cold was so not in the cards. I was—Hey! What is this?"

She came out of the bathroom holding up the bloody towel he'd used for his feet. "Is your wound bleeding again?" she demanded, running over to him, but he grabbed her hands and kept her from raising it.

" 'Tis nothing. Now hurry up and get into bed wi' me. We need tae conserve what li'le warmth we have left."

"In bed with . . . oh." Clearly she hadn't thought that far ahead. "Maybe we should get separate—"

"No," he said, hard and short. " 'Tis no time for you to be quailing about. You'll sleep wi' me."

And that apparently was the end to it. And, gratefully enough, worrying about getting into bed with him was enough to keep her from remembering the blood on the towels. Not willing to press his luck he made sure all the drapes were as tightly closed as possible and then shivered his way into the cold bed. When she was done drying the dog off as best she could she shucked off her snow pants, and climbed gingerly beneath the covers as well. Then before he could reach for her and drag her up against him she whistled for Karma and the big dog lumbered up into the bed and, bless her heart, crawled right up between them.

"Och, lass, a Newfoundland chaperone?"

"Yup," she said grinning at him through the dark. "Plus, she'll keep us warm."

He couldn't argue with that. *It was probably for the best,* he thought. He really needed to keep his distance from her. He was no good for her. Despite his cravings otherwise, she would be better off the sooner she got him out of her life.

But hours later as he lay there in excruciating pain listening to her snore, he couldn't keep track of that fact.

He whistled and snapped his fingers beside the bed. Karma obediently perked up and after a minute lumbered down off the bed. Clearly she was used to the big animal moving in and out of the bed because Kat didn't so much as flicker an eyelash at the departure. Once he had gathered her up against himself, rolling her to the center of the bed, he patted the bed on the other side of her and called up Karma. Karma came back eagerly. Now she would be swaddled in warmth from back to front and he would have the feel of her to add even more pain to his already agonizing existence. Despite having warmed up a modicum, he was still feeling cold and his side and feet were on fire. The idea of putting on those snowshoes again was unbearable. As it was he would need to get boots when they finally made it to Walmart and he had no idea just how swollen he was going to end up being by then. It didn't matter. As long as he got through to the next leg of their trip.

Soon after his exhaustion caught up with him and he fell asleep.

He wasn't aware of when his stone skin began to ripple along his body in alternating waves.

CHAPTER TWELVE

When Kat awoke it was to the feel of something hot and rough surrounding her. She started and the roughness immediately dissipated and melted into heated male sinew in an arm locked around her. As her movements stirred him, she twisted around to face him.

"Were you just stone?" she asked.

"Hmm? No, I . . ." Then he went very still, seeming to think about it and doing an internal check of some sort. Then his expression grew shuttered and shadowed. He pushed away from her, backing out of the bed until he hit the nearby wall on that side. "We better get going," he said after a moment.

"Wait a minute," she said, scrambling after him. "You did! You did turn to stone. And you were lying to me weren't you? You don't have as much time as you led me to believe you did, do you?"

"Leave me be," he said darkly, moving to push past her.

"That's it!" she cried. "I'm right! You *lied* to me!"

"Doona fash yourself, lass. Now let me by . . . unless, of course, you'd rather help me with the raging cock-stand sleeping again' you has given me. Maybe that's the stone you were feeling?"

"Oh!" She hauled off and smacked him on the shoulder . . . and she didn't pull the punch. Not that it hurt him. And that was the problem. Nothing hurt him. Not his side, not his feet. Nothing. And that could only mean one thing. He'd turned to stone while he slept. Turning completely to stone state increased his healing time exponentially. "You are not going to try and use sex to scare me off. That's what you've been doing, isn't it? With the towels and now with this. Where was that blood from anyway, if not your side?"

"My feet. They were cut up something fierce."

"Were?" She immediately knelt down at his feet and began to inspect them. This time the groan he bit back proved he hadn't just been using sex as a device to keep her at bay. Kat down on her knees before him while he was hard as nails erect sent desire clawing through him. He shook his head and tried to stay focused.

She's mad. Remember she's mad, he thought to himself.

"There's nothing wrong wi—"

She chose that moment to look up and with a gasp she realized his loosened towel was doing very little to hide the state of his body. In fact, she was so close to his erection that all she would have to do was rise up a little more on her knees and she'd be able to kiss him on it.

No! No kissing! No thinking about kissing a large, hot, incredibly hard penis, she reminded herself fiercely.

Nope. Not her. No, sir.

"I warned you, lass," he said, one of those shit-eating grins spreading wide across his face. "You doona wish for me to lie tae you? Well, I want your mouth on me fiercely bad an' there's no lie abou' it."

Just speaking the words made his cock ache twice as hard with need. He would never have allowed it of course because she would deserve a lot of attention long before he could even think about her gracing him in such a way, but there was no curbing the hot flash of fantasy seeing her on her knees in front of him was riding hard on him. He could just imagine what the warmth of her wet mouth would feel like. The stroke of her tongue. The touch of her hand.

"Jesus woman, stand up. You're killing me."

Kat hastened to her feet and backed up a careful step.

"Your feet are healed," she said. She swallowed, clearly trying to pretend he wasn't sporting the most stellar erection of his long long life.

"When I turn stone it hastens healing," he told her. The reminder that he'd lost control over himself did wonders for cooling his ardor. Still, ardor was becoming a constant state around her. "My side is near healed as well."

She stepped forward at that, forgetting to be cautious as she lifted his shirt and pulled back the bandage. It had blood on it from the rigors of yesterday's travels, but beneath the bandage his wound was knitted and well on the way to forming a fresh scar.

"Will you scar permanently or will that change as well?"

"It will most likely scar. We carry the mark of severe wounds. But only the most severe. Everything else we heal completely from." He didn't realize it, but when he spoke of severe wounds his hand automatically rubbed at the brand on his chest.

"What's that called?" she asked, drawing his attention to it.

"An ouroboros. When a Bodywalker is made a tattoo of an ouroboros appears somewhere on their body. My master chose it as his brand to identify me as belonging to him so no one would question me or give me a hard time if I made demands of them. You see, no one likes a lowly Gargoyle to give them commands."

There was anger in his eyes as he said that, but there was also a determined sort of pride as well. He would not allow his past to drag him down. That was what the lift to his chin meant. Nor would he accept any pity she might be feeling for the life he'd been forced to live. It had been what it had been. Nothing they did, nothing they *felt*, would change that.

She moved away from him, moving to the tightly drawn drapes. She gingerly peeked around one to look at the sky. It was nearing dusk. She stepped back.

"We have a little time. I'm going to see about getting us some food and—"

"No! You canna go out in the light!"

"I can bundle back up, use my scarf to cover my face. There'd be no—"

"I said no!" he said, his tone final and fearsome. "You'll no' risk yourself on account of me. Any one of a thousand things could happen and you'd get hurt. You've no sunglasses tae shade your eyes. 'Twould be madness and I'll hear no more of it. We wait."

The truth was she didn't want to go out in the light. But she did need to check the roads and maybe see about renting a car, if it were at all possible. But she nodded to him and figured another hour wouldn't make too much of a difference. The car rental place would not be likely to be open in any event. She looked at her watch. She was anxious to get to Walmart. She wanted to see if her ghostly friend would be able to find her note. In order for that to happen they needed to get there before nine.

"All right, we'll wait," she said.

She stood there for a moment longer, long enough to shiver in the stark cold of the room. It was so cold she could see her breath on the air. Clearly the electricity was still out and for some reason Clemmons, the motel owner, did not have a generator. She hoped he was just as cold as they were. It was very thoughtless of him, especially knowing what the weather could be like and the fact that this was ski season and he was more likely to be full than not this time of year.

After another second, whereupon she had begun to rub at her arms for warmth, Ahnvil cursed roundly and marched up to her. He grabbed her hand and with a jerk sent her crashing up against his body. He enfolded her in his warmth while yanking the coverlet off the bed and wrapping them both up into it.

"You're a bloody stubborn woman," he scolded her, rubbing her arm for her as she gratefully cuddled up close to him, her chilled state causing her to forego all demurring and protestation about allowing him to hold her close.

Oddly enough it wasn't sexuality that entered his awareness right then. There was something about her, something so different from any woman he'd been near in such a long time. Probably because he was used to incredibly strong women with phenomenal abilities, and yet here she was with her incredibly dangerous vulnerabilities and she was bravely wanting to venture out into the world in order to further their cause. And that was perhaps why he thought her so much braver than all the rest. It was one thing to be strong and face a challenge, it was another to face one knowing without a doubt you were going to be hurt in the process. For some reason he found that to be the most amazing thing about her. He suspected that she thought she was weak because she was hiding away where it was safe and dark, but what she had done was find clever ways to live with her disability and, he had no doubt, to the maximum of her ability. Of course she was afraid of hurt and pain, she'd be an idiot not to be.

As he held her he found himself breathing in the clean warmth of her hair, and by the time she'd stopped shivering his nose was drifting down past her ear on a direct course for her neck. Something about the graceful line of it beckoned to him, like the finest lure to the trickiest of fishes she was reeling him in faster and faster every time. How the hell had she gotten under his skin so quickly? Even knowing he was the worst thing for a woman as fragile as she was. But honestly, how was her susceptibility to the sun any different from those of any Nightwalker? Did it really make her any more or less fragile? Other than the fact that she was human and that if he were to climb on top of her and suddenly turn to stone he would without fail crush the life out of her. But she smelled so damn good. Why did she have to smell so damn good?

"Warm enough now?" he asked, his voice rasping out of him.

"Yes," she whispered back. "But we can't just stand here like this for another hour."

"Want to get back in bed?" he asked.

"No! No, that wouldn't be a very good idea."

He glanced around. There was a small chair in the far corner of the room. It was dubious whether it would hold both of them, but he took a chance, swept her up into his arms, and carried her over to it. Sitting down with her, he tried not to groan when she snuggled back against him, her bottom wriggling across his lap in little twitches.

Don't get hard. Don't get hard. Don't get—

"Hey! Stop that!"

"Sorry," he said, not sounding all that repentant. "I canna help it when you shimmy abou' like that in my lap. Sit still."

She did. Too still. He could tell she was holding herself rigidly, as though she were afraid to relax.

"Relax, Kat," he soothed her gently. "I willna bother you. I swear it. I just want you to be safe and warm. Relax."

After a minute she did, her weight coming to rest

comfortably in his arms. He just contented himself with the smell of her and the rhythmic sound of her breaths.

"What's it like? Being a Gargoyle? Is it hateful? Do you look the same as before or did that change?"

"I look the same as before. Maybe a bit more buff. More muscle, you know."

"Yes."

"And overall, now that I'm no' a slave to another man's whims and ways, I like it fine. I get to fly."

"I still don't understand how that's possible . . ."

"Doona ask for I doona know the how of it. All I know is it works. I can fly in the night air as easily as any feathered friend."

"Wow, I'd like to try flying like that one day."

"I can take you if you like."

"Oh wow. Really?" She sounded as eager and as scared as anyone could possibly be at the same time. "I'd like that. Yes. I'd like that," she reiterated, this time sounding more sure. "And how long does it take for you to turn to a statue once sunlight hits? Is it gradual or instantaneous?"

" 'Tis nearly instantaneous."

"What does it feel like?"

"Truthfully? 'Tis terrifying. No matter how many years you've been a Gargoyle, and I'm told 'tis true for others, your first instinct is tae fight it. Mainly because your breath is the first thing you feel seize after the first blush of stone begins. You think you'll suffocate and I suppose if we dinna turn tae stone immediately afterward, no longer needing oxygen, we might do so. But 'tis just like drowning for that brief window of time. And for a man like me, a man who fights everything headlong, that kind of powerlessness is a tough pill tae swallow."

"I can imagine. I think it would be the same for me, too. It's like that for me if I feel the touch of the sun. The reaction is instantaneous. Wait! Did you hear that?"

It was a rumbling rush of sound, scraping and loud.

"Plows! It's a plow!"

"Nay. Stay here," he commanded when she would have run to the window and risked a peek out. "Right or wrong you'll know in an hour. I'll no' have you risking as much as a single wisp of sun touching this fair, precious skin." He found her hand among the blankets and lifted it up to his lips, kissing her gently across the knuckles. "Ask me something else."

"Well . . . how rich are you? Like just stinking or ultra-stinking?"

"Besides the fact that I get paid for protecting my Bodywalkers as well as other benefits, I'm three hundred years old and have learned tae look for long-term investments. What do you think?"

"Ultra-stinking. I knew it." She sighed.

"Doona worry, Kat, I'll pay you back for anything you need to buy for me." And it was clear it bothered him that he was depending on her like this.

"It won't be a big deal," she assured him. "I have a small little nest egg and I do medical transcription to keep solvent." She paused, fidgeting a little. "It's something I can do it at home at any time. With technology I just send things over encrypted emails and voilà! Paycheck without sun exposure." She quieted and said, "You know, I don't hate my life. I don't want you to think that I do."

"I dinna think that. But I do think you miss your work wi' patients. You've too much of a knack for it."

"Sometimes I do. But not all that much. Like I said, I'm happy. I don't miss getting yelled at or puked on, that's for sure."

"I canna imagine why."

She laughed at that. Then another moment of silence ticked by. "Did you try to kill your forger?"

He sighed. "No, lass. Though I wish I could some-times, I canna do so. Circumstances have put the bastard right within my reach but have also made it so I canna have satisfaction. He's a powerful man and my Pharaoh needs him tae help fight an even more powerful evil. I doona want tae get into it because the less you know the better you'll feel."

"Ignorance is bliss? I don't know if I agree to that. I think I'd rather know. Hey, what do you make of the ghost-girl Bella?"

"I doona know, lass. As far as I could see you were writing tae yourself."

"How strange. So am I like psychic or some—hey!" She smacked his hand when he made a grab for her breasts. Or rather the pendant between her breasts. "Oh. Sorry," she said, realizing she'd judged the worst of him.

"'Tis the pendant," he said sharply. "I'll bet it has something tae do wi' it!"

"Hey, how come you could touch it now and nothing happened?"

He thought on it a second. "Because I wasna trying tae take it off you?"

"Let's not try and find out, shall we?"

"No. Let's no'" He fingered the cold metal slowly. "How do we know the spirit is no' malevolent?"

"Oh please," Kat scoffed. "She drew a little heart in the snow. She's as malevolent as cotton candy."

"Even cotton candy can cause something rotten. A cavity. A bad bellyache. There's two sides tae every coin."

"Well, she didn't feel bad. But I'll be careful, okay?"

"Telling the spirit where we'll be next is no' being careful," he pointed out.

"I suppose not. But I just have a feeling about this." She looked at him. "Just like I have a feeling you're not bad either. I was a little scared at first, but . . . something just told me not to be afraid of you."

"Oh aye, was that before or after I tried tae strangle you in your own bed?"

"Both," she said with a stubborn lift of her chin. "I know you're not responsible for that. You were hurt and you were having a nightmare. It was a stupid thing to do. And I could tell you some stories about violence from otherwise perfectly mundane people. People I knew to be harmless coming in injured and behaving like demons had caught hold of them. Injury does funny things to a body. Even more so, I imagine, when that body has been so long without its succor. Are you going to tell me how long you have before permanent being?"

"I promise, I doona know. There's been times when only two days have passed and I feel in danger of it. And then times when a week has passed and I'll only just be starting to get symptoms."

"What are the symptoms? Besides turning to stone involuntarily. I got that much."

"Madness," he said grimly. "Nightmares. One leads into the other. Weakness. I start tae get run down. I'm stronger in stone skin, strongest in Gargoyle form. The more I stay flesh the more energy I burn. That's why I keep eating so much. Speaking of which, I'm powerfully hungry. And no, you canna go get food. We've a li'le over half an hour yet." He paused a beat. "There's one other thing. We start tae . . . Gargoyles are part beast. As we weaken the beast comes out more and more. And the beast is usually . . . in heat. We become voraciously sexual. Gargoyles are lusty to begin wi', but . . ."

He trailed off because there was nothing left to say. The implication was clear.

"I admit, I had noticed that," she said, a warm flush creeping over her face in spite of the chill in the room. She wriggled one hand out of the blanket cocoon and touched it against his face. "Is that why you feel feverish? I thought it was an infection."

"Aye. But make no mistake," he said, burrowing his

face gently into her hair, "I'd want you as powerfully even in my sane mind."

How had he known that was exactly what she'd been thinking? That she had felt a sinking feeling in her gut thinking that his desire for her was nothing but a matter of Gargoyle madness and circumstance. When had it become so important to her to know that he wanted her? And why was it that the simple act of feeling his face and breath against her neck gave her a thrill of pleasure equal to the moments he had cradled her breast in his hand.

"If no' for you, my pretty Kat lass, I wouldna' be sane right now. The wound would have been a constant drain on my energy. The stone skin constantly trying to take me over . . . and likely succeeding. And while it might have helped heal the wound, as you see, it risks permanent being."

"You're fighting it constantly, aren't you?"

He hesitated in his answer, but that in itself was an answer. He remained silent and she bit her lip. She was incredibly worried for him. Afraid they wouldn't get him to his touchstone in time.

"What if you turn to a statue on the plane or somewhere in public? Won't people find out about you?"

"No. We feel it coming on soon enough that we find a hidden place for it. Then if someone happens upon us they think they've found a mysteriously appearing stone statue. We doona look human at all. I fear it will frighten you when you see it. And as for the plane, it's controlled and flown by Bodywalkers or humans who know what we are. It willna matter then."

She looked up into his warm amber eyes and said, "I won't be afraid of you. I'll know what you are on the inside, no matter what you become on the outside."

"How do you know what I am on the inside?" he wanted to know. "I'm well on tae being a stranger tae you."

"No. You're not a stranger anymore. And if you weren't good on the inside, then you wouldn't care about frightening me or worrying me. And I know you do."

He was silent for the next several minutes.

"The sun is down," he said after a while. "Come along. Let's get something tae eat. And then a vehicle."

"But by now the only car rental place will be closed, if it even opened at all what with no electricity."

"Doona worry about that." He paused a beat. "Is there someone in town who's ever done you a wrong?"

"Well . . ." She thought about it. But she knew the answer right away. "Bill Morrow. The jerk. I was in town with Karma twice and on both occasions he threatened to run her over with his truck. He hates her for some reason, even though she never did anything to him. He called me a little freak, too. The jerk," she reiterated.

"And where does he live?" Ahnvil's tone was quiet . . . almost dangerous.

"Above the old five-and-dime. He owns that whole row of stores. He owns a lot of the buildings in town and he thinks that gives him the right to do whatever he wants."

"And this truck he threatened tae run you over wi'. Do you know what it looks like?"

She scoffed. "It's the biggest, reddest piece of overcompensation that proves he is hung like a newborn baby in the arctic cold."

That made him laugh out loud and she grinned at him. "I used to tell him that if he didn't clean up his act, Karma was going to bite him in the ass. Get it? Karma? Ass?"

He chuckled and nodded. "Verra well. You will go and get us some food. I will go and get us transportation."

"In a towel. At six p.m.? And just how are you . . ." She narrowed her eyes on him. "Are you going to do what I think you're going to do?"

"Oh aye. I have skills," he confided to her, standing up and putting her on her feet.

"But that's—" She cut herself off, thought about it for half a second and then said, "Well, you know what, I think I'm kind of okay with that!"

"Doona worry. Just be ready tae go as soon as I pull up."

"Right. Any food requests?"

"Whatever you can find is fine."

CHAPTER THIRTEEN

They parted ways, anxiety crawling around in her belly the whole time she was searching for food, which proved to be harder than she thought. The restaurants were all closed because of lack of electricity, and the small market a few buildings down was the same. She was desperate to get something, knowing what it meant for him if he didn't eat regularly. In the end, the lack of electricity worked in her favor. As soon as the street was quiet she found a cinderblock from a nearby wall and then hauled it through one of the side windows to the market. Silence followed. No alarms, no cameras. She regretted what she had to do instantly, but it didn't keep her from grabbing things off the shelves. She bagged everything then left. She thought about leaving money or a note, but feared the reprisals if she did. She knew Bill Mackinzie very well, and she would somehow make this up to him. She didn't know how, but she would.

She escaped unseen back to the motel and was just opening the door to her room when the familiar loud rumble of Morrow's truck pulled up beside her.

"Grab Karma and let's go. We're a li'le conspicuous."

"I'd say so!" She whistled for Karma and hopped in the truck with her. Luckily it was one of those extended cabs so there was plenty of room for Karma. "Part of me wants to ride past the five-and-dime and blow his horn. The jerk has the *Dukes of Hazzard* horn installed. It makes it unmistakable."

"You have a vicious streak in you, do you no'? Remind me never tae piss you off."

"I'll be certain to."

Ahnvil threw the truck into gear and they trundled off down the reasonably plowed roads. She immediately burrowed into her stolen booty and started by handing him several doughnuts in a row. Then she moved on to canned chili. She had commandeered plasticware and a can opener and soon she was spoon-feeding him while he concentrated on keeping the truck on the icy mountainous road.

"I'm sorry I couldn't get you any real meat. Everything was either frozen or raw or needed a slicer in order to get at it. I didn't really want to take the time to figure it out. But I got lots of junk food! I love me some junk food!" She unwrapped a candy bar and bit into it.

"Ah, so now I see your true weakness. You have a sweet tooth."

"It's true and I'm proud of it." She deflated a little. "Except it makes my butt a little too jiggly. But I'm not going to worry about that right now."

"Oh aye, doona worry abou' it at all. I like your butt just fine."

That made her cheeks burn with color, but secretly she had to admit that it pleased her. She thought she was silly for reacting that way, but there it was nonetheless. It was just nice to have someone look at her and see so many things they felt were positive about her, rather than focusing on her flaws, shortcomings, and freakish weaknesses. But, of course, he wouldn't see anything wrong with her. He had to avoid the sun, for the most part, as well. He would be just as sensitively aware of it as she was.

"The road seems all right for the most part. If it continues on like this we should make it to the Walmart with plenty of time to shop before I have to try and contact my ghost friend."

"I doona know why you want her tae follow us," he said with a frown. "I doona like it."

"Your opinion is duly noted. I don't know why I want her to follow us either. I just . . . do. There's more to this. I'm not experienced with this sort of thing, but you said you know people who are powerful and understand things like how to get this Amulet off me. Maybe they can understand why I can see the ghost and you can't. Maybe they can tell me if she really is a ghost or if she's something else. I don't know, and I won't know unless we can get her to follow us to . . . Hey, where are we going exactly?"

"New Mexico. Tae a li'le town called Portales. We have a huge ranch out there. Lots of land and lots of property. A big house full of people. Bodywalkers. Gargoyles. We have a Djynn staying with us now. I doona know if I trust him. And if we get there and you meet him, doona make a wish. Ever. You never know if you'll get an honest result or some manner of trickery. Grey seems to be aboveboard, but he's also got his own agenda and none of us really knows what that is. And . . . I doona want you tae stay long. I want tae get the Amulet off you and send you back home immediately. 'Tis dangerous where we are and . . . you doona ken what we're dealing wi' but tis verra bad and I doona want you tae get hurt."

She understood the sentiment, even was grateful he was looking out for her. So why was it that a part of her was disappointed, almost hurt by the idea that he would want to be rid of her as soon as possible? *What a foolish thing to think!*

Kat shrugged the sensation off as best she could, reminding herself that she didn't want to be away from her home any more than he did. Home was safe and, even under his protection, the world was a frightening place to be caught out in. Every dawn brought horrible dangers with it; would potentially force her to face her fear of it. A fear that was rightfully justified.

By the time they reached Walmart, she felt exhausted from worrying about so many things and the dangers of the slippery roads besides. There had been places not plowed well enough and only the truck's four-wheel drive had allowed them to pass through. But in the end they arrived safe and sound and, delightfully, the store had electricity! Whether from a generator or that they had not been affected by the storm as Stone Gorge had been, it didn't matter. He was going to get some clothing and they could get more food. Something better and potentially more nutritious. She wanted to take care of him, she realized. It was very important to her that he get to his touchstone in time. He was far too beautiful to be lost to the world. To be frozen into the state of an ugly Gargoyle. She had not seen him like that thus far, but she could easily imagine what that meant. She had seen her share of Gargoyles over time and they were anything but the handsome man she was now sitting next to.

"Come wi' me, lass," he said after jumping out of the truck and walking over to her side. He held out his hand to her and helped her down to the slushy ground. "Karma, stay there," he said, giving the dog a brief rub at the ears. "We doona want anything tae happen tae a fine lass such as yourself."

To her, it was the sweetest thing he could have possibly done. He was understanding of how much Karma meant to her. It wasn't necessary for him to be kind, and yet he was.

If anyone thought anything of a man walking around the store in a towel in the dead of winter, no one said anything. Although she suspected there was more than one covert cellphone picture being taken. Ahnvil bee-lined for the men's department and after a brief search through a pile of cargo pants he bent over right there in front of God and country and pulled them on under his towel. Once he was clothed he popped off the tag and dropped the towel to the ground. Then he grabbed up a pack of socks and tore into them. He had them on his feet and was heading for shoes a moment later. On the way past the rounders of shirts she grabbed one she thought would fit, a handsome button-down in the fairest shade of pink, so fair it was almost white. As he tried on boots, she pushed the shirt at him.

"Your shirt is stained with blood. If you want to be less obvious . . . A bloodstained shirt will attract attention."

"No. I'll no' wear pink," he scoffed, taking a brief walk in the boots he had on. "Find me anything but pink. A T-shirt preferably."

Grumbling about men who were insecure in their own masculinity, she went back to the men's department and found him a T-shirt that said, I'LL STOP BEING DISRE-SPECTFUL WHEN YOU STOP BEING STUPID. He eyed the shirt dubiously. It was a bright red with white lettering.

"It's not pink," she said smugly.

"Aye," he agreed dryly.

On the way to the register she stopped for some pens and a pad of paper. The paper was a bright pink color. Hard to miss.

"Now this," she said, once again being smug, "is pink."

After they had checked out she went to the entrance of the store with him, realizing there were two. Dismayed she decided to leave a note inside both entrances. She wrote:

> *Hi! My name is Katrina Haynes. I am not a ghost. We are heading to Portales, New Mexico. If you can follow us there, maybe we can find out what is happening here. Do you think that's possible?*

Then they waited in the truck for nine o'clock. As time ticked past he grew increasingly restless. "Let me try your phone again," he said. It was a phrase that was becoming familiar. He had asked her to try it maybe ten times since leaving the house. "What's the nearest airport?"

"But—"

"It doesna hurt tae try," he said before she could point out that phone communication might be down still.

She handed him the phone and once he dialed and put it close to his ear she saw the profound wave of relief that washed over him.

"Jackson," he said on a sigh.

"Ahnvil?" Jackson asked in surprise. "What in hell happened to you?"

"'Tis a long story. Suffice it tae say I'm in a spot of trouble."

"You've been over a week without your stone, my friend," he said, knowing it was a needless thing to point out.

"Aye."

"We were afraid . . ."

"No. No' yet anyway. I need the jet though. I doona know how much time I have left." It was clear he didn't want to say it out loud, didn't want to remind either of them of how dangerous his situation was.

"Where are you?"

"Washington State."

"Wash—you mean the same Washington State that is in the middle of the blizzard of the century?"

"Aye," he affirmed grimly.

"Ahnvil, of course I'll send the jet, but I'm not certain flights are going in and out yet."

"They will be," Ahnvil said. They had no other option. They *had* to be.

"Right. It's on its way. It'll be there before sunrise, but I'm not sure we can get you back here before the sun comes out."

"We have to. If no' we'll close the shades and stay on the tarmac until you can get my stone tae me."

"All right. Don't worry. We'll figure this out and get you back here in time. Are you going to tell me what happened?"

"No' now. I'm no' alone and I'll be bringing a guest."

"We'll be waiting for you."

He hung up the phone.

"I'm going to go check." Kat bolted out of the car and headed for the entrance to Walmart. She checked one and the note was still there untouched. Then she checked the other and saw beneath her writing:

Where in Portales? We'll be there with bells on. I'm Isabella and I'm not a ghost either.

Kat responded with the exact address and wrote:

If neither of us is a ghost, then what is going on here?

As she watched, the note floated into the air and opened up. It flattened up against one of the giant claw machines and a slow, beautiful script began to fill the page.

I have no idea. Maybe we will figure it out in Portales. Why are we going there?

Kat wrote:

I have new friends there. Friends who might help us find a solution.

The response came only moments later. Bella wrote:

All right, we'll meet you there!

At the last minute she was struck with a moment of brilliance. She grabbed the arm of a man walking into the store.

"Excuse me, sir, do you see someone standing there?" She pointed to the place where the note still lay flat on the machine.

"Is this a joke?" he asked. "Young lady it's too cold to be—"

"Please. Just tell me what you see."

He sighed. "I see a lovely little brunette, curling black hair . . . purplish eyes. Cute figure. And her male companion who is glaring at me for ogling what is no doubt his wife."

"Oh. Can you speak to her?"

"Yes, and so can you," he snapped. Then he jerked free of her and went on into the store.

Kat brought the note to Ahnvil and showed it to him. Once again Ahnvil said all he could see was her responses. She told him how the letter had seemed to float of its own volition and telling him that the man had been able to see Bella but once again she had not.

"I thought about telling her how you're a Nightwalker. I mean, what could it hurt, right? She's not even in the same dimension as we are. At least I don't think she is. But then, that man saw her. I don't know what to think anymore."

" 'Tis best that you dinna tell her about Nightwalkers. No' until we learn more abou' this. Now, let's be on our way."

She nodded vigorously in agreement. Nighttime was burning and she knew time was growing short for him. He seemed to grow exponentially more agitated as they drove. By the time they had entered the airport he had broken into a sweat. When she ventured to touch his chest, his shirt was damp with it.

She had never been on a private jet before. As they stood at the hangar and watched the plane land several hours later, she had grown just as anxious as he was.

"What if the sun . . ." she said hoarsely, unable to comprehend what would happen.

"We draw the shades tight and we wait until dark."

"You don't have that long." She turned a hard look on him. "Do you?"

"I doona know," he said tightly.

"You said you wouldn't lie to me."

"I doona know if I'll even make the flight," he bit out on a growl, looming over her for a frightening second. The sound he made in his throat was shocking, as were the hands he wrapped around her upper arms as he stared hard in her eyes, the amber of his hot with fever. "If I doona make it, I doona want you tae fret. My friends will have a care for you. They will figure out how tae get the Amulet—"

"I don't give a flying fig about the Amulet!" she cried, wishing she were strong enough to give him a good shake. "Now, shut up and get on the plane. You're going to make it."

"I feel the madness creeping over me. 'Tis all I can do tae keep focused." And even as he said the words the hands that held on to her arms rippled into solid stone.

"No!" she cried, gripping at his shirt, pounding her fists against his chest. "You will not let it win! You are going to make this flight! Do you understand me? I-I can't do this alone."

"You can."

"I can't. I can't so I need you to stay with me. All right? You have to stay with me." She knew it wasn't so much about her fear as it was about giving him a reason to stay with her. Maybe if she did that it could help him fight off the inevitability of this thing. It was going to be hours before they made it to New Mexico and she could only pray he could hold on that long. Pray they beat the sun. Pray for everything.

The Gargoyle had escaped him somehow, had managed to leave the area, Panahasi realized. And every moment he was out of reach was a moment closer to his own destruction. If Odjit found out about the Amulet, he was done for. If she found out that the Gargoyle now knew the location of their secret enclave, all hell would break loose and he would not be the only one who would forfeit his life. Her rages were becoming more and more violent the further her pregnancy advanced. They were afraid of what she might do and even if she had logical reasons for doing it. A vicious madwoman was one thing, a pregnant one was quite another.

So there was only one thing left for him to do and that was to send sentries to the Bodywalker enclave in Portales, New Mexico. Maybe there . . . maybe there he could recapture the Gargoyle and keep him from getting back to Kamenwati . . . . the one man on earth who would truly know what Adoma's Amulet might be capable of.

He quickly went about putting his plan in action.

CHAPTER FOURTEEN

They boarded the plane and Kat stopped short, stunned by what she saw. But then she ignored the opulence of the jet and moved quickly into the cabin in order to allow Ahnvil the room to bring Karma on board. A short time later they were buckled in and taking off. She watched Ahnvil closely the entire time they were ascending, frustrated that they were seated apart from each other. She could see him hunching over into himself, running his hands through his dark hair repeatedly, sweat shining on his exposed skin. It was when he seemed to start talking to himself under his breath that she reached an all-new level of fear and concern. The minute the ding sounded that allowed her to take off her seat belt and go to him, she did, kneeling between his feet and rubbing his legs along his thighs.

"It's all right," she soothed him. "It's going to be all right."

"You doona know that!" he snapped roughly.

"I do know that!"

"If you know what is good for you, you'll keep your distance," he growled at her, another one of those animalistic sounds escaping him. A cross between a huff and a snarl.

"I know what's good for you and I'm not going any-where. I want you to talk to me. Tell me more about who you used to be."

"A slave! A murderer! The sort of man who gets women killed!"

"What does that mean?" she asked carefully, anxiety in her belly in response to his dangerous words.

"There was a Templar woman. Jan Li. She helped me escape my captors . . . only . . . she paid for it with her life. She trusted me tae help get her free of those bastards and I failed her. Just like I'm going tae fail you. Only this time 'tis going tae be worse. Much worse. Because you never asked for any of this. You never knew you were going tae be risking your life. 'Tis my fault you're here at all. That cursed necklace. I would rip it off you if I thought I could do it wi'out hurting you."

"It's my fault for putting it on in the first place," she said softly.

"How the hell would a mortal woman like you even know something like an Amulet came with a curse and certain power attached tae it? In your world things like that should only be make believe."

"I'm glad I'm not in that world anymore," she said fiercely. "I'm glad I know it's all an illusion. I'm glad I'm aware of the nature of things in the world around me."

"You could have gone the rest of your life, safe and content and no' knowing abou' any of it."

"But I didn't and I won't and that's okay," she in-sisted.

"'Tis no' okay tae me," he said, his tone softening as his hand came out, running along her head and through her hair, the roughness of his calluses catching on the strands. "Jesus God, you're beautiful," he said after a moment. It made her smile.

"You're just saying that because you're going crazy."

He laughed. "Doona insult my woman so. You doona want an angry Gargoyle on your hands."

"I'm not afraid of you," she whispered fiercely.

"Aye, but you should be," he whispered back, his forehead coming to touch hers. He took in a slow breath, his lashes fluttering closed before he groaned. "You shouldna be so close tae me. You smell too fine for words." He opened his eyes and she could see the raw appetite within them. Her breath snagged in her throat and her heart began to pound.

She knew he was going to drag her up to his hungry mouth long before he did it, and she did nothing to stop him. His kiss was like a virulent thing, a beautiful disease that grew and grew and overwhelmed every last defense she had to throw at it. She felt herself melting between his hands as he held her tightly to his body, bending her back over in her kneeling position.

His hand ran up her side, along the curve of her waist, over the ridges of her ribs and then, as gently as he could, he closed his hand over her breast. She drew breath straight from his lungs, her tongue, startled at first, suddenly leaping into the fray, tangling up with his in such an energetic attack that it was like setting fire to stone. Anything that could make stone burn was a powerful force, and she was literally wildfire to him. His mind was hazing over with the passion that was trying to overwhelm him, but he fought it back. He would not be the beast with her.

"No! Get away!" He shoved her away, reaching to unclasp his seat belt and stumbling away from her. "I willna do this tae you! Do you no' ken? I'll be a beast wi' you. I'll *hurt* you. You have to keep away from me. Please," he said, his tone and body settling into quiet. "Please doona let me hurt you."

"I won't," she promised just as quietly. "And you won't. You couldn't hurt a woman even if you tried."

"But I have! Jan Li . . ."

"It sounds like she knew exactly what she was getting into. And you weren't the one who hurt her. You have to stop blaming yourself for that."

He looked up and met her eyes.

"There's no one else tae blame."

"There is. You blame those who attacked you. Those who hurt her. You didn't—"

"I failed her!"

"You didn't do it on purpose!"

"Neither will I do harm tae you on purpose, but it'll happen just the same! Now keep your bloody distance woman!"

"Fine. Fine, I'll keep my distance. I won't let you touch me." And Kat tried not to let his actions feel like a rejection. She understood his logic, and yes, he probably was right, but just the same it made her feel as though she were somehow lacking. Because she was a frail mortal. Even frailer than most. She had known that all her life, but not until now had it truly meant something to her. Meant that she honestly could not have something she wanted. Everything else had been easy to live without. Sun. The daylight world. Friends. Normalcy. But none of it had hurt like this. Never had she felt so inadequate. She knew that, had she been a Gargoyle female he wouldn't be trying to hold back. He would probably take her right then and there, as hard as he could. As mad as he was. And it made her so angry that she couldn't give that to him. He needed it, and she couldn't provide it.

Most of the rest of the flight passed in tense silence. He paced the length and width of the cabin so constantly she thought *she* might go mad.

But she knew that if he didn't do it, that if he stopped for even a second, he might not move ever again. She could see his hands, again and again rippling into stone.

Sometimes it climbed all the way up to his shoulders. He would grit his teeth and fight it back.

She had reseated herself in the cabin, but at last she got up and crossed over to him. She reached to touch him and he jerked away.

"Stop," she said softly. "Just stop." She stepped up against his body, fighting his initial resistance and wrapping her arms around him.

"You promised tae stay away," he ground out.

"And you're burning energy every step you take. Quiet now. Be still. Shh . . ." She hushed him and quieted him, hugging him around his middle. After a moment he relaxed in her arms, his hands tentatively resting on her back and shoulders. They stood like that for almost thirty minutes, and never once did his hands flicker into stone. He calmed so much that he sat down with her, pulling her into his lap. He was wary at first, clearly afraid it might spark off something more than just comfort, but in the end he was able to remain peaceful with her in his arms and him in hers.

They passed the remainder of the flight exactly like that.

It was close to daylight by the time they landed.

"There should be someone waiting for us. One of our human companions. Most likely Max. I doona expect any Bodywalkers because—"

"They would be paralyzed by the sun," she finished for him. "I remember."

And it turned out he was right. When the jet pulled up there were two men waiting near a big SUV. One was relaxed back against the front bumper and hood of the car, his legs crossed at the shins and his arms were crossed over an athletic chest. He was black-haired, with a short, almost military-style cut and wore reflective sunglasses. The other man was big and burly, only slightly smaller than Ahnvil was and he stood in a hard stance with feet apart and arms over his chest. He had blond hair and also wore sunglasses, even though it was still dark. The sun was lightening the sky already.

"How far is it?" she asked nervously as she alighted from the jet and worked her way down the steps. Karma and Ahnvil came down hot on her heels.

"Fifteen minutes at best," Ahnvil said. He was anxiously looking at the sky as well. "We'll make sure you're covered, Kat. I'll no' let any harm come tae you."

She laughed incredulously. "It's not me I'm worried about!"

"Let's go folks. Night time is a-wasting," the dark-haired man said. He reached out for Ahnvil's hand and they shook.

"You didn't have to come yourself, Jackson," Ahnvil said reproachfully.

"Of course I did," he said, looking at Ahnvil as if any other idea would have been preposterous. "And who is this?"

"This is Katrina Haynes. Kat, this is Jackson, the Pharaoh of the Bodywalkers, and Ram, his first lieutenant."

"Good to meet you, Kat." Ram greeted her.

"She needs to be protected from the sun just as we do. She has a disease. The sun will cause her to blister and burn."

"Right. The windows are polarized. There will be no sun. We'll pull directly into the garage." Jackson turned and met her eyes through the tint on his glasses. "Let me introduce you to Max. He's human, so he'll be driving us in case we get caught in the sun."

"We have tae go," Ahnvil said. "I canna risk turning wi'out my touchstone. I'm too close."

"I can see that," Ram said when Ahnvil's hands briefly shifted to a stone state. "Let's go."

But no sooner were the words out of his mouth than a searing blast of red light exploded between the group, blowing them all off their feet. Then another hit, this time catching Jackson dead in the chest. Kat couldn't help the scream that erupted from her lips, even as Ahnvil got to his feet, grabbed her and thrust her behind himself.

Just in time for him to catch one of those beams right in his chest as well. He roared in pain and Kat could swear she heard his flesh sizzling as though it had been cooked. Yet he remained on his feet, only staggering back a step or two. She looked up and to her shock she could see two men and a woman literally floating in the air. The beams of light were being cast from their hands.

The light was called the Curse of Ra, and Ahnvil knew it well. It was a violent burning energy that could damage even a powerful Nightwalker, as was evidenced by the agonizing pain in Ahnvil's chest. Jackson was down and Ram was under attack by two of the three Templar assailants. Cloud cover began to rush over them and thunder roared as Ram used his power over the weather to generate a tremendous lightning blast. It hit the first Templar and radiated to the second one, causing the both to falter and fall out of the sky. That left the female and she was focused on Ahnvil. Or rather the woman behind Ahnvil, who was the only one uninjured. Outside of Max, who was still in the car and wise enough to stay there. He was mortal and there was nothing he could do. Their attackers were keeping them back from the car and Ahnvil couldn't risk sending Kat in that direction. Especially not when he was pretty sure the Templar woman was mistaking Kat for a Nightwalker. One hit by the Curse of Ra would kill a mortal human where they stood. It was Ahnvil's worst nightmare come to life, and if he remained in flesh form there would be nothing he could do to protect her.

"No! Don't do it!" she cried, somehow sensing his only course of action.

"I have no choice," he said darkly before closing his eyes and calling his stone skin. It rippled over him at lightning speed, as if gleefully delighted to be let out of its cage. She had her hands on his back and felt it turn into rough stone. With one tear Ahnvil ripped away his T-shirt and his whole body seemed to grow even bigger. He caught another blast, this one to the face. The Templars on the ground were regrouping, but so was Jackson. He used his massive power of telekinesis to pick up both men and send them slamming into the fuselage of the plane. The ringing of the metal echoed into the pre-dawn sky. The woman in flight was completely fixated on Ahnvil, and she beat him back with blast after blast. Finally, he roared with utter fury, his back hunching up and suddenly . . . suddenly wings were growing out of the rear of his shoulders, below the scapula and near the spine. His entire body began to distort, growing ever larger and now more and more misshapen. When he turned to look at her he had horns curling back from his skull, his face was distorted and grotesque, wide lips and deadly fangs for his mouth and dark sunken eyes . . . but eyes that were still the beautifully warm amber she recognized and allowed her to see the man and soul beyond the flattened nose, flared nostrils, and sharp cheekbones.

"Go! Run tae the car!" he snarled at her through a mouth full of fangs.

She was frozen in place, but not from fear of the attackers. She was terrified because he had been forced to become this thing and it was possible he would not be able to change back. And all because he had needed to protect *her*. Once again she was too frail and too weak. Well, she wasn't going to fail him. Not this time. She ran, watching all of the attackers from all corners and dodging one blast and then another. The second came so close she could smell her hair burning. Why were they trying to attack *her*? She was a nobody!

As she rounded the car, Max jumped out and protected her with the shield of his body as he shoved her into the back of the town car. Karma was hot on her heels and bounded into the car along with her. Then Max scrambled back in behind the wheel, his eyes darting back and forth and watching for anything he could do to assist the situation, she presumed. But now that he had wings, Ahnvil was becoming a force to be reckoned with and looked to be the only one of the three under attack who could take flight and meet the bitch in the air head-on. With a massive pumping of stone wings he launched himself into her like a huge granite missile. He plowed into her, tackling her like a linebacker and then pile-driving her down into the ground, tearing up asphalt and earth in a three-yard strip.

Meanwhile the other two men were back on their feet and now that the attackers no longer had the element of surprise Kat could see exactly why Jackson was the leader of his people. His power was phenomenal. He was throwing the men around like rag dolls, and at the same time pummeling them with objects from the ground. Ram waited until Jackson held them pinned in one place then aimed another bolt of lighting directly into their heads. After that it was apparently game over for those two attackers.

But she barely noticed. She was transfixed on watching Ahnvil fly and then the sheer power it must have taken for him to tear up airport asphalt down into the dirt. When he stood up again, he grabbed the female by the front of her shirt and hauled back his fist . . .

. . . and hesitated . . .

"Beat the bitch!" she screamed at him, knowing why

he was hesitating. The last Templar female he'd been near had needed his help and he had failed to provide it. And while his need to protect Kat had driven him this far, it was almost impossible for him to beat his fist into the dazed woman's face.

He seemed to hear her scream and turned to look over his shoulder at her, but he couldn't see her through the reflective glass.

He shoved the woman back into the ground and got to his feet. Ram and Jackson joined him and they helped to pull him back.

"Do we take her and question her?" Ram asked Jackson.

"No. There's no time and no room in the car. Just leave her here. We'll have drawn human attention by now. We need to leave before anyone can investigate. Whoever did this was damn foolish and impulsive."

"This doesn't seem like something Apep would do," Ram said grimly. "It's all a little half-assed."

"I think I know the why of it," Ahnvil said, his breath heaving from him, his big stone body shuddering. "But the sun is coming. If it touches me while I'm like this, there will be no coming back."

"Change back to flesh, Ahnvil," Jackson commanded of him. "The threat is neutralized. You don't need to stay like this."

"Doona tell me what tae do! I willna let them come for her!"

"Her?" Ram echoed. "You mean the girl."

"Aye, I mean the girl!" he growled savagely, his body everything that was threatening. "I willna . . ."

Then he staggered, nearly dropping to his knees. Both men reached out to help him but he threw them off savagely.

"Ahnvil."

The sound of her voice made him still, but his breath nonetheless came hard. She moved in closer and both men held out hands as if to stop her. She ignored them, pushing past them both. She knelt down and then moved her entire body into Ahnvil's arms. She pressed herself to his granite rough chest, wrapping her arms around his sides and pressing her hands to his back. After only a moment his hand came to her back and he held her to himself desperately, and yet it seemed as though he were afraid he was going to hurt her at the same time.

The men watched with no little awe as this tiny little mortal woman calmed her big beast of a Gargoyle. His breathing eased and very slowly the roughness beneath her began to smooth out and soon she had her face pressed against warm male flesh. His shirt had been ripped away in the battle. His pants remained in spite of how much larger he had grown, but it was obvious they had been stressed to a near breaking point. They now hung loosely on his hips.

And yet stone still rippled over him in waves, more and more frequently. She could see it in the light of dawn.

They realized at the same time the danger that meant.

"Get her in the car. Cover her with the blanket. Go! Now!"

"We'll make it before the sun crests," Max promised after ushering them all in the car. He hit the gas a moment later and with a spray of dirt and gravel tore off the tarmac.

They sped the entire way there. Ahnvil knew if the sun crested and pure daylight touched him he would turn to a statue instantly. The windows were polarized on either side of them to keep the sun out, but still he was anxious. Any number of things could happen before they got to the compound. Not the least of which was another attack by Apep's forces. If indeed it was Apep responsible. Ahnvil had a suspicion that this was far more about Panahasi than it was about Apep. Still, it was nothing to take lightly for any reason.

Ahnvil didn't even relax when they reached the compound borders. He would not until she was safely ensconced within and he was finally in touch with his stone. Pain had begun to claw through him, as though his body realized the sun was over the horizon and calling for him to rest . . . yet he must resist. If he turned without his stone he knew nothing would bring him back this time. Not even the woman who still held him tightly. Truthfully, he had no idea how she had managed to bring him back the first time. It had felt like magic, the soothing sensation she had sent into him. Just as everything she made him feel seemed like magic. Because God knew he had never felt anything like this overwhelming hunger he seemed to have for her. Maybe it was because of the threat of permanent being and the madness it brought. Maybe come the night, after his touchstone had recharged him, he wouldn't feel the same for her.

But as he ran his hands gently down the length of her back he found that incredibly hard to believe. Damn it, he barely knew her! What else could it possibly be? Perhaps it was that he didn't want it to change. Didn't want to lose the hunger he felt every time he smelled the warm chocolate scent she seemed to carry around with her everywhere she went. How did she do that? How did a woman manage to smell like warmed chocolate? It was only one of the many mysteries of her. Mysteries he wanted to unlock one by one.

By the time they pulled into the garage he had broken into a cold sweat. He hurried her into the house, ignoring everyone and everything around him, including Marissa and Jackson's sister, Docia, as both tried to greet him warmly and with relief to see that he was okay. The house also had polarized glass so not a stitch of daylight could get in, but still he worried. Glass was fragile. Even reinforced as this glass was, all it would take was one little chink.

He should have gone straight for his stone. It was kept in the center of the house. Jackson's ambient energy recharged the stone every day, so it had to be kept centrally in order to draw the most energy from him. It only took a small amount, but still, as with all things, the more the better.

Ahnvil brought Kat and Karma directly into his rooms.

"This is my suite," he said roughly. "Doona worry, you'll be safe here wi' my friends. All the glass in the house is protecting everyone inside. The forces again' us canna attack in daylight any more than we can go out in it so we should be safe . . . unless there is a human attack. But I doona think they would dare. As long as we're behind this glass we're too powerful for them by far. These are my private rooms and I want you to sleep here today. Come the night I'll be regenerated and back to my normal self and I'll be able to protect you myself."

"You said yourself your friends will be here. I'll be more than safe enough. They are amazingly powerful."

"Aye, but so are our enemies." He ran an anxious hand through her hair, fingertips touching her face so delicately. But she could feel him shaking hard. He was using everything he had to stay in his flesh state.

"Go," she said on a soft breath. "I'll be fine. Please go."

He did, reluctant the entire time, but eventually went for the stairs and hurried down. As soon as he reached the ground floor, Jackson was there. He had Ahnvil's touchstone in his hands. Ahnvil took it, the sudden wash of relief he felt nearly bringing him to his knees. But he wouldn't be safe until he had regenerated with his stone for several hours. He opened the front door and walked out into the rising sun. His landing, what they called the place they chose to sit on while they turned to statues and regenerated, lending a sense of normalcy to their appearance by making them look like any other normal statue, was a thick shale slab reinforced by concrete beneath him. It was still cold from the night, but he hardly felt it. What he felt was the clawing pain of turning to stone. He settled down onto his hands and knees and as his wings burst free and his touchstone was absorbed into the flesh of his hand, he moved as if to lunge forward, so that when he froze into his stone visage at last, he looked like he was a Gargoyle statue ready to leap free at any moment.

Kat watched all of this from above, and even for many minutes longer after that. She knew she couldn't truly relax until he'd been out there several hours. She wouldn't until she could see him move again. Until she could be certain he wasn't permanently turned to stone.

Jackson found her there, with her hands pressed against the glass, staring down at her Gargoyle worriedly.

"Don't worry," he said gently. "He has his touchstone now. He'll be just fine by the time the sun sets. Now come with me. Before we sleep I would like you to meet my wife and the others who reside here. I don't know how much Ahnvil has told you . . ." he hedged a bit awkwardly.

"Everything," she said. "I know you're a Bodywalker Pharaoh. I know there's a Djynn living here and that he or she would turn to smoke in sunlight. I know you are all called Nightwalkers and that you can't live in the sun any more than I can."

"You're right," he said with a bemused smile. "He has told you everything. But we know nothing about you, will you help us get to know you?"

"Of course. And then . . . I'm very tired . . ."

"We'll leave you to sleep. You can use Ahnvil's bed until we can get rooms set up for you. You'll have your own by night's end tomorrow. Come. Come meet everyone."

CHAPTER FIFTEEN

Bella was chewing on a nail anxiously as she waited for her husband to check them into a hotel in Albuquerque, New Mexico. Portales was apparently another three and a half hours away by car. Luckily they didn't need a car. Jacob could just turn them to dust and they could ride the currents of the wind. But it was daylight now and he was severely weakened in daylight. So they had decided to wait until dusk before finishing their journey.

"I don't understand it," she said for the thousandth time. "I know what she did. She pulled that man aside and asked him to describe me. Which meant he could see her as well. So what that means is . . ."

"Only *we* cannot see her," Jacob said. "I cannot even see her written responses to you. So what makes it possible for you to communicate with her? And why can we not see her in the first place?"

"I don't know," she said in exasperation. They had gone over and over this and still they couldn't figure out a solution.

"I cannot believe we have come all this way," Jacob said. Bella knew it wasn't a complaint. He was more perplexed than anything. They wondered what it was that coming here was supposed to do for them. Who

were these people that the mystery woman was supposed to know? How were they supposed to help them?

The only way to know was to see this task through to
its very end. Jacob didn't know how he felt about all of
this. He thought he should feel uneasy, but he didn't for
some reason. Probably because Bella didn't seem to feel
that way. If she didn't have a sense that there was any
trouble, then there probably wasn't any reason to feel
that there might be something to worry about.

So here they were, close to their goal, hindered only
by the light of day.

Some vacation this was turning out to be. But, on the
plus side, he'd never been to the Southwest before. He
was finding it to be quite beautiful with its low scrubby
vegetation, the large dark mountain in the distance that
signified the tail end of the Rocky Mountains, the sweeping roadways and overpasses done in soft pinks, and the
adobe houses. There was nothing but wild country in
any direction outside of Albuquerque.

"Come on. Let's get a little bit of rest," he said, drawing his wife beneath the wing of his arm. She raised a
brow at him.

"Only a little bit?"

He grinned, unable to help himself. "Well, you have
to help me salvage this vacation somehow."

"Oh. I see," she said with a laugh. "So you want me
to use my body to mollify you for dragging you around
all over creation when you'd much rather have been
making love to me?"

"That about sums it up," he said, his grin full of bold
mischief.

"You know, I'm all right with that," she said with a
grin of her own.

They headed up to their room.

The hotel staff couldn't figure out why the lights, the
heat, and the elevators suddenly decided to go on the

fritz, seemingly at the same time. They had no idea that Demon physiology was playing havoc with them.

Panahasi didn't find out about his failure until the next night at dusk. He was beyond enraged as the sole survivor, the female Bodywalker minion he had sent, related the tale of what had happened. He realized belatedly that he should have sent more forces, but he hadn't thought there would be more than just the Gargoyle to deal with. He screamed out like a temperamental child. He would have beaten the underling messenger if not for the fact that she already looked like she was close to death. The last thing he needed was for Apep to find another dead body in close proximity to him.

"You will keep yourself hidden from sight until you heal," Panahasi commanded of her.

"Yes, my lord," she mumbled, still fighting to breathe from the lungs that had been bruised and the ribs that had been snapped. She'd had to hide from the sun in an old, unused hangar for the entire day, which was no mean trick when airport security had been combing the area for whatever it was that had torn up the tarmac and killed what appeared to them to be two humans. Eventually, they would come to the conclusion that it had been some kind of freak lightning strike, an autopsy revealing nothing except human remains that had been struck by lightning.

Panahasi paced, trying to think of his next course of action. He didn't have the resources to attack the Politic stronghold. And even if he did he couldn't because he knew that Odjit was planning some kind of attack on them at some later date. He suspected she was waiting until after the birth of her child so she could spearhead the attack.

There was a great deal of speculation about the child. Odjit kept saying how the offspring would be the most

powerful child of all time . . . which made no sense because Bodywalker children were mortal children and
did not carry the power of their Bodywalker parents. So
that called into question the father of the child. The
running bet was Kamen. Kamenwati had been her first
lieutenant. For many reincarnations now their followers had suspected they were lovers, but there had never
been any outright proof. And if Kamen were the father
the same question arose. The child would only be mortal.
There were many who believed it was another Nightwalker. What kind was a good question, but no one
would know, he supposed, until after the birth and
right now Panahasi had more things to worry about
than who his mistress had been screwing and getting
knocked up by.

This was going to take some thinking.

"My lord," the useless female underling said.

"Do not speak to me. Your failure disgusts me! Now
be gone from my sight."

"But my lord, the pendant you asked about . . . the
one you sent us to retrieve . . ."

Panahasi turned to her with a vicious glare, unhappy
to be reminded of his failed goal. "Speak and then be
gone from my sight," he snarled at her.

"It is being worn by a mortal girl."

That gave him pause. "A mortal? Are you certain?"

"As certain as I can be. The Gargoyle was protecting
her as if she were in jeopardy . . . taking the Curse of Ra
fully, risking death for himself just to protect her."

"That's his job," he ground out to her. "The Gargoyles protect us."

"This was different. And she didn't use any power
against us. She ran to a car and cowered within."

This was an interesting piece of news, Panahasi realized. If the girl was mortal then that meant she could
easily be killed or taken captive. The trouble would be

getting her away from the other Nightwalkers and Gargoyles in the complex. But surely she would want to leave eventually. Sometime when she would be unescorted? Yes. That was entirely possible. All he needed to do was wait.

"Tell me everything there is to know about this female mortal. Then go and send in Morris, Havamati, and Skylar. I have a task for them. Maybe they can accomplish what you failed to do."

"Yes, my lord."

Katrina awoke shortly before dusk. She had borrowed a shirt from those in Ahnvil's closet to sleep in, but had no clothes to change into other than what she had worn the day before. She showered in his bathroom, touching his razor, smelling his shampoo. All of it seemed to suit him, right down to the T-shirts that engulfed her yet were no doubt snug across his muscled chest. She donned a fresh shirt, and, intent on asking one of the other women for clothes, she made her way out of his bedroom and down into the main body of the house. The only person she found was Ihron, another Gargoyle from the force that guarded the house. Apparently he had foregone rest and regeneration in order to protect the interior of the house while everyone else slept. As she understood it, they often chose one of the Gargoyle sentries to do this. He would be the first line of warning and defense if anything should happen within the house. He would then either regenerate in the dark for several hours or forego regeneration until the next day at dawn.

The only thing she was concerned about was Ahnvil. She would not relax until she could see him for herself at nightfall. She had only slept because she had been exhausted after such a long trip and the tension and effort necessary to keep Ahnvil from changing into permanent being. But it had been worth it. Worth saving him. She wished she could go out there and touch him. Wished she could hold him until he changed back in her arms, back into the warm flesh and blood of a man. Just as he had done the last time they had been together.

"Is everyone still sleeping?" she asked. She kept looking at the clock. The polarized glass made it impossible to judge the height of the sun. To them it looked like it was night outside.

"They'll be stirring soon enough," he said soothingly as he made her a cup of coffee. She noted he had the exact same accent that Ahnvil did and it made her very curious. "Sugar?"

"Yes. And milk." He dutifully prepared the cup and handed it to her. She perched nervously on the barstool of the counter and blew on the hot beverage. Karma had come up to her, nudging her big head under her hand and, getting the message, she absently began to pet her. She looked at the clock again.

Ihron chuckled at her. "Soon," he said. "He's fine. Doona worry."

She laughed sheepishly. "Does it show? I guess I'll feel better when I see him alive and breathing again."

"He made it in time," he assured her. "He has his touchstone."

"I'm sure you're right." But she looked at the clock yet again. "You would know, right?"

"Aye."

He came around the counter and rested a hand on her shoulder. "Trust me, coming to see you will be the very first thing he does. If I know him he will look on you as his tae protect. 'Tis what we're bred for."

"Bred for?"

"Our sole purpose was tae protect the Bodywalker who made us. With every generation the instinct was bred into us deeper and deeper. Sort of another way of keeping us loyal tae our makers. I'm happy to say it doesna always work. But 'tis in our nature tae protect with all of our heart and soul what we deem needs protecting. That is what the Gargoyles here are doing. Protecting the Pharaoh and the body Politic."

"How many of you are there?"

"Five at present. Diahmond, Ahnvil, Hector, Stohn, and myself."

"Where is the *h* in your name?"

"He told you about that?" he asked, looking surprised. "'Tis in the second position."

"So you're the same generation as Ahnvil? You had the same maker?"

"More than that, we were clansmen before being turned. We were captured together, turned together, enslaved together. We even escaped together. No' in the way that the recent Gargoyles are liberated. There's a sort of an underground railroad for Gargoyles now. Gargoyles who are already freed help tae liberate those who are still captive or newly created. It gets more and more difficult, however, with every generation as the Gargoyle design is improved and their loyalty more deeply rooted. 'Tis hard to turn them away from their makers, even though they are slaves."

"Was it hard for you?"

"Verra. Especially considering the skill of our maker. The story goes like this: Ahnvil had just stolen his touchstone. I was coming down the hall just as Ahnvil was running from the scene of his crime. I saw Ahnvil with his touchstone in hand and I had every intention of blocking his way, of keeping him from escaping."

"But you didn't?"

"No. I dinna." He smiled with remembering. "He grabbed hold of me, threw me up again' the wall, and said. 'Your bloody stone is in that room for the taking. You can raise the alarm or you can come wi' me, brother.'" He grinned. "Guess which one I chose?"

"Wow. I mean . . . wow."

"Aye. Believe me when I say this, he could have been done wi' me right then . . . killed me where I stood. We're of different beasts, for all we're alike. Mine made for grace and speed, his for brute strength."

"What's yours?" she asked, completely enthralled.

"A jaguar. Make no mistake, I'm plenty powerful, but in a head-to-head, hands down he's the stronger of the two of us."

She eyed his powerful physique, but she could see the lean grace in the lines of his body. "I can believe that. All of that."

"I owe that man my life, my freedom, and more. I may be the leader of our tribe, but he's the strongest of us. He doesna have the patience for it . . . leadership. Or so he says. And he may be right. But he's always taken the initiative in all things and I depend on him for his advice a great deal."

"He does seem very smart," she said. And then, for inexplicable reasons, her eyes welled up with tears.

"Hey now. Doona be doing that. There's a good lass," he soothed her, drawing her close and patting her on the head. "What is it?"

"I just want him to be all right. You have no idea what he went through to get here."

"I can imagine. He's—"

A vicious snarl filled the air suddenly, cutting Ihron off. He went so tense so fast that it was like she was suddenly being held by iron, the real, legitimate metal. They both turned their heads and saw Ahnvil standing there, air rushing out of him in bullish huffs.

"Get back!" he snarled at Ihron. "Remove your touch from her this instant or you risk losing a hand. Nay, the whole bloody arm," he threatened, his voice the darkest, hardest thing Kat had ever heard.

"Don't be ridiculous, Ahnvil!" she sputtered, her face

flooding with embarrassment as Ihron loosened his hold on her. Karma skittered away, backing off, the big dog sensing the sudden danger in the room. "We're just talking!"

"Looks tae me like you're touching," he growled, that gravel in his voice grinding low and deep. His accent thickened, just as it did every time he was aroused to some strong emotion or another. Or when he was making outrageously lewd propositions to her.

He moved forward that last step and grabbed Ihron's hand at the wrist and seeing the other Gargoyle, big as he was, solid as he was, just as able to turn to impenetrable stone as Ahnvil was, flinch . . . it had Katrina swallowing hard.

"I'm no' hurting her," Ihron said placatingly, speaking to Ahnvil as though he could try and tame the beast with a level tone of voice.

"I never said you were hurting her," he said, a rumble of warning trebling out of him.

Ihron opened his arms and let Kat go.

Kat was breathing hard, awash in so many emotions and so much fear she could barely catch her breath. But just the same, self-preservation made her move. She backed away from the two of them with haste, never taking her eyes from them as she fumbled at the door for escape. Ahnvil had been glaring holes through Ihron with his eyes, but the sound of the doorknob rattling made him blink and he looked in her direction. There was no describing the dismay that washed through him when he saw the fear on her face. He hastened toward her but when she cried out he froze in place.

"No, lass, doona be afraid of me. I'll no' hurt you."

"Don't tell me to not be afraid! I'm afraid, okay? You come in here all intense and hostile and maybe it makes me weak or pathetic or whatever, but unlike you I'm human and unlike you I'm mortal and unlike you when two big men who are part wild animal start growling at each other I'm really freakin' afraid!"

"I dinna say you've no cause for fear, thrown into this situation you find yourself a part of, but you dinna need tae be fearing *me*. For I'll no' hurt you. In fact, I'll protect you. I'll protect you from all of this you've been thrust into." He made sure she saw the shame in his features. "Thrust into by me."

She hesitated, but he could still see her white-knuckled grasp on the door handle. She glanced over at Ihron, who wisely raised his hands and backed away from the situation. Good thing, too, because Ahnvil wasn't sure he wasn't still of a mind to kill him for touching her.

He didn't examine the ferocity of the feeling. He was there to protect her, at all costs, and he would not fail her. Not her. Not this time.

"I swear tae you," he vowed deeply, making sure she felt the depth of it. "I will no' let anything happen tae you."

"B-but . . . *you're* happening to me," she said shakily. "You're *always* happening to me! Every time I turn around you're there doing something that pushes me and pushes me! I haven't had a single second to catch my breath before you're there *again*! Ihron wasn't doing anything!"

"He was!"

"He wasn't!" she yelled at him, suddenly forgetting about the door, forgetting all about her fear and lunging up into his face. "We were *talking*! I was upset. He touched me to reassure me, which is a hell of a lot more than I can say for you!"

To his shock she reached out and stabbed him in his chest with her finger to punctuate the accusation . . . right before she shook it out and muttered, "Ow," under her breath. Apparently poking him hard had hurt her, whereas he'd hardly felt a thing. It just made him all the more aware of how fragile she was.

"I brought you here tae protect you!"

"I don't need protection! I don't want your protection!"

"You're a damn fool if you really think that!" he shouted back at her. "Do you think I'd go through all this trouble for my own amusement?"

"Oh, so now I'm a fool, right? I'm trouble. And how am I supposed to know what goes on inside that thick skull of yours?" She scoffed at him. "Fool. You know what, I *am* a fool," she agreed suddenly. "I'm a fool for ever trying to help you in the first place! I knew *you* were trouble the minute I laid eyes on you, but nooooo . . . I had to get all Good Samaritan. And now look at me!"

"You're safe behind protected walls with nigh over a half-dozen immortals to protect you."

"I—" She cut herself off and looked at him funny for a minute, clearly taking stock of the picture from his perspective for that minute.

"Aye, that's it, lass. Go on and think on it for a moment. I canna help that you were the one tae find me in those woods, and I canna help that by helping me you've thrust yourself in the middle of a war. But I wouldna have left you behind for trackers tae find so they could torture answers out of you in order tae find me. Think what you like, but I couldna have that on my conscience. I've a damn site too much on it as it is. Enough blood has been spilt for my benefit already, and I'm sick tae death of it." He turned from her and glared at Ihron. "Doona put your hands on her again if you know what's good for you. We're friends, you and I, and I'd like it to stay such. But doona touch her again unless 'tis to save her life. Am I making myself clear?"

"Crystal," Ihron said. Then he turned his back on them both and left the room through the other door. He shut the door behind himself, leaving them closed into the room together.

She had her arms crossed under and over her breasts, in a kind of self-induced hug. Her eyes seemed so large in her delicate face and he was angry with himself for putting that fear in her life.

"I'll be going, too," he said quietly, turning to do just that.

There was something defeated in the sketch of his body and in the vitality of his normally bold presence in a room. It was as though something key to what he was had just abandoned him. She didn't have to be especially intuitive to feel it.

"Wait," she said, rolling her eyes, wondering why she was such a glutton for punishment. She should just let him go. She should just push him away and keep him away until she could figure a way out of the mess her life had become. "I'll go. This is your house . . ."

"*Our* house," he corrected clearly more harshly than he intended. "Damn it!" He ran a hand back through the thick, black waves of his hair, growling in frustration. "You doona understand! I canna . . . I just canna . . ." He floundered, looking so helpless that she felt another twang of sympathy for him. Then he looked at her hard, his fierce golden topaz eyes pinning her to the spot. "It's no' all about protecting you," he said intensely. "I . . . you ken I'm . . . I'm wanting you fiercely bad, lass. In ways I have no right tae feel. If I had an ounce of sense or honor I'd leave off you and that would be the end of it, but I just canna seem tae make myself! I take one look at your bonny face or that delicious body you're constantly trying to hide away from me and . . . you just doona get it. They've yet tae make an article of clothing effective enough tae keep your beauty under wraps. There's nothing that'll hide the lush scent of you from my senses. There's no way for you tae erase the way you've felt in my arms, knowing that just a kiss can light you tae fire like kindling. How can I know all of that, *feel* all of that, and then just be expected tae walk away? I'm no' that noble and I've never claimed tae be. I'm selfish, Kat. Selfish enough tae want you for myself. Myself and no other."

He reached out, lifting a hand as if to push back that lock of hair that always seemed to catch his attention, but he stopped himself and drew back. When he turned she leapt for him, grabbing for the hand he'd just tried to touch her with.

"No, wait! Please!" She pulled on him, but he kept moving away from her.

"Just let me go now."

"Ahnvil, stop!"

"Jesus, woman! I'm giving you your freedom! Do you bloody want it or no'?"

"No!" *What?*

"What?" he echoed, sounding equally shocked aloud as she had in her own head.

"I mean . . ." What did she mean? "I mean . . . I've never . . . I mean . . ." When he went to move again she said hastily, "I mean I've never had anyone think about me like that before!"

Well, that was true. All of her life she'd been "Little Kat." Tiny, dwarfish, weird little Kat. Freakish. Sometimes sassy. Sometimes brilliant, given a good moment. But . . . desirable? Never. Irresistible? Absolutely not. But to listen to him say it, he thought she was the most desirable, irresistible woman on the entire earth. And as scared as he made her feel sometimes, it was nothing compared to how those words made her feel. That she made him feel strongly, that it moved him to make rash choices and behave irrationally. He scared her mostly because she didn't know what in hell to do with that! What to do with *him*.

As he turned to look at her, his face and expression

were entirely incredulous. Her heart thumped upward in her chest, leaping into a dance of delight just to see it. He truly believed his words! He wasn't just saying things for the sake of getting on her good side, but he truly believed them. It was written all over his handsome visage, his bright eyes burning with it as he closed the distance between them once more, reaching for her, ringing the back of her neck with a strong hand and pulling her forward slightly . . . yet not enough to come into contact with him. Just enough to make certain she was looking into his eyes.

"I canna believe this is true," he said, his sentiment so low, making the *r* on the word "true" spin hard on his tongue. "That the world can be so blind. Anyone can just look at you and see how fine you are. Any man wi' blood in his veins can see the lush weight of your breasts and the wicked curve of your arse and start to feel his blood boil hot wi' need of you. Aye, you're a tiny thing by and by, but you pack a lot in this fine li'le package."

For the first time in her life she felt the honest truth of those words blossom inside of her, making her entire body curve toward him in newfound sensuality, wanting to tempt him as he said he was tempted, needing to wield that power over him.

"What else do you like about me?" she asked, hearing the breathy nature of her voice and pleased with the sound of it. It too sounded suddenly sexy to her ears and she hoped it sounded the same to his.

"Good God woman, doona speak tae me so. I'll be fixating on every last part of you then craving you as I go. 'Tis all I can do from this moment tae next tae keep my hands from you. You made me promise no' tae . . . tae touch you like that. I may be many bad things by and by, but I'm a creature of my word and I will no' go back on it wi'out your permission, as I've said before."

"Yes, as you've said before," she breathed softly. "And before I wanted you to be that man. But right now . . . right now I don't want you t-to keep your word anymore."

It was by far the most provocative, most dangerous thing she'd ever said. She knew what he was, knew the world he was from, and yet she was inviting him into her. Inviting him to do his worst and his best. She began to breathe hard as she recalled the heat of his body and the bold passion of his touch before she had set limitations. It was awesome and shocking to realize she wanted that more than anything. She wanted him to overwhelm her with his hunger.

"Och, lass! You canna say such things tae me! You doona ken what you're saying!" He dragged her into the press of his huge body, towering over and around her until she felt very small and very fragile indeed. He was breathing hard, and she knew this because he had burrowed his face against her neck once again and the hot spill of his breath was swift and fierce. "Jesus, you smell so good," he rumbled. "Can no' you see? Just the smell of you has me running away from myself and has me mad wi' need of you." To prove his point he ran a hand down her arm, gripped her hand in his and brought it to the front of his jeans, to the raging hard erection lying just beneath the denim. He used her hand to rub himself hard, used her to put pressure against himself. There was nothing about him that could be considered even remotely small, this least of all, and she had to admit that frightened her, but not half as much as it excited her. She uncurled her fingers, cupping them around him and pressing her palm into him of her own accord. She could feel the heat of him burning against her palm and now she was the one breathing hard and he was the one catching his breath in a gasp.

"Ah fuck," he groaned, that guttural tone returning

with a vengeance. "If this be a game, lass, you'll be sore regretting it in another minute or two." He drew back far enough to catch up her gaze with his own. The sight of the fire that was burning in his eyes took her breath away.

"I . . . I'm not saying I want to . . . to . . . Not yet I mean. But I want to . . . I want you to . . ."

"You want me tae want you," he ground out. "You want tae cocktease me, no? 'Tis a dangerous pastime, Katrina Haynes. And I can make no promises of controlling myself. I'm a beast, Kat. Was once a man, but now . . . I'm a beast and I'm starting tae look on you as a mate . . . Hell, I have been for a while now. Why else would I work so hard tae respect whatever you wish of me that was in my power tae give tae you?"

"I'm not . . ." Kat flushed so hotly she was afraid her face would burst into flame. "I'm not trying t-to . . . t-to tease you. I didn't mean . . ."

"I speak plainly, and that is what it is. Maybe no' with the conniving connotations the term sometimes implies, I ken you're no' like that. But you're afraid of me yet. Afraid, but curious. Afraid but hungry for what I can give you." He leaned into the press of her hand again, his eyes shuttering closed a moment as a low groan filtered up from deep in his chest. "Verra well then. I'll take whatever you can give me and give whatever you can take of me. But I'll warn you now. I'll press you. I'll press for what I want every single moment I can. If that scares you then best you back out now, though I'm no' sure I can let you go even so."

She swallowed noisily. "I don't want to back out. And I think I can hold my own. I have so far."

"Ah, do you now?" A darkly devious smile spread over his lips a moment before he yanked her off her feet and strode into the next room, then up the stairs . . . all the way until they were back in his bedroom. Her heart was thundering louder and louder every step of the way, but never as loud as when he threw her down onto the bed so hard her body would have caught air if not for the fact that his weight came down on her immediately after. He propped himself up over her with his weight leaning on one arm. He straddled one of her legs and with a powerful hand he pulled her thigh up into the seat of his jeans, rubbing himself against her. "I'll make you a deal, Kat lass. You keep doing this tae me, tae keep me busy let's say, and I'll be doing other things tae keep *you* busy."

"O-otherwise?" she hitched out nervously.

"Nothing for you tae fear, Kat lass. Nothing at all." His free hand came up and he touched her, two fingers, in the hollow of her throat. Such a sensitive, vulnerable part of her, and he touched it with a soft sort of reverence. Then he drifted those two fingers down to her breastbone, slowly riding the length of it until he reached the edge of her shirt. She watched breathlessly, anticipating, waiting. His big fingers slipped the button free with a whisper of sound and an incredible lightness of touch. One might expect a man as big as he was to be ham-handed and brutish, but whenever she expected it to be that way he proved her wrong with this grace and gentility.

"I'm going tae touch you, Kat lass. Slow-like and as long as you'll let me. Tell me that's what you want."

"I do," she breathed in a rush, sounding overly eager to her own ears. It was probably why he chuckled. But she couldn't make herself feel embarrassed about that. She was too far beyond embarrassment. She probably had been since she'd first seen him naked in her house. Naked and male and erect and dominant and . . . "Oh my," she whispered.

He chuckled again, the sound low and rich and companionable, not mocking. It made her smile in spite of herself.

And then she felt him slide his hand beneath her shirt, cupping her breast in his fingers and palm. All of a sudden she felt so small. Small beneath him. Small within his hands. Small and inadequate. Who was she kidding? She *was* tiny. Diminutive. Itty-fricken-bitty. All these years of fighting to make people see beyond her height and build and suddenly she was facing the truth of it. Probably because he was the polar opposite of her. *Good God, what could he possibly see in me?* A man like him needed a buxom lass with wide hips and a big fat booty. She had a tiny booty. Practically no booty. She was booty-less.

"Ah, Kat lass, look how fine and full you are," he invited, his tone sounding strained as if he were somehow holding himself back. "I want tae devour you, lass." His fingers curled into the fragile lace of her bra and pulled it free of her, exposing her breast and nipple to the open air. "I'm going tae taste you now. I'm going tae have you on the flat of my tongue and between my teeth."

She swallowed hard. There it was again. That feeling he could create in her. The feeling that she had all the power in this thing between them. But she didn't, did she?

She had no further time to think about it. Her nipple was between his teeth that next instant and the sensation was so outstanding that she cried out. His mouth was bold and wet, hot and strong, sucking her in, toying with her in quick little flicks, letting her go to cool in the air of the room. Her entire spine turned to butter, melting away beneath her as she squirmed with pleasure. Then he ramped up the sensation by exposing the opposite breast and closing his mouth over her with a voracious sound of hunger.

"Kat lass," he said, his breathing rolling hot over her

dampened skin, "you're so bloody fine. Can you no' feel how much I'm hurting for you?" He pressed the rigid length of his erect shaft against her thigh to make sure she was certain of his meaning. "Jesus. Jesus," he groaned, burying his head in her neck, his breath hard against her. "I canna do this. I canna be this close tae you, tae feel you, wi'out wanting tae be inside you. But you're such a wee li'le thing."

"Say that again and I'll knee you in the nads," she said breathlessly.

That made him laugh, the sound gusting hard against her. He raised up again and looked down into her bourbon-colored eyes. So brown with the slightest tinge of red. It was as beautiful as the rest of her.

"I want tae make love tae you, Kat. If not entirely, then enough tae give you the pleasure you deserve. I want tae taste you on my tongue, feel you from the inside on the tips of my fingers. I want tae hear you cry out in my ear. Maybe you'll say my name rough or maybe soft-like. Maybe you'll taste like chocolate, just as you smell."

"Ch-chocolate?" she asked, her mind reeling from his words. She had never heard anyone want anything from her so passionately. Just hearing all of his suggestive desires had made her wet with response.

"Yes. Warm, sweet . . . delicious." His lips brushed ever so lightly over hers. His tongue came out to drift over her lush bottom lip. Her breath caught, her throat tight with a thousand emotions. How could he ever know what his desire for her meant to her? How could he understand that she had never, in all of her life, felt more like a real, normal—even better than normal—woman in the eyes of another. It had taken finding this man and this dark little world for her to learn that normal was such a subjective thing.

"Do it," she said with soft ferocity. "Do it all. I want it all. I want to give it right back to you, too. I want to

know what you taste like, Ahnvil. What you feel like."
She reached between their bodies and ran a hard palm
down the length of his zipper. He bucked against her
touch, his hips lurching forward almost frantically.

He reared up then, ripping away the clean shirt he
had donned, exposing his bare, massively beautiful
chest. She reached out and grabbed at the buckle of his
belt, her nimble fingers undoing it swiftly. She pulled it
free and his loose waistband slid down to ride low on
his hips. She could see the strong cut of muscles stretched
taut over his hips, disappearing suggestively beneath his
jeans. Equally suggestive was the furry line of hair that
drew downward from his navel. Oddly enough he
hadn't a speck of hair on his chest. It was all just tight,
gorgeous muscle and a pair of flat, buff nipples.

He only let her look at him for a short period of time
before he was bracing a hand on the bed by her head
and looming over her. His fingers were at the buttons of
her shirt, undoing them in rapid succession. Within seconds he was parting the fabric, exposing her midriff,
her bra, and her panties. Next he went to the front clasp
of her bra and snapped it open. Then he lifted her limp
body up and shucked it all away. She lay there naked
and vulnerable, nothing but her panties to protect her.

"Look. A wee li'le bow," he said with amusement,
touching the tiny bow at the top center of her panties.
"Gods, I canna decide if you're adorable as hell or sexy as
hell. I'm torn betwixt the two and was never happier for
it."

That made her smile.

"I like the idea of being both for a change."

"For a change? You ever were," he insisted. "Nothing
has changed on you from the time before I met you tae
today. You are what you ever were. Beautiful, amazing,
sensual. All that and more adjectives a brute such as me
has little access tae."

"You're not a brute. No more now that you ever were. Not to me."

He unbuttoned his jeans with a single hand. "I doona want tae frighten you," he said after a moment's hesitation.

"I've seen it before," she reminded him.

"Aye. Only this time you'll know my aim is to put myself inside you and that's more than enough to frighten any lass."

"I'm not just any lass," she said on a whisper of breath.

"Oh aye," he agreed, then slowly unzipped his jeans and pushed them down and away from himself. His erection was an astounding thing of beauty. Bold and thick, flushed and taut. She couldn't help but to reach out and touch him, and the moment she did she felt him shudder hard. He said something unintelligible under his breath and even though she didn't know what it was she understood the sentiment behind it.

Slowly she wrapped her hand around him, just lightly at first, drifting her touch up and down the length of him, learning every single taut vein and bump. Then she went to stroke the head of it and was instantly rewarded with a bead of fluid against her fingertips. She rubbed the fluid back into him and he cursed.

"Nay. You'll make me come just as we are, that's how eager I am for you," he said after snatching her touch away from himself. He reached for her panties and in one swift jerk of movement he'd shucked them off her. And now she felt truly vulnerable. Truly exposed. She wasn't made perfectly, had no supermodel figure. She had some good curves in some places and some bad ones in others. But looking into his eyes she could swear he didn't see a single one of them, and that made her doubts about herself instantly evaporate. His hands were on her body then, running up her entire length from kneecaps to shoulders and touching everything in

between. It brought her skin to life and her nipples
tightened, jutting up toward him and eagerly begging
for his attention. And he gave it gladly. First with the
touch of his fingers. A brush. A stroke. A pull. A pinch.
Then he wrapped a hand around her ribs and jerked her
torso up about six inches and brought her directly to his
mouth. Teeth. Lips. Tongue. All of it in parts and then
together. The feel of it making her go wild with need.
How was he able to do this so easily? How was it as
smooth as water over glass with him when before, with
others, it had always seemed like so much effort?

He shifted from one nipple to the other, cuddling and
cradling each breast in their turn. She arched her back,
pressed back her shoulders. He tasted her until she was
raw with need and her fingers were nearly tearing the
hair out of his head.

"Ahnvil, please . . ." she moaned softly.

"No' yet, love. No' yet."

And then his touch drifted down over her belly, causing it to contract under the attention. He found the soft
mink curls guarding the treasure he was truly seeking
and scraped through them with the tips of his finger-
nails. He imagined himself doing the same with the
claws he grew when he changed and it was all he could
do to keep himself from doing so right then. He didn't
want to frighten her. Not when he was so close to having her. And anyway he didn't feel things as finely when
he was turned to stone. It was one of the reasons he
could take hit after hit after hit and just keep coming.

But now he didn't want to be so rough and so tough.
He was afraid of being that. Afraid of hurting her. God,
she was so small! But fiend that he was he couldn't make
himself walk away. He was going to do everything in
his power to make her sing. Everything he could to see
to it she felt nothing but the sweetest pleasure the world
could offer. So he touched her gently, felt how wet she

already was, and groaned as the flowering flesh gave way beneath his fingertips.

He immediately stroked her in short, languid circles. Her knees drew up instinctively, then one fell aside, completely opening her to him. He could see her, so pink and so pretty. He wasted no time sliding a probing finger into her. But even his fingers were big in the face of her smallness so he went gently. She made a sound and with the sweep of her hips pushed him into herself faster than he had planned on.

"You're tormenting me," she accused him on a soft cry.

"Nay. I just doona want tae hurt you."

"You won't. I know you won't. Just . . . please . . ."

So he thrust his finger into her and felt her give way. Her hips rose again, along with the erotic scent of her. That left him with only one option. To taste her while he touched her. There was really nothing else he could do. Nothing else he wanted to do.

When his tongue unerringly touched her clit Kat gasped loudly into the room. To her it sounded as though it echoed. But none of that mattered. What mattered was the pleasure that was echoing through her. She rolled her hips, chasing his mouth, rubbing herself against the tongue that was laving against her. It took no time at all before she reached a high point of pleasure, trembling on the very brink of release, needing so badly to fly. And then she was gone. Soaring beyond him, beyond the room, beyond everything she'd ever thought she was or could be. With him there were no limitations.

There was absolutely nothing weird to be found anywhere.

"Ah, Kat, you're the prettiest picture a man ever saw," he said as he carried her back down to earth with languid little strokes of the fingers inside of her. Two fingers, she realized. When had that happened? Did it matter?

No. Absolutely not.

Then he pulled them free of her, the wetness of it so obvious to them both. He took those two fingers and touched them to the head of his shaft, rubbing her wetness into himself there. It was the most erotic thing she'd ever seen in her life. And there was nothing she wanted more than to feel him inside of her, she thought as he moved over her, his cock heavy in his hand as he aimed himself carefully against her.

The instant he came into contact with her they both gasped aloud. He bent for her mouth, kissing her fiercely, all the while bathing himself in her wetness. He groaned as he thrust against but not inside her. Running himself over her again and again until he was sure she and he were both as wet as they could be. It was the hardest thing he'd ever done in his life. Even escaping from captivity had never been as hard as trying not to come against her before either of them was ready. He felt green and eager, as though she were his very first, and in a way he supposed she was. She was the first mortal woman he had allowed himself to be with since his forging. Ihron had been less discerning, but he had not been made as big as Ahnvil was. For him . . . he'd always been afraid his ferocity would hurt them.

But here ferocity was and yet it played in perfect tandem with gentility. And it was with leashing one and letting loose the other that he began to slide inside of her. Inch by excruciatingly lovely inch.

"Yes!" she cried, once again lifting those mobile hips of hers up into him. It brought him ever deeper inside of her. And deeper still with another undulation. And that was how it went, with her working herself along the length of him. It was torturous and sweet. Lush and violently needful. He wanted more and more until he was flayed apart from the pleasure of it.

And then, with a thrust he could not control, he shoved himself into her. She sucked in a hard breath, as if she had been hurt and he immediately cringed and went to pull back, but she grabbed hold of his shoulders and dug in her nails.

"No," she said, groaning tightly. "Don't move yet. I just want to enjoy this for a moment. Enjoy the first time you're inside of me."

"Oh, lass. My Kat lass," he said with a relieved wash of breath escaping him. "Doona take too long because I doona want tae spend myself wi'out so much as a thrust. And as it is I'm a hairsbreadth from it. God, oh God you feel like . . . like . . . like I've never known anything could feel. Can I move now? Please," he begged her.

"Yes. Please do," she said with a laugh. "You do beg so well."

"Oh aye. And soon you'll be doing the same," he said with a grin.

"Promises, promises," she sing-songed.

"You've got that right. And I'm a man who keeps his word."

And he kept it with a long, deep thrust that took her breath away. And then another. And another. A volley of them so stunning and so arousing, each to the highest degree. She knew within seconds that she was going to come again. There was nothing she could do to prepare herself, no hope of even stopping it . . . if she might ever want to stop anything like it.

She didn't.

Ahnvil felt her contract around him just as a cry of pleasure exploded out of her. Again, she worked her hips against him, using him however she could to derive the most out of her pleasure. It was absolutely maddening for him. He lunged into her then, the feeling like ripping free of chains and launching into freedom.

He was now thrusting into her in earnest. He needed it, couldn't stop it, rode into her like a madman. He forgot all about being gentle with her, forgot how small she was, forgot everything but the pleasure her body was giving to his. His hands gripped at the bedding on either side of her, just as indulgence was gripping at the very heart of him. He needed to indulge himself in her. Every last part of her, both physical and the ethereal. And as he pushed her into her third orgasm that was exactly how she looked. Heart-stoppingly, grippingly ethereal. And that was, in the end, what gave him the deepest pleasure. He lunged into her and started to come, thrust after thrust sending more and more of his seed deep inside of her. She had done it. She had taken everything that he was and had done it spectacularly.

And as he slowed to a stop, as he tried to catch his breath, he prayed he had not pushed her into something she would regret doing. When they had come up here she had said she didn't want to take this big of a leap, and he had threatened to push her to the limit of what she would allow. Would she regret this now? Would she try to backpedal away?

These were the worries that filled his thoughts as he moved free of her slight body and rolled onto his back, drawing hard for breath. He had given her pleasure, and that would have to comfort him for now.

"Oh my God," she gasped. "Oh my God. I can't wait to do that again!"

Startled he looked at her, his disbelief obvious because she laughed at him. "I know. I'll let you catch your breath first!"

"You sound as if . . . You doona regret what we've done then?"

"Regret it?" she was incredulous. "I'm lying here replete and asking for seconds and you're afraid I am feeling *regret*?" She laughed at him again.

"But a li'le while ago you said you dinna want tae do this. You dinna want tae ... not all the way, in any event."

"I'm a woman. I changed my mind." She smiled beatifically at him. "And a damn good thing, too!"

"Aye," he agreed. "A bloody damn good thing."

CHAPTER SIXTEEN

Ahnvil trailed a finger down along the braided chain of the Amulet, until he reached the shining pendant itself. He carefully lifted it from between her bare breasts and examined it. He didn't want to give the impression he was trying to take it off her. He didn't want it to jerk her away like last time, possibly hurting her.

"Come," he said after a moment, "Let us see a man about this bloody thing. The sooner we get it off you the better it will be."

She hesitated before agreeing with him. She sat up and retrieved the shirt she'd been wearing from where it had landed on the corner of the bed.

"What is it?" he wanted to know as he reached for his jeans, studying her face all the while.

"Nothing," she said. Which was a lie. She was worried suddenly. If they removed the pendant, then there would no longer be any reason for her to stay. She suspected she knew exactly what Ahnvil's first reaction would be. To protect her . . . even if it meant sending her away. And if anything was obvious, it was that this was a dangerous place for a mortal woman to be.

But she was in danger every damn time the sun came out. Life wasn't about avoiding dangers. She had spent her entire existence avoiding dangers, but never could it have been considered living a life. She'd just been making her way through, carefully, cautiously. She didn't want to live like that anymore. At least when she'd had her job in the ER she'd been doing something exciting and useful with her life. But then she had let the opinions of others chase her back into the darkness where she had thought she belonged. For the first time she was feeling as though she were out in the sun.

"Now, I can see that's no' true," he said seriously. "Are you hurt? Did I say something—?"

"No. Stop," she soothed him with a hand on his chest. "You've done nothing wrong." She looked down at her knees. "I'm just worried."

"Doona worry. We'll get it off somehow."

"No. No I mean . . . I'm worried that . . . you'll send me away after it comes off."

He frowned. "Well, of course I'll send you away. This is no place for a mortal girl."

"Max is mortal," she pointed out angrily.

"I doona decide what Max does wi' his life."

"Oh. You'll just decide what I do with mine?" she bit out.

"That's no' what I mean."

"Then what did you mean?" she wanted to know.

"I just meant that you're very fragile. And Max is . . . Max is . . ."

"A man?"

"Yes."

"Oh my God, you're a sexist pig on top of everything else!"

"What 'else'?" he wanted to know. "What's so wrong wi' me? You dinna think there was anything wrong wi' me a few minutes ago!"

"A few minutes ago we were equals. Now the only thing we're equal at is being equally pissed off at each other. Only *my* reasons make sense!"

"And mine doona? You doona think there's any danger in staying here?"

"That's not the point! For the first time I'm somewhere where my affliction doesn't make me stand out. For the first time I've found somewhere where being me is 'normal.' Do you really think I want to give that up?"

"You do if you've any sense in your head! 'Tis dangerous here!"

"'Tis dangerous anywhere there's a goddamn *sun*!" she spat out.

"Och! I doona believe you're talking like a madwoman. And here I thought you were a sensible girl!"

"I am not a girl. Nor am I a madwoman. You're just a boorish pain in my ass who thinks his way is the only way and screw what everybody else thinks!"

She got up and scooped her panties up off the floor. "And now I'm going to go find a shower and some decent clothes. Because God forbid someone even looks at me the wrong way, you'll be wanting to rip their arms out of their sockets! Then I'm going to call my mother. At least she'll be happy to hear what I've got to say."

"But . . . I doona want you tae go," he said suddenly, his tone quiet and low. "Is that what you think? That I *want* you tae go?"

She frowned and looked down at her toes. "Well, what am I supposed to think? You're having sex with me one minute and the next you can't wait to ship me off to where it's 'safe.'" She looked up at him. "I don't want to be safe. Not anymore. Safe is . . . safe is . . . kind of boring. You know? I've played it safe all of my life but these past few days have been like . . . like something out of an adventure story. And it's been happening to me." She pointed to herself. "Me. The queen of hiding and playing it safe." She frowned again. "And if I had played it safe that morning in the woods I would have called the cops and left you out in the cold until they got there. I would have hidden in my house until it was all over with. But I didn't, and I'm glad I didn't." She rubbed her hands together. "So don't ask me to throw it all away. I don't want any take-backsies. I don't want to go backward. Can we please . . . please just take it one night at a time? If I feel I'm in too much danger believe me I'll be the first to cry uncle and I will lead the charge in the other direction."

He was frowning as well, and it was clear it was a difficult thing for him to wrestle with, the idea of letting her remain in an unprotected state.

"I know," she said softly, climbing back on the bed and straddling his thighs. She took his face in between her hands and looked down deeply into his golden eyes. "I know it's ingrained deep inside you to protect. I understand that you were made that way. Ihron told me your forger made you that way in order to force your loyalty."

"Aye. He did, the bastard." He sighed. "And now I'm going tae take you tae him."

"You're going to . . . ?"

"Up!" He lurched up to his feet, taking her up with him. Instinctively she clutched around his shoulders and her legs wrapped around his waist.

"But why would you—?" She huffed in frustration. "I don't understand!"

"Do you remember when I said there was someone here who would know how tae help us get this bloody thing off you?"

"Yes, but . . ."

"His name is Kamenwati."

"Kamenwati. Your *forger* is *here*?"

"Aye. And from what I heard he knows what this is and verra likely can tell us how tae get it off you. Will you let me take you tae him?" He stopped moving, waiting for her reply. Doing his best not to force her to his will. Realizing that, she smiled softly at him and touched warm fingers to his serious mouth.

"I trust you to know what's best . . . in this particular instance."

He had to grin at her obvious stipulation. "Verra well. But first you'll be putting on some decent clothing. We've a closetful here, just in case a new Bodywalker comes tae town and needs a wardrobe. It's a thing," he said at her quizzical expression. "The Bodywalkers like tae be prepared for everything."

"Oh, I see. Yes. Clothes would be very nice." As he walked them into the hallway she asked, "How is it that your forger is under the same roof as you are? I mean, how do you even keep from killing him where he stands? It seems to me that would be your first reaction."

"Aye. First, second, and last. But he's a powerful man and has defected from the Templars. A man like that, with his power, could help sway the way of the war. But there are other reasons, even more dangerous ones why we need him on our side. You see, there's an evil god who—"

"Did you say a *god*?" she interrupted incredulously.

"Aye. I did. Kamenwati cast magic and accidentally resurrected a demon god named Apep into the female Templar leader's body. Her name is Odjit. This god has more power than you can possibly imagine in him. Kamen says it will take time tae come tae fruition, and when that happens we'll all be the first thing on his hit list. Now do you see? Do you see why I canna have you here? You've no defense again' a regular Templar, never mind a demon god."

"I see," she said with a tight swallow. "But I still won't go."

"Gods, you're stubborn, woman."

"Aye," she said smugly.

After he brought her to the closet of all women's wet dreams, allowing her to find a pair of jeans that fit— almost, they were too long—and a pretty russet blouse that flattered her eyes, she fluffed her hair in a nearby mirror . . . then smoothed it . . . then fluffed it again.

"Ye gods woman, you're no' going out on a date!" Ahnvil said in exasperation. And she detected a hint of jealousy in the remark as well. For some reason that tickled her pink.

"Right. Well, I just want to make sure I look good for when I kick him in the ass. He deserves it for what he did to you."

"Aye," Ahnvil said thoughtfully. "But if he had no', I wouldna have gotten tae meet you."

She hadn't thought about it like that, and again it gave her pleasure that he had.

She went to walk out of the room, but he stopped her, moved in front of her, and kept her a step behind his back as he led her down the stairs. The entire time they moved through the house and down the stairs he kept her in a protective position, making sure his body was guarding hers at all times.

She thought about saying something, about showing her exasperation, but in the end it was kind of soothing to feel so well protected. There was something strongly pleasing about it. It seemed as though for the most part all of what he was doing was giving her pleasure. In one form or another. And just thinking about some of the forms that pleasure had taken had her flushing rosy red as she followed him.

They went down to the second story, and she realized there were more suites of rooms down here. The main house itself was enormous, and she had noticed a couple of other houses situated behind it a little distance away. All and all the property was mammoth. The driveway to get to the house had been very long. And all around them for as far as the eyes could see was land. Allowing them privacy, she realized, against whatever paranormal activity might happen there.

"Wait! I forgot about Bella! I have to leave her a note. She could be here anytime."

"After," he said. "Then we can write your note and tack it tae the door. I'm still no' comfortable wi' you talking tae the spirit."

"She's not a spirit," she felt the need to point out.

"Whatever she is, I doona like it."

"Well, maybe we'll find out something about her from your forger."

"Aye. That's a possibility. Here we are." They stopped at a closed door and he rapped his knuckles against it.

"How do you know he's in there?"

"He's confined tae his rooms more often than no'. We're still wary of his intentions, so he has limited access tae the house. But we have grown more lax abou' it over time. I doona agree with it, but I doona question my Pharaoh all that much. He's a wiser man than I and has proved it over the many incarnations I have been with him for."

"But everyone deserves questioning," she said with a frown.

"Aye, but like I said, he's proved to be right more often than no'."

The door opened just then, revealing a tall, athletically built man with dark hair, bright blue eyes, and pretty astounding good looks.

"Jeez, do all of you have to look like you just stepped off the cover of a romance novel?" she muttered.

"Kamenwati," Ahnvil said, ignoring her remark. "I need . . . I need a favor," he gritted out from between his teeth. She knew how much it took for him to say those words. Even Kamen raised his brows in surprise.

"Do come in," Kamen said with politesse, swinging the door open wide and stepping back to allow them to pass. After they had filed into the room, Ahnvil once again put her slightly behind him, but lifted the pendant around her neck, displaying it against his palm for Kamenwati to see.

"It's called Adoma's Amulet," he said tightly. "And she canna get it off."

"I know what it's called," Kamen said, a cultured nearly British accent coming from him. Maybe a little more . . . South African? He came forward slowly, presumably not to spook the big Gargoyle standing between her and him, and lifted the Amulet into his own hand. "It has something like a curse on it. 'When the child of dark dons the Amulet of Adoma, it shall forever bring insight and protection to the wearer, but will never be removed.' How is she a child of dark? Is she a Nightwalker? I always presumed that was what it meant."

"No, she is no'. She canna go out in the sun though. She has a disease." He looked to Kat for help.

"Xeroderma pigmentosum," she supplied dutifully.

"I see. They call you the children of the night."

"You've heard of it?" she asked with surprise.

"I have many centuries' worth of medical knowledge."

"Oh. Okay."

"I had originally thought 'child of dark' meant a Nightwalker. I was researching it more carefully before donning it myself. I did not want to be reckless." The remark was pointed.

"Hey! How was I supposed to know it had a curse on it?" she grumbled.

"I'm not sure I can get this off for you," Kamen said. "But perhaps with access to all new spells, incantations, and research source material I will find something I didn't find before."

"Our recorded histories," Ahnvil explained to Kat, "or rather, those of the Bodywalkers, were separated when the war began. Each faction commandeered different storage areas and relocated what they found there. That left the historical sources split in two. They only have access to partial resources and so do we."

"My research thus far was unsatisfactory, but . . . how did you come about possessing this? The last I saw it it was in my quarters at the Templar stronghold."

"A Templar named Panahasi stole it from your belongings," Ahnvil explained, the bitterness in his tone growing. "He was the one who captured me and held me. He seemed tae think I was the 'slave, born of the infinite Nightwalkers.' I thought it said: 'The slave, born of the infinite Nightwalkers, will set free the power wi'in. The one that harnesses Adoma's Amulet will have such power as to make a god weep.' What you're saying is different."

"There was more to it than what you heard. And you may be the slave. I certainly thought you were. Or rather, a Gargoyle in general. I don't really understand, and these things are really subjective when it comes to interpretation. As for breaking the curse and removing the Amulet, I'm not entirely sure I can do that, either. But as I said, I will need access to your stored resources."

A look of utter suspicion crossed Ahnvil's features.

"I doona think that will be allowed."

"Then I can't help you," Kamen said, looking genuinely regretful. But she could tell Ahnvil would never trust him in this.

"Maybe this is something you ought to take up with your Pharaoh," she suggested. "Because I really want this thing off . . . oh wait. But not yet. There's the girl . . . the woman. I keep communicating with a woman who I can't see, who Ahnvil can't see, but other people can. It's complicated," she said dismissively, realizing how it must sound. "What if this Amulet is the reason why this is happening?"

"Now this is interesting," Kamen said, looking genuinely fascinated. "You say you communicate. How?"

"By written notes. Oh, and I can see the note float up and stuff, as if someone were picking it up. As if she were the Invisible Woman, or something."

"Intriguing," Kamen mused.

"And she's coming here. To Portales."

"Now this I would like to see," Kamen said. "I am curious if any of us will be able to see her or if it is just the two of you she is invisible to."

"Provided she ever gets here. I have to write a note to her. I thought I would put it on the door."

"So you are bringing this unknown element right to our doorstep?" Kamen queried archly.

"I doona like it any more than you do," he said to Kamen. "But I dinna see any other way of resolving this."

"I see. Well, there's no changing it now in any event. Let me know what Jackson says about the source material and if he agrees I will get to work straightaway. Also, let me know when this woman begins to write back to you. I have a few spells I can try to help lift whatever obfuscation—"

"No! No spells!" Ahnvil said sharply. Kamen raised a brow, clearly undisturbed by the hulking, bristling giant.

"And just how do you think I am going to be removing the Amulet? I rather doubt writing sonnets to it will do the trick. Spells are what I do, what I know. And you know that or you wouldn't have brought her to me. This Amulet is of the supernatural. It will take the supernatural to remove it."

That made Ahnvil glower, the anger in him evident. "We'll talk to Jackson," Kat said, pulling at the seething Gargoyle, trying to get him to move down the hallway with her. After a moment he relented and followed in her wake.

For a minute.

Then he was putting her behind himself again, leading the way.

"You know, this better be you protecting me," she muttered, "because if this is some medieval the-woman-walks-ten-paces-behind-the-man bullshit, I'm going to be really pissed."

" 'Tis no' bullshite," he said. "I doona want you hurt so 'tis best you remain where I can protect you."

"That's what I thought it was," she said with a soft sigh. "But you can't protect me every minute of every day."

He stopped and turned to look at her. "Aye. I can. 'Tis what I was created tae do. And I'll be loyal tae it and tae you till the day I die. Do you ken that?"

"I . . ." She swallowed. There was something so breathtaking about the intensity of his words. And there was so much feeling behind them as well. To say it made her feel special . . . treasured . . . was an understatement. "All right," she said. Then she touched a hand to his back, urging him onward.

They found Jackson and explained what was happening and what Kamen's request was.

"I'm leery about giving him access to our source material as well," he admitted to them. "But if we want to see this thing off you I don't see any way around it." Jackson frowned in spite of the fact that the lovely redheaded Marissa entered the room and immediately found her place under his arm, snuggling against his body. Watching the two of them was like watching a romantic movie come to life. He was sweet to her, his fingertips touching and then holding her hand, his lips brushing the rise of her cheek as he thought on his problem for a moment. "The fact is, if we want to have any hope of defeating Apep when he decides to come for us, we will need Kamenwati to have full access to all of the material we can provide him. But I am still not sure I trust his motivations completely. He says he is here to help right the wrong he has committed, but there is always the chance that he is working his own agenda for the benefit of the Templars."

"Wait . . . Apep? The demon god? And the Templars are bad. The war you're in. Have I got that right?"

"Yes." Jackson said.

"Why would Kamen want to atone? What'd he do?"

"He resurrected the god Apep while trying to re-awaken his mistress, Odjit," Jackson explained. "He says he regrets this and will work with us to help defeat her. We are gathering strength, and Kamenwati is part of that strength . . . provided he is sincere." He paused thoughtfully. "But there might be another resource besides Kamen that we can use. Grey. Only he isn't here at the moment."

"Grey?" she echoed.

"A Djynn. Very likely the most powerful Djynn in the North American continent. He is ruler of all the Djynn here. There are others just as powerful ruling over the other continents, but we recently came to know him and he has visited us since then, from time to time. He knows that Apep is a force to be reckoned with and might lend a hand if we need him to."

"Might?" she asked Jackson.

"Djynn are notoriously capricious. They always have their own agenda."

"Is that why it's bad to make wishes?"

"Aye, it is," Ahnvil said gravely.

"Then I'm not sure I want to meet a Djynn," she hedged worriedly.

"Doona worry. I willna let him hurt you."

"He sounds much more powerful than you are," she said cautiously, not wanting to insult him but knowing no other way of voicing her opinion on the matter.

"I'm tougher than I look," he said, chucking her under the chin with a curved finger.

"That's saying a lot," she said with a laugh.

"Aye." He turned to Jackson. "So how do we get in touch wi' Grey?"

"There isn't a way. We'll just have to wait. He didn't say when he would be returning, but I got the impression he would not be gone long."

"I hope not. The sooner she's away from here the happier I'll be."

That earned him a smack on the arm. "I told you, I'm not leaving!" Kat cried.

"We'll see," Ahnvil said.

"That means 'We do it my way, woman!'" she scoffed. "I'm not going to let you boss me around. God! You can be so infuriating!" She pushed away from them and, spying a pad and a pen she scooped them up and marched toward the entrance of the house.

"And just where do you think you're goin'?" he demanded to know from her.

"For a walk! And you're not coming with me! I'm just going down to the road and back and I don't need you following me. I have to think about what to say in my next letter to Bella and I also need a break from a lumbering, pigheaded Gargoyle!"

"Lumbering?" he echoed. Then he shook it off. "No. I forbid you tae go. You willna leave this house wi'out me."

"You *forbid* me?" she said, her voice raising enough octaves to make him wince. "No one forbids me from doing anything! And even if I agreed to take someone with me it sure as hell wouldn't be a jackass like you!" She turned her back on him and marched out the door, muttering the word *forbid* under her breath and scoffing.

Ahnvil turned to look over at Jackson and Marissa helplessly, seeking some kind of guidance from them. "Tell her 'tis no' safe for her! She willna listen tae me!"

"She said she wasn't leaving the property, so she should be fine," Jackson said.

"You can't tighten your grip on her," Marissa advised. "She'll just slip through your fingers if you do."

"But 'tis no' safe. Surely you know that!"

"There are Gargoyles all around the property," Marissa reminded him. "And she doesn't have anything anyone would want."

"What abou' the Amulet?" he asked even as the front door was slamming shut. He looked back at it worriedly, seemingly torn between staying and going. "I doona think that attack yesterday was meant by Apep. I think it was Panahasi trying tae get the Amulet back."

"It's true Apep would have sent a stronger force," Jackson said with a sage nod. "And it's likely he would have been in the middle of the fray. Just the same, I could have been the target just as much as it could have been about the Amulet. There's really no telling. But she's mortal and fragile, Ahnvil. *Anything* out in the world could hurt her. You can't protect her from all of it."

"She could bump her head against a door and develop a brain bleed and die," Marissa posited. "There's no way you would ever be able to protect her from something like that. And if you constantly smother her you'll as good as kill her anyway. You have to let her make her own choices, let her choose to take her own risks. The disease she has is dangerous and deadly. She knows what it means to live a life of caution. She won't just throw it away for no reason. Just give her a little time alone. She'll be back in a few minutes."

Ahnvil didn't look happy with that idea. He had begun to fidget the minute the door had shut behind her. It was in his blood to protect that which he felt loyal to. It was almost impossible to fight the impulse.

It made him wonder when, exactly, he had begun to feel so utterly loyal to her. It had happened so gradually. While he wasn't paying any attention. One day he'd been a stranger to her, and the next he couldn't move three feet away from her because his soul was screaming out to him that she needed and deserved protection. A feeling that had only intensified since the attack at the airport . . . and since he had made love to her.

Christ, just thinking about that made him want her again. It reminded him of the way she had felt, the way she had smelled. He had loved the taste of her on his tongue. The feel of her surrounding him when he'd been deep inside of her. He began to grow hard for her right where he stood and he turned away from his Pharaohs with a flush.

Now he wanted to follow after her all the more. But he couldn't, he realized. He couldn't or she'd just grow more and more angry with him. And he didn't want her to be angry with him. He wanted her to forgive him for his boorish ways and maybe let him touch her again.

He couldn't follow her, but he might be able to get someone else that could.

He went off in search of them.

Kat sat down on the porch swing, Karma at her feet, in order to write a note to Bella. It was short and sweet. A simple "We're here, are you?" It seemed like a good place to start. She would check the note in about fifteen minutes and every fifteen minutes after that.

As for these first fifteen minutes, she was going to use them to take a walk. She stuck the note in the front door and leaving her writing implements on the swing, she stepped down off the porch and started walking, Karma close at her side. The driveway was very long, the landscaping cultured and beautiful. Someone had a very green thumb and an eye for making the land around the house look neat and tidy and yet it blended in almost seamlessly with the land that stretched outward beyond them.

She was really feeling like her head was starting to clear by the time she had almost reached the end of the driveway. It was also about the same time she heard footsteps behind her.

She turned and saw a man she hadn't met walking toward her. He was just under six feet tall, had black hair that curled slightly and almost touched his shoulders. He had chocolate-brown eyes and a very lean athletic build.

She sighed.

"He sent you to follow me, didn't he?"

"Mmmyup," the man said with a boyish grin. "I'm Leo. Leo Alvarez."

"Hi, Leo," she said, reaching to shake his hand. She narrowed her eyes on him a little. "Why haven't I met you yet?"

"I was away. Just got back a few hours ago."

"Oh." She paused. "You're different. You're human . . . I mean mortal . . . aren't you?"

"Yes. How can you tell the difference?"

"I don't know. I just can."

"Do I carry myself like I can die any minute?" he asked with another grin.

"No," she said with a laugh. "Like I said, I don't know how I know. If you're mortal, what good could you do if I got into trouble?"

"You'd be surprised," he said mysteriously. Then she found herself thinking he might be able to handle himself after all. *That* was how he carried himself. "So you're the girl who has our boy tied into knots. You look pretty harmless to me."

"I am harmless, believe me." She paused. "He's tied in knots?"

"I've never seen him like this. Mind you, I've only known him a few months, but he always seemed coolheaded. Intense, but coolheaded. Definitely the sort you want at your back in a fight. The only time I can remember him getting hot was when Kamen first came here, and I have to say I know the feeling." He paused and absently rubbed a hand over a spot on his chest. She didn't think he realized he was doing it, but for some reason she knew it was connected to what she was saying to him.

"I'm going to guess and say you were part of Kamen's former damage path as well. I have to say, I don't see . . . That is, he doesn't come off as this evil person."

Leo paused a beat, but only a beat. "I don't trust him, if that's what you mean. I don't think he deserves trust. But he does seem genuinely repentant for what he's done. I think he wants to right his wrongs. But I also feel once he's done that . . . he'll either go back to what he was doing before or just disappear off the face of the earth."

"What he was doing before?"

"Being one of the main leaders of the Templar faction. One of the reasons why they've been at war so long. He brought a lot of power to bear against the Politic, as I understand it."

"What's it like for you?" she asked. "Being human among all these immortals."

"I hold my own," he assured her. "And there are things I can do for them that they can't do for themselves. And my girl is a Nightwalker, too."

"Really?" she looked back to the house as if she could see his girl. "Where is she?"

"Visiting her brother," he said. "She's a Night Angel."

"Black skin, yellow eyes," she said softly.

"Yeah. Ahnvil told you about that?"

"He told me a lot of things. But there're also a lot of things he hasn't told me." She lifted the Amulet into her hand, running it absently up and down the chain. As she did so she headed back toward the house, walking in step with Leo. "And what's it like, being the lover of a Nightwalker?"

"You mean you don't know?" he asked with an amused gleam in his eye.

"Well . . ." She blushed. "Is he a Nightwalker? I mean, I thought he was just a weapon a Nightwalker devised."

That seemed to give him pause. "You know what, I never looked at it that way. I suppose in a way you are right. They've only been around a few hundred years or so. I thought there was seven Nightwalker breeds, but that would make it only six, if I looked at it that way."

"Six? I forgot who they all were. Djynns, Bodywalkers, Night Angels . . ."

"Wraiths."

"Oh yeah! Them."

"Trust me, you don't want to know them. Mysticals are another, though I'm not sure what they are. And Phoenixes. Never seen one of those, either."

"Phoenixes! I think I'd love to see one of those."

"I hear it's very rare. They're a bit reclusive. But they are going to have to get over it because if this god Apep is getting as powerful as I think he is, we're going to need help from every corner."

"I see." She shuddered. "It's so fantastical. Gods and monsters and such. Now that I know they are real, I want to meet all of them. I've already got a phantom of sorts following me around."

"You mean besides the dog?" he asked, giving a purposeful look at Karma.

"Yes, besides the dog," she laughed.

"I heard about that. I'm really curious to see . . ." He trailed off just as they were coming up on the porch. "Can I help you?" he asked, sounding a little stunned.

Kat looked in the direction he was staring and saw nothing. Then she heard the sound of a gun leaving its holster and for the first time she realized he was armed.

"What is it?" she asked tensely.

"A man, and a woman. They just came around the

corner of the house and onto the porch but they came out of nowhere. I was just looking that way a moment ago and there was nothing." Then, speaking to the invisible people he said, "You might want to rethink getting closer to that house, mister." He raised his gun and drew a bead.

And that was when she realized what was happening.

"No! Don't!" she cried. "It's her! The phantom. Ask her what her name is."

"What's your name?" he asked dutifully.

"Bella," Bella said from around her husband, who had stepped in front of her to protect her from the gun being aimed at them. "I'm looking for Kat."

"She's standing right beside me," Leo said, nodding in her direction.

"She can't see me, and I can't see her," Kat said. "You say there's a man with her?"

"Yeah. Kind of looks like me. Same build, same coloring . . . a little taller," Leo said.

"Ask her who she is. Tell her . . . tell her . . ." She floundered a moment, thinking furiously. "Tell her magical people live here. Nightwalkers."

"I am not telling her that!" Leo bit out to what seemed like nobody, from Bella's and Jacob's perspectives.

"Tell her!"

He grumbled. "Magical people live here. Nightwalkers."

Bella's jaw dropped and, frankly, Jacob looked just as stunned. He stepped forward and narrowed his eyes on the Hispanic male. "What kind of Nightwalkers?"

"*We're* Nightwalkers," his wife piped up from behind him. Her husband turned to glare at her. She shrugged, put up her hands and said, "What? Like any of this is normal? Like we're dealing with the average mortal or something? It's a leap of faith."

"He's mortal. I can tell," Jacob said, his preternatural senses making it clear.

"All kinds," Leo said finally. "You're right. I am mortal." His brow furrowed. He looked at Kat. "But so are you. Why can't you see them?"

She shrugged.

"We can't see her, either. But Bella and Kat are able to write to each other."

"I know. I heard," Leo said, slowly lowering his weapon. "So now what?"

"What kind of Nightwalkers?" Bella repeated, stepping as if to go around her husband, but he held her back again.

"What kind are you?" Leo countered.

"He's a Demon and I'm a Druid."

"A Demon?" The gun came up again.

"Bella . . ." Jacob warned.

"But the good kind!" she added hastily.

"There's a good kind?" Leo asked, completely sounding like he didn't believe it for a second.

"Yes," Jacob said. "Your turn."

"Bodywalkers. Not me, but inside the house."

"We've never heard of Bodywalkers," Jacob said with a frown.

"And we've never heard of Demons or Druids. Not as Nightwalkers in any event."

"You said Nightwalkers, as in . . . more than one?"

"Yeah. As in Djynn, Night Angels. More," Leo said cautiously.

"Vampires? Lycanthropes?" Jacob suggested.

"Right," Leo scoffed. "Like they're real." Then a beat went by. Leo seemed to remember that a few months ago none of this had been real to him. "How many do you know about?" he thought to ask.

"Six breeds," Jacob said.

"We have seven . . . or wait . . . maybe just six. Long story," he said at Jacob's questioning look.

"The prophecy!" Bella yelped suddenly.

"What?" Jacob and Leo asked at the same time. "What prophecy?" Leo asked.

"'. . . And so it will come to pass in the forward times that the nations of the Nightwalkers will be shattered, driven apart, and become strangers to one another,'" Bella began to recite. "'Hidden, by misfortune and by purpose, these twelve nations will come to cross-purposes and fade from each other's existence. In the forward times these nations will face toil and struggle unlike any time before and only by coming together once more can they hope to face the evil that will set upon them. But they are lost to one another . . . and so will remain lost, until a great enemy is defeated . . . and a new one resurrects itself . . .' It's from the Lost Scroll of Kindred. I found it not too long ago. I think . . . I think there's something keeping us from seeing each other."

"But Kat isn't a Nightwalker," Leo said. "So that shoots that theory all to hell. Unless . . ." He looked at Kat, his eyes falling to the Amulet. "Unless it's that Amulet you're wearing." Leo slowly put his weapon back in its holster and held out his empty hands. "Look, maybe you should come in the house and meet some of the others. Maybe they can see you."

As it turned out, by the time all introductions were done, only Max, the other mortal in the group, was able to see the newly arrived couple. Everyone, including Kamen, Max, and Leo, was sitting in the main living area and Max and Leo were taking turns translating between the two kinds of Nightwalkers.

"The scroll must mean our six breeds of Nightwalkers can't see your six . . . for some reason," Bella said. "Although, from what you said there's only Bodywalkers and Gargoyles here. And you don't think Gargoyles are one of the breeds, so why can't they see us, either?"

"Because they are made from the energy, the Bodywalker spirit, of their forger," Kamen said. "If we can't see then it stands to reason they can't see. I have to say, this has all the earmarks of a curse. It feels unnatural like a curse."

Kat fingered her pendant. "Like this is cursed," she said.

Ahnvil was standing beside Kat's chair and his hand went to the back of her neck in a gesture of comfort.

"If this is a curse then there is a way to lift it," Kamen said. "Just as somewhere there is a way to lift the curse of that Amulet. It's just going to take time and research to find out what it is and how to lift it."

"We can't lift it unless we know first the nature of it," Ahnvil said.

"Yes."

"So together there are twelve Nightwalker nations. Six have no idea the other six exist . . . until now. Until Kat," Bella said.

"Yes. Until Kat," Kamen said thoughtfully. "Docia, I want to see if the other breeds are blind to this couple. Can you get SingSing here? SingSing is a Djynn we know," he said aloud in explanation.

"Sure. She said all I have to do is put on her scarf and she'll know I need her." Docia rose and hurried off to her bedroom. A few minutes later she returned, wearing a lovely colorful, silvery scarf. She was a bit breathless for her effort. "I don't know how long it'll take . . ."

"Well then, I guess we just wait until she comes," Leo said.

"Let me make sure I have this right," Bella said. "Mistrals, Lycanthropes, Vampires, Demons, Druids, and Shadowdwellers can't see or hear Bodywalkers, Djynn, Mysticals, Phoenixes, Night Angels, and Wraiths."

"In theory. We'll have a better idea when SingSing gets here."

"You rrrrrang?" a perky voice asked on a rolling *r*. A moment later a diminutive young woman with corkscrew ginger curls appeared in the center of the room. "Ta-da!" She snickered. "That never gets old." She looked around the room. "Jeez. Why so serious?"

"SingSing," Ram spoke up, "how many people do you see in the room?"

"Is this a trick question?" she asked, climbing up onto the arm of one of the chairs and perching there like a bird. As a stunned Kat watched, a small dragon head peeked out of the nest of curls adorning the little woman's head. "I see eleven."

Everyone looked at each other.

"Name them."

"What? Why?"

"Just do it," Ram asked in a pained tone.

"Fine fine. Crab-ass Ram. Sweet Docia. Jackson, Marissa, Max, Leo. Ihron. Hey, handsome." She gave him an exaggerated batting of her lashes. "Girl, I Don't Know. Ahnvil. By the way, I am so mad at you. I thought I was your girl. And there you are cheating on me with another Djynn. Kamen and Stohn. Is this a game? I like games. Are we all going to hide now? Who's it?"

"You don't see a dark-haired couple other than tha—? Wait." Ahnvil said. "What other Djynn? You mean Grey?"

"No, Grey isn't here. And unless you're gay, I don't have to worry about him. I mean the Djynn you're all touchy-feely with over there." She pointed to Kat.

Djynn?

"But I'm not a—" Kat looked even more perplexed than everyone else. "I'm human."

"Mmm, mostly. But you're definitely a Djynn. Half-sies. Not wholesies. Ooo . . . some naughty Djynn musta banged your momma. No offense to your momma. I'm sure she was quite bangable."

"My—but . . . my mother? *Mom*?" Kat was entirely incredulous.

"Oh, she probably had no idea. It's against the rules to *you know* with humans"—she pumped her fist in and out—"but it's not unheard of."

"That's why I can't see her!" Kat cried. "I'm an effing *Nightwalker*??"

"The sun! That's why you're allergic to the sun. Why you blister!" Ahnvil said with no small amount of shock.

"Well, sure," SingSing said. "I would think that might happen."

"But then how could I talk to Bella?" Kat wondered. "Because I'm a half-breed?"

"Talk to who now?" SingSing asked.

"Bella," Ahnvil said, then rapidly explained the situation.

"Or because of the Amulet," Kamen put in. "It's helping you to see partly beyond the curse."

"Wow. Curses. Spells. Amulets. Lions, tigers, and bears, oh my!" SingSing said. She poked the dragon head until it disappeared back into her hair.

"I have a headache," Ahnvil grumbled. "She gives me a headache."

"Humph, I know when I'm not wanted," SingSing said with a pout. She reached up and with a snap of her fingers she disappeared. Then an echoing, "Ta-da!" was heard.

"Great, you scared her off," Leo said dryly. "We learned more from her in the past minute than we have in the past hour."

"Sorry," Ahnvil sighed.

"Djynn. I'm not weird, I'm just a Djynn," Kat was marveling.

"Partly. I wonder if that means you can use magic," Kamen mused.

"Magic!" Kat gasped.

"Djynns derive their powers from objects that harbor magic. Like the Amulet," Kamen said. "It's imbued with magic. You could probably use it to perform a trick . . . like maybe SingSing's disappearing act."

"Oh. No. No disappearing," she said hastily. "I might not be able to reappear again."

"I can teach you some magic that would—" Kamen began.

"No!" Ahnvil cut him off sharply, putting himself between Kamen and Kat. "You'll no' teach her anythin'!"

"Better she be taught than to do something accidentally that she has no control over," Kamen said darkly. "Rather like putting on an Amulet without recognizing its power. She put it on for a reason. It called to her. Attracted her. But instead of using it as a power resource she put it on and now is stuck wearing it."

"I doona care. If she has to learn then it will be from SingSing or Grey or *anybody* else but you."

"Whoa. Hostile much?" Bella asked when Max finished interpreting him. "I don't mean to get in the middle of this, but clearly she couldn't see us, either. What do we do now? I mean, maybe it's because I'm half human and half Druid just like she's half human and half Djynn that we can sorta talk to each other. But that doesn't change the fact that none of our world knows about yours and there's something standing in the way of it. And the only people who can communicate with us are human mortals . . . who none of the races I know have told about themselves so on our end it's out of the question. So maybe one of you guys"—she indicated Leo and Max—"can help us out? We need to contact the Demon King the Vampire Prince, the Lycanthrope Queen. There's a lot of people out there who need to learn about this."

"On our end as well," Jackson said. "We'll need to get in touch with Grey, the Night Angels. The Phoenixes, too . . . although it is beyond me how to do that. Same goes for the Mysticals. Do they even have a leadership?"

"They do."

The room turned as one to see a new male had entered the room, although how he had entered was a mystery to Kat.

"Grey," Ahnvil said, answering the question. Another Djynn! Someone she could potentially learn a lot from, Kat thought with no small amount of eagerness. Someone Ahnvil already said he would not mind her learning from. Someone she suspected had to be incredibly powerful to be the leader of the Djynn in all of North America.

After Grey was brought up to speed he was utterly intrigued. "Something beyond my scope of power. Fascinating," he said, only supporting Kat's perception that she would have a lot to learn from him about being a Djynn. "SingSing told me to come to you, but didn't mention why. I am so glad she did. She's a good girl. Always able to tell when she is over her head." He eyed Kat thoughtfully. "I've heard of Adoma's Amulet," he said, moving closer to her and lifting the object into his hand. "Yes, it's really quite powerful. Why ever would you want to take it off?"

"Because I *can't*," she said dryly.

"Humans. Always wanting what they can't have only to realize they don't want what they've gotten after all."

"Well, luckily I can always put it back *on* again once I figure out how to get it *off*," Kat said.

"Are you so certain of that?" he asked archly.

Kat wasn't certain about anything anymore. She was in this surreal new world where she didn't know a damn thing about herself . . . where she was even more normal then she thought she was all of this time.

"Look at me," Grey instructed, touching her under her chin and lifting it. He examined her on one side and then the other with his eyes. "Sun sensitive?" he asked.

"Very," Kat said.

"For a full-breed Djynn, we turn to smoke at the touch of the sun. You blister and burn because you need to learn how to voluntarily become smoke. You have enough power for it, I believe, but we will only know in time. It will have to be the first thing you learn. In order to protect yourself."

Kat gaped at him a long moment. "Cool." That was all she could think of to say in response.

"As for the Mysticals, I have the Empress of the Mysticals in my care. In fact, Leo and his Night Angel helped to rescue her from her captives."

"You mean the winged *horse*?" Leo said, gaping at him. "She was an Empress?"

"Yes. Is. It is taking her some time to recover from the poison they were giving her . . . the eggs. Mysticals cannot eat eggs. It freezes them into either their mystical form or their human form, depending on what state they are in at the time. The Tsar of the Phoenixes will also want to know about this. I recommend we all inform these Nightwalkers of the curse and then, perhaps, we can figure out a way among us to lift it. And if their prophecy is correct, a great evil is upon us and we will need to be in tandem in order to fight it off."

"Even the Wraiths?" Jackson asked dubiously. Wraiths were pure evil in his book.

"We'll cross that bridge when we come to it," Grey said.

"Do you think it's Apep? The great evil?" Docia asked.

"Perhaps. The thing about prophecy is it is often unclear how to interpret it until after it is too late . . . or has run its course."

"Agreed," Kamen said. "It would seem I would best serve this action by researching the magics and prophecies."

"There we are again," Ahnvil said harshly. "With you trying tae get at our knowledge stores. You're pushing pretty damn hard for it, are you no'?"

"It's what I'm best at. If you don't want me to do my spellwork, then what good am I to you?"

"None at all," Ahnvil said with dark punctuation.

Kamen turned to lift a questioning brow at Jackson.

"Very well," Jackson relented. "You could hardly do any more harm than Apep can."

"I've told you," Kamen said quietly. "I brought this evil onto this earth and I will not rest until I have eradicated it. I know my duty here. I also know you have little reason to trust me." He looked pointedly at Ahnvil. "But it has been a long time since you were in my care. Things have changed."

"Your care? Your bloody *care*?"

Kat leapt up and put herself in between Ahnvil and Kamenwati, probably the only reason why Ahnvil's hands were not presently around Kamen's throat.

"You. Come with me," she commanded, grabbing up his hand. "All of you," she pointed to the room. "Talk among yourselves and figure this out."

She then pulled Ahnvil out of the room and headed for the stairs. When she had him in his rooms at last, she shut the door hard behind them. Then, hands on her hips, she frowned at him.

"Look, I get that he pisses you off. I get that you hate him. You have every reason to. But you have to see the bigger picture here."

"No, I doona! I—"

"Hush! I'm talking! You will listen to me or . . . or . . . or there will not be a spectacular blowjob in your future. Got it?"

Oh, he obviously got it all right. His jaw dropped nearly to the ground for several beats, and then his eyes darkened with what could only be described as pure, blistering desire.

"Spectacular?" he repeated, moving slowly in her direction.

"Out-freakin'-standing," she promised with a lift of her chin. "But only if you stop being such a thickheaded pain in the butt. I just found out I'm a Nightwalker, like, ten minutes ago. And then I found out I can learn how to turn to smoke! Do you have any idea what that feels like? It's really fricken scary, that's what it feels like! So instead of being all mad and grumpy and stuff, can you please please *please* help me out here?"

Ahnvil had been standing there, fists clenched, body ramrod straight, but at the sound of the pleading and desperation in her voice he sighed and relaxed, his hands falling open.

"Of course I can. But I have tae tell you, I doona trust Grey all that much either. I always feel like he knows more than he's letting on. I dinna like the way he was looking at you."

"Well, be that as it may, I need him. I need him or SingSing or somebody to teach me how to be . . . to be a Djynn. God, I hear myself say it and I can't even believe it. To be honest I'm starting to think I'm back at home in my little bed having, like, the coolest dream *ever.*"

"I'd much rather have you here," he said, his voice rich and low. "In *my* bed."

The remark made her eyes widen a little, but then she felt herself smiling slowly. Naughtily. "Oh, really?" she asked.

"Yes, really."

She moved forward, her body falling against the intense warmth of his as her eyes drew up slowly to meet his amber ones. "I wonder . . . How would you like to make love to a Djynn?"

He chuckled at that. "That's a bit like asking me if I want that spectacular blowjob. 'Tis what I would call a no-brainer."

"I would call it that, too," she said, her eyes lighting

with merry mischief. "So which will it be? Door number one"—she reached to run drifting fingertips up the length of his fly—"Or door number two?" She reached next for his hand and drew it up over her belly, over her ribs, and then settled the weight of her breast in his palm.

"Christ," he muttered, the light in his eyes nothing short of virulent fire. "Do I have tae choose? Why canna I have both?"

"So greedy," she said with an exaggerated pout. Then she smiled. "Okay, you talked me into it." She reached for his belt buckle, her fingers nimble as she unhitched the two sides of it. The hand on her breast tightened briefly, as if he couldn't help himself, but then he turned his knuckles to her and ran them up the length of her breastbone. He traveled up her throat as she pulled his belt free and was touching gentle fingers to her lips as she reached to unbutton his fly.

"I doona know if I can even bear the idea of it. I think of your mouth on me and—" He grabbed hold of her hand and turned her palm in toward his body. He rubbed the heel of her hand tightly down the length of a very hard erection. "Just the idea of it and I'm randy enough tae come in my pants like the greenest lad in the township. You're too new tae me for me tae have an ounce of control. I'm afraid I'll . . . I doona want tae hurt you."

"You won't hurt me. You'll let me do this, you'll let me give you all the pleasure I know how to give, and then you're going to return the favor. And we're both going to love every. Single. Minute." She leaned in and kissed his mouth in punctuation with the last three words.

"Oh, I doona doubt that, Kat lass. No' for a second. I—" Ahnvil stopped before saying he loved every single thing about her. Love was a very strong word to use, and a man shouldn't use it lightly. He didn't want to lay false groundwork, giving her ideas about the future that just might not be possible. The future was a dark, murky place. He didn't know what he would have to offer her in it. He barely knew how to keep himself in the present from day to day. So much of his life came out of the past. Out of his mistakes and misfortunes. Out of his hate and his anger. He wasn't even sure he would know how to give a lass things like love and contentment. Didn't one have to be content before one could offer it to someone else?

Oh, but she was tempting him with far better things then contentment, he thought as she drew down the zipper to his jeans. She reached with strong little hands to push his pants down off his hips. He felt her nails scraping gently against his skin as she bared his backside and then his thighs. His erection had fallen free of the denim and, as she worked his jeans free, her body brushed against him again and again and again. She dropped to her knees and guided his feet free of his pants. He was forced to bear the gorgeous sight of her in that submissive serving position. Then she looked up. First into his eyes and then at the jutting length of his erection. She reached out and touched gentle fingertips about midway along the shaft, then drew them slowly down and then back up the length of him. It was nothing, a touch of so little consequence, and yet it made him tighten and harden even more. He had to touch himself, to squeeze himself as though in warning, to try and control the intensity of his reaction. If the lightest of touches could spin him so out of control, what would the feel of her kiss do to him?

"No. Let me," she scolded him softly, taking his hand and drawing it away. Then she imitated the touch he'd used, squeezing him at the base of his cock.

"Jesus," he groaned, his hand feeling lost in the open air until he finally rested it atop her head, his fingers burrowing into the dark roots. *Be gentle,* he warned himself. *Doona hurt her.*

She was, he decided, the most beautiful thing he'd ever seen. Not just because of what she was doing to him, but because she was genuinely *beautiful,* with her bourbon eyes and her mink-colored hair, her berry-red lips and lightly freckled pale skin. He was glad she couldn't be touched by the sun. He wouldn't trade her porcelain prettiness for all the world.

She wrapped her hand fully around him, drawing up to her fullest height on her knees. But their heights were so disparate that she could not reach him. All he would get was the feel of her breath washing over him. Slowly, allowing her to continue to keep him in her wee hand, he knelt down, his knees spreading wide on either side of hers. She smiled at him and he thought he might die from the way it made him feel. He felt suddenly invincible. Oh, he had learned what it meant to feel invulnerable as a powerful Gargoyle, but with the smallest of courtesies she made him feel that he was able to conquer worlds. She leaned forward drawing him up to her lips. At the last moment she stuck out her tongue and touched it to him instead of just kissing him with her lips. Light exploded into his vision and he was convinced the only thing possibly better was when he was deep inside of her.

She slowly licked him, as if he were a piece of hard candy, and everything in his body grew tenser and tighter as pleasure washed over him. His hand in her hair fisted against her scalp, crushing strands into submission. It was an attempt to keep himself from pushing her forward in an endeavor to hasten her torture to a better point of pleasure. But he didn't want to make her do anything before she was ready. Not when everything was so new and he didn't yet know all of her boundaries as a lover. But he was learning more and more as every second ticked by.

She licked him down to the base of his shaft and then back up several times, each stroke bringing more nerves alive than he'd ever realized he had. Her tongue toyed against the head, sweeping away the welling fluid that seeped from it more and more with each passing moment.

"Gods above, Kat lass, you're killing me."

That made her smile with an unholy satisfaction. And that made him all the more impatient to have her. He was just about to grab her and throw her to the floor when suddenly she opened her mouth and took him inside with a sweep of her tongue.

Had she said spectacular? It was stellar. Utter nirvana. Now he knew he had never felt anything like it in his life. What made it so different? What was it that brought him to his knees even though he was already kneeling to her?

Kat. It was all Kat. She was beyond everything a woman should be. So brave in the face of what she had thought of as a crippling disease, making her way in the world as best she could when the world looked at her with cruel, judgmental eyes. She had hidden away to protect herself, and yet it was a defiance, too. A way of saying she could live her life on her own terms and screw what everyone else thought.

And yet he knew she thought she was weak. That she had let them win by forcing her to run and hide. He saw it differently. Very differently. And her bravery and brilliance was just as bold as the way she held him in her mouth.

"Kat . . . oh, my sweet Kat, you have tae stop," he groaned, as she worked him into her mouth again and again and yet again. "You'll have me spending in another minute and I want tae be inside you when I do."

She responded by moving quicker, taking him deeper,

sucking at him a little harder. Now both of his hands were clutching into her hair and in spite of himself he was beginning to thrust up against her palate more and more with every second.

"Kat, I'm going tae—" He was going to come. He knew it with barely an instant before she made it happen. He roared out with pleasure, letting go of her so she could move free of him if she chose to. But she did not. She took everything from him. His seed. His pleasure. His sanity. He was humbled by it, even as he was drained by it. He was sucking for air, barely able to keep upright on his knees as she pulled away from him at last. He nearly fell over at the sight of the bright satisfaction in her eyes. She was entirely pleased with herself, and had every right to be.

He reached for her, turned her onto her back on the floor, threw a leg over her, and went nose to nose with her.

"Your turn," he rumbled fiercely.

He kissed her then, thrilling at the taste of himself on her tongue, sensual and salty and sweet all at once. When he came up for air she was flushed and pretty and all things irresistible. "Come and give us that tongue again," he said before touching his lips to hers and kissing her as deeply as he already had, and yet it felt as if he never had before. It was like that every time he kissed her.

And that was when he realized he was falling. Fast. Too fast. And too hard.

Panic touched him. He couldn't do this. Compared to her with her kindness, generosity, and boundless bravery, he had very little to offer her. Danger? Threat? A life where he would risk his life day in and day out to protect the lives of others with no regard for himself and the woman who would be waiting for him to return?

He drew away from her. From her mouth, from her entire body, rising up on his knees as he tried to catch his breath.

"What is it?" she asked, sitting up and looking at him with innocent, questioning eyes.

"I have to . . . There's something . . . I forgot to . . ." All of it fell flat as he grabbed his pants off the floor and pulled them on with as much haste as was possible. "I'll be back soon," he said once he was fully dressed. But it was a lie. He couldn't come back. He couldn't risk the emotions he knew were building inside of him. They were not his to give. His life, his duty, had been given up to Menes, the man he had sworn to protect in exchange for the energy he so willingly provided to his touchstone.

No. He had nothing to give her except maybe sex and amusement, but it had gone beyond that already. He had to be honest with himself and admit it. He could only pray it had not gone beyond it for Kat as well. She wasn't a casual sort of woman. She took these things very seriously. She would not give herself to any man lightly. If he had learned anything about her it was that she didn't do things lightly.

Even as he walked out the door, unable to meet her eyes or even look at her face, he knew he was hurting her. She didn't realize it yet, but he was hurting her. But there was nothing he could do about that.

Nothing at all.

CHAPTER SEVENTEEN

It wasn't until twenty minutes had passed before Kat began to get the picture that Ahnvil wasn't coming back. *Well*, she thought, *perhaps he's being held up by something important.* Or maybe he'd sensed some kind of threat. Hadn't someone told her that Gargoyles had a built in alarm system that had them sensing threats before they even fully materialized?

Picking herself up off the floor, she went to the window. It faced the front of the house. Looking outside she saw nothing more than a woman she had not met yet playing with a dog. She was pretty and tall and, like everyone in this place, really attractive. She was realizing that the perk of being a Bodywalker was that you got to pick and choose who you came back as. That included looks. But that was understandable because good looks got much further in this shallow world of theirs. That was a fact.

But the playing woman told her that there was no obvious threat taking place. At loose ends, she decided to go back downstairs and look for him, trying to figure out what had happened. When she passed through the living area it was devoid of the gathering she had left behind. Now she was curious on two fronts. She thought one should have been more important than the other, but for some reason it was Ahnvil she fixated on.

But after nearly twenty minutes of searching, she did not find him. Instead, she ran into Kamen in the kitchen. Full-bodied ran into. She was so preoccupied that she crashed into him like a crash-test dummy. He reached out and steadied her.

"Oh. Hi," she said distractedly.

"Hello, little Djynn."

"I'm sorry but . . . have you seen Ahnvil? You know, big Gargoyle. Hates your guts."

"Yes," he said with amusement, "I am aware of who he is. No, I have not seen him." He studied her. "You left earlier. Are you not curious as to what transpired afterward?"

She nodded to him.

"Leo Alvarez has accompanied the new Nightwalker couple off the grounds. They will return to their Demon King . . . Noah, I believe is his name . . . and they will tell them of finding us and this curse that seems to be separating us. Eventually I believe we will need to figure out a way to dispel this curse. It will not be an easy solution. It might take years before we discover it. Unfortunately, I do not believe we have years. Fortunately, Menes has allowed me permission to begin to research this matter on my own. He has finally come to realize that I am his best hope in dispelling this problem."

"I don't doubt it." Kat let go of her distractions and focused on the man in front of her. "Did you mean what you said? That you can help me learn about who I am?"

"You would be much better served to ask Grey for assistance in that regard. He knows what it means to be a Djynn. Far better than I do. Though I admit, he is mercurial at best. Most Djynn are. Between him and perhaps SingSing . . ."

"I get the feeling I won't get anywhere with SingSing.

She isn't the instructive type. I'm not entirely sure she's all there." She whirled her finger around her ear.

"Perhaps," he said with a small smile. She wondered if the man had ever laughed. He seemed incredibly serious. Then again, she would be serious, too, if she were under house arrest and untrusted by the entire household. She couldn't imagine what that would be like. Here she was a total stranger and already she had been trusted with high levels of information. Before they had even known anything about her. Based solely on the word of her Gargoyle.

"Can I ask you something?"

"Why would you stop now?" he queried.

"Oh. Right." She gave him a self-effacing laugh. "Well, I was wondering. Do you regret anything you've done . . . I mean outside of this whole resurrecting a demon god thing."

He raised a brow. "Is that not enough?" he asked.

"I suppose it is."

"I am going to guess you are asking if I regret making and owning Gargoyles." At her nod he said, "I have not made a Gargoyle since creating Stohn, and even he was not something I wished to do. After so many escapees I realized there was nothing I could do to breed in true loyalty. My compatriots are convinced otherwise, but I did not need to have my head bashed against the wall in order to see the writing upon it. A Gargoyle caught escaping was put to death without question. And escaping Gargoyle tells you he no longer has loyalty to you, that there is a flaw in the forging process. At least, that was the general belief. I have other abilities that if brought to bear could reel an escapee in, had I truly wanted to."

"And you didn't want to?"

"Better they escape than stab me in the back while I slept. Once they attempt escape it is very clear they will be focused on nothing else for the rest of their days, rendering them useless to me."

"You are so cold about it," she said with a frown.

"I am merely stating facts. It does not follow that I approve of my actions in retrospect."

"Oh. So you regret them?"

"Regret applies emotion. I do not feel that strongly about it one way or another. But I can see the flaws in my thinking."

"And I can see why Ahnvil hates your guts," she said with another frown.

"Would you rather I affect an emotion that does not exist? I would much rather be honest with you."

"I would much rather you feel something. Anything. You don't feel anything about anything from what I can see."

"I feel, I assure you. And quite deeply. I just do not feel appropriately according to you on this topic. And I do not cast my feelings about like one strews trash upon the ground. Emotion must be kept, savored, and contemplated. I have thrown emotion too easily and that is how we have ended up facing off with such powerful evil. And I have, I realize belatedly, thrown it in the wrong direction. Emotion clouded my judgment. A mistake I will not repeat."

"You felt a great deal for this Odjit, didn't you?"

He looked uncomfortable with the topic, for the first time showing her a glimmer of the emotion he was trying to hold in check. "I felt for the ideal. She was . . . not what I thought she was. Had I . . ." He trailed off and shook his head. "What I felt is of no consequence. It is not real. That is what matters."

"All right. I accept that. Regret is regret, whether you think it requires a deep show of emotion or not. You wish you had done otherwise. Whether in hindsight or not, doesn't matter. That's what regret is. Looking back and seeing what we've done is wrong. Now, let's get back to this magic thing." She took hold of the Amulet and lifted it into his view. "Tell me about this."

"It came with a prophetic verse. I will try to recall it exactly. 'The slave, born of the infinite Nightwalkers, will set free the power within. The one that harnesses Adoma's Amulet will have such power as to make a god weep.'"

"Wow. I still can't get over that."

"Indeed. Would you like to know how I am interpreting this?"

She nodded eagerly.

"I believe that the prophecy has come to pass. The slave has set the Amulet free. The Gargoyle liberated it from those fools who thought they could use it to their own will. And the one who will harness the Amulet is you."

"Me?" She knew she looked as incredulous as she sounded.

"You," he confirmed. "Clearly the Amulet has chosen its owner. I donned the Amulet myself and it did nothing for me, no matter how much I put it through its paces."

"But you said . . ."

"I had forgotten I had tried that. Not until later. And learning you are part Djynn has altered my perception of things. So that means you are special in some way. Very likely it has to do with you being a Djynn. Now, what the Amulet does . . . that I cannot say. That is for you to discover. Perhaps when you learn to draw the power from your niks you will learn how to hold that power to your will."

"Wait. Nik?"

"A nik is an object of magical power, either living or dead. Inanimate niks are called niknaks. Living ones are called nikkis. This is a nik." He pointed to the pendant. "What happened when you tried to remove it?"

"Well . . . when I tried it was like . . . I couldn't make

myself do it. When Ahnvil tried it threw me across the room to get me away from him."

"Ah. And yet you were not hurt?"

"No. Just got the wind knocked out of me."

"It protected you from injury and protected you from being divested of it. It would seem it has your best interests at heart. Don't try and remove it. It's too valuable to you while on you."

"I told you, I *can't* remove it."

"You can't remove it *now*. There will come a time when you will learn how. And that is when others will seek to take it from you. There are always others who will seek to take your niks from you. Especially other Djynns. You see, as soon as a Djynn touches a nik, it becomes theirs . . . until another Djynn touches it. However they can touch all they like while you wear it and nothing will come of it. It may not even allow them to come close enough to touch."

"You know, is it possible for something to be so cool and so terrifying all at once?"

"Clearly so. But you are not as afraid as you profess."

"No, I'm not," she said, realizing his insight was correct. "I think it's because all my life the human world felt a little bit *off* to me. I didn't know what it was then, but in hindsight I guess I do now. I wasn't meant to be in the human world." She laughed. "You know, there isn't a kid alive who doesn't wish they had superpowers at some point. I'm not yet sure if it'll be all it's cracked up to be. But all my life I've just dealt with being a square peg in a round hole. Maybe as I grow more powerful . . . more able to control what I can do . . . maybe then I'll start to feel normal."

"But you are a half-breed," he seemed to feel it was necessary to point out. "Even Grey knows it won't be as easy as it sounds. Mixing gene pools is a frightening variable when it comes to Nightwalkers and humans. It's why we don't do it very often. Usually our worlds don't even coincide enough for us to be attracted to humans, but there is always an exception. You realize you cannot share this with your mother?"

"I-I hadn't thought about it." She bit her lip.

"The less people who know about our world the better. It is a rare human being who can cope."

She thought about her mother, the woman who couldn't tolerate a new cell tower being built a half a mountain away from her, and realized he was correct. She would never understand. Hell, she probably wouldn't believe her and would try to have her committed. Mom, bless her heart, was strong. She had to be to raise a child of darkness, as children with her disease were called. She had gone to bat and fought more times for Kat than even Kat had probably realized. To add one more thing to the mix just might be one thing too many.

Or maybe she would feel the same sense of relief that Kat felt. The same sense of finally understanding where she fit in the world.

She shook her head at her own thoughts. No. Kamen was right. It was better left unsaid.

"I wanted to hate you, you know," she told him. "Because Ahnvil does. Because he has good reason to."

"And yet you don't?"

"No. I pity you. You've made terrible mistakes and yet aren't even sure if you know the right way to atone for them. You want to. I can tell you want to. But you don't know how. That's why you keep pushing for this research. You think that this is the way to absolution."

"Perhaps. Or perhaps I realize there is no absolution. That nothing I do or say will ever make up for lifetimes worth of sins. Ask your Gargoyle friend. There is nothing I can do that will ever make what I did to him right in his eyes."

"No. I don't suppose there is. So . . ." She looked

around, checking to see if Ahnvil was in earshot before leaning in closer to him. "Teach me one little thing I can do. I just want one little thing that proves to me I can do what everybody says I can do. I just . . . I mean I'm sure it's true . . . but . . ."

"But you want to see it for yourself. To make it real."

"Yeah. To make it real."

"Very well. Pick up the Amulet and hold it in your hand."

She did so readily, gripping her hand around it tightly.

"Ease up," he said, resting a hand over hers and coaxing her to relax. "Now, inside the very heart of this Amulet is power. It's like when I do spellwork. I have to seek inside of myself and then seek inside of the spell and somehow bridge the two together. The more experience you develop, the faster you will be able to build the bridge. Each item will require a new bridge, each bridge unique and constructed in its own way. For now, focus on this item. Imagine yourself stringing lines from the heart inside of your chest to the heart inside the Amulet."

She nodded as she did so, afraid to speak. There was something about the intonation of his voice, the reverence of it that both excited and soothed her. She felt herself stringing those lines, but it took a great deal of focus to do it so she closed her eyes.

"Once you feel those lines are true, lay planking across them. Like that of a bridge. And with every plank you will take a step closer and closer to the heart of the Amulet's power."

She nodded as she slowly struggled to do what he asked. Sometimes it was easy to lay the plank. Other times she would take a step, feel unsteady, and have to step back again or . . . or it felt like she would fall away and have to start all over again. And yet, before too much time had passed she envisioned herself growing closer and closer to her goal.

"Almost there," she whispered.

"Once you reach your goal, I want you to open your eyes."

"I can't. I'll lose it," she said, her voice still soft, as if speaking too loudly would ruin everything she'd achieved. It very probably would. She didn't want to have to start all over again.

"No. You won't. You have a strong will. I can sense it on you. The way you have lived your life in spite of the light has forced you to be strong. You will learn this control with ease because of it. Slowly open your eyes, all the while holding your bridge together."

Kat could almost feel the difference when she touched the heart of the Amulet. It was like receiving a rush of energy, like a sudden breath of fresh air blowing back her hair. She didn't realize that was exactly what happened, her hair stirring wildly for that brief instant.

"Very good. Come now," he urged.

She slowly opened her eyes and he reached across the counter for a ceramic coffee mug. Placing it in the center of the counter he said, "Try and levitate the mug from the counter. Levitation, like turning to smoke, is one of the easiest tricks a Djynn can master. This should be simple for you. Slowly push the energy from the heart toward the mug, wrap it around as if you were grasping hold of it with a lasso and then use it to lift it up. Don't worry about grace or keeping it upright, just lift it."

By the time she felt she had come into contact with the mug she was actually growing a little tired. She was tensed from head to toe, trying to hold on to her focus.

"Breathe and relax," he coaxed her.

And slowly, if only by a few millimeters at a time, the mug began to lift off the countertop.

"What the bloody hell is going on here?!"

The sharp command in Ahnvil's voice was punctuated by the sudden explosion of the coffee mug. It shattered into pieces, each one a sudden projectile. Kamen flinched, throwing up a hand that was immediately peppered with sharp debris. As for Kat, it looked at though the pieces fell just shy of hitting her.

"I have told you tae stay away from her!" Ahnvil reached for Kamen, grabbing him by the front of his shirt. "She does not need your black, manipulative lessons!"

"Stop it!" she cried, shoving her body in between the two men.

Kamen hit Ahnvil hard in the chest, pushing him off himself just as she was doing so. She could see bright red streaks of blood smearing over Ahnvil's shirt.

"I am tired of you whipping me like a bad puppy!" Kamen growled. "If you want to throw down with me I am happy to oblige! But you are not this woman's keeper and she is free to do what she wants. And what she wants is to learn how to control her power!"

"Why you fucking weasel!" Ahnvil seethed, launching himself forward once more to go for Kamen's throat. "I'll kill you where you stand for even looking at her!"

"Enough!" she shouted at him, as up in his face as she could possibly manage from her height and in the storm of his rage.

"You doona understand the man you're dealing wi', Kat! Doona make the mistake of thinking anything abou' him is worth trusting. He is evil, pure and simple and I'm going tae—"

"What? Kill him?" she demanded. "You couldn't do it before and for the same reasons you can't do so now! Whatever you think of him, you *need* him. You need him to fight Apep and to figure out this curse thing! And it should count for something," she said, her voice coming down as he stopped pushing his body against hers as though he were going to lunge for Kamen's throat at any second, "that he's even here at all. He could have just as easily walked away, never to be heard from again, letting you all get spanked by Apep without any warning whatsoever." She pushed him back even more. "And Kamen's right. You don't own me and you can't tell me what to do or who to pick to teach me how to do this stuff." She pointed to the cup. "That was the very first thing I've ever done as a Djynn! And it was going great until you came in here and went ballistic!"

Kat turned her back on him and reached for Kamen's arm, realizing it and his face had been peppered by shards of ceramic and were now bleeding freely.

"It will be fine," Kamen assured her. "I will remove the debris and it will heal in short order." His hand covered hers to reassure her there was no reason for her to worry.

"Doona touch her," Ahnvil hissed, "if you are wanting tae keep that hand. You doona need both of them tae help us fix your fuckup."

"That's it!" Kat whirled around and faced him angrily, "I've had it! You won't let people help me, you won't even let them touch me, and you don't even have any right! Especially not after you just left me to my own devices for reasons I'm not all that sure were all that important!" Unable to help herself, she threw all her weight behind a punch into his shoulder. Then another. She knew she was as ineffectual as a fly, but she couldn't seem to help herself. She began crying by the fourth time she hit him and she didn't even know why. Finally she shoved at him, shoved him out of the way as much as she could with her tiny stature and suddenly he moved, as though she were his size and had shoved into him like a linebacker. With much surprise, he was pushed back hard into a near wall. Far enough out of her way to allow her to pass, running out of the house.

Ahnvil looked at Kamen with shock apparent in his amber eyes. He had felt that push from head to toe, not just in his midsection like she had physically done. What she had done was more. It was power. Pure power.

"What have you done tae her?" he asked Kamen, his voice low and terrible.

"It was done the day she was born. It has been there all along. Only now she has a tool to access it. And I would be careful," Kamen warned. "She shattered that cup because she is raw and inexperienced and *powerful*. Halfbreed or no, she will be a powerful Djynn once she starts to acquire more niks."

"Your lessons will stop. She will learn from Grey or from—"

"SingSing? Let me know how that works out for you," Kamen said dryly. "If she asks me to tutor her then I will. Threaten me all you like, it is her choice, not yours. Your issues with me are outside of this subject. Are you interested in fighting it out? I'm happy to oblige."

Ahnvil clenched his hands into fists twice, his jaw working. Clearly he wanted to take Kamen up on the offer with every fiber of his being, but as reckless as he was, Ahnvil was a Gargoyle. He had been bred with the instinct to protect the man who held his touchstone in his care. That man was Jackson. Their ruler. And if Jackson needed Kamen to protect their little enclave, then he must be protected as well. It burned him, burned him badly to know that once again he was in the position of having to protect Kamenwati, just as he had when he had been Kamen's slave.

Kamen stepped a step closer to him, leaning in to say softly, "I am no longer your enemy. Leave the past where it belongs. Only then can you move forward and find what you need."

With that Kamen moved past him, leaving Ahnvil to stew in his words.

Kat hated crying. She almost never did it. She had learned long ago that tears did nothing to change things and were a waste of some perfectly good energy. But for some reason this had all crept under her skin. As she walked angrily down the long drive, blowing off steam through her pace, she tried to make sense of her emotions. She was so angry with Ahnvil for his antagonistic behaviors! He had ruined her very first attempt at being what she was born to be. Instead of lifting the cup she had blown it to bits and it had been his fault. Where did he get off, trying to tell her what she could and could not do? Yes, she understood he had bad history with Kamen, but that was exactly what it was. History. And it wasn't *her* history.

And maybe he was right and she should be cautious around Kamen, and she would be, but having him teach her a few basic activities couldn't really hurt anything. Could it? Then there was the issue of his disappearance. Where had he gone. Why? He'd made like he was needed for something but there had not been anything going on since the new Nightwalkers had left.

New. Old. Hell, they were all new to her. But she had brought them all together and that was something to be proud of. If not for her they would never have come this far. Would never have come to understand there was a curse at all. Whatever happened afterward she had done that much at least.

None of that had anything to do with her and Ahnvil.

What about me and Ahnvil? she wondered after a moment, her pace slowing considerably from stomping to a mild march. Just what was it she was expecting here? He had never made any declarations of any kind of feelings for her, and she had never asked him for any. She didn't even want any. Why *would* she want any? He was so possessive of her as it was, she could just imagine what it would be like if he had actual feelings for her. It was understood, wasn't it, that theirs was just a physical relationship? If that were the case, it had felt just a little one-sided a little while ago.

That wasn't fair. So far he had been very attentive as a lover. And he had even made as though he were going to reciprocate . . . but something had gone wrong.

Before she knew it she had reached the edge of the drive, at the farthest end of the property. The house was very small in the distance now, and she was amazed at how far and how fast she could move when in high temper. She stepped out onto the main road. It could hardly be called a road, she noted. It was a dirt ranch road that led deep in toward the property. It made her wonder if all of the land was theirs. It might have to be, if attacks like the one at the airport were a common occurrence. They wouldn't want to draw attention to themselves.

She was only a few feet down the road when she had that thought. All of a sudden she felt exposed, as if she had bitten off more than she could chew. She slowed, turned, and stepped back toward the drive.

Right when she did that, like a magician jerking back a cloth covering a levitating lady, a man appeared in her path. She sucked in a breath to scream, but he got hold of her in the next instant, slapping a hand over her mouth as he grabbed her throat. He barreled into her, taking her down to the ground, his full weight behind a knee that jammed up under her ribs. Her breath left her in a rush and it was all she could do to suck it back in through her nose. The next thing she knew he was grabbing for her pendant and went to rip it off her.

The punch of energy that left her body was tremendous. It sent the man flying up into the air with a scream of surprise. The necklace fell back down against her chest. Just as she was sucking in a breath to scream, a second man appeared.

"Aaaahhhnvil!!" she screamed as loudly as she could. She was set upon again, and by the time a third attacker appeared, the first one had regained himself and was coming back down to the ground.

"It's hexed or something!" the first announced. "Take the girl. We'll let Panahasi figure it out for himself."

"Done!" The second and third man grabbed her by an arm each and she felt torsion, as though they were going to rip her in two between them. It was so painful that she was afraid to move for fear of ripping her own arms out of her sockets. In desperation she tried to think, tried to focus on what she had learned.

Build a bridge. To the heart of the pendant's power, she heard Kamen's voice in her head.

But before she could do so, the world around her just disappeared. The sprawling desert landscape vanished from her sight and all she could see was streaking black and charcoal darkness. She felt like she couldn't breathe. All the while they were dragging her forward. She could feel the rush of the harsh wind against her, as though they were dragging her at a superfast speed from one point to the next. As they went the temperature began to drop to a point well below the crisp night air of New Mexico, until she felt as though she were out in the bleak exposure of Washington state, or some place like it, once more. That supposition was supported when they suddenly stopped and she found herself knee-deep in snow, light flurries falling down around her. No sooner had she made out the stars in the sky than her whole body heaved with the most profound nausea she'd felt in her life. She vomited into the snow, her arms twisted again as they held her, as if she might try something while puking up her guts.

"That's the streak, missy," one of them said in a guttural back-alley cockney accent. "They always belt up on the first run."

She was yanked forward toward what looked an old prison or mental institution, but instead of the front entrance she was brought off to a wing on the far side. As they were going, however, she could see an object hanging from the roof of the building. She felt her gorge rise when she realized it was a body. She looked around frantically, but like the house in New Mexico, this was located at the top of a very long drive and there was nothing but wooded land all around it. They could hang bodies in the open because there would never be anyone to see them except those who lived there. She was dragged inside and then down the stairs. She tried to fight then, even in spite of the painful way they had her arms twisted around, but it was impossible. Before she knew it she was being thrown into a cell. They strapped her in with heavy metal manacles connected to chains that fed back into the wall. The heavily barred wall on the front side of the cell was the only exposure. There were no windows, no source of light other than the industrial overhead lighting outside of her cage. On the other side of the bars was what looked like a workshop. There were tables laid out with all manner of things. From a half-dissected animal on one side, to a pile of books on another and bottles and bottles of objects and powders on the third. It was a massive room overall, but it was jammed full of stuff. And the person who kept the cell was clearly something of a slob. Half-eaten food on a plate was on one of the tables, a discarded shirt hung off a desk chair. There was a desk, but it could hardly be seen under the piles and piles of papers and envelopes and other paraphernalia. On the wall were shadowboxes filled with butterflies and various other insects.

"Oh my God," she whispered to the now empty rooms. "I'm in *Silence of the Lambs*! I'm going to be putting lotion in the basket!"

She was left alone for quite some time. The only sound outside of her frantic breathing was the drip of water. It was cold, cold enough to have her walking back and forth in an attempt to warm herself. There wasn't so much as a cot or a blanket. Only the floor and the questionable sanitation of a single toilet/sink combination. Just as she was trying to figure out what she was expected to use in the way of toilet paper, a short man entered the room. Or maybe he just seemed short because she had grown so used to Ahnvil towering over her. *Oh God*, she thought frantically. *What I wouldn't give to have him here right now!* He would know what to do. He would have the power and strength to get her out of this horrible situation.

"Well, what have we here?"

"A really pissed off woman is what," she groused, for some reason feeling like she shouldn't show any fear. But she *was* afraid. Without Ahnvil, she had no clue how to navigate this dangerous paranormal world. He had been right. It was dangerous to be involved in their world. But the truth was, if the necklace was what they were after, that house had had nothing to do with it. She would have called trouble to her no matter where she went.

"Charming," he said drolly. "Now, we can make this a very simple transaction, my dear. You give me my Amulet and I give you your freedom."

"Yeah, right. You're going to just let me walk out of here and go on my merry way?" she noted. *Oh shut up, Katrina! What is the matter with you?*

"Well, aren't you clever. But I promise," he said, holding up a hand and giving the most fake sincere smile she'd ever seen. "You will be unharmed and let go if you hand me the pendant."

"I can't," she said, fighting tears and trying to keep them out of her voice. "It won't come off. It's like cursed or something."

"Do you mind if I try?" he asked.

She knew what would happen. An evil part of her stepped back invitingly and smiled. "Be my guest," she said.

He looked cautious as he entered the cell. "How is it a human girl like you has this pendant?"

"I got it from a Gargoyle."

"Oh. Him. I figured it might be that. Now, let me see." He reached for the Amulet and picked it up. He examined it for a moment and then, clearly, made the decision to try and pull it over her head. The minute his intent became obvious, the pendant sent out the repulsion field and they both were shoved in opposing directions. She hit the wall and he hit the bars. They both picked themselves up, groaning.

"See. I told you," she said.

"Hmm. This is going to take some doing. The obvious solution might be the best way. I will have to think on it."

Panahasi left her cell and went to walk out.

"Wait! I need something."

"What?" he asked wearily.

"Toilet paper. A blanket and a cot or something. Maybe if I'm more comfortable I'll be able to figure out how to get it off me."

He rolled his eyes. He didn't believe her any more than she did. "Very well. What harm is there in providing some last creature comforts."

That was when she realized what the "obvious solution" was.

He was going to kill her and take the necklace off her corpse.

Ahnvil had felt the danger only moments before he had heard Kat scream for him. Somehow they had cloaked themselves from his senses, making it possible for them to come undetected to the borders of the property. He had run for her, stone rippling over his body, wings exploding from his back. He had seen them attacking her, but before he could reach her they had all disappeared together.

When he had reached the end of the drive there was nothing left for him to find.

He stood in the dirt road and roared with fury.

He should never have let her leave the house. Should never have let her go off on her own! Now she was gone and there was nothing he could do about it except stew in the most incomprehensible paralysis he had ever known in his life. By the time Ihron and Jackson made it to the end of the drive he was on his knees, breathing hard, unable to catch his breath no matter how hard he tried. Tears filled his vision, tears he couldn't understand because he couldn't remember the last time he had shed them. Not even when Jan Li had died, burning to a crisp in his hands as the Curse of Ra was thrown against her from three separate quarters. Maybe one, even two simultaneous hits she could have survived, but not three. She had not been strong enough for three.

And Kat was nowhere near as strong as Jan Li. He didn't even know if she was immortal or even had immortal traits. She was a half-breed. That meant any number of variables. Any number of weaknesses.

"Please," he rasped hoarsely. "Oh God, please . . . she's just a li'le thing. She doesna know how tae fight them off. 'Tis all my fault."

"Ahnvil," Jackson said, reaching to put a hand on the Gargoyle's shoulder. He roared out, in pain and dismay and what felt like a hundred other feelings. He was responsible for her. He was responsible for her and he had let her down. He threw Jackson off himself.

Think! You have to think!

"Panahasi! It has tae be Panahasi."

"The Templar?" Jackson asked.

"Yes." All three of them looked up to see Kamen standing there.

Ahnvil surged to his feet, unwilling to be caught kneeling before his nemesis.

"And what do you know of it?" Ahnvil asked scathingly.

"He's a weasel," Kamen said simply. "Weak. A low man on the totem pole."

"Even a low man can hurt her," Ahnvil growled. "He was the one who took the Amulet from your quarters. The one that captured me. I canna believe he even managed it and now I'm answering for it. I've committed one blunder after another and she pays the price."

"How did he capture you anyway?" Kamen asked. His affectation was flat, but Ahnvil took it as smug.

"They drugged me. Before I could process the poison I was out cold. Woke in a cell. I doona know anything about it from here to there. But . . ." He looked away, his mind obviously working. "But I could find the place again wi' a li'le luck. I was injured . . . burning and weak, but . . . just the same . . . if I use Kat's house as a starting point and took tae the sky, surely I could find it."

"It's as good a point as any," Jackson said. "I'll call the jet."

"It will be hours before you get there that way. If they are using the method I think they are it will only take them minutes. If it is who you say it is and he's working under the radar, he can't afford to deal with her for very long. He's going to use the fastest way possible to get to the Amulet." Kamen made sure he met Ahnvil's eyes. "The only way to get it off her is to cut off her head."

"Gods above." Ahnvil was shaking, a cold weight settling into the pit in his belly. He was paralyzed with fear. Couldn't move. He was the take action sort and he should be moving but all he could do was stare dead into the bright blue eyes of the man who had created him.

"I can travel as fast as they can. But only to a place I've seen. And from the sound of it they've moved Templar headquarters far and away from where it was last I saw. We were in the southeast before. Now it appears they are northwest."

"That doesna help us!" Ahnvil growled.

"What about a satellite photo?" Jackson asked quickly.

"That will do. Do you think you can find Kat's house?" Kamen asked.

"She left her wallet in the house. No doubt it has her address in it."

"One other thing . . . I can only take a willing person. It took three of them to take her while she was kicking and screaming. Someone who resists me will do no good."

"I'll be going," Ahnvil said. "And make no mistake about it."

"I figured you would want to. But that will leave it to me and to you to get her back," Kamen pointed out. The unspoken was clear. Ahnvil had shown no aptitude for trusting Kamen. "I have the skills to get us in and out of the stronghold . . . perhaps without anyone even knowing we are there. Provided you allow me to do what I know how to do."

"Magic," Ahnvil scoffed. "Spells, prayers, and incantations."

"Yes. Spells that hide. Prayers that bring luck. Incantations that can steal us away from there to here without anyone being the wiser. Are we agreed?"

Ahnvil narrowed his eyes a moment, but then with a clenched jaw he nodded with a short dip of his head.

"Verra well. Let's do this."

CHAPTER EIGHTEEN

The Bodywalker male with the cockney accent made yet another appearance about an hour later with the cot and the blanket in tow. He also had toilet paper but held it out of her reach.

"What you gonna give me?" he wanted to know. "Here I brought you all these nice gifties. Do somefin' for me, yeah?"

"Like what?" she wanted to know with narrowed untrusting eyes on him.

"Well, you're a bit small for my liking, but you've got tits just the same. C'mon then. Show a little."

"Over my dead body," she hissed at him.

"Well then, I'll be going." He went outside of the cell, taking the paper with him. Then he chuckled as the door closed. "You know what? The master is going to kill you for that bauble you're wearing. After that, I will look at your tits well enough." He leaned in with a leering grin. "And I'll touch 'em, too."

He laughed loud and raucously, dropping the paper on the worktable well out of her reach.

Honestly, it was the last worry on her mind. She scrambled over to the cot and wrapped herself up in the thin, smelly blanket. It was vile, but she was freezing. It took twenty minutes before she brought her shivering down to a small tremor. Then she fixated on the roll of paper on the table. Checking the door carefully, she slowly picked up the Amulet, wrapping her hand tightly around it.

"Build a bridge. Build a bridge," she whispered to herself fiercely. She was still cold so it wasn't very easy to focus, but she was very motivated. Not to get the paper, but to see if she could harness this power and do something with it. Anything. Maybe somehow she would be able to get herself out of this mess.

"Build a bridge . . ."

Suddenly something bright and hot and white seemed to light up her mind. It was nothing like the first time she had tried it. This was ten times more powerful. She looked down at the Amulet, stunned to think so much power was stored inside of something so relatively small. Then she looked up, looking for the roll of paper. Maybe if she could levitate it . . . maybe even bring it to herself . . . maybe then she could try and focus the power into doing other things. But instead of fixating on the paper, she realized something on the workbench was glowing a bright, fluorescent pink. It brightened and dulled in throbs, almost like a pulse but much slower. She narrowed her gaze, trying to make out what it was . . . and that was when it began to lift up off the table.

"Holy shit!" she whispered softly, carefully to herself. She didn't want to disrupt herself. Didn't want to ruin a good thing. Once it was in the air she tried to concentrate on bringing it to her, but hard as she tried she couldn't make it move in any direction except up and down. She narrowed her eyes on it, trying to see what it was. After a moment it began to tumble over slowly. Once it did she could see it was a bangle bracelet.

Well, shit. Another piece of jewelry? What would happen if she put that on her wrist?

No sooner did she have the thought than the bracelet whipped through the air and thrust itself onto her hand.

The minute it was around her wrist it settled down and the glow disappeared.

"Ah crap," she said softly, a sigh escaping her. She knew even without trying that this one wasn't coming off her, either. On the plus side . . . *way* pretty. And it had diamonds on it. What girl didn't like diamonds? She hadn't owned a single diamond in her whole life because diamonds were purported to look best in sunlight and the idea had just been too depressing. But now, she was thinking anything that looked this good under fluorescent lighting was worth having no matter what. But now she was stuck with two pieces of jewelry and had no idea what to do with either of them. But there had been a very different feel to the energy she had just used and she suspected it was the bracelet and not the Amulet that had supplied it. She wondered if this Panahasi even knew what he had in the bracelet. Did he even realize it was powerful?

And it *was* powerful. Her arm was literally humming with it.

"A nik," she whispered softly, turning it around on her wrist slowly, looking at all the perfect rows of gems. It seemed like a fairly new design, unlike Adoma's Amulet, which had a more beaten look to the metal and a rougher polish to the onyx stones. Is it possible for new objects to be imbued with power? *Well, of course they could*, she thought, rolling her eyes at her own flaky brain. New or old it was the power of the maker that imbued them and if there were powerful Bodywalkers in this time then it was possible.

But who had made this one?

"What's your name, pretty little thing?" she murmured. Then a sound outside the door made her start. She hastily yanked the manacle down over the bracelet and then her shirt cuff after that. She moved back to the cot and wrapped herself in her blanket, doing everything but whistling innocently.

"Well, I see you are comfortable," Panahasi said, moving to his worktable. Her heart lurched up into her throat at the idea of his discovering she had pilfered the bracelet, but as he settled in to work at his books, he kept his back to where the missing piece of jewelry had come from. He began to flip through pages from a very old-looking book that had to be the biggest and thickest book she had ever seen.

"Are those spells?" she asked, trying not to sound too interested. She rolled her eyes inwardly at herself. Just how does one ask a question without sounding interested?

"Yes, and if you don't mind they are very old and very complex so I would appreciate you not interrupting my concentration."

"Sorry." She paused a moment or two. "Can anyone learn how to do a spell?"

He sighed. "Humans such as yourself can try, but it very often corrupts those of weaker spirit. It poisons you. You are better off not trying it."

"But it doesn't corrupt you?"

"I suppose it could if it was the right spell done for the wrong reasons. But most of the magics I use are . . ."

"Wimpy?" she suggested.

"No! Just more benign."

"Oh, are you not powerful enough for the big guns?"

"No! Will you shut up?"

"Sorry."

"If you know what's good for you—" he warned.

"Yeah, yeah, otherwise you will have to kill me . . . like you're not planning it already. What's wrong? Can't figure out what to do with the body? I hear lye is a good way to go."

"Enough!" He slammed down his pen and pad of paper and rushed up against the bars. "I can get rid of you in a second, missy, and wouldn't care about the body. Or didn't you see the remains of the last person who crossed me hanging from the rafters?"

That made her heart miss a beat. But when it came down to it, she'd been afraid of something a lot worse than dying for the whole of her life. The sun. A burning ball of pain and death that filled the sky hour after hour, trapping her within the walls of her home. To her, this man was nothing. He was small. And with that thought all of her remaining fear simply vanished. She was not small. She was powerful. She had two objects of power right there on her body, untapped resources that, if she could just learn to control them might possibly get her out of this situation. But, she realized, she would be wise to stop poking the bear.

She affected the fear he was looking for. The fear that would make this small man feel big. She cowered down under her blanket and spent the next hour very quietly watching him toil over his notes and books. Over time she got the picture that a lot of what he was reading was escaping his understanding. He kept running his hands through his hair then brushing away the bits as they fell onto his work. It explained why his hair was thinning in places. After all, what Bodywalker would choose a balding man when a handsome head of hair was just as easy to come by? But he was so thoroughly aggravated by his hardship of understanding that it was affecting him physically. This was supported by the red patches around the fingertips clutching his pen. He had chewed his nails down to the nubs, leaving only the cuticles to work on. Apparently he did it so frequently even his Bodywalker body didn't have time to heal from the abuse. She watched him gnaw and spit more times then she cared to count over the next hour.

"So you must be pretty powerful, to have all these books," she fished gently, affecting genuine interest as she leaned forward on her cot. "And this workroom. And you clearly keep prisoners from time to time. Does your boss depend on you a lot?"

"She does," he said, his shoulders lifting back as he slid a cautious look in her direction. "She is very powerful and only trusts a select few with her care and tasks. Especially now, with her condition."

"Her . . . condition?"

"Yes. She is expecting a child."

The Bodywalkers had not mentioned to her that the god Apep was expecting a child. *Did they even know?* she wondered. Known or not, the ramifications of such a thing had to be tremendous. A god giving birth to offspring? That could *not* be a good thing. What if it was as powerful as its parent? Then they would be facing the threat of two gods, not only one.

Now she knew she had to get out of there. She had to somehow get this information to them as quickly as possible. They had to know! They had to know or they all would be in danger. And Ahnvil was their protector so he would be the first to meet that danger. That couldn't be allowed to happen. He would be killed for certain and if he died . . .

Oh god. *Oh god, oh god, oh god.* This couldn't be happening, she thought frantically. She had to do something!

"Are you the father?" she asked.

"Oh no," he demurred. "I don't know who it was. But I do know she considered me as mating material."

"Oh? How do you know that?"

"Because she . . . well, she has flirted with me on many occasions. Quite seriously. You know . . . touching and such," he responded.

Oh gross.

"Well then. What an honor."

"Yes, I thought so," he said, preening ridiculously.

"Well, you also seem pretty fair. I mean, I'll give you

the necklace if I can. Can you help me find a way to get it off that doesn't involve chopping my head off?" *And that gives me time to learn how to get the hell out of Dodge!* she thought.

"I don't know . . ." he hedged.

"Oh, come on. As smart and powerful as you are . . . you can't figure this out?"

"Of course I can!"

"Of course you can," she agreed with him.

"I've already been researching Adoma's Amulet and haven't come across anything about it being hexed, never mind how to get it off or negate the hex."

"Well, there must be something. Just . . . give it another day or two. You can just as easily kill me then as now. Right?"

"Right. Perhaps I will," he said thoughtfully. "I must admit, it is a puzzle and it does intrigue me."

"See? Everyone loves a puzzle."

He frowned and glared at her. "Don't think I don't see what you are trying to do here. I'm not an idiot!"

"I never said you were," she said. *You're a total fucking idiot,* she thought but, obviously, did not say aloud. "And I'm not one, either. Of course, I'm going to try and get you to approach this from a different angle. But since it doesn't hurt either of us to try it another day or two maybe we can just wait that long. Honestly, I'll be pretty damn impressed if you can figure it out in that short amount of time. I am really not holding out any hope."

"Well, you should. If anyone can figure this out it will be me," he said, trying to come off as smooth and confident but looking small and desperate. He was no more convinced of his abilities than she was. Which really kind of pissed her off. To be captured was one thing. To be captured by a total moron was just downright embarrassing.

She was going to get out of this somehow. And it had

to be soon. If she was right, she was in the same strong-hold that held Apep and *that* was a being of true power and cutthroat insanity she did not want to come up against. If she could just fly under the radar. That fact that she hadn't been dragged in front of Apep already told her that she wasn't the only one wanting to fly under the radar. She was pretty sure this whole kidnapping thing was a little side project for Panahasi. Just as his theft of the Amulet from Kamen's belongings had been done on the side. Panahasi's greed and deception were two things working in her favor. The third and fourth things were sparkling and pretty and resting on various parts of her body.

Maybe there were keys to the manacles left on the table somewhere. She wished he would leave so she could prac-tice some more with levitation.

"I'll be leaving you now. I have some things to do," Panahasi said.

Whoa. Awesome! I wish I had a peanut butter sand-wich, she thought with an inner snicker.

"I'll have them bring you some lunch," he said then.

Oh. My. God.

"What's on the menu?" she ventured to ask.

"Nothing special," he snapped at her. "You are a pris-oner, remember? You'll be fortunate if I send a peanut butter sandwich."

Okay . . . what the hell is going on here? She said aloud, "Oh, that's fine. I understand." *I wish you'd let me out of here*, she thought a bit frantically. And for just a minute he toyed with the keys at his belt but then rubbed at the back of his neck and marched out of the room, muttering under his breath.

"What the hell was *that*?" she asked aloud, pulling back the cuff of her manacles and looking at the bangle. What was it Ahnvil had said? *Never ask for a wish from a Djynn.* But she was a Djynn. Did that mean she could grant wishes? For others *and* for herself? Oh, why hadn't she had more time to practice her new abilities? She needed to know what to do! Could she convince a Bodywalker like Panahasi to simply unlock the door to her cage and let her go free? It was clear that the one thing working in her favor was that he had no idea she was a Nightwalker. A Djynn. If he had thought her anything more than a simple mortal female he would be on his guard against her. He might even kill her right away to protect himself.

So she wondered if it was more practice that made the difference or just more powerful niks.

"Damn, if only I knew what to do!" she said fiercely to herself. She waited until he was gone for a good fifteen minutes before she went back to the bars and started looking around for things on the workbench that might be able to help her. Maybe more niks or even a set of spare keys. She would get far more use out of a set of spare keys. But there was nothing. Outside of all those jars full of weird things it was nearly impossible to figure out what was on the slovenly bench.

Then she started to wonder about the books them-selves. Would there be anything of any use to her in them? She nixed that idea right away as well. Even from a distance she'd been able to tell he'd been trying to trans-late them from another language. And if he was having trouble in spite of having lived hundreds of centuries, then she wouldn't have a chance.

So she decided to just practice with what she already had. She picked one thing on the table, a heavy mortar and pestle, and then tried to build a bridge to the store of energy in the bangle nik. When she finally reached it the influx of power was so strong it hit her like a sucker punch, blowing back her tangled hair, making her chest hurt and her hands go numb and tingly by turns. The sensations filled her with trepidation and she nervously backed away from it. Almost immediately everything returned to normal.

Come on, come on! Get a grip if you wanna get out of this mess, she told herself in a fierce sort of pep talk. By the time she got the nerve up to try again, someone was coming down the corridor outside and came into the room carrying a tray. It was the crude man with the cockney accent again. And sure enough, there on the tray lay a peanut butter sandwich and a glass of milk.

Note to self: Do not wish for pink hair.

Surprisingly he didn't hassle her. But before he could leave she said, "I really wish you'd give me that roll of toilet paper."

Then, without any fanfare, he reached for the paper and handed it to her. Just like that. No arguments, no quid pro quo. She was tempted to wish for him to open the door, but she didn't have a plan for what to do after that. She needed to practice levitation. If she could bring things to her, then maybe she could learn how to push them away. Maybe she could repel anyone who tried to come after her once she got free.

She was pretty certain by then that she could get them to open the door for her. They seemed easily suggestible. Especially this one. He was an underling to Panahasi, clearly, so it stood to reason that he was weaker than he was. If she could manipulate Panahasi that easily, then surely she could get this one to set her free when the time came.

The brute left and she hurriedly began to eat her sandwich, only then realizing how hungry she was. She ought to have been afraid they were going to poison her, she supposed, but the fact was Mr. Cockney was too eager to spill her blood. He would encourage his boss to let him resolve things in a far more violent manner. Or at least that was what she hoped.

And she was right, there was no poison in her food. And that was very disquieting.

She was tired, but didn't allow herself to doze off for even a minute. Not even when she had expended so much energy tapping into the two ornaments on her body in alternating trips, learning the feel of the different levels and flavors of energy. But she was miserly about it because she began to get the feeling that the energy was finite. That she might expend it all. Whether or not it would recharge over time was anybody's guess, but she wasn't going to waste her resources just in case it was a one shot deal. The bangle's power was still overpowering every time she tried to touch its heart, but she made herself get used to it, exercising her mind until it started to come easier and easier for her to connect with it.

But she knew that doing it while sitting quietly in a cell was one thing and doing it while in the midst of a dangerous escape was quite another. And even if she made it out of the building, it was brutally cold outside and the snow was as deep as it had been when the storm had ended near her home. She suspected she was very close to her home. That was why Ahnvil had ended up on her doorstep after escaping. It was quite possible this was the very same cell they had been keeping him in. It saddened her to think of him. She knew what his reaction would be once they realized she was missing. He would blame himself for it. And while he was responsible for the anger that had driven her from the house, she was the idiot that had left the protection of the compound. It had been a stupid, thoughtless thing to do. She had been made well aware of the danger that was lying in wait, and she had forgotten to be more cautious. Her. The queen of caution.

But she knew he would blame himself. He was so incredibly hard on himself and took on so much responsibility. And she had been just as hard on him. He couldn't help the instincts that had been forced upon him. His territoriality was something he clearly struggled with and she should try to understand that. She should try to be more patient. Especially where Kamen was concerned. She was being wholly insensitive to his feelings to turn to Kamen for help right in front of his face like that. It had to sting very badly for him. But the truth was Kamen was responsible for her being able to do the things she now could do. These things that might now save her life. If she ever got out of this mess, maybe that fact would help to soften his hatred of Kamen a little.

She hoped, but seriously doubted. Her Gargoyle was not known for his ability to forgive. Not in her estimation anyway.

She missed him, she realized with no little surprise. And not just because of the astounding protection she knew he could afford her. She had done more protecting of him throughout their time together than he had of her. What she missed was the deep sound of his voice. The overwhelming presence of his body. She found she had already grown used to walking in the shadow of it, of feeling protected by it, of feeling wanted by him.

And yes, he did want her. The fiery physicality of what he wanted from her was outrageous. They had only made love a few times, but every time had been explosive and addictive. Even now she was craving the smell of him, the feel of him and the taste of him. She was craving what it felt like to have his hands and lips on her body.

Panahasi walked in on the heels of that thought and she flushed hotly. She moved back to her cot, huddling around the feelings she'd been feeling, protecting them from his acrid presence. It was obscene to have him there while she was thinking about how much she—

Cared, she thought with haste, covering over the unthinkable word that wanted to pop up in its place. She didn't want to think about things that simply could not or would not be. Ahnvil was only interested in the physical. She was not going to be one of those foolish women who fell head over heels for an inaccessible man.

Not that it mattered right then, she thought as she watched Panahasi go back to his work. She might be dead in just a few hours. What did it matter what she did and did not feel?

Oh hell, she thought. She *did* feel. She felt a lot. She just had to envision his handsome face and his warm, vital amber eyes and she felt her entire body go soft with desire and emotion. No, it wasn't just about sex. It was more. She felt for him. Felt his pain as he struggled with his harsh past and the responsibilities he had then and on into the future. She loved that he was such a powerful man of honor, that she knew he would rather die than dishonor himself. He would lay his life on the line to protect her and Jackson and everyone in that entire compound. All without prejudice. And that included Kamen. Because Jackson wanted him protected, Ahnvil would do so even though he hated his guts.

If that wasn't honor than she didn't know what was.

Ahnvil fell to his knees and vomited the instant they were out of Kamen's streak.

"It's like that the first few times," Kamen said. He did not try and help the Gargoyle in any way, knowing any hand of friendship he held out would be immediately rebuffed.

Ahnvil pushed himself up to his feet, staggering a little as the world spun and then tried to right itself.

"Give it a minute," Kamen advised.

"I doona have a minute," he snapped. "Kat doesna have a minute. For all we know the sword is already at her neck."

"We will find them when we find them. We will either

be on time or we will be too late. You need to be prepared for both instances."

"I doona need your bloody words of wisdom! Just take tae the air and help me find this place!"

"Since I don't know what it looks like, we will go together. All right?"

What Kamen was thinking was that there was no way he was going to let the Gargoyle go off on his own. The minute he found the location they were looking for he would try to go in with all barrels blazing, with no thought to his own safety. His protective instincts were just that strong. Kamen had made him that way. What he found interesting was how deeply Ahnvil had allowed himself to fixate on this little Djynn half-breed. There was much more to it than the need to protect all who were in the house and under Jackson's care. He had not missed the undercurrent of sexual energy the Gargoyle was expending toward the Djynn. Gargoyles were sexual by nature, but this went beyond mere lust.

But far be it from him to analyze this overmuch. He was there to help. He had no goals, looked for no respect or forgiveness via the task at hand. He would simply do what he had the skills to do and would leave everything to lie where it would. He was not asking for nor was he seeking forgiveness.

"Verra well," Ahnvil said after obviously trying on and then discarding about a half-dozen mental arguments. He extended his wings and with two powerful steps of thickly muscled stone thighs he launched himself into the air. With ease, Kamen levitated into his wake.

Together they began to circle out, using Kat's house as their center point.

CHAPTER NINETEEN

Katrina waited until Panahasi left the room for what she deemed the final time that night. Daylight was soon approaching and for the first time she realized that the internal clock that told her was as much due to her Night-walker blood as it was due to her years of dealing with an allergy to the sun. She had thought she had developed one because of the other when in fact it had already been there all along.

If she was going to do this she needed to do it now. She needed to get out and then, hopefully, run to the same place Ahnvil had run to. Her home. Hopefully she could get there before the sun came out and started to cook her flesh into boils and bubbles. She had not yet learned how to turn to smoke to protect herself and didn't have the first idea of how to begin to try.

Mr. Cockney came down the corridor with her tray of food, which held the bowl of tomato soup she had mentally wished for in order to exercise her skill. She waited until he was just about to leave and close the door.

"I wish you would unlock the cuffs," she said, holding up her wrists. "It's not like I'm going anywhere."

"All right," he said immediately. He pulled out a key and unlocked her cuffs. "It's not like you can get one over on me, yeah?"

"Yeah," she agreed with an innocent and winning smile. "And when you go, I wish you'd leave the door unlocked. I promise I won't go anywhere."

"Well, as long as you promise," he said, closing the door shut and failing to lock it. She had realized it was easier to get someone to do something she wished for if she gave them a reason, a logical reason, for doing it.

She had a moment when she thought he would come to his senses . . . and then a moment when she wanted to wish him into locking himself up and dropping his drawers down around his ankles so his humiliation would be complete, but it would be hard to logic things like that out. When it came right down to it, it simply was not worth the risk.

She moved carefully out of the cell, wincing when the metal creaked. She had to get out of there as soon as possible. What if Cockney came to his senses and came back to lock her up? Wishes, she knew, could be mercurial things at best. Ahnvil had warned her to never make a wish to a Djynn, but *she* was a Djynn so did that count? And the more important question was, was this possibly because of the bracelet or was this something innate within her that she was only now learning to use?

No time. She had no time to worry about this. She had to run. Had to flee. And all the while she had to hold on to the bridge to the two power sources on her body in case she needed them.

She hurried into the corridor outside, inching and creeping down it several feet at a time. She tried to remember that as far as anyone knew she looked just like any other Bodywalker out there, but most of the ones here had been wearing saffron-colored tunics and robes, like some kind of demented Hare Krishna movement.

She made it all the way to the stairs before someone noticed her.

"Hey! What are you—?"

Panahasi. She came right around the corner and ran smack into Panahasi. It took him only one moment, a fraction of a second, for him to realize who she was and the significance to her being there, out in the open, unconfined.

There was nothing to describe what she was feeling in that moment except to say it was pure and utter panic. So when she intended to use her power to push him away, she got an entirely different response. A rush of power bolted out of her and directly into the center of his chest. Not outside of his chest, but dead center inside of his chest.

He exploded from the inside out.

Kat was doused with blood, bits of flesh and bone also flinging in her direction. But it was as though she were in some kind of bubble. Everything washed down around her, streaming to the floor as if it were sliding down off some bizarre sheet of protective glass.

She sat there, horrified, gasping for breath. Her panic was complete, freezing her in place.

Run. Run! *Run!*

Finally the screaming in her brain propelled her body into action. She ran. She didn't stop. Didn't look back, barely looked where she was going. All she knew was that she had to go up. She was in a basement and had to go up. She found the stairs easily. They were clearly marked by the old signage. As were the exit signs. She found the very first one and slammed her whole body into the door. She promptly was thrown back on her ass, the padlock and chains she'd not noticed holding true. She was starting to hear shouts of warning, the raising of the alarm and she knew she was going to fail. It was that knowledge that slammed the bridge to the Amulet into place and that fear that sent the power against the chains. Like Panahasi they exploded into shards of metal, the links falling free of the door. She ran at them again, this time using the bridge to help her push her way out. They flung open hard and she was dumped out into three feet of snow.

She didn't even feel it. She ran, slogging through the thickness of it, her heart in her throat as she realized she was leaving a perfect trail for them to follow. She wasn't going to make it. Even though Panahasi was dead, someone would raise an alarm, alert Apep, and surely then she would die. And she had no doubt in her mind that it would be slow and agonizing.

And that was when something slammed into her body from behind driving her down into the deep snow. She screamed, tears rising frantically in her eyes, her breath thundering out of her as she clawed at the snow and tried to escape with every fiber of her being.

"Kat! Doona be afraid. I've got you!"

And in the next instant she was airborne, snow falling away from her body as the arms he had wrapped around her chest pulled her in tight. She could feel the wash of air from the powerful pumping of his wings. She should have been terrified. She was flying in the air at breakneck speed with nothing but a pair of hands to hold her safely.

But they were *his* hands. His. Her Gargoyle. And she had never felt safer in all of her life.

That was when she was aware of a second person in flight beside them. Kamen.

"You came together?" she asked, her teeth chattering from her wet, cold state.

"Aye. We were just trying to figure out a way to find you. Then suddenly there you were. Hang on." He dipped and reeled, drawing them down low, into the trees.

Okay, now she began to worry. Limbs and branches were everywhere, sometimes just a hairsbreadth from striking her. He flew so swiftly she had no idea how he was able to anticipate them. She suspected he didn't exactly have a flight plan, either.

"Oh my god! Go up! You need to go higher!"

"No, I canna. There's no one chasing us yet, but that doesna mean Panahasi willna send more of his minions after us. Flying low keeps us out of easy sight."

"Panahasi is dead! I-I killed him. And the ones who know I was there, I don't think they even knew why. Except that he wanted the Amulet."

He seemed to absorb the news of Panahasi's death quite well. He slowed, bringing them back down to the snow. Kamen followed until all three of them had settled into the cold, icy fine softness of it.

Ahnvil turned her to him, quickly inspecting her. Finding she didn't have a scratch on her, he seemed to exhale in relief. Then his eyes fell on the diamond and ruby bracelet she wore.

"Now, doona tell me he was giving you gifts. Was he trying tae kill you or woo you?"

"I found the bracelet myself on his workbench. I honestly don't think he knew what it was or he wouldn't have left it out in the open like that I'm sure. Then again he is something of a moron. Or rather, *was*."

"Time for tales of conquests are for later," Kamen said. "Right now, we need to leave this place behind." He reached out to put his hand on Ahnvil's shoulder and his other hand on Kat's arm. He closed his eyes and in an instant they were streaking.

By the time they came to a halt both she and Ahnvil were so nauseated and dizzy they had to cling to one another to keep upright. After a moment, Kat lost one peanut butter sandwich . . . or rather what was left of it. Which was not very much so she was heaving hard without much production. She felt Ahnvil's stone hands in her hair, holding it back, slowly turning to flesh as he patiently stroked her neck and back.

"There now. Easy now, Kat lass," he soothed her softly until she finally was able to see straight.

"God, I am never doing that again," she vowed.

"Which part?" Ahnvil asked with a gentle smile. "Kick arse and rescue yourself or the streak?"

She laughed shakily. "I'll never put myself in the position to have to do the first again, and I'll never do that second thing, period."

"I doona blame you. Come, lass, let's get you inside where it's safe and warm you up."

His kindness and his caring knew no bounds. He did not yell at her for her stupidity as he helped her undress and get into the tub, brush her teeth, and do all the little things that would make her feel more human and at rest. He did not question her about the bracelet or how she had managed to escape as he dressed her in a clean T-shirt. He did not remind her of her close call and the fact that she had just murdered a man as he drew her onto the bed, holding her up tight and close under his arm.

He waited until she was fully quieted, until she was feeling safe and completely under his protection, before he began.

"Tell me everything," he said softly. "If you're ready."

"I am," she said. She began to describe everything that had happened, and every time he realized how close she had come to danger, his hold on her tightened. Whether it was to control his temper or to give her comfort, she didn't know. But she suspected it was a combination of the two.

"I have come to realize," he said after she had fallen quiet, "that Panahasi was acting completely independently of Apep. Thanks to all of the good gods for that. If Apep had gotten a hold of you . . ." He closed his eyes, suppressing the tremor that threatened to wash through him. *She is safe,* he kept trying to remind himself. *She is protected in your arms.*

But it didn't change the fact that he had failed to protect her in the first place.

"I'm sorry," he said with heartfelt sincerity. "I was
wrong. If not for Kamen's teachings you might be dead
right now." He reached down to finger the newest bauble on her wrist. "It is because of him that you are safe
right now, and that is no' a debt I will forget."

"And you'll let him teach me more? I mean, I will
want to know most of the serious Djynn stuff from an
actual Djynn like Grey, but Kamen can teach me more
of the basics. You're okay with that?"

"You were right when you said it is not up tae me.
You do what you need tae do, Kat. I willna interfere."

She looked up into his face, sliding around so she was
lying on his chest and looking into his eyes. "I understand why you hate him. I don't want to upset you."

"I admit, I hate him less at the moment." He touched
her at the corner of her lips, the stroke endearing and
warm. "He's brought something back to me that means
far more than the ills of being enslaved."

Kat felt her throat tightening up and unexpected tears
jumped into her eyes once more. She'd been an emo-
tional wreck since this whole adventure had begun, but
this was an entirely different feeling.

"I'm surprised to hear you say that," she whispered.

" 'Tis the truth of it," he said with a simple shrug.

The words had an incredible effect on her, but she
reined herself in, tried to be careful with her soaring feelings. She didn't want to get too far ahead of herself. Didn't
want to thrust herself out there, exposed to whatever pain
he might throw her way. She was on uneven ground as it
was. Every step she took was one step closer to falling flat
on her face. There was just too much uncertainty in the
future.

So instead of filling the air with insufficient words, and
the possibility of dangerous disappointment, she reached

to touch her mouth to his. He pulled her up tightly into the kiss a moment after that, his mouth warm and strong against hers. She closed her eyes, just wanting to feel the strength of him, to absorb his vitality deep into herself. That, more than anything, made her feel safe again. That and the surrounding feel of his arms, the strong press of his hands against her back.

Safe.

And warm. No. Not warm. Hot. It only took a moment for the heat of his kiss to stir up the heat he always seemed to carry with him. Then, with a sudden movement, he rolled her onto her back, his hips driving up between her thighs as they instinctively bracketed him, his elbows propped on either side of her shoulders, freeing his hands to be in her hair and against the sides of her face.

"My Kat," he said, leaving her mouth for just a moment to speak the words. Then he was back again, this time speaking fire against her.

My Kat. His Kat. Was she his Kat? Or was that just something he was saying in that moment? Was it a way of getting his way? Were his words thoughtless or were they full of thought, full of emotion? Gargoyles were a lusty lot, he had told her. Did that mean they would do or say anything to make their way into a woman's bed?

She put the questions aside and decided to simply accept what he was giving physically and leave off questioning. She couldn't trouble her mind with the rest. She had been through so much that night. Now it was daylight beyond the polarized glass of his bedroom and they were safe from all the evil members of the Nightwalkers, imp gods included, and they could rest easy.

Kat accepted a series of kisses so deep she could barely catch her breath. He made love to her mouth with his lips and then deep sweeps of his tongue. He tangled his up with hers, traded tastes and fever until she was lost and thought she would never be found. She felt everything she was go wet and soft with growing need. She had never wanted anything so much, she realized, as she wanted him right then. Nothing had ever been so clear. She very quickly came so far from the fear she had been immersed in just hours earlier. But both places were places of strength. She had fought for her freedom and had won. Now she was fighting for feelings far more frightening. She was coming home in a way she had never known before. All the pain of that place and time was washing away and being replaced by this passion. Doubt and hate had no place, no home, in that moment.

His hand brushed from her face down onto her throat, his fingertips tracing along the line of her collarbone. There was something about the softness and starkness of the caress that made her look into his darkened amber eyes, seeing things she wasn't sure she understood. He looked a little lost, as though pieces of the moment were missing. But she didn't know how to fill the holes. She didn't think she had what he needed. So she filled the blanks with kisses, with the touch of her hands drifting across the wide breadth of his shoulders.

He was without his stone armor, and yet felt just as durable; a strength that amazed her. She had never known anyone so strong, and to feel it under the brush of her hands was an amazing thing. To feel his warmth growing hotter at her command was something so remarkable that she could speak with nothing but her hands. She used her hands to draw him closer, to tell him how amazed she was by his strength. To tell him she wanted every part of him, every contour and every breath with everything that she was.

And he wanted her just as much with just as demanding an extreme. He burned for her and in that moment was unafraid to show it to her. There was no room for lies, no room for fighting. Why would either of them want to anyway? They gave truth to each other, naked and needful. He unbuttoned her shirt, parting both halves of it evenly, exposing first her belly and then each of her breasts. Her nipples contracted with the brush of the disappearing fabric and then the touch of the room air. Then she was tethered to him by the touch of his fingertips running down the length of her breastbone, inch by inch, every one tangling her up in an expanding need.

When he touched her belly it contracted with both surprise and expectation. She wanted his touch and yet was shocked by it just the same. His hand flattened against her for a moment, pressing into her, as if he were trying to reach inside of her. Then he pulled his palm away leaving just his fingertips against her once more. He drew them down, all the way to the very edge of the light hair at her mound. But instead of threading into the curls he pulled away, running back up her body in the other direction. He drew a line in the crescent under first one breast and then the other.

By the time he cupped her left breast she was breathing as though she'd run a quarter mile. He smiled a little, and she knew he was taunting her on purpose. And frankly she didn't care. She wasn't in any kind of rush. Well, maybe she was. But she wasn't. Oh, how the hell was she supposed to know? If there was one thing Ahnvil was good at it was turning her inside out.

"There's a fine sight," he said, his voice thick with the need she could see in his eyes. "You've the prettiest breasts I've ever seen."

"That's such a lie," she said breathlessly.

"No' a lie. I'll no' pretend I'm a virgin, Kat lass. I've seen my share over three hundred years. When I tell you yours are the prettiest breasts I've ever seen, you can know I doona say it lightly. They're fair and pale, the wee freckles just at the tops of them," he stroked his fingertips over them, "and then the darkest pinkest nipples . . . so tight and puckering so prettily. Aye. I've never seen the like. And now I'm going tae love on them as greedily as ever a man could."

And he started by laving each nipple with the flat of his tongue, wetting them so they grew even tighter in the cool room air. Then, with a strong intake of his breath he closed his mouth over her right nipple while taking the other up between his fingers. He overwhelmed her by sucking and pinching at her simultaneously, continuing to do so until she was dizzy, then switching and doing it all over again. Her knees drew up, her feet climbing all the way up the backs of his legs. Had he pulled his body up a few more inches he would have been cradled directly in the warmth of her core, but he remained frustratingly out of her reach.

He knew she wanted him to move up, to be more blatant in his lovemaking, but he was taking his time. Feeling her squirm and hearing her pant and moan for him was enough for him for now.

Ahnvil left off her breasts and pressed his lips to her solar plexus. Then again to the area above her navel, and then again to the spot just below it.

"Christ, I can smell the heat on you," he said fiercely. "It makes me want tae . . . I'm going tae taste you soon, Kat lass. And I'm going tae make you come while doing it."

"O-okay," she said.

That made him laugh.

"Well then, now that I have your permission . . ." He briefly dipped his tongue into her navel, making her giggle through the ferocity of her desire. Then he wedged his shoulders between her thighs, his hand stroking down the length of first one, then the other. He used the knuckles of his hand to run the full length of her, from curls to backside, letting her buck up against him as she tried to encourage him to move faster than he was willing to. Then, much to her relief, he touched her. The relief was short-lived, however, as fire seared across her flesh everywhere he stroked against her.

Ahnvil could feel just how wet she was, and how wet she was growing with each passing touch of his fingers. It began to make him impatient as well. He found the lip of her entrance and pushed his finger inside of her, groaning at the tight, sweet feel of her. As she clutched at his fingers, first one and then quickly two, he could well imagine what she would feel like around him. It was as though they had never made love. As though it were the very first time he would be getting to learn her. The perception amazed him. Shouldn't this be familiar territory already? They'd made love several times before this, why did it feel so . . . so *novel*?

That was when he realized it would never feel old or tired. Not with her. He didn't know why, he just knew. It was a humbling sort of thing to realize. He closed his eyes briefly, absorbing what it meant to him, knowing she was well beyond anything he deserved and yet unable to be selfless enough to let her go and find what she deserved somewhere better.

Yes, he was selfish. There was no two ways about it. And once realizing it he decided to be resigned to it. If she wanted something other than what he could give her, then it would have to be her that drew an end to things. He knew it wouldn't be him. *Couldn't* be him. For now, she was allowing him time with her, loaning him her sweet body. So he would do whatever he could to see to it she was pleased, to make her happy. He would not be running away from her again, would not be leaving her unfulfilled. He already had to repay her for what had passed before.

He heard her gasp, knew he was giving her pleasure,

so he chased the sound down, touching her deeper, stroking his thumb around her clit until she made the sound again. Then that wasn't enough and he had to aim for a long, deeper, throatier sound, so he dipped his head down between her thighs and moved his thumb away from her, replacing it with his tongue. He teased her a little . . . then a lot, not doing what was best for her but bringing her right to the edge of it once . . . twice . . . again. Until she ground out a sound of frustration. He chuckled and then she was on to him, thrusting a punishing set of toes into his ribs.

"Doona fash yourself," he murmured against her thigh, giving her a brief kiss there. "I know what I'm doing."

"You couldn't tell from my position!" she grumbled.

He laughed again. "You feel what I want you tae feel. And now I want you tae feel more. So you will."

And so she did. She cried out to the heavens as he worked against her with skilled flicks of his tongue and the occasional sucking of her swollen clit. Then he was swirling his tongue around her, driving her to the very edge of orgasm. All it would take was just a little . . . bit . . . more . . .

She whipped into the release sharply, for all she had been building up to it, and she unthinkingly clawed her nails over the flesh of his shoulder and through the roots of his hair. She clutched him in spasm, holding him to herself, as if he might escape her should she give him a single moment's chance. She couldn't have been further from the truth.

"Doona let go, lass," he said huskily. "I'm no' through wi' you yet."

"Wait!" she cried breathlessly.

"No. I'll no' wait."

"Shouldn't I have some . . . oh God . . . some say in this?"

"No."

"Oh. Okay," she said with a swallow he could hear.

"I want to give, you want to get. Where's the harm?" he pressed.

"But I—"

"No."

"Oh. Okay," she sighed, finally relaxing back and letting him have his way. She didn't complain again until she was rounding the bend of her third orgasm. "Please," she said. "I can't do it again."

"Aye, you can. But doona worry, I've something else in mind."

He pushed her thighs farther apart, making room for himself as he surged up the center of her body. He felt his own heavy weight in his hand as he took himself within his own fist and brought himself to the edge of her entrance. He kissed her, waiting for her to relax, which took a fair minute because she was locked up tight in anticipation. But he waited . . . waited . . . and when she exhaled and finally realized he was in charge and nothing she did would sway or hurry him unless he wanted to be swayed or hurried, then he moved forward, pushing into her in a sudden surge of strength. She blended a cry in with his, both of them stunned by the way the other felt. It took a bit of doing, getting himself fully inside of her without spilling himself too soon. She had just that much power over him . . . and was just that tight besides. It reminded him of their disparate sizes, made him worry for her for a moment. But then he reminded himself that this was the lass who had blown Panahasi to kingdom come and had managed to escape Apep's stronghold. And now, thanks to her, they knew exactly where that stronghold was. It had been moved since Kamen's defection from their camp, and although he had escaped from there as well, he might not have found it again without her as motivation. Without her having saved his life in the first place.

No. He was selling her short to think of her as fragile. Not after all she had been through and survived. A trap he had almost lost his life to. A situation that Jan Li had not made it out of even with knowing the grounds like the back of her hand.

He pushed the memory away and focused solely on her. Focused on the feel of her and the strength of her. He tried to introduce himself into her gradually, in order to give her better pleasure, but in the end it was so easy. She was so sexual, so passionate, that she simply couldn't help herself.

With every deep, languorous thrust into her he felt his own control spinning away like a frenetic little top. There was no particular rhythm to the way he moved, but there was a beat to it. Deep. Hard. Punctuating.

"Oh yes," he ground out. "You're so fine, my wee Kat. Sometimes it feels like making love tae daylight, the way you harden me, the way you make me feel invulnerable and able to conquer the world."

Her reply was a soft, ramping sound of pleasure. Every time she made it, it grew in intensity. He could hear it . . . feel the place she was cresting to. He knew then that if she came there would be no helping him. He would be equally thrown into it. And it was a fight he willingly gave himself over to. He never sped up, only moved deeper, harder, making her body shimmy with each impact. It wasn't a frenetic orgasm like the ones before, but it was a deeper one . . . and a more soulful one . . . as he forced her to look dead into his eyes the entire time.

He kept her head between his hands, directing her gaze to his as she cried out and tried to close her eyes and roll away into it. But he refused to let her, forced her to be present, with him, in every single instant of it.

She tightened around him, making it beautifully hard to push into her. In the end, though, it was watching her pleasure explode in her eyes that sent him over the edge. Knowing she was there with him was all the aphrodisiac, all the foreplay, he would ever need.

CHAPTER TWENTY

"Leo has sent word from the court of the Demon King," Jackson said. "I hung up with him a little while ago. Apparently," he said with bemusement, "several of their Nightwalker races don't get along with technology and basic things like electricity. So he has to leave the court and travel a distance in order to make a call. It brings to mind Wraiths. They too have difficulties with advanced technologies. Normally this might worry me, but Leo is more convinced than ever that these are good, honest Nightwalkers. And Leo, as you know, does not trust anyone. That impresses me. He's not of a mind to turn his back on them just yet, that kind of trust will take time, but on the surface he has a pretty good feeling."

"So what's the next step?" Kamen asked.

"You and the Druid Bella are the next step," Jackson said. "She will be researching in their library, since she can read any language apparently, and you will research in ours, since you would know more about identifying and reversing magics of that magnitude."

"The key is to figure out its origin. Once we do that the rest should fall into place," Kamen said.

"My thoughts exactly." Jackson paused a beat. "However, I agree with Ahnvil and am unwilling to extend complete trust to you. You will have a keeper. A warden, if I have to put a name to it. Another former Templar like Docia's Bodywalker, Tameri, who will keep you honest and will make certain you are not working merely for your own ends . . . or for the ends of the Templars."

"I would expect no less," Kamen said quietly.

"Well then"—Jackson clapped his hands together and rubbed them almost eagerly—"let the games begin. We'll see if we can figure out this curse before Apep gives birth to . . . gods know what he will bring forth onto this planet. The very thought of it scares the hell out of me."

The entire household had to agree. They were all sitting around the living area after Jackson had called them there. Even Grey and SingSing had joined them. And apparently Faith, Leo's Night Angel lover, had joined him in the court of the Demon King.

"There was one other thing I wanted to mention. According to Faith, her brother, a Night Angel of great power and ability, was . . . raped by a powerful Bodywalker recently. We believe this was Apep and that Faith's brother was being forced to father this child Apep now carries. We must take the creation of this child even more seriously because of that. Faith reports that if his offspring has any fraction of his father's power, plus whatever he will gain by being Apep's offspring . . . soon we will be facing the potential of an even greater threat than before.

"A being of this much power alone might be a challenging adversary, but in tandem with Apep's power it could make them unstoppable and, curse or no curse, we might not have a chance in hell of defeating him. Apep is, after all, a god. No one knows the bounds of his power yet, but I have a feeling that we will find out very soon."

"We will find a way," Marissa reassured them, remaining calm and sure in the face of it. Much in the

way her mate was responding to it. There was a reason
each was Pharaoh in their own right. They were meant
to be leaders and had proven themselves over and over
throughout their many incarnations.

"We need to," Grey said quietly. "My magic is powerful, to be sure, but on its own it would be no match
for a god. I am not so vain as to think it would be."

"That's just it. We can't think in terms of individuality. The whole point of lifting this curse is to allow us
the ability to join with others in order to defeat a common enemy," Marissa said.

"I will feel better once this curse is lifted," Grey said.
Although, if he had not voiced it, Kat wouldn't have had
a clue that he was feeling any unease. The Marid Djynn
was lacking in any affectation. He was like watching a
placid pool. Kat wondered if one day she would have as
much power as he did and if it would make her feel that
calm and secure in the face of great danger. Even admitting his own weaknesses he seemed unconcerned. Perhaps it was like Jackson and Marissa, the face of an
experienced leader trying to remain calm in the face of
adversity.

It had been a week since she had escaped Apep's stronghold. They had all been holding their breath, waiting for
some kind of retaliation from Apep or the Templars, but
the more time that passed the more the idea that Panahasi was working alone was supported.

After the meeting finished and the group had pretty
much disbanded, Kat got up the nerve to talk to Grey
directly. Frankly, he intimidated her. His power. His
position. She felt as though she might come off as an
upstart, this awkward inexperienced girl asking such a
powerful Djynn for a lesson in how to be what she was.

"Excuse me," she said, her hands nervously twisting
together.

Grey looked at her. He had been sitting perched on

the arm of the couch and had just risen to his feet. But when she addressed him he sat back down again, relaxing as he gave her a small smile of encouragement.

"You would like to learn something?"

"No. I mean yes! I mean"—she sighed in frustration with herself—"Kamen told me there are different castes of Djynn. From weak to most powerful. I was wondering . . . what class am I? No one seems to be able to tell me."

"That is because it is hard to tell," Grey said. "Being a half-breed it is not easy to define what you are. But I have my suspicions."

"What are they?" she asked eagerly.

"Are you certain you wish to know? You may not like what you hear."

Kat swallowed noisily at that. That definitely did not sound good *at all*. She shored up her courage. "Yes," she said.

"What has Kamen told you about the castes?"

"Marids and Afreets are the most powerful. Janns are the weakest. Sheytans . . . well, I got the feeling they are very spooky. To be avoided."

"Sheytans are definitely 'spooky,'" he said with a small light of amusement in his eyes. But then that light faded. "Sheytans deal in the darkest of magics. Death magics. Curses. Power-stripping. They have magic that rains fire down on those who anger or offend them. They draw power from the darkest of niks. Cursed objects, violent things. Weaponry. Objects like those you are wearing right now."

Kat reached out to fiddle with her necklace nervously. "This is cursed. Y-you're saying I-I'm a Sheytan?"

"My guess is you were sired by a Sheytan and that you have Sheytan abilities. How far you can take it remains to be seen. But you dealt a tremendous death-blow to Panahasi without even trying to, and that should tell you something."

"Does that mean I can accidentally blow someone else up? I've been afraid to practice because I don't want to—"

"You were threatened by him," Grey reminded her. "You dealt out what was due. I doubt you can deal death to someone who does not deserve it. There are rules to Djynn magic."

"You mean . . . it was self-defense. So it was justified."

"Exactly. If you've been giving yourself a hard time about that, you shouldn't."

"I'm not," she assured him. "I was a little shell-shocked at first, but I know I had no choice. I would never have gotten out of there alive if I hadn't fought. I'm okay with what happened."

"Good! So let's teach you a key skill, shall we?" At her eager nod he said, "Djynns turn to smoke at the touch of the sun to protect themselves from the burning and blistering you suffer. If you turn to smoke it will not hurt you. The only trouble is that you will also lose cohesion the longer you remain in smoke form, so you need to find a protected place as soon as possible once you turn."

"I want to learn that very much. Can you give me a minute?" she asked, holding out a staying hand.

"Of course. I need to speak to SingSing before she flits away again. She is quite . . . mercurial, at best. Shall we meet here again in ten minutes?"

"Okay," she said with a nod.

Once Grey left, Kat turned to Ahnvil, who had stood silently behind her the entire time. She realized just how important it was that he had not interfered. It must have taken a great deal for him to control his impulse to protect her from everything. "Are you okay with this?" she asked him.

"I already told you. I have no right tae stop you from

learning about who you are," he said, moving up to her and cradling the side of her face in one of his large hands.

"That isn't what I asked you," she said, covering the back of the hand that touched her face with one of her own. "Are you okay with this? With me. With me possibly being . . . a Sheytan. A death-dealing Djynn." She shuddered. "I mean, I would understand because frankly I'm not entirely sure I am okay with it myself. But I know how you feel about magics . . . and I don't want . . ."

" 'Tis no' magic I detest," he said softly. "And even if it were I would no' detest it coming from you. 'Tis one magic user in particular that rubs me wrong."

"Kamen."

"Aye. Kamen. But, as I said, I doona look on him wi' as much hatred as I once did. No' since his actions allowed you tae come back safe tae me. I will never like him. I will no' *ever* trust him. But . . . well, I've said my bit on it. And truth be told . . . if it were no' for magic . . . I wouldna ever have met you. I would have long ago been dead and dust. That alone made it worthwhile tae be forged."

"Oh," she said, her eyes dropping down as she flushed with pleasure. "I didn't think of that."

"I've thought of nothing else," he said softly, his knuckles caressing her gently over the rise of her cheek. "No' since I got you back from Panahasi. I—" He broke off and then seemed surprised to hear what his own mouth was saying. "Anyway, 'tis time you learned how to turn to smoke and protect yourself."

He turned her by her shoulders, making her face toward where Grey had disappeared to.

"But—"

She turned back, but he was already on his way out of the room.

Well, hell.

What did he mean he'd thought of nothing else? Surely not . . . not the way he made it sound. He made it sound as though he had been severely emotionally affected by what had happened. But in order for that to be true he had to have felt strongly for her in the first place. And sure, they had grown very close this past week. They had certainly been engaging in the most physical relationship she'd ever had. He had a way of making a girl think she was the be all and end all of his universe, but . . . that had all been perception. Hadn't it?

No. This was dangerous. He had never said anything about having an actual relationship with her. Outside of the sexual? No. She was just reading too much into it.

Well, what was she supposed to think, she thought petulantly, when he kept saying things like that? If she was reading too far into things he only had himself to blame. It wasn't her fault and he shouldn't keep doing things or saying things like that when he really didn't mean them to mean what they might have meant from any other man on the planet.

Damn him.

She sat there stewing, running it over and over in her mind, for another five minutes before Grey came back.

"Is something troubling you?"

"No," Ahnvil said to Jackson, frowning at the Pharaoh even though his reply was absentminded.

"Then why the frown?"

"I was just thinking abou' something. 'Tis no' a matter of concern."

"Oh?" Jackson smiled, his eyes light with amusement. "Anything that has my chief Gargoyle frowning like that might have to be my concern."

"No. 'Tis nothing. 'Tis just that . . . I doona like the idea of Grey making my Kat feel like she might be something to be fearful of."

"Fearful? Why would she think that?"

"He thinks she might be Sheytan."

"I see," Jackson said, his amusement tempered with a measure of seriousness. "Sheytans are a very serious business. Not to be messed with. I don't think her being one is a bad thing at all. However, I, for one, wouldn't mind having a Sheytan Djynn in my camp."

"I dinna think you would. 'Tis no' you I'm worried abou' 'tis Kat. She's had tae learn abou' so many wild and strange things these past days. I doona want her tae think she should fear *herself*." He frowned. "I've seen how she's behaved this past week. Afraid tae use her power. Afraid she'll blow someone up."

"A healthy fear to have, considering. At least until she learns more about her abilities and how to control them."

"I doona see the health in it." His frown deepened. "No' for her. She's feared herself enough. 'Tis time she got to revel in what she is."

"And she can't do that if she's a Sheytan."

"No. I mean . . . no. I doona mean—" His brow wrinkled.

"Seems to me the only one not liking her being a Sheytan is you."

"That's no' true!" Ahnvil snapped. "I'd love her no matter what she is!"

Jackson leaned back against the counter, folded his arms over his chest and raised a brow. He waited.

It took a moment. A very long moment.

"Oh, bloody hell," Ahnvil said, shock widening his eyes as he ran a hand down over his face. "This is no' good," he said, taking a deep breath. Then another. Before he knew it he was practically hyperventilating.

"Hey. Easy, big fella," Jackson said, amusement in every line of his body as he went over to the Gargoyle and thumped him on the back a few times. "Take a good breath. Easy now. It's always like this the first time you figure it out." He suppressed a chuckle, simply for fear of getting decked. "It'll be okay."

"No, it willna!" Ahnvil bit out at him. "This is horrifying!"

"Ahnvil . . . it's not as bad as all—"

"I have nothing to offer her!" the Gargoyle snapped. "What do I have for her? A life here, ground zero for Apep's next demented scheme? You barely survived Apep's last incursion onto this territory. She's got nothing to protect her from him!"

"She has you. And if I'm not mistaken, she protected herself pretty good from Panahasi . . . and she wasn't even trying."

"Panahasi is one thing, a god quite another," he returned sharply, although not sounding as convinced as he had a moment earlier.

"And you do have something to offer her. You said it yourself. You love her. From what I hear, that's more than enough for a woman."

Ahnvil scoffed.

"You know, I won't hold you here if you do not want to be here. You are free to take her somewhere safer any time you like. I am sure any one of the Bodywalker nexus houses would be happy to have you."

Again, Ahnvil scoffed. "And leave the center of things when you'll be needing me most? I doona think so!"

"You know what it sounds like to me? Excuses," Jackson said. "You're afraid. And you should be. It's a big responsibility, to love and care for someone."

This time Ahnvil looked at him with interest instead of reactionary emotion.

"How do you do it? I mean, how do you keep from being afraid?"

"I don't. I'm terrified. All the time. And so is she about me. It's just the nature of the beast. If you think you can reap the glories of love without paying the price, then you clearly aren't willing to do the work and you should end it right—"

"No," Ahnvil said hastily. "No, 'tis no' that. No' at all. I just . . . I doona want tae . . . I'm afraid I'll . . ."

"Hurt her?" Jackson filled in for him.

"Oh aye," Ahnvil said on a big, gusting breath.

"You will. You'll fight. You'll make up . . . one of my favorite parts, by the way. But if you want to find out *your* favorite part . . ." Jackson trailed off. But he could already see the fever of excitement laced with fear in the Gargoyle's eyes.

"I'll fuck up. I just know I will fuck up."

"Oh aye," Jackson said with a chuckle.

"How . . . how do I tell . . ."

"Sorry, big fella. There you are totally on your own," Jackson said with a grin as he turned and looked in the refrigerator.

By the time he turned back, the kitchen was empty.

"Dude, you were so just looking for an excuse," Jackson said to the empty room.

"There, see? Just imagine your fingers floating away on the air . . . but not too far from the rest of you. Cohesion is important," Grey said.

"Whoa. This is so cool," Kat murmured as her fingers dissolved into smoke. "I thought this was going to be so much harder!"

"When the sun hits you your body is naturally trying to do this, but since you are a hybrid something in the instinctive mechanism is mis-wired. Now bring yourself back to cohesion. That's very well done. Not bad for an hour's work."

Once her fingers were solid, she beamed at Grey . . . only he wasn't looking at her. He was looking with obvious surprise at a point above her shoulder behind her. Curious, she turned and saw . . .

A very big, very tall . . . Scot. And she did mean Scot. As in, a kilt of green and black with strands of violet, a matching sporran with a white furred beard around its base and a white shirt with pirate sleeves dressing up her big Scot. All he needed was a bag of pipes and he'd be complete.

"What is going on?" She looked around the room, looking for the joke. And while she was doing that her big Scot dropped to both his knees before her . . . which almost brought them eye to eye. She snickered out her nose. "Have you been drinking scotch with Ihron again?"

"No. Though I wish I'd thought of it. I need tae speak wi' you."

"Well, I . . ." She looked over her shoulder only to find Grey had disappeared. She sighed. "I wish people would stop doing that," she muttered.

"Doing what?"

"Nothing," she said dismissively. "What is all this?" she wanted to know.

"You canna tell? I'm on my knees before you, lass."

"Well, I didn't really think . . ." She frowned in consternation. "Can't you just speak plainly?" she almost whined. But she hated whiners, so she didn't. Barely.

"Och, lass, doona be so blind tae me. Canna you see how much you mean tae me? I'm trying tae ask you . . . can you no' be my wife or am I just too stupid tae deserve you?"

"You are not too stupid!" she snapped off. "Why do you have to put yourself down like that? Why can't you j—"

She stopped.

Blinked.

"I'm sorry, can you repeat that?"

"Kat lass, I love you wi' all my heart. You have tae understand, my heart was made of stone, but now . . . you make me feel things I never thought I would. Things I doona deserve tae feel."

"Why not? Why don't you deserve it?" she numbly wanted to know.

"Because . . . because I have nothing to offer you, Kat lass. No home of your own. No true security or safety, no normalcy. Life with me would be . . . hard."

"Life is hard, period. Life for me, as a Nightwalker, is going to be hard." Suddenly a thread of true under-standing slid through the eye of the needle. "You're . . . you're serious? This is serious?"

"As a bloody heart attack, woman," he said, looking completely offended.

"I'm sorry. I'm sorry," she said hastily, squeezing the hands that now clasped hers. "Just give me a minute to catch up. Just . . . just a minute." She took a deep breath. Two. She closed her eyes and exhaled through her teeth. She opened them.

Yup. He was still there. Still real. Still looking for all the world like he was expecting an answer.

All this time . . . he had meant it. All those times he'd made her feel as though the sun rose and set with her . . . they had been *real*.

"You doona love me," he said dejectedly, his breath leaving him on a deflating sigh. "I'm sorry. I thought maybe . . . Och, I'm an ass!" He went to get up and she lunge forward to keep him on his knees.

"No! No, I do! I . . . I . . ."

I do! Kat thought. *I do love him! All this time I kept telling myself I was seeing too far into things, that I was making things up in my head . . . but all this time . . . I do!*

"You do?"

"Yes, I do," she breathed.

"So . . . will you please marry me, Kat? Or is this too soon?"

"No! Not too soon!" she said hastily, gripping his hands harder as tears leapt into her eyes. "Just soon enough! Oh my God. Oh my God! I never thought . . ."

She began to cry in earnest and he hastened to his feet, wrapping big arms around her.

"Never thought what, Kat?" he asked gently as he comforted her.

"I never thought I would get married," she sobbed. "I was always thinking . . . what if I pass this disease down to my kids? How can I expect to find a man who would put up with living in the dark? And now . . . here you are . . . all handsome and big and . . . *here*."

"Oh aye. I'm here. And I'm no' going anywhere," he promised her.

"A-are you sure? I mean, you never even said or acted like this was something you might want."

"Are you trying tae talk me ou' of it? Because it willna work," he warned her.

She sighed and smiled. "Okay, then. Just checking."

He chuckled. "You still have no' answered my question. Will you marry me?"

She grinned up at him.

"Oh. Aye," she said. "A great big aye!"

"Good," he said with a relieved sigh. "Now give us a proper kiss."

"Aye."

"Stop that. You sound like a bloody pirate."

"Aye."

"Kat . . ."

"Aye! Aye! Aye!" She whooped and jumped up into his arms. He accepted the leap with a laugh. He hugged her tightly to himself, as always careful not to hurt her.

"I'll always be careful no' tae hurt you, Kat lass."

"I believe you," she said with a smile as she hugged him back. "I really do believe you. And I promise not to hurt you, too."

"You canna hurt me. I'm forged from stone, lass."

"Mmm. Just the same. Some parts of you, while hard, are not always made from stone."

"Here I am being serious and you're being lewd and dirty."

"I am not!" she gasped. "I didn't mean that!"

"Sure. Whatever you say, dear."

"Ahnvil!"

"No, I mean it, I believe you," he said kindly.

"Stop it!"

"I understand, you're no' that kind of girl . . ."

"Ahnvil! I am, too, that kind of girl!"

"See, I knew it all along."

Kat threw back her head and laughed. "You're horrible."

"Oh aye. But you said aye, so now you're stuck wi' me."

"That I did," she said with a happy sigh as she hugged him again. "And that I am."

Read on for an exciting preview
of the first book in
Jacquelyn Frank's new Immortal Brothers series

CURSED BY FIRE

The heat was unbearable, searing and constant, burning his skin until it crisped. He could smell the aroma of cooking flesh and knew it was himself that he smelled. It was all too familiar, singeing and sinking into his nostrils, a vile stench he would never forget. Would never be allowed to forget. As usual the metal around his wrists burned first, glowing a hot red . . . as though it could melt away or be smelted along with his flesh. But it never melted away . . . it held true time and time again. He had torn at them, strained against them. Every time the fire came he prayed it would melt his hands away first, allowing him to slip free.

But that was not how things worked here. There was never going to be freedom for him. His was an eternal damnation. He had sinned against all of the gods and they, who usually warred among themselves, had come together to see him punished. That was how deeply he had sinned.

He and his brothers had been chained and entombed in this forsaken cavern, and their immortal lives, the ones they had dared to wrest from the secrets of the gods, were now their curse as they died again and again. Death by fire. Or rather, as near to death as was possible for an immortal. He suffered and singed and crackled to a crisp until his lungs could no longer breathe in the flames, until his marrow boiled within his bones and until his chains held only a desiccated corpse turned mostly to ash.

And then the flames would subside and slowly, ever so excruciatingly slowly, his body would heal. Flesh would rebuild itself along the lines of his bones, cell by cell, one healing piece of sinew after another. Immortality repairing itself, birthing him new again, making his skin supple and whole and preparing him to be fresh and healthy and ready to be burned all over again.

The chains he wore went around his forearms in a gauntlet from wrist to elbow, and for good measure a bolt had been shot through each, spearing through the flesh and bone of his forearms from one side to the next, making certain there was no way he could slide free of them. Not that it was necessary. These were chains forged by gods. If you were dressed in the chains of the gods there would be no freedom from them until the gods decided to set you free.

He laughed, the sound hollow in the echo of the abated flames. But they were growing again, he could hear them with his newly healed eardrums. He had long ago ceased begging the gods for mercy. They had not heard him although he had screamed for it endlessly for hours. For days. For decades. For centuries. He no longer knew how much time had passed and it had ceased being important to him. Nothing was important to him. His lot in this existence was merely to burn and to suffer. Again and again, over and over.

You thought you deserved eternal life. Now see what your ambition has won you. See it. Feel it. Deserve it.

No. No one deserved this. True his crimes were brash and arrogant, but they had been crimes of hubris, not unabashed wickedness. He had never been evil incarnate.

But he dared not think to himself that he was blameless for his lot. No. Nor did he dare blame the gods. Oh, he had cursed them. Screamed their names and damned them. Renouncing them one moment and yet pleading to them with utter devotion mere hours later. Such was the nature of torment like this.

But he had not tried to blame the gods or bargain for his release or promised to be the most devout of men should they set him free. No. He knew that freedom would now be wasted on him. His mind was so scorched, so torn, it was nothing but a wasteland.

No. He would simply sit here and burn. He did not even think of his brothers any longer. How often he had wished he could turn back time, wished that he had heeded Garreth who had tried one last time to recall them from the task they had set for themselves. But by then they had almost reached the mountain's pinnacle. By then they had already fought and killed two manticores. By then they had almost frozen to death exposed on the face of Mount Airidara and even then Garreth had been dying at their feet and the only way to save him was to continue onward. But all of that had been excuses, for at the heart of it all had been nothing but selfish desire for the power of immortality. As warriors they faced death every day and without fear, but what they wanted was the glory of being invincible. Like the stories of the demigods, the gods own children or special heroes that had been awarded immortality as a prized gift for their service to the gods. And he had first tried to obtain the gift through his deeds. Winning battles and waging war, overtaking heathen lands and building monuments to the gods, teaching their ways to the untaught. They had converted land after land into the lands of the shield goddess or the god of peace and tranquility. But the gods had been unimpressed and had offered no reward for their service.

And now he knew why. He knew it was because they

had never really done any of it in the name of the gods. They had done it for their own ends and for no other reason and the gods had seen through them.

The four brothers had grown tired of waiting for the gods to get around to rewarding their so-called faithful servants and instead had researched a tale, told to them all through their lives growing up, about the hero Gynnis, who had climbed a great mountain and had found atop it a fountain of gold and gems and within that fountain had been the waters of immortality. One sip of these waters and they would be gifted with youth, health and life everlasting. The waters would heal all wounds, new and old, they would erase the hardest years from face and form, and again . . . life everlasting.

And through much work, much research, much capturing of holy scrolls from holy cities, Jaykun had finally concluded that the fountain was on Mount Airidare. It could not be anywhere else for all other mountains had reportedly been conquered by other men and there had never been tales of success of finding the fountain. No mortal other than Gynnis had ever gained immortality by drinking its waters. So by process of elimination and by the use of many signs and landmarks in those holy scrolls they had known it would be there.

After days of deadly progress, days where they could have and should have failed dozens of times, they had seen the pinnacle and there, running free and gleaming of gold and gemstones, had sat a fountain where water should be frozen solid, but was not. They were in the thinnest air the world had to offer, that was how far up near the field of heaven they were. They could barely breathe it was so thin.

But laying eyes on that fountain had been like a bolt of pure oxygen and exhilarating, revitalizing energy. Just from the sight of it.

And still Garreth had tried to stay them. Upon seeing it he had hesitated and asked them to rethink this, had claimed a sense of foreboding. But they had ignored him and had pressed on and in the end all four of them, even Garreth, had drunk deeply of the fountain's waters.

It had truly been the most miraculous thing he had ever known. His battle scarred and weather frozen body had healed before his very eyes. Frostbite that had claimed at least three of his fingers had reversed itself, revealing warm pink flesh once more. Old battle wounds, like the one that had nearly severed his left leg from the rest of his body had rehealed, the tightness and pain he had dealt with every day since evaporating with alacrity. The scar itself had disappeared from beneath his many layers of clothing. He had not needed to see it because he had felt it. And in the reflective surface of the fountain's waters he had seen the years melt away from his face until he looked as he had looked fifteen summers past, a younger man in the prime of his life, no more then thirty no less that twenty five from what he could see. Garreth, previously near death, had sprung up to his feet laughing and full of life once more.

And then . . . then the gods had come. With a mighty storm of fury and clouds full of lightning and thunder, snow driving them down to the ground, the ground itself hauling and shuddering with rage. Oh yes, they had come.

You dare steal this reward when you have not deserved it in Our eyes? You dare to do so without permission, without honor? You will pay for your folly, foolish, arrogant worms. You will pay for your immortality with blood and bone and flesh. We cannot take this gift back, but We can see to it that you wish you had never dared to think you could push the hand of the gods to your will and your liking.

Then he had been thrown down from that mountain

and into the deepest chamber in the eight hells and had been left there to burn. He did not know what had become of his brothers, Garreth, Jaykun, and Maxum. He could only assume they had been thrown into similar caverns and were suffering similar fates. He had been alone ever since, day after day, with nothing to keep his interest and nothing but the fire for company.

So Dethan was not prepared when, just as the fires were about to roar to life once more, the softest waterfall of sparkling light appeared before his eyes. It started small, with just a falling dot of light, then two, then twenty, then hundreds. The sparkling bits of light began to fall into the shape of a woman. Then, in a flash, a woman of dark hair and blinding beauty was standing before him.

He blinked hard several times, trying to rid himself of the vision. It would not be the first time he had hallucinated under the stress of his torment. But there she stayed and there she stood, wearing a dress so glittering and beautiful it refracted the firelight like diamonds might do. Or perhaps kitomite, which was harder and more brilliant than diamonds. Yes, that was it. The dress, he realized, was a suit of chain-mail armor, fitting her form with perfection and looking as stunning and impervious as it must be if made from kitomite.

That was when he knew it was Weysa, the goddess of conflict. The shield goddess. He had erected statues of her above her altars where spoils of war were frequently laid upon it in homage to her when an army or fighter was victorious. He had prayed to her before every battle and he had seen her fury when he had drunk from the forbidden waters, so it was no wonder that he knew her at first sight. He shuffled about on his hands and knees, rolling himself into obeisance, his forehead touching the scalding hot rock, his palms doing the same, his flesh searing against the stone like a cut of fresh junjun beast is seared in a pan.

She seemed to regard him in silence and as she did so the fires remained completely abated for the first time since he had come there. He was grateful for the reprieve, no matter what the reason, no matter what further curses she might rain down upon his head.

"Low beast," she said after long moments.

"The lowest," he agreed with her, fearful as he spoke that she might grow angry with him for speaking aloud to her.

"What have you learned here, in your time spent?"

He did not know how to answer her. He did not know what she wanted to hear. So he fumbled for the most honest of answers he could come to.

"Never to cross the mighty gods, for their will is the only will."

"Do you beg for mercy?"

"No, Mistress," he said, "For your will will be done and there is nothing I can do to change it."

"Good, because We have been merciful thus far. Your fate could have been much worse, but We took into account all that you have done in Our name."

Merciful? This torment had been the gods' idea of mercy? Dethan felt a wash of rage overcoming him, and he struggled to fight it back. What if she could divine his thoughts? He would anger her and then she would show him what it meant for a god to be unmerciful.

"So," Weysa said, "your time here has not cowed you completely."

Dread filled him. Surely she would become angry with him now. What would she do with him?

"Good," she said then, surprising him. "I need a true warrior. A man loyal to me who will fight in my name."

She wanted him to fight for her? Yes. He would fight for her. Anything. Anything to be free of this hell.

"Fortune has told me that you are my one true hope in this matter. And so you will be. Rise."

He did so, leaving strips of his flesh behind, burned to the floor, all the while keeping his eyes cast downward. Partly to honor her, partly because her armor was too brilliant for his eyes to bear.

"I have grown weak," she said, surprising him. "Things have changed greatly since the times you have fought for me. My strength lies in those who worship me and so many have fallen by the wayside, worshipping false gods instead or . . . following my enemies and giving them the strength I need. You see, the gods have split into two factions, low beast. We war. We war violently. But We cannot win or find advantage unless We have devotion to Us. I need you to find me that devotion, to win over those who do not believe and those who would worship my enemies over me."

Dethan remain silent as she relayed this, but all the while his mind was racing. A war between the gods? This did not surprise him. They had always been a contentious lot. But things must have fallen desperate if she was coming to him for help.

"I will give you these gifts and you will not squander them or you will pay dearly for it," she said. And suddenly a suit of plated armor appeared at his feet. It seemed to be made of hedonite, a black, shining stone known for its lightness of weight. It was far too fragile to be of use in an armor.

"Do not let the look of it deceive you, for this is god-made armor, forged by my own hands and imbued with my strength. It will protect you against any weapon. It will make you invulnerable. Invulnerability coupled with immortality will make you nigh invincible. But be warned. You can die if your head leaves your shoulders by way of a god-made weapon, and my enemies will make gifts of such weapons to stop your progress. Do you understand?"

"Yes, Mistress," he said.

"Good. Then there is this." A sword appeared at his feet. It too seemed to be made of the black hedonite. "This is a mighty weapon. In your hands, be your intentions true and just, it will cut down your foes, of which there will be many. It can pierce god-made armor, no matter how strongly imbued. This was forged with the strength of six gods. All of our faction together."

"Mistress, may I ask which six gods?" he asked, knowing there were twelve gods over all and this meant they were split exactly down the middle.

"Our faction consists of Hella, the goddess of fate and fortune; Meru, the goddess of hearth, home, and harvest; her brother Mordu, the god of hope, love, and dreams; Lothas, the god of day and night; and last is Framun, the god of peace and tranquility."

"So you war with Xaxis, the god of the eight hells; Grimu, the god of the heavens; Diathus, the goddess of the land and oceans; Kitori, the goddess of life and death; Jikaro, the god of storms; and Sabo the god of pain and suffering." He swallowed. That Kitori had sided with five of the darkest gods did not ring true to him, and she was the queen of all the gods and demanded much respect.

"Your thoughts do you justice, low beast. Kitori has been swayed by these other gods. I believe she is held hostage more than she had sided with them. They together have the power to subdue her in spite of her great powers. And that is part of your goal. By gaining me, and these other gods that side with me, worshippers, I believe I will be able to rescue Kitori from their influence. Such a coup would no doubt turn the tide of this war. And there is something else . . ."

"Yes, my mistress," he encouraged her. His mind was

racing. If she was rescuing him from this fate worse than death then things were as dire as they appeared. He would fight for her, as he had done in the past. This in spite of the rage he felt toward all of the gods for the suffering they had subjected him to. Especially if it meant freedom from this torment. It was the only choice really, because there was nothing he could do in the face of their power. But perhaps . . . perhaps he could convince her . . .

No. He would not try to manipulate his goddess. That was a slippery slope and he would not risk angering her. But he would ask . . . he would beg . . .

"There is a great weapon that can be used against Xaxis's faction."

So, it was Xaxis leading the faction, Dethan thought. That figured. Xaxis had been trying to wrest power from the other gods for time immemorial.

"This weapon is surrounded by a great city, a city that guards the mouth of the eight hells."

"Olan?" he asked.

"Olan," she agreed. "I need you to conquer this city and to wrest control of this weapon."

Suddenly she looked over her shoulder, as if she heard someone coming. She turned to him quickly. "This is Xaxis's territory and he is beginning to sense that I am here. I must leave before I am captured by him. But you are freed. I will bring you above the hells and you must begin your work. But be warned, you do not go freely. You are cursed ever after, a memory to make you remember where you have come from and where you will return should you fail me. Every night, at dusk, you will conflagrate and burn until the juquil's hour. If you perform well for me I will consider lifting the curse. Do you understand?"

Dethan's fists clenched in anger, but he controlled the emotion with an iron will. So he would be made to suffer this same hell again and again even while he worked for her honor and ends. But the rest of the time . . . the rest of the time he would live in reprieve, and that was far better than what he suffered now.

"Yes, Mistress, I understand. But . . . if your humble servant might ask . . . my brothers are great warriors. If you were to rescue them from this torment as well they too could fight for your faction."

"Your brothers, unlike you, are not here in the hells. However, like you, they are made to suffer in the territories ruled by the other faction. I have risked all coming here and cannot do so again. The only reason I was able to come at all is because the others have distracted Xaxis in order to free me to do this. Your brother Garreth is chained to the very mountain where you found the fountain, freezing solid again and again. The territory is controlled by Diathus. Jaykun is chained to a star and, like you, burns again and again. This is Grimu's territory and I have no access to the heavens. Maxum . . . I do not know where Maxum is. He was given to Sabo to be dealt with and Sabo never shared with us the punishment he meted out. Probably so no other god could do what I am doing now." She looked over her shoulder again and this time he saw true anxiety on her features. "I must go now. Fight, warrior, as you have never fought before. Find an army. Fight to bring my name to the people. And never forget who has set you free and who can set you down again."

"No, Mistress, never."

"The fires will see to that. Remember, dusk every day. It will do you well to make sure no others are nearby when this happens or they will be consumed by the flames as well. Now we are off."

In a flash of speed and burning light that sickened him, he found himself standing at the mouth of one of the entrances to the eight hells, easily recognizable by the dragon's head carved into the massive stones surrounding it, the mouth of the creature leading downward to the fiery pit. He could assume this was not the entrance in Olan. Weysa would not put him in the heart of the very city she wished him to conquer. So it was one of the four other entrances placed upon the face of Ethos. One he knew was under water. One, like the fountain, was set high on a mountain, and since it was not cold but more summery climes around him, that left the largest opening, the one in Hexis. His armor rested at his feet and he hastened to pick it up. He was still seared and wounded, and had no clothing so he stood bare and naked, knowing nothing of the world around him.

He could have hidden back within the cave, but he could not bring himself to step toward it, his muscle and sinew screaming in fear of moving toward the fires below in even the smallest of increments.

Luckily the closest thing to the mouth of the cave was an altar upon which sacrifices to Xaxis were made. He hurried over to it, hiding and skulking behind it as he looked around with wide, wild eyes. The altar was laden with all manner of things, from fruits to beasts. Things going to rot and waste. And thanks to that the first thing he realized was that he was starving . . . famished from who knew how long without food. But to steal from the altar might mean an insult to the god it was meant for, so he touched nothing there, not wishing to incite any further wrath from the gods. Especially not Xaxis. He was to be working covertly for his goddess's interests. He could not draw attention to himself until it was time to begin to war in her name.

But she had given him no army. She expected him to find one on his own. It had taken years for him to build the forces he had once used to march across the world. But what of those lands he had once defeated? Would they still be his to command? How long had it been since he had been locked away?

No. He could not hope that any of them would know who he was. None but perhaps . . . home. Perhaps where he had once sat as warlord and master they would know who he was. But it did not follow that they would accept him. And he was a very long way from the massive walls of Toren, his home. It would take travel across a desert, a lush living valley, and an ocean before he could get there.

It felt strange to use the term *home*. His home for so long had been that fiery cavern. His home had been a pair of chains.

That was when he looked down at his arms.

Free. *Free*. His skin, raw and ragged as it was, pale, damp and weak it might be, but it was in the open air for the first time since . . . well . . . since. Naked in the cooler air after being in the scalding heat he was shivering so hard his teeth clacked like heavy sticks knocking together.

There was no one nearby. That did not surprise him. The entrance was located well above the sprawl of the city. Xaxis was not the sort of god one wanted to spend too much time on or get too close to. He was worshipped out of fear. He was worshipped whenever someone died, the idea being that he could be convinced to turn a blind eye to the departed, allowing them to bypass the eight hells and be risen up to the heavens where they would reside in the house of brightness and glory. He was worshipped by those who dealt in death, who thrived in the causing of it, the needing of it. He had been considered to be a worshipper of death because he had dealt in war. And in war there was always death. But in truth it had been Weysa, the goddess of conflict, who had earned his devotion, and that was probably why she had come to him and none of his other brothers. They were all warriors, but in their own way. Garreth had not even been a part of his forces, preferring to take on quests of honor. Maxum was a gold-sword. Selling his sword for gold and going wherever the money was best, whether the cause was good or bad. And yet, Maxum had his own set of morals, his own limitations, his own rules.

That left Jaykun. Jaykun had been his right arm, his first lieutenant. His successor, had it come to that. But it never had. They had taken on the folly of finding immortality, in spite of all the riches and glories they already had in the world.

Riches. *Yes,* he thought with sudden elation. He had hidden caches of wealth all over the Red Continent. All he need do was get to one of them, hoping above all that they had not been discovered. He could buy an army if he had those monies. Or at least he could start to buy one. The one thing he had learned in his days as a warlord was that war was an expensive undertaking. Tactics and planning were all well and good, but without the funds to support ones troops, the effort would come to a standstill.

But one step at a time. He needed clothes. And then a horse. With a horse and some proper provisioning he could cross the Syken Desert and see if one of his largest caches were still intact.

He looked around and found some thick shrubbery to the side of the folly, the opening to hell. He grabbed his sword and the armor and dragged it all behind a bush, hiding it well. The weight of it was light, but it was still cumbersome. He hid it as best he could, looking around furtively to make certain none were watching. But set so far from the town he was alone.

Once he was free of encumbrance he crept toward the city. A piece of fruit had rolled down the hill, presumably from the offerings above, and he snatched it up greedily. He ripped through the thick skin, shoving his entire face into the sweet pulpy heart of it. He devoured it as he moved, but it was gone all too quickly. He threw the skins aside and wiped his face.

It was daylight, late afternoon, by the position of the blue sun. It was told that the sun burned blue because that was the hottest part of the flame . . . although the songs of the gods said that the sun was the blue of the eyes of Atemna, the mortal woman who captured Lothas's heart, the heart of the god of day and night. The moon and sun were his to command, bringing day and night, and he had the power to change the color of the sun in remembrance of his love.

Of course, Atemna met a tragic end when Diathus, Lothis's wife and the goddess of land and oceans, drowned the girl in a fit of jealousy.

It wasn't the first story of mortals suffering because of the tumultuous whims of the gods. But he would know that better than anyone. He wondered if he and his brothers were now one of the songs of the gods. A cautionary tale for those who reached too high.

The worst part of the city was closest to the folly.

After all, who wanted to live nearest to hell? The children that ran in the muddied streets wore tatters and rags, the stench of poor sewage reeked heavy on the air, and the noise was very overwhelming the closer he got to it. The stench was harsh in his singed nostrils, but welcome after years of smelling nothing but soot and crisping flesh. He had crept well into the edge of the mess of it without anyone taking notice of his lack of clothing. They had stronger worries, these impoverished people, and no doubt he wasn't the first naked beggar they had ever seen.

But he would not beg. No. Not that he was above it. He was not above anything anymore. But beggars would be cast down on, would earn nothing but negative attention. Especially one like him who looked so vulnerable on sight. Begging would not get him what he needed.

Thievery would.

The first order was some kind of clothing. He snuck down a back alley and immediately he could see clothing lines had been drawn up high between the buildings. But they were a good two stories up.

This did not sway him from his course. He found a strange metal tube that ran from ground to roof, water running out of the opening in the bottom. He wrapped a hand around it and pulled, studying the fastenings that held it to the stone. With a shrug he began to climb it. After all, if he fell, he would not die. Oh, it would hurt . . . it might slow him down, but he would heal and then he would walk away from it.

Because he could walk. Because he was free.

Only . . . the sun was lowering. If the fires were going to return . . .

The thought leant him speed. Because his muscles were still burned and shriveled it took all of his strength to climb the tube up to the nearest line and the clothing he found upon it. There was a pair of pants, worn and barely patched in places, but clean and ten times better than what he had right then. A hundred times better. He snatched them from the line and like a rat that steals the sliver of cheese he scurried back down the pipe and slipped back into the late day shadows of the alley. Scrambling, he shoved first one leg and then another into the pants and then held them clutched to his body for he had no belt and they were meant for a much stockier man. But now he was clothed and could walk around freely. What he needed was to find a horse. He would scope out barns or smithies, places where horses could be found, and when night fell he would come back . . .

After the juquil's hour, he reminded himself. Because from sunset to the juquil's hour he would burn. And he had to find a place where he could do so and not bring danger to others . . . or notice to himself. And the only place he could think of that would fit that need was . . .

Just thinking about the entrance made him break out in a cold sweat. The idea of voluntarily stepping into the mouth of hell all but paralyzed him with fear. He had not been well acquainted with fear during his life as a warlord. He had even been called fearless in bardsong. But he was well acquainted with it now. And he didn't dare step back near hell and Xaxis's territory. What if he could sense him then? What if he came for him and dragged him back down and chained him once more?

The thought of it made him shake with terror. Bone chilled, flesh scorched terror. He had to stop, sinking down onto his haunches in the shadows of the wet, smelly alleyway, huddling into himself and trying for all he was worth to remind himself of who he had once been. A man of courage. A warrior. A warlord who had ruled with an iron fist.

But he was not that man any longer.

After a minute he rose up again and then made his way out into the open streets. The deeper he went into the city the thicker the traffic. Pedestrians and horses, carts and coaches lined the roads, kicking up mud and grinding it down again until he found himself sticking in the sludge as it sucked at his feet and ankles. It was a wonder anyone managed to get anywhere at all. The wheels of one of the heavier coaches must have sunk a good four inches or better into the muck. It was only the team of stout ginger merries that kept it from slogging down. And beautiful horses they were. A perfectly matched set of four ginger colored steeds with white manes and tails. They were called ginger merries because of their sweet, playful dispositions. They were usually a woman's horse and, indeed, the coach was full of highborn women.

At least that much was the same. The rich still lived better than the poor. Ginger merries still existed. But already he was seeing things he'd never seen before. Like the metal tube he had climbed. It was a clever thing, he realized. It kept water from accumulating on the roof of the building.

The buildings were another thing. They were well made, not just of stone but of wood and some kind of plaster. Whitish in color in some of the buildings he was now passing, brown in those where he'd just come from. Still others were made even better with wood planks nailed to the sides. He couldn't help himself. He stopped and pulled at one. The wood shingle held fast. He could not comprehend its purpose so he simply let it be and left. He had many other things to accomplish. Although he understood that he could not hope to conquer a world he did not understand. So he would pay attention as he went.

Dethan found a stablery after a short while and

within it a horse of fine flesh. If his fortune ran well, the horse would still be there come the juquil's hour.

"Beauteous Hella, look upon me this night, so I may aid your cause," he prayed with fervor to the goddess of fate and fortune.

He turned away and heard a loud shout. Fearing someone had noticed him he cringed at the sound. He turned just as the sound of a cracking whip cut through the air. There, not too far down the partly cobbled road, was one of the fine coaches . . . this one led by dark stallions with shining coats that showed the musculature and fine breeding of the foursome. Now there, he thought, was a horse worth stealing.

The whip cracked again and a man cried out. Dethan moved a little further down so he could see better because it was very clear the whip was not being used on the team of horses. The coachman raised up his arm again and Dethan could see the man, wearing little better clothing than he wore, cowering away from the coming blow, two stripes of red showing through the mud on his skin where the whip had struck before.

"Dog! Foul thing, you dare interfere with his lordship's horses!" the coachman yelled.

And then, when he looked into the open coach windows to see who was within, he could see a pair of dark eyes watching the exchange rapaciously. The man within did not intervene, did not stop the abuse. It was more like . . . he hungered for it. Was eager to see it. The smile that touched his cruel lips only solidified the impression. Dethan had known men like this before. Wicked men. Cruel men. He had fought both with and against them in the wars he had engaged in. Though he had had no tolerance for it in his own camps, there were those he had discovered later on who had a thirst for such cruelties.

Dethan did not know why he stepped forward, did

not know why he thrust his hand out, blocking the next strike of the whip's tail from hitting the man, letting it wrap around his wrist instead. He yanked back as hard as he could, testing the strength of his healing muscles to the maximum. The coachman had such a grip on the whip that Dethan ended up yanking the lot of them, man and whip, from high above and down into the wet of the mud. The coachman spluttered and spat, getting to his feet in a state, his face mottled red with fury.

"How dare you!" he gasped. "Do you not see the sigil on this coach? It is the lord high jenden's vehicle! You will be whipped for your insolence!"

"Would that be with this whip?" Dethan asked, rolling the whip up slowly in his hands. His manner was mild on first glance, but anyone who looked a bit harder realized what the coachman realized and that was that Dethan, for all he wore baggy rags and a thick layer of mud, was the one fully in charge of the altercation.

"You there! You let my man go or you will find yourself without a head!" barked a voice from within the coach. He turned to look over his shoulder and saw the man leaning out of the window of the conveyance.

Dethan turned to face the man. "Oh, I'll let him go," Dethan said. "Only, not with his whip. The whip is mine now."

"How dare you commandeer anything of mine! How dare you interfere with—!"

He broke off suddenly when a delicate, gloved hand appeared from the darkness of the coach and rested on the hand of the man within. It was wearing a glove of white and there was a sprig of flowers ringed around the wrist.

She, for it was obviously a woman, must have said something—Dethan could not hear what—for the angry man subsided somewhat, though it was very clear he was not happy about it. He looked to the left and right, seeing the crowd they were beginning to draw.

"But . . . my dear . . . he is an upstart of a peasant and we cannot suborn—"

"Is this truly worthy of your time?" she asked, this time loud enough for Dethan to hear, though in no way with strong emotion. More like she might scold a puppy. Then she finally appeared in the window, and Dethan felt his breath lock up in cold shock in his chest.

She was the most beautiful woman he had ever seen . . . save the goddesses themselves. Her only flaw, immediately noticeable, was the burn scar along her lower cheek and jaw on the left-hand side of her face. But he hardly saw it because the rest of her face was stunning, her eyes dark and bottomless, her nose small and delicate and her lips lush and smiling over perfectly white teeth. It was a shock to him that she had all of her teeth. Women of his time hardly made it to her age with all intact.

Her hair was dark and curly, piled high on her head with a jaunty little cap set amidst it. The teal cap had a stiff veil that dropped down over the left side of her face, presumably to hide the scar, only it had been pushed back either by accident or design and she could be seen quite clearly. She had the longest of necks, the whitest of skin. Her gloved hand was graceful on the man's.

"Can you not see how out of line your carriage driver was, Lord Grannish?" she asked him gently. "This man was only doing what was right. Those with power should not use it to press down those without," she said, almost pointedly. No. It was with a point. Something he did not fully understand was being passed between them.

"Very well," Grannish groused, his narrow face with its curling moustache looking a cross between angry and deferential. Whatever it was, he was not happy about it. "Driver!"

"Sir." the lady addressed Dethan. "The driver cannot drive without the whip."

The unspoken implication was clear. She was trying to manipulate him the way she had just managed the other man. But he had no intention of being managed.

"A whip should not be applied to such fine horseflesh, woman. If he cannot control them with reins alone then you are in need of a better driver. And I am in need of a belt." With a sharp movement he whipped the whip around his waist, effectively belting up his pants and tying the end tightly to his body.

"This is a woman of the highest born blood," the man Grannish hissed. "You will refer to her by her title—!"

" 'My lady' will suffice," she cut him off.

"Your pardon, *my lady,* I am a foreigner to these lands and things are different here than where I come from."

"Then it is understood. Truly, you are forgiven. Driver, ride on!" she said in loud command.

The driver had since climbed out of the mud and back up into his seat, Dethan having kept a sharp eye on him the entire time. He made a sound to the horses and they drove on with a jolting start. Dethan watched them go, his eyes on the woman and hers on his the entire time. It took him a minute to shake himself free of the trance in which he found himself, and then he found himself questioning why he had done what he had just done. He should be worrying about his own skin, his own tasks, and not what happened to a lone man in the filth of the street.

"Thank you, sir," the man said then, coming up to him and grabbing his hand. He touched the back of his hand to the back of Dethan's pressing them together. "I owe you much. Come let me reward you."

"I have no need of reward," Dethan said. He eyed the other man. "And you have little to give, I think."

"Any other day that would be true, but today is the fair and I have been saving my silver to go. I think I might find me a wife today, if I can be so lucky."

"You intend to buy one?" Dethan asked.

"Oh well . . . I suppose I could. From one of the slavers. But my money is so little that I wouldn't be able to buy any woman of passing health. It takes a strong woman to be a mudfarmer's wife."

"You might be surprised," Dethan said. "A sickly slave might be made well with good care. I've seen it done."

"It might be cheaper at that!" The man chuckled; it was a low raspy sound. He ran a hand back through his hair, obviously a habit because there were streaks of mud in various stages of wetness from the times before. "By the time the courting is done a man can be begging in the streets. Your idea has merit, that's what! So, to the fair then? I'll buy you a roasted gossel leg for your trouble though I wish it was more."

"A gossel leg is more than fair and will be more than welcome."

"Very well then." The man pressed the backs of their hands together again. "My name's Tonkin. You are new around here."

"Yes. Why does that matter?" Dethan said uneasily.

"Well, no one who knows would step in to interfere with his lordship the high jenden's business. He's a cruel bastard, make no mistake about it. If I hadn't fallen I would never have come close to that vehicle of his. He rides it round here all fine and fierce looking, making sure all us drudges know our place."

"Jenden?" he asked cautiously. He didn't want to seem too strange to this individual. But by the look the man sent him he could tell he was very much so strange.

"Advisor to the grand. You know, advisor to the *king*," he stressed when, no doubt, Dethan's expression remained blank. "And anyways, that was the grandina, the grand's daughter, with him. I guarantee you had she not been with him the whole business would have gone much differently. It's rumored that once the jenden killed someone right in the middle of the street. And the grand is so enamored with all the jenden says and does he can do no wrong. I suppose that's why he's given his eldest daughter and heir to the jenden to marry. Though some say he's getting the raw deal, what with her being so ugly and all."

"Ugly? That's ugly?" Dethan asked incredulously, cocking a thumb in the direction the coach had disappeared in. "She's nearly as beautiful as Kitari. And I do not make that case lightly, for I've seen Kitari with my own eyes!"

He regretted it the minute Tonkin looked at him as though he'd grown boils all over his face. After all, what manner of man claimed to have seen the unattainable queen of the gods? But then Tonkin's face relaxed and he chuckled.

"Oh aye, she is a beauty at that. *I* agree with you. But 'round here that burn makes her ugly to most. Some said she will be unfit to rule after her father's death . . . no doubt some like the jenden himself. Jenden Grannish wouldn't be marrying her, you could wager, if he could think of any other way of becoming grand for himself. As it is the grand's children have been cast a sad eye by Hella. Misfortunes have fallen on the royal family in terrible ways. The grand's sons dying like that. And his two youngest daughters taken by the plague just this past summer. That leaves only the grandina Selinda and grandino Drakin. But the boy prince is only two and of poor health." Dethan's companion tsked his tongue and shook his head gravely.

As though to say that was the whole of it and there was nothing to be done about it. But surely anyone could see that there was something dark at play in the grand's household. Of course, Fate was as capricious a goddess as any and Hella had been known to toy with entire families, entire bloodlines, especially if she felt slighted in some way. It was hard to say what moved Fate and why her whims fluctuated so wildly. There were those who said Hella had gone mad, her mind crazed by the many things she could see and feel unfolding in the world. From all the choices she had to make every day that could save a person or bring about their demise or worse.

But fate could be changed or altered under the right conditions. One just needed to know all the elements at play.